P9-CFO-896

Also by Jean Stone

SINS OF INNOCENCE

FIRST LOVES

IVY SECRETS

Places by the Sea

Jean Stone

BANTAM BOOKS
NEW YORK TORONTO LONDON SYDNEY AUCKLAND

PLACES BY THE SEA
A Bantam Fanfare Book / April 1997

FANFARE and the portrayal of a boxed "ff" are trademarks of Bantam
Books, a division of Bantam Doubleday Dell Publishing Group, Inc.

ISBN-13: 978-0-553-57424-1

ISBN-10: 0-553-57424-8

Published simultaneously in the United States and Canada

Bantam Books are published by Bantam Books, a division of Bantam
Doubleday Dell Publishing Group, Inc. Its trademark, consisting of the words
"Bantam Books" and the portrayal of a rooster, is Registered in U.S. Patent
and Trademark Office and in other countries. Marca Registrada. Bantam
Books, 1540 Broadway, New York, New York 10036.

PRINTED IN THE UNITED STATES OF AMERICA

OPM   10 9 8 7 6

In Memory of Snuggles

1981–1995

THE BEST LITTLE DOG IN THE WORLD

Acknowledgments

Many thanks to the gang at The Outermost Inn in Gay Head, Martha's Vineyard: Hugh and Jeanne Taylor, Barbara, and Nancy for the warmth of their laughter and sharing their stories, and Hollis, for introducing me to lucky stones, shark's teeth, and sassafras roots; to the girls at The Daggett House (no relation to Tim!) in Edgartown: Kathy, Vicki, Nanette, and Pat; to my tireless editor, Wendy McCurdy and her always-supportive friend, Elinor; to my energetic, idea-generating agent, Loretta Weingel-Fidel; to Steven Cooper for chicken fried rice, black and white cookies, and listening; to my medical expert, David Page, M.D., who never hurt a character he didn't like; to my research sidekick, Carol Zombik, for traipsing to lighthouses and going in wrong doors at restaurants; to Aunt Shirley, Aunt Lois, Linda, Jane, Cindy, Mo, and Maripat for putting up with me; and, of course—always—to E.J., for being E.J., for being there.

Places
by the
Sea

Prologue

 "My mother will kill me if she catches me up here." Jill crept up the stairs, her heart racing, her adrenaline pumping. Up the stairs, to the widow's walk—an act as forbidden as climbing the cliffs of Gay Head.

"She'll be at the rummage sale for hours," Rita said from behind her. "Besides, you've been dying to do this for years."

"It's just a widow's walk."

"It's your house, Jill. And anyway, we're not going to hurt anything."

As she reached the top stair, Jill stopped and tapped the wide-board floor with her fraying Keds. "My mother says it's not safe."

"Bullshit. We know how to be careful."

Jill hesitated. She wondered if her best friend was right. They were, after all, twelve years old. It wasn't like they were kids anymore.

Rita moved up to the step below her. "Chicken."

Slowly Jill picked up her other long, skinny leg and placed her foot on the floor. Then, she looked up into the small square room. Cartons were stacked everywhere. Cartons, and an old black trunk, its top covered by a handmade quilt.

Cautiously Jill stepped inside and tiptoed to the

walls of glass, to the view she'd never seen. Three stories below, the shops lined the streets of Edgartown; next to them stood the white-steepled church, across from which stretched the water: Vineyard Sound, the harbor, even Katama Bay. A rainbow of sails dotted the blueness. Then she realized how quiet it was up here, so quiet it was hard to believe it was August, that there were tourists far below.

"Wow," Rita said as she moved into the room. "What a great hideout."

Jill gazed across the water. "Do you suppose my great-great-grandmother stood here waiting, watching for her husband to return from the sea?"

"More like watching him stagger home from the tavern."

"Rita! My family owns the tavern. They aren't drunks."

"My mistake. I forgot. The Randalls are perfect."

Jill kept her eyes fixed out the window, wondering what lay beyond the water, and why she'd never been brave enough to venture up here before.

"Hey—I wonder what's in this old trunk."

Quickly Jill turned. "Rita, I think we'd better go back downstairs."

"Wait. I just want to see . . ." She squatted in front of the trunk and tugged at the latch. "Shit. It's locked."

Just then a voice bellowed up from downstairs. "Jill!"

Jill's eyes widened. "Oh, God," she whispered. "It's her. Did you close the door?"

"Sssh," Rita mouthed, the flush on her cheeks as red as her hair.

Footsteps pounded up the stairs. Jill froze. Her heart felt as though it would fly from her chest. Suddenly Florence Randall appeared, her housedress askew, her face flaming pink, the sickening scent of her lavender-crocheted hankie surrounding her in a puff of deceptive sweetness. "Get out of here!" she screeched.

Jill backed against the window. Her mother marched toward her and grabbed her arm. Jill winced at the hurt. Then, Florence spotted Rita at the trunk. "Don't touch that!" she shrieked. She broke her grasp from Jill and lunged toward Rita. "Get out . . . you . . . you troublemaker!"

Rita sprang up; her small frame darted past Florence.

"Get out of this house!" Florence shouted after her. "Get out this instant!"

Jill twisted quickly and ran down the stairs behind her best friend, the shouts of "You'll be sorry!" and "Wait 'til your father gets home!" reverberating in her ears.

They raced to the second floor, rounded the corner, sped down the hall, dashed down to the first floor, and flew out the front door. Outside, they sprinted toward the lighthouse without stopping, scrambling to their special place in under the private docks, their safe place, their escape.

Her stomach cramped, her breath was short. Jill collapsed on the rocks. "I hate my mother," she cried.

Rita slumped beside her. "Yeah," she grumbled, "no shit."

"Someday," Jill gasped between breaths. "Someday, Rita, I'm going to get away from her. I'm going to get off this damn island. And I'm never—*ever*—coming back."

Chapter 1

"This is Jill McPhearson . . ."
"And Christopher Edwards . . ."
"Good Night, Boston."

The beat of their theme song rose; giant spotlights crisscrossed the set; twin cameras rapidly cut from angle to angle in split-second close-ups: Jill's honey-gold hair, huge green eyes, and peach-blushed high cheekbones; Christopher's loose, tawny hair, spa-induced tan, and bright white smile. In the monitor, Jill noted the sparks of chemistry that shot between them and bounced off the cluster of pavé diamonds on her earrings and matching gold choker. Thankfully the cameras did not betray what was really going on in her mind.

"Now," came the director's voice, and quickly, on cue, Christopher winked at Jill.

The wink, of course, had been Addie Becker's idea—Addie, their unstoppable publicist who had defied the critics and catapulted *Good Night, Boston* to a prime-time TV slot with meteoric ratings. Addie had believed in their show: believed that television audiences were tired of talk shows, bored with TV news magazines, and fed up with the fluff of entertainment offerings. She'd also believed that Christopher and Jill had something innovative, something powerful: *Good Night, Boston* featured *good* news about *real* people who accomplished extraordinary, caring, human things. The *Globe* called it "Refreshing." The *Herald* said "Long overdue." And two months ago, they had swept the New England Emmys.

Clearly, Addie Becker had been right.

Without hesitation, Jill smiled back at Christopher now, responding to his wink the way Addie had instructed, in the choreographed gesture guaranteed to whet the romance appetites of their viewers—proof that love over forty, indeed, was possible, and that bliss could be made in media heaven. Christopher, after all, was more than a co-host. The five-carat, pear-shaped diamond on Jill's left hand was glittering proof of that.

The credits rolled. The cameras pulled back for the softly lit, closing long shot. Jill unclipped her microphone and set it on the desk, wishing that the show could go on forever, that she could remain forever seated in the studio, doing what she loved best, beside the man she loved so much.

But this was her last show for a month. The viewers had been told she'd be off making wedding plans, but that was a lie. Instead of picking out bridal gowns and selecting invitations, Jill was headed for Martha's Vineyard to clean out her parents' house— the house where she'd been raised. She had only returned once in over twenty-five years. Now, she had no choice.

"Good show tonight, honey," Christopher said.

"You're only saying that because you're going to miss me."

"You'll be back before you know it. Besides, we'll have a great time this weekend."

Jill sighed. Christopher had no idea how difficult this trip was going to be for her. Sure, he was going for the weekend. But he would return to Boston Sunday night, carry on with the show, and leave her to deal with her past. Alone.

"It doesn't seem like the right time for me to leave," she protested. "We've only been on the air six months. . . ."

Christopher laughed. "Are you worried about the show or going to the Vineyard?"

Aware that the red light of the camera was still aimed at them, she turned her head to avoid the viewers. "I'm worried about the ratings." But she'd been in the business long enough—slugging her way from street reporter to news anchor to the desk at which she now sat—to know that summers were nothing more than rerun-packed lineups and that most viewers turned off their sets.

"It's August," he said, as if reading her mind. "People are at the ballpark, not watching TV."

"Not everyone plays baseball. Difficult as though that may be for you to believe."

"And out," the director spoke through her earpiece.

Christopher laughed again as the studio lights dimmed. He undid his wiring, leaned over, and put his arm around her shoulder. "You're right about one thing," he whispered, kissing her neck. "I am going to miss you."

The tingle of his kiss made her smile, this time for real, this time not for the cameras. "And you'll be running around Boston all month without me."

"One of us has to work, remember?"

"And both of us better get out of here if we're going to make it to Logan on time." Jill hadn't seen her children in a month and hoped that three weeks with their father in London had left them smiling, cheerful, and getting along. It didn't hurt to believe in miracles.

Christopher shook his head. "Sorry, honey. I have to stay here and meet the woman who's filling in for you. Addie's going to ride with you, though. She has some things to go over before you leave."

Addie was not what Jill had in mind. She had wanted this to be a family time—a night when the kids could get to know their soon-to-be stepfather. Between being away at their schools in New Hampshire and their time in London, they hardly knew Christopher at all, except what they saw on TV, if they bothered to watch at all.

"But I'll be at your house in the morning," he continued. "Is eleven okay?"

Eleven o'clock would, indeed, give them plenty of time to catch the one-fifteen ferry out of Woods Hole. The ferry that would take her home. Whether she liked it or not.

Moving his hand to her cheek, Christopher traced the curve of her face. "Get it over with, Jill. Sell the house. Be done with it, once and for all."

She looked into his eyes—the pale blue eyes that for years had captivated the hearts of millions of baseball fans. There were still times when Jill was amazed that Christopher Edwards—the Miami Blazers' legendary pitcher—had handpicked her to be his co-host, then to be his wife. With a career in which image meant everything, she couldn't have asked for a better partner—nor could Addie have devised a more effective team.

As Jill opened her mouth to tell him she loved him, a breathy voice resonated across the studio. "Mr. Edwards?" the voice asked.

Christopher turned and shielded his eyes against the remaining studio light. Jill's eyes followed his, toward a shadowy figure that stepped over a cable and into the light.

It was a young woman. Blond, gorgeous, with long, long legs and full, high-riding breasts. "Mr. Edwards," she breathed, "I'm Lizette French. Ms. McPhearson's summer replacement."

. . .

"For God's sake, Addie, she looks like a *Playboy* bunny," Jill muttered as the limo maneuvered its way through the urban clash of cobblestone streets and high-rise buildings. "*Lizette.* What kind of a name is that? Lizette *French.* It's absurd."

Addie lounged beside Jill, her bright yellow caftan folding over her portly lumps and spilling onto the seat, the daffodil sash of her wide-brimmed white hat draped over one sloping shoulder. She peered at Jill through cerise-framed eyeglasses. "You're jealous."

"I'm forty-three years old, Addie. It's the show that concerns me. Not Christopher." As she spoke, Jill twisted the pear-shaped diamond for reassurance.

"The show will be fine. Lizette comes across as a professional on camera."

Jill snorted. "A professional what?"

Reaching across to the softly lit bar, Addie uncorked a bottle of champagne. "Let's not be catty, darling. Lizette is from California."

"That figures."

"She's been working for *Focus.*"

"*Focus* is a national show."

"Owned by RueCom. Yes. I know." Addie poured champagne into one flute and handed it to Jill. She filled another for herself.

"How'd she wind up here? Swinging her body around my fiancé, stealing my place on my show?"

Addie laughed. "She's not 'stealing your place,' Jill. She's filling in while you're away. As far as swinging her body, I think that comes naturally."

"If she's from California, I doubt that any part of her is natural." She stared out the dark-tinted window, wishing the wine would quell the trembling inside her, wondering if her trip to the Vineyard was going to ruin her life in more ways than one. She silently cursed her mother for dying; for leaving her with this responsibility at the worst possible time.

"Forget about Lizette. We have more important things to discuss."

Jill took another sip from her glass.

"First, Ben Niles will be at your parents' house tomorrow at ten o'clock."

"Who is Ben Niles?"

"The contractor. Renovator. Whatever he calls himself. The man I hired to fix up the house. His signature alone will get you top dollar."

Jill nodded, vaguely remembering that Addie had located someone through an article in *Yankee* magazine. She was glad Addie had made the arrangements: the less Jill had to do with the house, the better. *Get it over with,* had been Christopher's words. *Once and for all.*

Addie's cell phone rang. She flipped it open and answered it. "When?" she asked into the small receiver, then paused. "How much?"

Jill shifted on the seat. She detested cell phones. They had a way of interrupting everyone, everything. Though Christopher had begged her to get one, she'd refused. He'd accused her of being a telecommunications snob. She'd told him maybe she was just an island girl at heart.

An island girl. The thought of it stabbed her stomach now. She set down her glass, folded her arms, and tapped her high heel-sandaled foot against the base of the leather seat.

Addie clicked off her phone. "It's all set," she said to Jill.

"What now?"

"We've landed a spread in *Lifestyles*."

Martha's Vineyard slid from her thoughts. "*Lifestyles*?" Her heart raced a little, her cheeks reddened and warmed. "Again?" The "People to Notice" section of the weekly magazine had recently mentioned *Good Night, Boston* and the engagement of the show's co-hosts. It had been Jill's first taste of national exposure—a taste she had found quite delicious. Like most things these days, the article had been Addie's doing.

"I've come up with a new angle. They'll release it November first—two weeks before the wedding," Addie continued. "You'll be a shoe-in for *Oprah*, or at least Regis and Kathie Lee."

"What's the angle?"

Addie leaned into her and lay a hand on Jill's arm. "The kids."

Through Addie's round glasses, Jill stared at the fifty-year-old lines that framed the woman's determined eyes. "What about the kids?"

"We're going to feature them."

She frowned. "Jeff and Amy?"

Addie took a long swig, then refilled her glass. "It's perfect, Jill. You and Christopher are going to be the family of the new millennium. Stepchildren, stepparents, everyone getting along. The new American dream."

"Step-families aren't new, Addie. Nor are they news."

Addie laughed. "You and your 'news' instincts. You're TV royalty now, darling. That makes you entertainment, not 'news.' "

Images of tabloids sprang to her mind, complete with hordes of paparazzi—the kind that floated around Princes William and Harry and the Kennedy kids. "I don't know, Addie. Jeff is sixteen. Amy's fourteen. They're so impressionable right now."

"Look, Jill, for months I've been telling you Boston is only the starting gate for your career. I haven't steered you wrong so far, have I?"

"But you haven't involved my kids."

"They're teenagers. They can handle it. Besides, it will give them new distinction at school."

"But Amy's just a child. . . ."

Addie's phone rang again.

Jill sighed inside, wishing she had a better idea of how to be the right kind of mother—with or without the entertainment spotlight. But she knew she had little to draw from. Her mother had hardly been a mother, at least not one she had ever related to or felt close to, even at the end. When Florence Randall died two months ago, Jill and Christopher were on the road, doing *Good Night, Boston* live from Moscow. Her mother's church friends offered to hold the memorial service until Jill returned: Jill suggested they go ahead without her. The ladies had quietly complied.

Outside the limo, the tile walls of the tunnel rushed by, compressing the air inside, squeezing Jill's thoughts into a claustrophobic vise—the same kind of vise she'd felt as a child, growing up on the Vineyard. She set the champagne flute into the small holder beside her and tried to remind herself she was Jill McPhearson now—successful, sought-after Jill McPhearson—with no link to Jill Randall, that inferior nobody-child.

Finally, Addie clicked off. "So, do I call back the editor and tell her it's a go?"

"I need to think about it," Jill replied. "I want to talk to Christopher."

"He already agreed. I ran it by him earlier today."

She snapped her head around. "You talked to him first? Jeff and Amy are *my* kids, Addie."

"They're about to be *both* your kids, darling," Addie said firmly as the car followed the sign to British Airways. "I'll need an answer by Monday."

The limo pulled to the curb at the international terminal, and Jill slipped on sunglasses. It didn't matter that the sun had long since set: the twenty-foot illuminated billboard atop the next building displayed her full-color head shot, smiling beside Christopher's, in an elegant, public-perfect pose that she didn't feel like living up to right now.

Stepping from the car and following Addie into the terminal, Jill wished she had someone—a mother, maybe, or even a friend—with whom she could talk about the *Lifestyles* article. But there was no one. No one but Addie who had everything to gain. Or lose.

She crossed to the gate from customs and spotted her too-tall-for-sixteen son striding toward her, dressed in his favorite Celtics T-shirt and faded jeans. She raised her hand and waved, then, with her arm in midair, Jill stopped. Walking beside Jeff was a heavily made-up, dark-haired girl she didn't recognize.

Then she did.

She put her hand to her mouth and tried not to gasp.

Addie grabbed Jill's elbow. "Well, well," she remarked, "Amy may have left a fourteen-year-old, but she's returned twenty-five."

Jill could not answer. She stared at the white leather micro-miniskirt that moved toward her, propelled by a haughty strut on four-inch, jelly platform shoes.

"But Daddy bought me this skirt in SoHo," Amy whined once they'd arrived home, bid Addie good-bye, and hauled three weeks worth of teenage suitcases into the foyer of the modest Tudor in Cambridge—the house Jill had found when she'd been promoted to her first anchor job.

"I don't care if Princess Di bought it for you," Jill barked, tossing her MCM bag on the sofa and heading to the kitchen for a much-needed glass of wine. "If I ever catch you in it again, you're grounded."

"All the girls wear them, Mother."

"All the girls do not have me for a mother."

"Lucky for them."

A tightness crept across the back of Jill's neck. She reached up to the wine rack and plucked a bottle of chardonnay. "I want both of you to get upstairs and unpack your dirty laundry," she called back to the foyer. "Then get your things together for the Vineyard. We're leaving at eleven o'clock."

"In the morning?" Amy sputtered, then mumbled something incoherent, though Jill distinctly thought she heard the word "bitch."

She opened her mouth to respond, then opened the bottle instead. If there was only one thing she had learned from her mother, it was that sometimes silence was more effective than words.

Rubbing her neck, she poured the wine into an elegant Baccarat wineglass, one of a set of twelve, an engagement gift from Thalia's, the exclusive French restaurant in Back Bay, a sponsor of *Good Night, Boston.* Hopefully, the vibration of Amy's feet stomping up the stairs wouldn't crack the crystal.

"Mom?" Jeff bellowed as he rounded the corner into the kitchen. "How many phone lines are there at the house on the Vineyard?"

Jill took a drink. "Why?"

"Because I can't be stuck away on some island without being able to get on-line."

She stared at her glass, disappointed that the wine had failed to soothe the tension. "I lived there almost eighteen years without going on-line. Without even owning a computer."

"Did they have phones back then?"

Jeff was a great kid, a fun kid. But he needed to work on his timing. "I'll take care of the phone. Now please, go unpack. I'd like to have the laundry done before midnight." She dumped the wine down the sink and wondered if her fans ever realized that she, too, had dirty clothes to wash, and if they would assume that the family of the new millennium could survive an entire month under the same roof.

Chapter 2

The Friday afternoon sun streamed through the blinds, painting thin yellow stripes across her naked stomach. Rita knew she'd better get moving: there was a house to show at one, and it must be close to that now. She'd have to hurry, but it had been worth it. She knew she'd said that the last time would be the last time, but Rita was glad she'd changed her mind. Joe had kept it up longer than usual today, and damn, he'd made her feel good.

She rolled onto her side and stared at the gray-haired man beside her. "What time you got, Joe?"

He moaned a little, then, without opening his eyes, reached beneath the sheets and stroked her thigh. "All the time in the world, honey."

Rita laughed at the lie. "All the time until the ferry comes in," she said as she sat up and pulled the comforter around her age-softened, though still small breasts. She'd hated being short—*petite*—all her life, until recently, when she'd noticed that other women her age had begun to plump out, their breasts obviously held in place only by the retaining walls of their bras, their hips leaking across chair seats like the waves over the tide line during a storm. "Will she be on the two o'clock?"

Joe sighed. "It's the same every week. She arrives on the two o'clock, Fridays, and leaves on the six-fifteen, Sundays." He coughed and lit a cigarette. "I don't know how much more of her I can stand."

"Surely you'll stand her until her father dies," Rita said, though she knew perfectly well Joe would never leave his wife for her, no matter what he said, no matter how much money he claimed he'd save in the divorce once his wife had her inheritance. As much as a small, hopeful part of her wanted to believe him, Rita knew it was just another line. God knew she'd heard enough of them to know. "I've got to get going," she said.

"Yeah. It's twenty 'til one now."

"Shit," she said, grabbing the comforter and leaping from the bed. "Why the fuck did you let me fall asleep?"

"Shit." He chuckled. "Why the fuck did you let me keep fucking you?"

Rita tossed the pillow at him as she walked quickly toward the bathroom, fluffing her overdyed hair, the white down comforter dragging behind her. "I won't have time for a freaking shower."

"Tourists like the smell of fish," he said. "It's part of why they come here."

She closed the door behind her, wishing he hadn't said that. Just because she was an island woman, just because she liked being in his bed, didn't mean she liked her men crude. As she slipped into her underwear, Rita wondered if Joe Geissel was that crude with his wife. Probably not. Summer people always felt they could go that extra mile with islanders. As if they thought they didn't have class. Or feelings.

Quickly dressing in the mint-green cotton skirt, white shirt, and matching green-and-white-striped blazer with the navy "SurfSide Realty" logo embroidered on the pocket, Rita checked her makeup in madam's oval mirror and resisted the temptation to leave a telltale sign: a mascara wand, perhaps, or a few strands of her short, curly red hair. *Ha,* she thought to herself. *That would teach him.* Then she sighed and wiped the counter clean, flushing away the tissue and the evidence. Teaching Joe's wife that another woman had graced her chamber would accomplish nothing, and could end up screwing Rita out of a golden chance to save her financial neck.

She clasped three gold chains around the deep "V" of her open shirt, pushed the matching wide bracelets onto her wrists, and decided she'd better forget it.

"See you next week?" Joe called from the bed as she crossed the bedroom and retrieved her briefcase.

"Sure. I'll call you." She poked long dangle earrings into her ears and raced down the wide, winding staircase of the old beachfront estate that, though in need of repair, would probably bring two million five, maybe six, on today's market because of its prime location in prestigious West Chop.

As Rita groaned her way toward Oak Bluffs, her eyes flicked back and forth from the road of stalled tourists to the red digital clock on the dashboard of her seven-year-old Toyota. Hopefully, the Martins were slowed by traffic, too. Joe Geissel or not, Rita couldn't afford to miss a potential sale. It was already August and prime time for sales was quickly waning. Once Labor Day passed, Rita knew the only action she'd get would be a few buyers looking to steal property, and a roster of new listings from people wanting to sell before winter. Real estate on the island, like all other action, ceased to exist beyond Labor Day.

She turned onto County Road and wondered if Joe would ever list the house. He'd mentioned the possibility when she'd met him at the tavern last month—hell, it was the only reason she'd agreed to sleep with him in the first place. That, and the fact he was on his fourth marriage, so it wasn't as though she was intruding on marital bliss. Besides, Rita knew that as she got older, the men became scarcer. Thankfully, the world was adapting to suit her needs. Roles were reversed now: men who used to work in the city and come out only on weekends to where their wives and children were safely ensconced for the summer now often stayed here, while the wives did the city-shuttle. Men like Joe, a semiretired financial consultant, did what little work they felt like from their phone/fax/e-mail setups in one of the musty rooms of the treasured summer homes, while their wives held down respectable jobs in the city. It was a demographic trend for which Rita was supremely grateful.

The Martins were waiting when she arrived. Rita started to apologize when she noticed the looks of disdain on their faces. No one had to tell her they hated the house. She pasted on her agent-of-the-month smile and got out of her car.

"Too small," Mrs. Martin whined.

"Too expensive," her husband snorted.

"Too far from the beach," the missus added.

Rita wanted to tell them to go screw themselves, that they'd known before looking that there were only four bedrooms and that the price was a million eight firm. And even though it was a hike to the beach, the property was in the freaking historic district, had an unheard-of full-acre lot, and overlooked Vineyard Sound.

She wanted to tell them. Then she remembered the mountain of unpaid bills on her desk.

"I'm sorry you don't care for this one," she said, adjusting the too hastily snapped belt of her skirt. "But I think there will be another place more to your liking which is coming on the market any day."

Mrs. Martin raised an overtweezed eyebrow. "Oh?"

"Yes." She averted her gaze from the woman's straw tote bag with the multicolored yarn flowers splattered across the front, and wondered if Mrs. Martin had a house filled with Vineyard souvenirs in her most likely sprawling estate back in Brookline. "I'm afraid it will sell fast, though. It's in an A-one location. A waterfront property." The words spilled as her thoughts raced. "However," she added, "it might be out of your price range."

"Where is it?" the mister asked.

Rita cautiously crossed her fingers. "West Chop."

Mrs. Martin stuck her elbow into Mr. Martin's thick side. "Can we see it before the papers are drawn up?"

Looking for the deal. Always looking for the deal. Rita had learned long ago that the most important key to real estate success was to make the client think they had found the deal of the century. "Well, I'm not sure . . ." She stammered a little—rule number two—in order to heighten their interest. "The owners haven't made a firm decision to sell."

"We'd like to see it, anyway," Mrs. Martin said.

Rita smiled again. "I'll see what I can do. Why don't you call my office . . . say . . . next Tuesday? I should know something more definite by then."

The Martins nodded and climbed into their Mercedes. Rita waved as they drove off, then got into her own car and said a quick prayer that she could get a commitment from Joe on Monday, after his wife had returned to the city and Rita had a chance to tell him that selling now was the smartest thing he could do.

As she turned over the engine, she wished she'd stayed in bed a little longer with Joe, but figured what the hell, she might as well drive home to Edgartown and pick up the mail. Maybe there was a letter from her mother who had moved to Florida a year ago and remained steadfast in her Yankee conservativeness to write—and not phone—except on special occasions and during off-peak times. Tonight she should pick up some good tips at the tavern, and tomorrow was Saturday and there were houses to clean, and hopefully another house or two to show.

God, Rita thought as she headed toward Vineyard Haven Road, *how I hate summers.*

The post office was crowded. Rita moved her way to the mailboxes, cursing herself for not having home delivery. Just because Vineyard Haven had yet to succumb to mailmen didn't mean Edgartown hadn't.

"Hey, Rita," a voice called to her.

She thumbed through a stack of mail and turned to Jesse Parker who stood behind the counter. He was unshaven and looked like he'd just come off another bender.

"Afternoon, Jesse. How's your mother?"

"She hates the nursing home. Other than that, about the same."

"Maybe I'll stop by and bring her some fudge. Does she still like penuche?"

"Yours is the best. I still haven't made a decision about her house."

"Take your time, Jesse. There's no reason to upset her." As much as she could use the listing, her commission on Mrs. Parker's small Cape wouldn't exactly change Rita's life. Besides, hustling tourists was one thing; islanders were different. They were family. She moved to the counter, glancing at her mail.

"Hey," he continued, "did you hear the news?"

There was no letter from Rita's mother. Only a few bills, an ad for a septic system, and a long white envelope from the Internal Revenue Service. She frowned, then looked up at him. "What news?"

"Your old friend's coming back to town."

"What old friend?" She walked to the trash bin and tossed in the ad, silently wishing she could throw the rest there, too.

"Jill Randall."

She clutched the envelopes and stared at Jesse.

"What's her name now? McPhearson? Yeah, that's it. Anyway, she's coming back today."

Rita's spine stiffened. "Why?"

He shrugged. "Who knows."

"You probably do, Jesse. You know everything."

He scratched his stubble. "Not sure. Maybe she and that fellow she's going to marry—you know, that baseball star, what's his name, Edwards or something?"

Rita shifted on one foot. If anyone in town said they hadn't followed Jill's life, they were lying. Her picture was plastered often enough on the front page of the Boston papers, a constant reminder of her success, screaming from news racks all over the island. "Christopher Edwards," she said dryly.

"Yeah. That's it. They're reopening her folks' old house. The one on Water Street."

The fact that the Randall house was on Water Street was no news to Rita. *North* Water Street. In the better part of town.

"Maybe they're going to be summer people."

She tucked the envelopes into her briefcase. "I doubt it. Jill hated it here. Couldn't wait to get away."

"People change."

As she snapped her briefcase shut, Rita noticed that her hand was trembling. "Well," she said coolly, "guess I'll have to pay them a visit."

She turned and quickly went out the door, knowing full well that she did not, or never would, have any intention of paying a visit to her old childhood friend. Jill had achieved everything she'd once wanted, according to anyone who ever said anything. Fine, Rita thought. But she damn well wasn't going to come back here and gloat and make Rita feel like a piece of worthless shit all over again. Rita Blair, the one who was never quite as good or as smart or as pretty. The last thing she wanted was to have Jill learn that she'd turned out exactly as Jill had probably expected: struggling to make a living the way her mother had done—waiting on tables and cleaning other people's shit.

And the last thing she wanted was for Jill to learn the reason why she had disappeared from the island twenty-six years ago.

Chapter 3

Amy hadn't spoken to her since last night.

The strong summer wind whipped Jill's hair in front of her face now, blocking the view of the coastline of Cape Cod diminishing against the horizon. She reached up and pulled back her hair, her hand catching a light spray of seawater as the ferry arched its way across the choppy sound. Though the sun shined brightly, the crossing felt surprisingly rough. Jill wasn't sure if it was because of the wind or the waves of trepidation that rumbled inside her.

"Wouldn't you think her father had enough sense to know Amy is too young for a skirt like that?" Jill asked Christopher as they leaned against the upper deck rail.

He spoke softly, his words floating in the wind. "Forget it, Jill. You told her she can't wear it. It's done."

Jill sighed. "Sometimes I hate being a mother."

"I don't believe that for a minute."

"Well, all right. It's not being a mother I hate. It's not knowing how."

"Really, Jill. I think you're overreacting."

She gripped the rail more tightly. A gull soared in the sky, swooped, then landed on the sonar mast.

"Am I also overreacting when I tell you I'm upset about the *Lifestyles* spread? That you agreed with Addie before asking me?"

Christopher lay his hand on her shoulder. "Look, I told Addie it was fine with me. I said she'd have to talk with you."

"She did."

"And?"

"And, I don't know." She turned her face from him and looked across the harbor. As Vineyard Haven grew larger, pressure began to build in her head. In the years since she and Richard had divorced, Jill had grown accustomed to making her own decisions. Accustomed to it, and tired of it. Still, it was difficult to change.

She glanced across the deck at Jeff and Amy. Jeff was leaning into the breeze, stretching to see all that he could see. Amy stood beside him wearing gray grunge and a pout. Jill wondered why the nineties had to be so complicated.

"Passengers return to your vehicles," came a voice from the loudspeaker.

"I'm going below for the car," Christopher said. "Why don't you get the kids and meet me on the dock?"

Jill nodded to Christopher as he left, and wished he would be more understanding. But he'd never had kids—he simply didn't know the balancing act it entailed. She threaded her way through the pastel-clothed, straw-hatted tourists, cameras slung around the pale indoor skin of their necks, toward Jeff and Amy—her kids, her problem, no matter what. And they were good kids, had always been good kids. It wasn't their fault they were teenagers.

Watching them now, it amazed Jill that she had produced such healthy, good-looking, intelligent children, with an easy sophistication that showed in their confident postures and private-school polish.

She knew she needed to remember that they were city kids, with global interests and worldly self-assuredness, with a mother who captivated New England TV viewers, and a father with whom they spent time at his impressive London flat. Jeff and Amy would never have to fight for what they wanted in life; they would never have to wonder what they had missed. After all, Jeff and Amy were not island kids. Jill had made sure of that.

"Thought we'd see a whale or two," Jeff shouted over the noise of the engines to his mother.

She followed his gaze to the water. "Sorry, no whales. A few scallops, maybe."

Amy turned her head away.

"Wasn't your father a fisherman?" Jeff asked.

Jill stared at the fast-approaching buildings: the Steamship Authority terminal, the Black Dog Tavern, the August-packed parking lot. She tried to ignore the nudge of guilt as she heard Jeff refer to "your father." She'd always meant to bring the children to the Vineyard. She'd always meant to have them get to know their grandparents. But something more important had always come up. Now, her father had been dead a decade, and her mother . . . *Well,* Jill thought, *now it's simply too late.*

"Your grandfather ran the 1802 Tavern," she said slowly, "named for the year it was opened by his family, six generations before him. He fished during scallop season. Like everyone else on the damn island."

Her last line drew a flash from Amy's dark eyes—the dark eyes that were eerily identical to Jill's mother's—the grandmother Amy had never known.

"Do we own the tavern now?" Jeff asked.

Jill wrapped her sand-washed silk jacket close against her as the ferry bumped the pier. "No," she answered, and let it go at that.

The ride from Vineyard Haven was little more than a blur. Stalled by the stop-and-go traffic of summer people, by the shifting rental tides of a Friday afternoon, the oversized Range Rover that Christopher had leased was a dinosaur crawling along the road. Though she'd first balked at the hugeness of the vehicle she'd be stuck driving for a month, one look at the suitcases made Jill shut up. There were six for her alone: five for her wardrobe and one for makeup, sable brushes, hot rollers—necessary essentials for Jill to achieve the "natural," viewer-pleasing look that she dared not be seen in public without.

As they wove along the narrow streets, she tried to tune out the comments that drifted from the backseat: "Wow, neat," Jeff said as they passed the gingerbread-style houses that hugged the road in Oak Bluffs; "Cool," he whispered when a couple of teenage girls crossed the road toward the beach, their youthful bodies tightly packed into string bikinis. Amy, of course, was not talking.

Through it all, Jill felt disoriented. Everything around her seemed so much smaller than she remembered: the houses were smaller, the dunes were smaller, the tourists, more plentiful. Heading into Edgartown, her head began to ache. She loosened the collar of her shirt.

"Tell me where to turn," Christopher said suddenly.

She sat up straight and stared ahead. "Stay to the left," she said in a voice that sounded like someone else's, someone with a headache, someone in pain. "When you get to Water Street, go left again."

The houses were the same: close to the road, white colonial structures, trimmed in black or dark green, all looking freshly painted, all bordered by neat white picket fences. The stores were the same, too. Different names, perhaps, but the same small, quaint shops, the same open doors, welcoming tourists and their MasterCards. Here, too, everything looked dwarfed.

At Water Street, Christopher turned left.

They drove a block. Then two. And then Jill saw it: the sea captain's house with the widow's walk on the roof, the small paned windows, the narrow brick walk. It was her house, the house of her father and grandfather and generations before them. It was the house on Water Street; the house, and the life, she had once escaped. Now she was home.

Slowly the ache in her head began to dull, replaced by the soft thumping of her heart in her throat.

The key trembled in Jill's hand. While Christopher and the kids stood impatiently behind her, she blinked her eyes quickly and rattled the lock. Finally, the brass handle turned. She pushed open the door and stepped inside. Stale air in the hallway crushed against her chest. She fought for breath.

"Should the bags go upstairs?" Christopher asked.

Jill nodded, unable to speak.

The hallway was dark, darker than she remembered. A layer of dust had settled over the mahogany staircase. She stood, staring up the steep stairs, at the veiled light that filtered through the white eyelet curtains hanging from the window at the top. She half expected to see her father come down the steps, a pipe in his mouth, a newspaper in his hand; she half expected to smell the sickish odor of lavender hankies mixed with the pungent aroma of quahog chowder, and to hear the strains of Benny Goodman droning from the sewing room. But as she stood motionless, Jill saw only the gray diffused light, smelled only a thick scent of must, and heard nothing at all.

"Which room?" Christopher asked as they bustled past her with suitcases and canvas bags.

"Amy, take the back bedroom on the right," Jill said quickly. The back bedroom had been her room. Once. Long ago. "Jeff, you can have the front one."

"And us?" Christopher asked, halfway up the stairs now.

There was no sense pretending they didn't sleep together. "Upstairs. To the left," Jill said quietly. The bedroom to the left. The spacious room with a view of the street, a view of the harbor, and a tall fireplace across from the canopied bed. Her parents' bed.

She shook off her thoughts. "I'll get the groceries." She turned back to the open door, stepped outside, and breathed deeply, not feeling at all like the new TV royalty, but like a little girl again, that same little girl, trapped in the middle of the sea.

Kyle wasn't home from work yet. Rita went into the living room of the low-ceilinged, warped-floored saltbox where she'd lived all her forty-three years, except, of course, for twenty-six years ago, when she'd gone to live with her aunt in Worcester, first hiding out with a pregnant belly, then hiding the baby she'd decided to keep. The baby, Kyle. The four-year-old boy she'd returned to the Vineyard with and had told everyone he was three. Big for his age. Advanced. With the help of some Wite-Out and one of those new plain paper copiers they had at her typist's job in the city, Rita had doctored Kyle's birth certificate, and made it "official"-looking enough to enroll him in kindergarten two years later and keep tongues from wagging from Oak Bluffs to Gay Head.

She flopped on the threadbare sofa now and rested her face in her hands. Those were the years she'd long ago chosen to forget. Those few people who knew the truth were, thank God, dead, except for Rita's mother who would never tell a soul. But Rita had never been sure if Jill had known. And now Jill was coming back to the island. . . .

"Shit," Rita said. She stood up again and pulled off her SurfSide Real Estate blazer. Kyle was nearly twenty-five . . . twenty-*six* . . . years old now. Did it really matter what anyone thought? Did it really matter if anyone cared?

She closed her eyes and clenched her jaw. If Kyle found out, what would he think of his mother? She had told him his father was a GI she'd married in Worcester, a soldier off to Vietnam. She'd said his name was William Smith, and that he'd been killed over there. After his death, the pain was too great for Rita, so she took back her maiden name and gave it to Kyle when he was born.

At least, that's what she'd said. It had seemed like such a simple lie at the time, a protective lie, an okay lie.

Kyle had never doubted his mother. And he never pursued more knowledge of his father. Now, it all seemed so long ago, so long that Rita herself had come to believe the lie.

The last thing she'd expected was that Jill would return.

She went into the kitchen, plucked two ice cubes from the freezer, and dropped them into a glass. From beneath the sink she took a half-full bottle of scotch, not caring that she had to change into her waitress uniform and be at the tavern in an hour and a half, not caring how many cottages she had to clean tomorrow. She poured in two inches, then turned on the faucet. It coughed and choked, then finally spit out a dribble of water. Damn, Rita thought as she let the water drizzle into her glass. If only she could sell the house on County Road, the farm in Tisbury, or the B & B in Gay Head, if only she could sell something, *anything*—never mind Joe's house—maybe she could afford to have the damn plumbing fixed. And the roof. And buy a new car.

"Fat chance," she said aloud as she took a deep swig from her drink. For even if she did come into a sum of money, a summer windfall, even if Joe decided to sell, Rita knew she could not risk spending the cash. Winter wasn't far off and she knew only too well that winters could be expensive, with far more outgo than income.

Two years ago, she could have sold her own house. It was hers free and clear, a parting gift from her mother. But when Rita's boss, Franklin, was diagnosed with cancer and decided to sell the real estate agency, Rita had bought into the American dream. She'd mortgaged her house to the max, paid off Franklin, and become the sole proprietor of Surf-Side Realty, complete with two secretaries and a downtown office.

How was she supposed to have known the business wasn't that great? How was she supposed to have known that within a year she'd have to let one, then the other secretary go, and that last month she'd be kicked out of her office as well?

Plopping back on the sofa, Rita put her feet on the magazine-strewn coffee table and knew that if the market didn't turn around soon, she'd be forced into living the way she'd been raised: renting out the house in summer, bunking in with her mother's friends.

As a kid, she'd pretended it was fun, bouncing from house to house, her bed often consisting of a sleeping bag on the floor of a cramped Cape, in a room filled with smoke and laughter and a boozy smell wafting from the crowd of adults huddled around the card table, playing pitch until dawn.

She'd pretended it was fun, but in truth, it was humiliating—an annual reinforcement of the fact that Rita was poor, that she was not quite as good as her best friend, Jill, who had a big bedroom all to herself, twelve months a year. The last thing Rita wanted now was to feel those feelings again, to beg for somewhere to live, to admit that her struggle was no different than her mother's had been.

Kyle, of course, was her saving grace. He had turned into a hard worker, had used his woodworking classes in high school to learn carpentry, and this summer had landed a good job with Ben Niles, the well-respected restorer of Cape and Island homes— *classy* Cape and Island homes, the kind that could bring in a year's salary with one commission. Hell, Ben even took Kyle on a couple of jobs to Nantucket this spring, and to Hyannis last month. Paid all his expenses in a nice hotel, bought all his food.

Yeah, she thought as she took another sip of scotch, Kyle had a good job. And if she sold a hefty property soon, she could manage to keep the house for him, summers included.

Rita swirled the ice cubes in her glass, knowing that Kyle had a good life ahead of him. As long as Jill McPhearson didn't screw it up.

"Jesus Christ, Jill," Christopher said as he stood beside her at the tiny window in the kitchen. "Is that the Chappaquiddick ferry?"

She finished unpacking the coffee maker with mechanical precision, a robot without emotion. "Yes."

"I can't believe you never told me it was in your backyard."

The milk came next, then the orange juice.

"This house is worth more than I ever imagined."

"Why? Does it give it some twisted sort of added historic significance?" As soon as her words were out, she wished she had clipped them. The sarcasm had not been intentional: Christopher, of course, was right. The location of the house did give it some kind of notoriety, warped though it may be.

She ran her hand through her hair. "Why don't you go look at the ferry while I finish in here?" she asked in her nicest tone. It had been a tedious day; her headache had not yet eased.

"You wouldn't mind?"

"Not at all." The kids had already dumped their suitcases in their rooms and taken off for the center of town. Jill wanted some peace right now, some time to herself.

"Great." He went out the back door, its screen slapping shut, the way it always had, the way Jill herself had made it slap so many times, so long ago, when she dashed off to school, ran off to meet Rita, or simply wanted to escape from the house.

She went to the window and watched him walk briskly toward the ferry, his long legs trundling toward excitement, as though if he didn't hurry, surely it would leave without him. She wondered how much restraint he would need to stop from swimming the channel to determine for himself if Ted Kennedy had done it so long ago, or was said to have done it.

Then she leaned against the sink and realized that if it hadn't been for Chappaquiddick, she might never be standing here now, with a hugely successful career, two wonderful—well, sometimes wonderful—children, and nowhere to go but up.

It all began that Saturday morning in July, 1969. Her father was in the front room, scanning the newspaper. Jill was upstairs in her bedroom, making her four-poster bed the way Mother insisted, the right way, with rigid square corners and no space for air.

Then, Mother came in from shopping, bearing more news than the *Vineyard Gazette*.

"A girl was killed last night," Florence announced

in a voice so loud Jill heard it upstairs. "In Ted Kennedy's car."

She ran to the top of the stairs and listened.

"Over on Chappy. The car went off Dyke Bridge."

Jill heard her father groan. "Oh, God. Why here?" The paper rustled. "I'd better get down to the tavern. All hell's going to break loose."

Her father was right. Within hours, the peaceful island was invaded by police and investigators, a tidal wave of gawkers, and, worst of all, by the media. The peaceful island, whose inhabitants always protected the privacy of others, U.S. senators included, and gave them a haven from the microscope of the world.

The people came, and for the first time the economy of the island flourished long past Labor Day, right through the January inquest. And though no one on the island enjoyed their usual post-tourist sigh that year, all reveled in the extra dollars they fed into their bank accounts.

Florence Randall wanted no part of it. She would not allow the "incident" to be mentioned at the dinner table. She would not allow George to bring home any gossip that the mainlanders shared in the tavern. And, had she known, she would never have allowed Jill to cut school with Rita that cold winter day of the inquest, park her bicycle across from Duke's County Courthouse, and watch, with stunned fascination, the army of outsiders clustered there.

Rita was enthralled with the men. But Jill was distracted by something else: the women who had come in from Washington to testify. They were miniskirted and teased-haired, and they smiled with somber graciousness when faced with the cameras. And then there were the female reporters. Even *they* held a sophistication Jill had only witnessed among the wealthy summer tourists. But these were not tourists.

They were working women with careers, with a place in this life and a sense of themselves that they could call their own, free from the confines of island life or the watchful eyes of hovering mothers.

Jill tucked her mousy hair beneath her hand-knit hat and looked down at her four-year-old sweater and worn Wrangler jeans—not even bell-bottoms, just jeans. "Rita," she said, "I know how I'm going to get off this island. I know what I'm going to do."

"Please don't say you're going to marry a Kennedy."

"Nope. I'm going to go to college. Then I'm going into television. I'm going to make it big."

Rita was quiet a moment. Then she shrugged. "Hey, you're the honor roll student, not me. Besides, your parents can afford it."

Jill stuffed her hands in the pockets of her jeans. She'd never thought she was smarter than Rita. She'd always felt her grades only reflected the long hours her mother forced her to stay in her room with no TV and no radio, with only her schoolbooks and her parents' expectations. No, she never thought she was smarter than Rita. But sometimes she felt guilty that she had a father, and that he, unlike Rita's, had not taken off when they were in the third grade. She studied the women reporters again. "You know how badly I want to leave here, Rita."

"Sure, kid," Rita answered as she walked back toward her bike. "I gotta get to work. The tavern's going to be jammed."

Jill had suspected many times that that day had been the beginning of the end of her friendship with Rita, that it had been why Rita had left the island right after graduation, with no explanation and no good-bye, leaving Jill with only an unsettled loss and an undefined ache of regret.

From the window now she saw Christopher board the ferry, probably wanting to feel the water beneath him, to imagine what had happened that night about which few will ever know the truth. She thought about Christopher, her long-awaited partner; she thought about Chappaquiddick and how it had shaped her life; and she thought about Rita, and wondered what had become of her, and why her best friend had never been in touch.

"Hey, Mom, I'm home." Kyle's voice resounded from the kitchen, sending waves of contentment through Rita, like no other sound in the world. He appeared in the doorway of the living room, all six feet two, broad-shouldered, sandy-haired masculinity, a vivid reminder that Kyle was no longer her "little" boy.

She drained her glass and smiled. "How was your day?"

"Great," he said, tossing his keys on the chair. "But you're not going to believe where I'm working Monday."

"Nantucket?" It would be wonderful if Ben liked Kyle's work well enough to keep him on in winter. It would help Kyle's confidence, as well as his wallet.

"Nope. Right here on the Vineyard. Jill McPhearson's house."

She set down her empty glass. The scotch rolled over in her stomach. "Jill's?"

"Yeah. Can you stand it? Ben keeps getting these jobs for celebrities. We'll be working there all month. I guess her boyfriend's here, too. Sure would like to meet him."

Rita dropped her feet from the coffee table. "They're only people, Kyle. They're not gods."

Kyle shrugged. "Still, it's pretty cool."

"A lot of celebrities come to the island, you know that. They come here for their privacy. They pay dearly to have no one bother them."

"I'm not going to bother them, Mom. I'm going to work for them."

She stood up. There was no way she was going to think about this now. There was no way . . . "I've got to get to the tavern," she said quickly. "Remind me to set my alarm early. I promised to make penuche for Jesse Parker's mother."

"It's August, Mom. Don't you have enough to do?"

"I like to be neighborly."

"The Parkers live a mile away."

"What can I say?" Rita said as she headed upstairs to change into her tavern uniform. "The old lady says my fudge is better than hers ever was." The truth was, everyone loved Rita's fudge. And Rita loved making it, because it made people smile: sick people, troubled people, people she knew, people she didn't. A batch of her sweet fudge made them all smile, and the way Rita figured it, people didn't have a lot to smile about as a rule.

Kyle followed her to the foot of the stairs. "Did you know her?" he asked. "When she lived here?"

Rita gripped the wobbly handrail. "Who?"

"Jill, Mom. Jill McPhearson."

She let go of the handrail and continued up the steps. "A little," she answered. There was no point in telling Kyle that Jill Randall McPhearson had once, in another time, in another life, been her best friend. There was no need to tell Kyle, because on this freaking island, he would more than likely find out soon enough.

Chapter 4

 "I can't," Jill said as Christopher slid his hand beneath her silk nightgown. It wasn't that she didn't want him. It was the damn house. The damn room. The damn bed.

He raised her nightgown and brushed his lips across her nipple. It stiffened. His erect penis pressed against her thigh. "It might make you feel better," he whispered. The scent of his breath drifted lightly toward her: minty toothpaste, not quite masking the dinner of pizza—take-out pizza, because Jill had been unable to bring herself to cook in her mother's kitchen.

She gently moved his head away and covered herself. "Maybe tomorrow, okay?"

In the soft glow of moonlight that seeped through the sheer white drapes, she saw Christopher run his hand through his hair. "Sure," he said. "Tomorrow." He lay back on the bed, turned his back to her, and fell into silence.

She was aware that tears had formed in her eyes. In the four months they'd been sleeping together, she'd never said no to Christopher. She'd never wanted to. There were, of course, times when she had been tired, stressed from the show, preoccupied with thoughts of the kids. At those times, Jill pretended to have an orgasm. *Faked it,* as the magazine articles said. She'd long since decided there was no harm in that, especially if the next day meant an early call or a tedious interview. It was sometimes better to have sex and get it over with. Besides, she reasoned, she and Christopher had so much more than . . . sex. They had a future together—a bright-lights, big-city future.

But tonight, Jill didn't have the strength even to fake it. She was too aware of the mattress beneath her skin, the subtle lumps and curves of the mattress where her parents—Florence and George Randall—had slept together for so many years. She could not stop herself from wondering if . . . when they slept side by side right here . . . if Florence had ever faked it, or known that she could. It was a concept Jill found disturbing, not for the answer but for the fact that she'd even thought it at all.

She pulled the sheet to her chin, her nostrils catching the stuffy scent of the linen closet, the oppressive odor of island must. She quickly pushed the sheet away. The tears rolled down her cheeks. She stared into the silhouette of the shallow fireplace and wondered if she had the strength to make it through an entire month, or if she should leave tomorrow.

At five minutes to ten on Saturday morning, Ben Niles parked his '47 Buick on North Water Street and took a last look at the note that lay on the seat beside him. It had been there since yesterday morning, after he'd stormed into the Edgartown Post Office, demanding to know who had mailed it to his house in Oak Bluffs. From behind the counter, Jesse Parker had looked at him blankly, said he couldn't help him, then asked if Ben had been working for any interesting people lately, as if the letter meant nothing, as if threatening notes were mailed out of Edgartown every day.

"Bastard," he muttered, then got out of the car and slammed the door. The note must have come from Dave Ashenbach—the one person with enough stupidity to try to intimidate him.

He marched up the brick walk, lifted the brass door knocker, and rapped twice, cursing himself for taking on yet another celebrity job, all in the name of money, as if he needed any more, as if he needed the name of one more celebrity goddess on his perfect-people-packed résumé. But when the pushy PR woman had called, Ben had seized the opportunity to stay on the Vineyard this month. It would give him plenty of time to finalize his plans, plenty of access to convince the town fathers to bless them. As long as Ashenbach stayed the hell out of the way.

The door opened and a woman stood there, looking as though she'd just rolled out of bed, yet still like the goddess of a perfect world. He wondered if beneath the silk-and-lace robe her body was as fake as her hair color.

"Jill McPhearson?" he asked.

Her eyes grazed over him as though she were expecting a guy dressed in a Brooks Brothers suit, rather than jeans and a T-shirt. As she pulled back her hair he noticed her hands—soft, uncallused skin, long, slender fingers, and a huge diamond ring that shouted "I'm taken. In case anyone hasn't heard." He tipped back the brim of his Red Sox baseball cap and looked squarely into her eyes. "I'm Ben Niles," he said. "The renovator."

"Oh," she commented. "Mr. Niles. Come in."

Her voice had the same overenunciated lilt of others he'd worked for, other show-biz, perfect types. "Call me Ben," he said as he stepped into the foyer, onto a worn oriental rug. She was nearly as tall as his five feet nine. *Christ,* he thought, *tall, pretty, and skinny.* He wondered if that was what had made her famous. *Calm down, Dad,* he could almost hear his daughter, Carol Ann, say. Carol Ann—who seemed to think it was now her duty to step in and keep him under control, the way her mother had tried, the way Louise had nearly perfected before her death two years ago. Well, he was fifty years old now, and quite able to take care of himself. He took a deep breath and tried to remind himself that Jill McPhearson had nothing to do with his problems. "I understand you need some work done."

His eyes quickly traveled from the faded floral paper in the hall to the drawing room on the left, the dining room on the right. It was a grand old home, Georgian style, rich with butternut and mahogany trim, the kind of solid Vineyard tradition he would showcase in his living museum—Menemsha House—if the variance ever came through, if Ashenbach minded his own damn business.

"I need you to make it salable," Jill responded. "I'm putting it on the market."

No surprise there, he thought, suddenly weary of the synthetic people he'd allowed to permeate his life. "That's a shame," he responded slowly. "Not many of these old places are so well preserved."

"My family has lived here for generations."

He resisted shaking his head. "Then it's even more of a shame."

She folded her arms across her flat stomach and tossed back her shoulder-length hair—her shoulder-length, uncombed, bottle-streaked hair. "What do you need to see first?"

Ben wondered if he had pissed her off. He tugged at the brim of his cap. *She's a customer,* he told himself again, *a customer whose money will help pay for Menemsha House.* He tried to smile. "I'll check the structure. The plumbing, the wiring."

Just then a man appeared at the top of the stairs.

He was dressed in a polo shirt and neatly pressed cotton shorts. *Ah,* Ben thought, *the other half of the perfect couple.*

"You must be here to refurbish the house," the man said as he came down the steps. "Well, you certainly have your work cut out for you."

Ben glanced at Jill and noticed what appeared to be annoyance flash across her face. "This is Ben Niles," she said. "Ben, Christopher Edwards."

He nodded toward Ben's cap. "I see you're a baseball fan."

"One who remembers that Christopher Edwards pitched three no-hitters against the Sox in '73."

"Don't hold it against me."

Ben laughed, the way his customers expected, part of *his* game that he knew so well. "I wasn't a Sox fan at the time." He wanted to add that he'd been nowhere near New England—or the Vineyard—until twenty years ago, a fact that was part, if not all, of the town fathers' problem. He was not a native, not one of *them.* But Ben cut himself off. For all he knew, Jill McPhearson, synthetic or not, was Dave Ashenbach's kissing cousin.

Christopher smiled, then turned to Jill, who still seemed annoyed by his presence. "Honey, I'll show Ben around."

"No," she answered brusquely. "Thanks, but why don't you fix yourself breakfast?"

He looked at her a moment, then looked away. "Fine. I'll be in the kitchen."

She turned back to Ben. "If you'd like to start in the basement, I'll get into some clothes and be right down."

Ben nodded and let her direct him toward the back of the house, silently pleased that paradise was never quite as perfect as it seemed. Then again, he reasoned, women like Jill McPhearson probably never had to worry about the Dave Ashenbachs of the world, or about their dream going up in smoke, burning to the ground, with them in it.

"I'd like to go up to the widow's walk," Ben said an hour after Jill had joined him, after she had finally begun to relax, having pushed down in her mind the fact that Christopher had practically raped her this morning. Ben's arrival had thankfully stopped him.

"The widow's walk?" she asked. A chill that was greater than the one emitting from the damp, crumbling, brick basement walls seeped through her. She leaned against an old metal pot that her mother had used for making beach plum jelly—her famous beach plum jelly that won first place every year at the fair, the same jelly that no one but Florence knew the recipe for, handed down from generation to generation of the Randall family; the same Florence Randall who once declared the widow's walk off-limits. "Must you go up there?" Jill asked, brushing a cobweb from her eyes.

Ben narrowed his blue—no, gray—eyes. "Only if you intend to include it with the sale of the house."

She wanted to ask if he thought he was being funny. Instead, she silently led him up the steep, winding stairs to the first floor, then the second. As she reached out to turn the knob on the door leading up, her heart began to flutter. She opened the door and turned to Ben. "You go ahead. I'll wait here."

He laughed. "Afraid of heights?" Then he ascended the steps.

Suppressing an urge to scream, Jill gritted her teeth and wondered if there were any sensitive men left in the world. The last, she suspected, had been her father. *Well,* she thought as she watched Ben's ass move beneath the form-fitting denim, *screw him. He's a* builder, *for God's sake, a common laborer.*

And she'd had all the male arrogance she could handle for one day.

She narrowed her eyes, then flinched with the realization that she was still staring at Ben's ass, his solid, sexy ass. *God,* Jill moaned, *why are the men with the best asses usually the biggest jerks?*

Pulling her eyes away, she ball-fisted her hands and climbed the stairs, blinking back the image of taut ass muscles and the ghost of her mother's wrath.

Once. She had only been here once, and yet the sensation of peace, the aura of quiet, had stayed with her throughout the years. Quiet, of course, until Florence had surprised her and Rita. Quickly scanning the room, Jill noticed that it was unchanged: the cartons remained, the old steamer trunk remained.

"This would make a great hot tub room," Ben said.

"I'll have the real estate agent mention that in the ad."

Ben shook his head and bounced up and down on his heels, as though testing the strength of the floor. Then he went to a window and applied pressure to the casing. "It's not in bad shape."

I know, Jill wanted to say. *I always knew it wasn't dangerous up here.* Her forehead tightened.

"You're going to need some structural reinforcement. Probably on every floor. That's where we'll start."

"How long will it take?" Her eyes drifted to the black steamer trunk. She slowly walked over and removed the old quilt, remembering when Rita had tried to open it, remembering it had been locked.

"I won't know that until we start."

"I want it done by Labor Day." She tugged at the lock; it broke off in her hand. Holding her breath, Jill carefully lifted the lid: inside were neat packages wrapped in old newspapers. She lifted one out and opened it. In her hand she held a footed pewter dish, round and sculpted in a feathered pattern, a peacock's image at the top. Jill had never seen the thing, had no idea what it was for.

Ben went back down the stairs, then stopped halfway down. Running his hand across the wall, he again bounced up and down again. "Labor Day might be tight. We'll do our best."

She rewrapped the dish. "I don't care how much it costs." As she returned the dish to the trunk, she spotted something else, something tucked in the corner. It looked like a book. Pulling it out, she examined the cracked leather tab and a small brass lock. She pushed a button; the book opened.

"Jill?" Ben called from the stairs. "I'd like to check out the bedrooms next."

She quickly flipped the pages. It wasn't a printed book, it was handwritten.

"Jill?" Ben summoned again.

"Wait a minute," she snapped, more sharply than she'd intended. She closed the book and replaced it on top of a vase. Then she realized that what she'd seen was her mother's handwriting. She frowned a moment, wondering what it could be. Florence Randall never relaxed long enough to read a book, let alone write anything. Jill shook her head. It was probably recipes, she thought. Maybe the prized beach plum jelly one.

"Coming," she muttered to Ben, closing the lid of the trunk, heading for the stairs, and wishing that all males over thirty years old would get the hell out of her life.

It was nearly one o'clock when Jill said good-bye to Ben, after signing his contract for an exorbitant fee. The paper, however, promised the inclusion of his trademark—a tiny stained glass whale to be set in a front window—proof that a Ben Niles's guarantee came with the house. Whatever that meant to whoever cared.

Standing at the soon-to-be-replaced back screen door, Jill noticed Christopher in the backyard, sitting on an Adirondack chair, a cup of coffee in one hand, a newspaper in the other. Her father had often sat there, watching the sailboats, watching the gulls, smoking his pipe in quiet repose.

She took a small breath and went out the door.

"I'm sorry about this morning," he said, without looking up. "I was a despicable rogue."

"Yes," she answered, sitting on the grass next to him. "You were."

He was quiet a moment. "I thought it would be fun to make love in the morning. I thought it might take your mind off this house."

"I was asleep. You startled me." She doubted his intention had anything to do with making her feel more at ease. Still, she decided to let it go. An apology, after all, was an apology.

"Addie called," he said.

Her mood shifted. She pulled at a blade of grass. "Does she miss me already?"

Christopher set down the paper. "She's waiting for an answer on the *Lifestyles* spread."

She stared out to the harbor. The Chappaquiddick ferry made its slow trek across the tiny strip of blue. "She said I had until Monday. I haven't had time to think about it."

"Jill, if we plan to build our career, this won't be the last time the subject of the kids will come up."

She didn't answer.

"She thinks the island is perfect for the photo shoot."

The energy seemed to drain from her body.

"Here? But you won't be here. You're leaving tomorrow."

"It's only a half-hour flight from Boston."

She didn't know what to say.

"Addie thinks it would be better to position you—us—away from the city. The Vineyard has a broader image. It would take us out of the local-yokel mode."

"What's wrong with Boston? God, Christopher, that's where we live. Our show is titled *Good Night, Boston,* if you remember."

He held up his hand. "Hey, I'm just the messenger."

Jill sighed, wishing she could believe him. "Tell her I'll decide before you leave tomorrow."

He nodded and set down the paper. "Let's take the kids out for dinner tonight."

"Afraid you'll get pizza two nights in a row?"

"No."

She chewed the bitter tip of the blade of grass: it was not sweet, not root-beer-flavorful like the sassafras root out at Gay Head. She let it fall from her hand. "Well, I won't turn down a dinner invitation. But I doubt that Amy will join us."

"I'll talk to her," he said. "Dinner at the tavern might help break the ice between you two."

"Where?"

"The tavern. The one your father owned."

She lowered her head and stared at the ground.

"I saw it when I went into town to get the paper. Didn't you say it was the 1802 Tavern?"

Her stomach churned. "Yes."

"They have a menu posted out front. It sounds good."

"I don't know . . ."

"Maybe it would give you a chance to see how the kids react to the *Lifestyles* piece."

She snapped her head up. "That's *my* decision, Christopher. Not theirs."

He sighed and picked up the paper again. "Well, at least let's have a decent dinner together."

"At the 1802?"

"You're going to have to face it sometime, Jill."

"Face it? There's nothing to face. It was my father's business, that's all."

"Then stop acting as though this house, his tavern . . . as though this whole damn island had some kind of sick claim on your brain."

The hot morning sun burned into her cheeks. "That's not fair. It's not true, and it's not fair."

"Prove it. Let's go to the tavern tonight."

Right now, Jill wondered if it were possible that she hated Christopher. He had no right to make her feel this . . . unsettled. Just because he'd been raised in a family that had doted on him, not by a mother who barely acknowledged his existence . . . just because his first marriage had quietly ended when his wife agreeably exited, not when she ran off with someone half her age as Richard had done . . .

God, she thought, she was so tired of always fighting for her place in the world. Since leaving the island, she had never stopped struggling to be the best. Struggling to prove she was the best—to prove to her mother, to prove to herself. And whether or not her mother had ever known, Jill was the best. She had been the best reporter, the best news anchor. She'd grabbed the brass ring with *Good Night, Boston*, and again when she'd won Christopher. She wasn't about to let him take it away from her now.

"All right," she said. "If you can get Amy to agree, we'll go to the tavern. I'm not afraid of it, Christopher. It's only a restaurant."

"Great," he answered as he jumped from the

chair. "Because Addie thinks it would be a perfect place for one of the *Lifestyles* shots."

"Give it up, Dad," Carol Ann said as she stood in the doorway of Ben's workshop—his blueprint-strewn haven, wedged in the alley behind his gingerbread cottage in Oak Bluffs.

He hunched over the plans for Menemsha House again—as if he didn't know them by heart, didn't know how every wide floorboard would be nailed, how every bit of woodworking would be carved. "I can't give it up," he replied.

"These people are your neighbors. Why are you fighting them?"

"Because they're wrong." He opened a wide, shallow drawer beside his workbench and slid out the duplicate set of plans. Ben had not fallen into the CAD-CAM trap of creating his visions on unfeeling computer screens: he craved the purist's touch of a pencil in his hand, the artist's brush, in number two lead. At his age, he was entitled to do it his way, even though it meant making two sets of plans for every project—two sets, just in case.

"You've always said you feel the islanders don't accept you. This is only going to alienate them further."

"Anyone not born here is an alien."

"Come on, Dad. They see the work you do for the celebrities, the tourists. It threatens them. They don't want Menemsha to become Oak Bluffs."

"My work is my livelihood, Carol Ann. And besides, Menemsha House isn't about show business. Or hawking T-shirts and pizza-by-the-slice. It's about preserving culture."

"There are plenty of museums on the island."

God, Ben thought, how could he expect the zoning board to understand when his own daughter didn't? He rubbed his thinning hair. "It's not a museum. It's an educational facility." And it *would* be educational—where tourists and islanders alike could learn the things he'd learned: the fine crafts of Early American building, using the authentic techniques from milling the bark off oak trees, to groove-and-tongue construction, and using the same tools from smooth wood chisels to hand-wrought nails. It was his dream. And it would be done.

"You're impossible."

"I know." He glanced at his daughter: her eyes as gray as his own were narrow with concern, the same deep dimple was tightly set in her same tanned, freckled cheek. Carol Ann might be the image of her father, copper-colored hair included. But it was her voice that always surprised Ben, for it was not his voice but Louise's, the soft, gentle voice of his now-deceased wife. Carol Ann had his features and his sturdy, not-so-tall frame, but she was Louise in both voice and spirit: quiet, cautious, and unliking conflict. She had married John Larson, a good man, but equally conventional, and their two preschool children would probably turn out the same.

He sighed. "The people of Menemsha think they still live in a fishing village. They're afraid of disrupting their sainted lobster pots. Apparently nobody told them the waters were fished out years ago."

Carol Ann frowned and glanced around the mess of tools and wood shavings in the workshop. "I wish you'd get a cleaning lady."

"A cleaning lady would screw up my system. Besides, I don't intend to act like a tourist, just because your mother's gone." He tried to swallow that little lump that popped from out of nowhere into his throat each time he admitted that Louise was dead.

"I didn't think you'd act like a damn fool, either, Dad. Mother would be so embarrassed."

"Your mother thought Menemsha House was magnificent."

"She didn't know it abuts Dave Ashenbach's property."

He shot a look at Carol Ann. He had not told her about the note. He hadn't wanted to cause her alarm. Or give her more ammunition to talk him out of it. "Look, honey," he said softly, "I bought that decaying old house for the way it sits atop the hill overlooking the bay, for the view of the sunset and the peace of the harbor. Now I want to turn it into something valuable, something worthwhile. If Ashenbach has a problem with that, it's not my fault. I'm not going to damage his precious land."

Carol Ann slipped her hands into the pockets of her jeans. "I only know that Mother wouldn't have wanted you to cause such a fuss."

Ben chuckled. "A *fuss*? God, Carol Ann, you sound like an old woman. You're spending far too much time at the Town Hall." The fact that Carol Ann—*his* daughter—worked in the clerk's office—worked for the *bureaucracy*—secretly amused him.

"Dad, don't change the subject. I think you should give this up now. John agrees with me."

"I'm sure he does. Well, the zoning board meeting is Monday night. It would be nice if my family at least pretended to support me." He snapped off the light. "Come on up to the house. I'll fix us some tea."

"I can't. John's waiting for me. We're taking the kids for ice cream tonight."

He nodded, but did not remark that it would be nice if his daughter had invited him to go along. Maybe his grandchildren and a double-decker fudge swirl would take his mind off the turmoil that no doubt lay ahead.

. . .

Jill scanned the tables that were jammed together, the whaling memorabilia that lined the stone walls, and the dark, low beams that stretched across the stucco ceiling.

"Quaint little place," Christopher said. "Has it changed?"

They were sitting by the fireplace. Although she had agreed to come, Amy was across the table from her mother—as far away as possible. Somehow, Christopher had coaxed her to join them.

"It's hard to say," Jill said. "I was only here a few times." It wasn't a complete lie, but she wasn't in the mood to reflect. It was all she could do to sit here, try to act natural, try not to feel like a young girl again, a quiet, young girl who hadn't been allowed to work here in summers, who hadn't been allowed to mingle with the tourists. Even her glazed linen skirt and matching silk shell—uptown, sophisticated attire that usually helped reassure her of her success—did not fortify her courage. Instead of feeling wealthy, successful, like *someone*, she felt overdressed and out of place.

"I thought your father owned it," Jeff said as he grabbed a menu and began scanning it.

"He did. But kids didn't go to taverns when I was a girl."

"God, Mom," Jeff said. "It's just a restaurant."

"I know. But my mother thought differently."

Amy, too, buried her face in a menu.

"I remember that there's a secret room, though."

"A secret room?" Jeff asked.

"It's where they used to stash bootleg liquor."

"Amy," Jeff said, "you'd better listen up." He looked at Jill, a smirk on his face. "Dad let Amy drink wine in London."

"Shut up," Amy said.

Jill clenched her jaw and continued. "My father had a hidden door installed in the kitchen. The original entry is through the bookcase beside the fire-place."

"Cool," Jeff said.

Amy rolled her eyes.

Jill glared at her daughter, wanting to tell her she had no right to be such a little bitch. Didn't she have any sensitivity at all? Didn't Amy know how difficult it must be for Jill to walk in here—to walk in and sit down and not feel a longing for the father she'd loved . . . for the father she'd abandoned?

A waitress appeared beside them. "Cocktails?"

Christopher ordered a bottle of Montrachet before Jill had a chance to say if she wanted wine. The kids ordered Cokes. Jill picked up the menu and glanced through the offerings: hamburgers, turkey clubs, grilled veggie sandwiches on focaccia bread. And, of course, the catch of the day, which a small blackboard said was halibut. She suddenly remembered how her father had loved halibut.

They waited in silence for their drinks. Jill stared into the small tin candleholder on the table and knew there was no way she could turn back the clock. But there was a way she could restore harmony in her own little family. When the wine came and her glass was poured, Jill looked at Christopher, then to the children.

"We have a family decision to make," she said, taking a slow sip from her glass, hoping she'd made the right choice.

Amy, Jill noticed, didn't bother to emit her usual groan.

Jeff perked up. "If it's about where we're going to live after you're married, I'd want a separate room for my computer station."

Jill set down her glass. "No. It's not about that." She looked at Christopher again. He let her continue. "With the coming wedding there's bound to be a lot of publicity. I was wondering how you felt about it."

Jeff shrugged. "It's no big deal, Mom. We're used to it by now."

She toyed with the stem of her glass. "What if it needed to be more? What if the publicity needed to include you kids?"

"Us?" Amy asked. "We get to have our pictures taken?"

Amazing. She had acknowledged that her mother was speaking. "Well, it's nothing definite yet," Jill said. "Maybe." She thought she noticed a slight smile creep across Amy's face.

"Do we have to?" Jeff asked.

"Grow up, Jeff," Amy piped up. "We're talking about *Lifestyles* magazine."

Jill blanched. She looked at Amy. "How did you know. . . ."

Amy looked at Christopher and bit her lip.

Christopher gave Jill a "sorry about that" grin.

Jill took a drink. "Well, apparently this doesn't come as a surprise to everyone." She glanced to the small bar, to the rich mahogany wood with its gleaming brass rail, and wished with everything she had that her father were behind it, smiling and happy, drying the tall glasses with a white linen cloth.

"Mom," Amy said, "don't blame Christopher. He tried to get me to come tonight by telling me you had some great news for us. But I made him tell me what it was."

Jill wondered if the stem of her glass might break under the pressure of her fingers.

Amy leaned across the table. "Mom, please. *Lifestyles* magazine! Can we be on the cover?"

Jill closed her eyes. She was probably being foolish. She was probably being too sensitive. The way Florence had always told her she was. She cleared her throat and opened her eyes. "No. Probably not on the cover."

"When can we do it? Oh, Mom. Please. Please, Mom. This would be the absolute greatest . . ."

Jill held up her hand. "I haven't made the decision yet. I wanted to talk to you both first."

"Count me out," Jeff said. "It's not my idea of excitement."

"You're such a geek," Amy shot at her brother. "You wouldn't know anything exciting if it bit you in the ass."

"Amy," Jill said sternly.

"Sorry, Mom. Oh, God. *Lifestyles* magazine. What will I wear?"

As Jill took another sip of wine, a sense of defeat flowed into her.

Rita watched them through the bookcase of the secret room. So Jill had really come back. Well, there was no way she was going to wait on her. Wait on her, like a slave to her majesty. Ha. She'd told Charlie she had a headache, that she needed to rest a few minutes. So she'd slipped through the back way into the secret room, where she could see for herself just how well Jill Randall McPhearson had done for herself, and figure out how the Christ Rita Blair was going to be able to avoid her for the next month.

Chapter 5

Ben steered the old Buick onto Lighthouse Road toward Gay Head. The sky was beginning to turn pink; the gulls were soaring with their early morning cries. It was his favorite time on the Vineyard: before the tourists awoke, before reality ruined another day. He checked his watch and hoped he hadn't missed Frank Lyfred—"Noepe" as he was called by his tribal family, after the original island name. Ben had learned that *Noepe* meant "amid the waters": an appropriate name, he felt, for a medicine man who healed the spirit by meditating with the tides.

Each dawn—as dependable as the frothy surf and the gulls overhead—Noepe practiced the ancient meditation ritual. It did not matter to Ben that when the medicine man was finished, he put on a Lands' End buttoned-down, collared shirt, turned on his computer, and went to work as the town accountant. Ben knew that deep in Noepe's soul lay the spirit of his people—and beyond. And, hell, somebody had to keep fiscal tabs on Gay Head.

Sipping coffee from his Dippin' Donuts paper cup, Ben wished he'd bought a muffin. Not one of those low-fat kind that Carol Ann was after him to try; no, Ben wanted the real thing, no substitutions. It was, he felt, one of the biggest problems with the world today: too much imitation, as though people had forgotten what anything real was about.

It was the same with Jill McPhearson. The woman was obviously more interested in her high-flying career than she was in what mattered. She owned an incredible house—a vintage, pure island house—and what was she going to do? Dump it. It apparently no longer suited her lifestyle. It apparently wasn't perfect enough.

"It's only a house," she'd remarked.

Only a house. The fact that it had been in her family for seven generations seemed to make no difference. Ben shook his head. *That's the trouble with the damn world, all right. Nobody gives a shit anymore.*

He pulled off the side of the road by the lighthouse and thought about Menemsha House—*his* house—a house *he* gave a shit about, no matter if the town fathers or his daughter agreed. He hoped Noepe would be able to give him some encouragement this morning—some words of support to reassure Ben that he hadn't totally lost his mind.

He got out of the car and climbed the rocky slope toward the lighthouse, turning up the collar of his denim jacket to buffer the wind off the sea. When he reached the top, Ben looked to the horizon—it was clear this morning, warm. Beyond the aqua water the Elizabeth Islands were crystalline drops, floating gems of green and sand.

Off to the right, atop the rust-colored cliff, sat Noepe, cross-legged on the ground, his long white ponytail caught by the breeze, his eyes closed in prayer. It had been that way when Ben had first seen the man . . . that Sunday morning six years ago when he'd just learned about Louise's cancer. He'd needed somewhere to go, to think, to search for strength. He'd come to the cliffs to be alone. But instead of solitude, he'd encountered Noepe.

Throughout Louise's chemotherapy, her remission, her relapse, then her death, Ben continued to come out to the cliffs at dawn. Carol Ann had wanted him to see a therapist, go to a support group, talk about his feelings. But Ben had always done things his way, alone, within himself.

He smiled now as he watched Noepe, and realized that, in fact, the old man had become a therapist for Ben, a man who shared his thoughts and often abstract wisdom through wizened eyes. As Ben watched Noepe in silent prayer, he wondered if the old man worshiped Moshup, the ancient Wampanoag god, or if the Methodists had ever converted him. But despite the inner depths to which their conversations traveled, neither of them had intruded into each other's private beliefs. It was an unspoken respect, a strange and wondrous bond.

Carefully navigating across the top of the cliff, Ben stood near where the old man sat, arms folded, chin high.

After a moment Noepe spoke without looking up at Ben. "The sun has blessed us this morning," he said quietly.

It was, Ben knew, Noepe's way of telling him it was all right to join him.

He walked closer to the man and crouched beside him. "It has, indeed. Sunday morning. The day of rest."

Noepe kept his eyes fixed on the sea. "And are you at rest, Ben Niles?"

Ben followed Noepe's gaze toward the horizon. "I've had a threat about Menemsha House," he said. "They want to burn it down."

"Men do not always share the same passions," Noepe replied.

"My passion is to honor the past, Noepe. I believe if we honor the past, our lives will be more solid."

A gust of wind rustled the fringe of the old man's long tunic. "You are a builder," he commented. "Building means progress. Progress can be frightening. Especially to island people."

"I'm not trying to build anything. I'm trying to rebuild. Rebuild the past."

Noepe encircled his arms through the air, then drew them toward his heart, as though gathering the spirit of the great ragged cliffs, melding the ancient knowledge into his soul. "My ancestors believed that a hundred million years of history is carved within these cliffs of clay. But history can only bring us knowledge if we seek to understand it. There is honor in what you attempt, Ben. But you will draw people to the site. They will tread upon the land."

Ben pulled off his baseball cap and rubbed his head. "Are the Wampanoags against Menemsha House?"

• "Fighting one's adversaries is difficult enough. First, you must be certain of who they are."

"But surely Menemsha House wouldn't interfere with the Indians. With your customs."

Noepe didn't answer.

"I think Dave Ashenbach sent the threat."

"Know your enemies first, Ben. If you feel you are right—if you feel you can conquer them—then do not relinquish your dream. That is the best advice I can give."

Ben looked out to the sea again and wondered if he had the commitment to conquer enemies, and why he couldn't be more like the Jill McPhearsons of the world—content to keep moving forward, to grab what the world offered, and not become clotted by the baggage of the past.

•   •   •

On the way back to Oak Bluffs, Ben decided to stop by Menemsha House. Maybe a walk around the grounds, a silent stroll through the decaying structure, would give him strength, renew his determination. Or maybe he needed to see if Ashenbach—or whoever—had already gone through with the threat.

The driveway snaked up and around, through the scrub pines and oaks, up toward the back of the house, toward the garage area, where there was plenty of room for his planned parking lot: twenty cars at a time, no problem.

As he rounded the last curve, Ben caught sight of the house, and as always, he smiled. Menemsha House did not lay in ashes: it stood, in all its three-story, twelve-thousand-square-foot majesty, keeping watch over the harbor, standing sentry against intruders as it had for over a hundred years—no longer on guard against looters and pirates, but now against faceless men with kerosene and Bic lighters. He tugged at the brim of his cap and scoffed at himself for being melodramatic.

He pulled to the side of the garage, thinking of Noepe's words: *Men do not always share the same passions.* Nor, Ben thought with a short laugh, do men and women. Jill McPhearson can have hers, Ashenbach, his. As for Ben, his passion stood here, in all its gray-shingled, leaky-roofed beauty.

He smiled and jammed the old Buick's shift into neutral when he noticed a reflection from the other side of the garage, something metallic, chromelike. At first he thought it was the propane tanks, but they'd been moved beside the house last week, waiting for him to find the time to call and have them filled. Then he realized what it was: a bumper. A bumper of a car. Or a pickup.

Frowning, Ben took off his cap again and tried to quiet the sense of foreboding creeping through him. *Know your enemies,* Noepe had warned. He glanced at the floor on the passenger side and wished he had a hammer or a baseball bat—something, anything, to help him conquer his enemy, if, indeed, his enemy was now parked beyond the garage, awaiting his arrival.

He rolled down the window and listened. But he heard only the gentle sound of the curling waves far below and the distant cry of a gull.

Slowly, Ben pulled the door handle and eased back the heavy door. As he started to get out, he saw the back door of the house open. He was caught; halfway from the driver's seat, halfway from the ground.

Know your enemies. Well, Ben thought, *looks like I'm about to.*

A figure emerged onto the back porch of the house. He was tall, he was disheveled, with hair sticking up in all directions and a T-shirt hanging from the waist of his jeans.

Ben snorted. "Jesus, Kyle," he said. "You scared the hell out of me."

"Ben?" Kyle Blair called as he tucked in his shirt and walked toward the car. "What are you doing here?"

"I own the goddamn place."

"Oh," Kyle said, "right."

"What are you doing here?"

Kyle turned and looked back to the house. "I, ah . . ."

"You, ah, what? You look like you spent the night here."

Kyle smiled. "Yeah, well . . ."

"Shit," Ben said as he tugged at his cap again. "You're not alone, are you?"

"Well. No."

"Christ, you should have told me. I wouldn't have interrupted."

"I thought it might be a good idea for someone to stay here . . . in case of, well, you know . . ."

Unfortunately, Kyle had been with him when Ben received the letter. He knew about the threat to burn it down.

"That was a pretty stupid thing to do, Kyle. What makes you think if someone's going to torch the place they'd care who was in it?"

"Well, I thought I could stop anyone . . ."

Ben shook his head. "I'm going to leave now, Kyle. And you are going to take your young lady and get the hell away from here pronto. I don't want you around if any trouble's going to happen. Do you hear me?"

"Yes, sir. I'm sorry. . . ."

Ben waved him off. "Just don't do it again. Not until we get to the bottom of this mess." He got back into the car and started the motor. "I'll see you tomorrow morning," he said through the open window. "Eight o'clock. Jill McPhearson's."

Kyle nodded and waved.

Ben backed up the car, then headed down the driveway, thinking that not only was Kyle a good worker, he was a good kid. In the short time since he'd worked for Ben he'd learned a lot. Yes, Ben thought, Kyle was a good kid. He wondered what it would have been like if Carol Ann had been a boy, a boy like Kyle, who understood the things Ben wanted, and appreciated what Ben was all about.

Jill opened her eyes with the slow ease of someone who's had a good night's sleep. She took a deep breath, letting the warm morning air fill her lungs, safe in the knowledge that everything was going to be fine. Although she'd been annoyed that Christopher had told Amy about the *Lifestyles* article, at least Amy was speaking to her again. And Jeff, Jill knew, would cooperate when the time came. He wasn't rebellious like his sister, and for that she was grateful. If only she could relax more often and let the kids be themselves, maybe she wouldn't be such a bad mother, after all.

She watched the thin curtain move with the morning breeze and, for the first time, felt good to be here. The ghosts seemed to have lifted; she was on track to the future. Tomorrow Ben Niles would begin work on the house, and hopefully, this would all soon be behind her. Then, life would really begin.

She stretched out her long body and smiled. Then she turned to Christopher who lay beside her, breathing steadily, on his side, away from her. Slowly, Jill pulled off her satin Dior nightgown and tucked herself against his back, skin upon skin, warmth upon warmth. With a gentle motion, she reached over his hip and took his penis in her hand. It was soft, sleeping. She held it, then softly squeezed. From within his sleep, Christopher murmured and turned onto his back. She rose up and moved her body over him, teasing his penis between her legs, urging his flesh to respond. He reached up and caressed her hair, his eyes still shut in dreamlike splendor. Then, his penis began to stiffen, his pulse began to beat. She lowered herself onto him, his rhythm merging with her own.

They made wordless, slow, good-morning love, the kind he had said he'd wanted, the kind that, only yesterday, she'd been unable to give. When Jill was certain that Christopher—with a small smile on his face—had fallen asleep again, she quietly got out of bed, showered, and dressed in her favorite linen capri pants and short-sleeved crop top. She wanted the good feelings within her to linger; she wanted the glow to last. And she was determined that nothing was going to ruin this day.

The house was quiet as she slipped outside and walked toward Main Street. At Bagel Heaven, she bought eight giant muffins—Sunday brunch tourist muffins—overstuffed with cranberries and blueberries and sprinkled with sunny bits of crystal sugar. She stopped at the corner market for peaches and strawberries, plus a copy of the *New York Times*, the way her father would have done.

"It's not Sunday without the *Times*," he'd often said when Florence complained about the piles and piles of newsprint scattered about the living room when she came home from church. "You celebrate your way, I'll celebrate mine," he added. The discussion was closed; Florence, as always, banished herself to the sewing room. Strains of Benny Goodman predictably followed, until it was time to retreat to the purgatory of the kitchen and the toil of dinner.

Jill returned home now, eager to surprise her family with a peaceful, luscious breakfast. She quietly hummed as she laid out plates, napkins, and chunky tumblers for orange juice. Even the sight of Florence's kitchen could not make her wince today: it was going to be a perfect breakfast, the start to a wonderful day. Christopher was not leaving until five o'clock: perhaps they could pack a picnic lunch and explore Chappy—as a family—or maybe drive to Gay Head, browse through the Indian shops, and have lunch at the clifftop restaurant overlooking the sea.

When the table was set, Jill took a pair of shears from the drawer and stepped out the back door where the hydrangea blossomed in August abundance. She clipped off several blue, then pink flowers, arranging a fat, round bouquet to brighten the table, then returned inside to the pantry, searching for one last item that would complete the perfect brunch: a jar of Florence's beach plum jelly.

"Jesus Christ, Jill, didn't you hear the phone?"

The sharpness of Christopher's voice jolted her. She bumped her head on a shelf lined with old Ball jars. Glass crashed, metal lids spun across the wavy wood floor. She stuck her head from the doorway. "What's wrong?"

He paced in the kitchen, his hair askew, his cotton duck shorts obviously hastily thrown on, his chest naked. He did not resemble at all the gently sleeping man she had left not more than two hours ago.

"It was Addie. For chrissake, Jill, she's been calling and calling."

She stepped from the pantry, a salvaged jelly jar in her hand. "It's Sunday morning. Doesn't that woman ever sleep?"

"The entertainment business isn't nine to five, Jill. I thought you'd figured that out by now." His words shot out like sparks from a firecracker.

"I went to the store. . . ."

"And there's no goddamn answering machine here. You'd better go out and get one tomorrow if you're going to stay here."

She set down the jelly and tried to calm her nerves. "What's going on, Christopher?"

He stood, hands on his hips. "I've got to get back to the city. How fast can I get a flight?"

Her patience was diminishing. "Your flight leaves at five."

He shook his head. "Too late. I've got to be back before two."

"What's happening at two?"

"Oh, God, honey," he cried, then stepped forward laughing. He threw his arms around her and squeezed. "It's happening. It's finally happening. Maurice Fischer's in town. He's going to meet me at the Copley before he goes back to Atlanta."

Jill tried to breathe through the firm hold of Christopher's arms. The name Maurice Fischer, indeed, was familiar—Fischer was a media mogul, founder and CEO of RueCom, the fastest growing independent broadcast conglomerate in the nation.

"Maurice Fischer?" she squeaked, and pulled herself from his grasp. "Why are you meeting him?"

"Don't you see, honey? He called Addie. She's been trying to get to him for months. And finally, he called her."

It was the first Jill had heard of it.

"Why?"

"*Good Night, Boston,* that's why. Jill, it's going to happen. I can feel it. RueCom is going to syndicate us. We're going national. Maybe international."

She put her hand to her throat. "What?"

Christopher grabbed her again, hugged her again. "I knew the show was special. I knew it would happen. We're going to do it. Fischer wouldn't waste his time if he didn't have a deal in mind."

She stepped back and looked at the simple arrangement of hydrangea. "If Maurice Fischer is going to talk to you about *Good Night, Boston,* shouldn't I be there?"

He shook his head. "I'll explain you're out of town on family business. Call the airport and get me on the next flight. I've got to take a shower and get the hell out of here."

He turned and raced from the kitchen, leaving Jill standing there, listening to the thump of his two-at-a-time footsteps on the stairs, wondering what had just happened and what this would mean for her future.

Suddenly Amy appeared in the doorway. "Christ, can't anybody get any sleep around here?"

"Watch your language, young lady," Jill heard herself mechanically say. "Now sit down. I have a nice breakfast for us."

Amy shook her head. "Not hungry," she said, then disappeared from the room.

Jill pulled out a centuries-old oak chair and sat down, wondering what on earth made her think anything was ever going to change. Then she remembered another reason that the RueCom name was so familiar—it was the conglomerate that produced *Focus!*—the show hosted by none other than Ms. Lizette French.

People are only as sick as the secrets they keep. Rita poured herself another mug of coffee, and decided to call in sick tonight: no amount of tips at the 1802 would be worth almost running into Jill again.

She glanced over at the calendar stuck on the refrigerator, trying to calculate if she could afford to tell Charlie to forget about her for August. Kyle had said they'd be working there the whole month, and surely by Labor Day Jill would be sick of the island and eager to get back to her charmed life in the real world.

She closed her eyes and thought about last night. Jill, of course, looked spectacular. Not that Rita would have expected anything less. Jill had always had the looks, always had the long legs the boys went crazy for, always had everything in her favor.

But did Jill give a shit? No. She'd always told Rita her mother wouldn't allow her to date. But Rita suspected Jill didn't think island boys were good enough for her. Well, by the looks of things, the guy she had now was far from an island boy.

And those two kids! *God*, Rita groaned as she took another sip of coffee, *Where the hell did she get those two kids?* The boy looked just like his mother; the girl was exotic-looking with all that long, black hair. And they both had those shiny, bright smiles— the kind that rich kids seemed to inherit, as though they'd never needed braces or fillings, or even tooth-paste, for chrissake.

As she leaned against the counter and took a sip from her mug, she wondered what Jill's first husband had been like. She remembered the day her mother had come home from work and told Rita the news . . . remembered it like it was yesterday.

"Jill Randall finally caught herself a husband," Hazel Blair had announced as she pranced through the door at midnight, untying her apron and throwing it on the chair. Rita was standing at the counter, making Kyle's school lunch. He was in the second grade, should have been in the third.

"Well, la dee dah," Rita answered.

"Now, Rita," Hazel scolded, "Jill was your friend for a very long time. You should be happy for her."

"Oh, I am, Ma. I'm just busting with excitement." She'd slapped the white bread over the bologna and stuffed it in a plastic bag.

"He's a man from Boston. A stockbroker or something."

"Is he rich?"

"Does it matter?"

Rita slipped the sandwich and two cookies into a small brown bag. She opened the refrigerator door, set Kyle's lunch next to the quart jar of grape jelly, and thought about how that figured, that Jill would end up with the husband and the money and all those things that someone like Rita would never have, that someone like Rita didn't, apparently, deserve.

The only time Rita felt avenged was when she learned of Jill's divorce: that Jill had *two* kids to raise alone, not one, like Rita, and that Jill didn't even have her parents to help, because she was still too damn stubborn to come back to the Vineyard, which was fine with Rita because who needed her anyway.

She poked back the ball-fringe curtains at the kitchen window now and looked into the driveway. Kyle's pickup wasn't there. She glanced up at the round clock over the refrigerator: 9:20. He must have had a heavy date last night.

She went back to the Formica table, sat down, and opened her appointment book.

There were two cottages to clean by noon, in case any Sunday house shoppers happened to find Surf-Side Real Estate in the yellow pages. Though she'd only dared to invest in one pair of season ferry tickets this year, even that had been a waste. The biggest firms had scooped up all the ticket blocks, luring their potential customers with the promise of coming and going from the Vineyard with ease—their customers, not Rita's. The results had been simple: no perks, no customers, no commissions.

Closing her appointment book and slipping it back into her briefcase, Rita noticed the stack of mail she'd picked up yesterday. She pulled it out and surveyed the windowed-envelope return addresses of Master and Visa cards, the electric company, the phone company. Then she saw the one from the IRS. Rita frowned and tore it open.

Delinquent Payroll Taxes, the title read. Her eyes scanned the sheet, the listing of her name, along with those of her two laid-off secretaries. There was a line for penalty charges, a line for interest. The total taxes due, by September fifteenth, was just over twenty thousand dollars.

She was still sitting at the table, staring at the notice, wondering why the IRS was picking on her when, surely, there must be huge corporations screwing the hell out of them, when the sound of Kyle's pickup revved in the driveway. Rita looked up quickly and realized her heart was pounding. She quickly stuffed the IRS notice in her briefcase and snapped it shut.

He breezed in the back door with a smile on his face and a donut box in his hand.

"You deserve a treat," he said as he leaned down and kissed his mother's cheek. "I brought you eclairs. Your favorite."

"Just what I need. Haven't you heard about fat cells?"

Kyle laughed. "Ben says . . ."

"Ben, Ben, Ben. That's all I ever hear about."

Kyle looked hurt.

She put out her hand and touched his arm. "I'm sorry, honey. I know how much you think of your boss. I'm tired, that's all. With a long day ahead. Forgive me?"

"Sure, Mom," he said in a voice that didn't sound quite as convincing as his words.

Rita pulled the box toward her and opened the lid. Inside were four fat eclairs, the kind they probably didn't serve at San Quentin, or wherever it was they sent tax evaders. Though the pit of her stomach felt like a rock pile, she plucked one out and took a big bite. "Mmmm," she accentuated. "I take back everything I've ever said. Ben Niles is a saint."

Kyle laughed. "You working today?"

She looked at her son. "It's Sunday. It's August. What do you think?"

He laughed again.

"You certainly are in a good mood this morning," Rita said.

Kyle dug out an eclair and ate it in three swift bites.

"Chew your food, don't swallow it."

"I am in a good mood, Mom. I had a great time last night."

"Anyone I know?"

"Nope. Her name's Carrie."

"Carrie. Not the one Stephen King wrote about?"

He rolled his eyes, then devoured another eclair. "You're not going to believe this, but it's Carrie *Wilkins*."

"As in Sam Wilkins?" Sam Wilkins was one of the famous celebrities who had been using the Vineyard as a summer refuge since his Grammy-winning days of the sixties and seventies, and since that nasty business about his dead wife.

"Carrie's his daughter."

"Well, la dee dah," Rita said. "Maybe you'll get to meet her famous father. Maybe he'd like to sell his house." *And maybe her famous father has about twenty grand he'd like to part with,* she wanted to add.

Kyle wrinkled his brow. "Mom? Is anything wrong?"

"Wrong? No. It's just that it's summer. Summers are tiring." Even though she fought it back, a freaking tear spilled from her eye.

"Mom!" He leaned over and wiped her tear. "Tell me. What's wrong?"

She shook her head. "It's nothing, honey. I'm just worried about making ends meet. As usual." She patted his hand. "It's nothing for you to worry about. Now tell me about your new girlfriend. I want to hear some good news."

"Well, they live in Los Angeles," Kyle said. "Carrie said her father's making a comeback."

"Just what the world needs. Another aging rock star."

"Mom, Carrie's really nice."

"Is she a singer, too?"

"She wants to be an actor."

"What's she doing hanging around with you?"

"I dunno. She likes me. She thinks islanders are cool."

"How old is she?"

"Well," he stumbled. "She's younger than me, but she's older, if you know what I mean. She lives a different kind of life."

"How old is she, Kyle?"

"Eighteen."

Rita sighed. "That's awfully young."

"Mom, she's only here for the summer."

"Just watch yourself, Kyle."

"Why, Mother, whatever do you mean?" he asked with a hint of sarcasm and a shit-eating grin that told Rita he knew exactly what she meant.

Rita stood up. "I've got to get to work," she said. "Thanks for the eclairs." She left the kitchen, heading for the shower, and wondered what Carrie Wilkins—or her famous father—would think if they knew Kyle was actually a year older than he thought . . . and what every "cool islander" would think if they knew Rita Blair was headed for jail.

Chapter 6

He took a ten-thirty flight. After dropping Christopher at the airport, Jill maneuvered the bulky Range Rover back toward Edgartown, trying to block out thoughts of Maurice Fischer and RueCom and Lizette French, realizing that, more and more, her life was being engineered by Christopher—and, of course, Addie.

The price of fame.

In the slow line of traffic, Jill stared at the bumper of a minivan in front of her, at the silhouetted heads that bobbed up and down, necks twisting this way and that, as if afraid to miss a sight along West Tisbury Road. Clutching the steering wheel, she realized she could not control the queue of cars, any more than she could control her life, now that Christopher was in it. The scary part was, the thought was exhilarating, above and beyond her wildest dreams, far surpassing the way it had been with Richard.

She remembered her early years with Richard: how she had fought to keep from becoming swallowed up in Richard's life, in his tantalizing world of international business, in his jet-setting from London to Boston, from Geneva to New York. For no matter how often she traveled with Richard, no matter how many worlds she saw, she was still nothing more than Richard McPhearson's wife, with nothing more to list under "occupation" than *housewife* . . . wealthier, perhaps, than her mother had been, but still just a housewife, with nothing to count on but a string of predictable days, then weeks, then years.

After the kids were born Jill insisted on going back to work as a TV reporter, insisted that she was not about to travel the world with two small children at home, nor would she stay home and clean and cook and, God forbid, polish silver with that smelly pink paste her mother had used every Saturday night, shining the silver as if the president were coming for dinner.

At first Jill had blamed Richard for the breakup of their marriage—he, after all, was the one who cheated, the one who found himself a mistress in Rome, a woman eager to cook for him, to coddle him, to make him feel "special." It wasn't until long after the divorce that she realized perhaps she'd been wrong. Perhaps she had "cheated" on Richard, too, cheated him out of the kind of wife he expected.

She wasn't going to do it again. Unlike Richard, Christopher expected her to be *someone*—a woman who saw no limits for her career, and would not get bogged down by the trivia of life.

Brake lights flashed red. Jill jammed on her own and resisted the urge to blow her horn. Then she suddenly remembered there was no reason to hurry: there was no need to rush home. The children were old enough to survive without their mother, and all that was there was work to do—cleaning out, sorting out, throwing out the possessions of her parents, remnants of her childhood. All that was there were old memories to dredge up, and wait until Christopher called tonight to tell her the news, to tell her if they were going to win even greater fame, and if her career, indeed, was limitless.

Her grip on the steering wheel eased, her thoughts

began to calm. She was not going to lose Christopher as she'd lost Richard: this time, she was going to make it work. Even if Lizette French thought otherwise.

She glanced at the stream of cars and wondered if the lives of the people inside were working out, and if, this time, hers really would.

As the line inched its way toward the center of town, Jill spotted a street sign on the left: Beauford Terrace. She recognized the name: Beauford Terrace was where Rita had lived.

Quickly she snapped on her signal and turned down the street. The houses had always been less grand than on Water Street; now, they seemed closer together, in more need of repair. She looked to the left—Rita, she remembered, lived on the left. One house, two, three . . . there it was. The fourth house on the left, the small clapboard saltbox with the peeling red paint and sagging front step.

She pulled onto the shoulder and stopped, staring at the house where she'd once spent so much time, remembering the kitchen table where she'd spent so many hours with Rita and Hazel. Those were happy times for Jill, especially, because of Hazel, the woman who had been more of a mother to Jill than her own throughout her lonely growing-up years.

It was a house filled with laughter, love, and acceptance, filled with Hazel Blair. It was Hazel who listened, Hazel who advised, Hazel who showed Jill and Rita how to wear makeup, who bought their first pairs of panty hose, and who was there with the flashbulb the night of the junior prom; while Florence kept busy in her kitchen, her silence letting Jill know she would have preferred she go to the prom with another boy, a more acceptable boy than Bruce Lindquist, a fisherman's son, the friend of Rita's boyfriend-of-the-week who, Jill remembered, happened to be Charlie Rollins.

Yes, Jill thought now, Hazel had been the perfect mother. She studied the house now and wondered if Hazel still lived there, if she ever thought about her daughter's friend, Jill, and if she knew all the good things that had happened in Jill's life. She wondered if Hazel would have agreed that she should let the kids' pictures be in *Lifestyles* magazine.

A horn blared behind her. Jill glanced in the mirror: her vehicle was in the path of a truck towing an enormous boat. As she began to turn the Range Rover around, Jill caught sight of herself in the rear-view mirror: her neatly groomed hair, her smoothly applied morning makeup, even though it was Sunday, even though she was on the Vineyard. Her eyes dropped to her huge engagement ring, then she slowly put the shift into Drive and headed back to the main road, back toward Water Street, knowing that it no longer mattered what Hazel Blair thought, because life on Martha's Vineyard was one thing; Jill's world now, quite another. She had been, after all, reborn: she had become a product, a commodity, of the spin-doctor nineties.

If only she could remember that, everything would be fine.

Armed with a box of plastic trash bags, a muffin, and a fistful of strawberries, the Jill-of-the-nineties marched directly toward the widow's walk to begin her task. Confidence, she knew, was her greatest ally. It didn't matter that when she'd returned to the house and walked into the kitchen, a small ache had crawled through her. It didn't matter that her breakfast had sat, sadly alone, awaiting the family that had not come.

Families, she'd groaned, and cleared the table to restore the room to Florence's order. Then she noticed that one muffin was gone. *Jeff,* she thought, *thank God for Jeff.*

When she reached the top of the stairs now, Jill decided there was no point in sorting out things to sell: if Christopher called tonight with good news, they might have to pack up and leave sooner than planned. A show going into syndication could mean a lot of work to do, fast.

Glancing quickly around the widow's walk, she decided to trash everything, starting with the trunk she'd opened yesterday.

Once again Jill lifted the lid and removed the pewter dish. She took out a trash bag and dumped it in. Next was a newsprint-wrapped vase, hideously decorated with a bright blue bird. She pitched it on top of the dish.

Then she spotted the leather-bound book again. Starting to fling it, Jill suddenly stopped. She stared at it a moment. It was a book, she decided, only a book. Still, it had been written in her mother's hand. She set down her plate and raised the book to her face: a faint trace of lavender wafted up from the cover. She flinched. Then, slowly, her palm skimmed the smooth brown leather. She wondered if she should open it; she wondered if she should look for the beach plum recipe. Then she remembered the Ball jars that had careened to the floor this morning: surely those were the last of Florence's batch. Jill should at least peek inside and decide if one family heirloom should be retained, though she could not imagine Amy standing over a cookpot, stirring homemade jelly, any more than she would herself.

She settled against the trunk and drew up her knees, remembering that she had not been allowed to help make the jelly.

"You'll burn yourself," her mother said.

"You'll make a mess."

"You'll ruin it."

The only chore Jill was allowed was to monitor the paraffin, watching it set into the same waxy expression of her mother's face and wondering why she couldn't be the kind of daughter her mother had wanted.

But that was then. And this was now.

With one unsteady finger, Jill pushed the button on the tarnished lock. As she turned back the cover, she looked at the flyleaf. Then she looked again. In her mother's uniform handwriting were the words "Florence Carter." Not Randall, but Carter. Jill stared at the name. Carter was her mother's maiden name. Carter—the New-York-City-Carters who most probably had never seen a beach plum, let alone made jelly.

Jill scowled. Then she turned the page.

The paper crackled but did not crumble: the ink on the first ruled sheet was faded but not illegible. At the top was a date.

Wed. Aug. 15, 1945.

A small chill ran through Jill. Her eyes quickly scanned the page. It looked like a letter, addressed to no one. She refocused her gaze in under the date and began to read:

The war is over.

She grasped the edges of the book. *My God,* she thought, *my God, what is this?* She began reading again, forcing herself to continue, to read each word slowly, carefully.

The war is over, the entry read. *I look down from my room and I can see the people dancing on Park Avenue. Taxi horns are honking, music is blaring from rooming-house windows across the way: Glenn Miller, Dizzy Gillespie, and Benny, Benny Goodman. The curfew has been lifted. The city breathes again.*

Jill sat up straight and pushed back her hair. She flipped ahead—page after page of handwritten entries, page after page of dated passages. *My God,* she thought. *A diary. My mother kept a diary.*

Gooseflesh crawled over her arms. She turned back to the beginning and picked up where she left off.

> *The war is over and I am twenty-five years old. I have a college degree in English. I have spent the past three years as a volunteer at the Red Cross, but doubt that my skills of keeping bandage inventories will help me make my mark upon the world. Mother thinks it's time to put my trousseau together. For those of us who didn't marry before the war we are old now, old to become brides. It no longer matters that we were the cream of the Park Avenue debutantes—others have passed us now, younger women, more beautiful. But the men are home now, and will be coming home, so perhaps there is still reason to hope that one has been reserved for me.*

Jill stared at the page, then quickly closed the book. She did not want to know about her mother's past. She did not want to waste time reading about a woman she'd rather forget.

Before she could change her mind, she tossed the diary back in the trunk, picked up her plate, and left the widow's walk, deciding to clean out the kitchen instead. After all, she reasoned, she really must be near the telephone when Christopher called with the news about Maurice Fischer and the prospects that RueCom held for her future.

Chapter 7

 She awoke to the sound of loud banging. Jill rolled over and looked at the old round clock on the nightstand: ten minutes before eight.

She groaned. Ben Niles had said he'd be there at eight, and she'd forgotten to set the alarm.

Pulling herself from the bed, she slipped on her lacy peach robe, threaded her fingers through her tangled hair, and went downstairs, cursing the fact she'd stayed up long past midnight, boxing dishes and heaving out cans, waiting for the call from Christopher that had not come. She had tried him three times; Addie twice. The only response had been voice mail.

She unlocked the heavy door and pulled it open.

"Morning," Ben said, his smile broad, his eyes alert, as if mocking her for laziness, mocking her, period.

"Morning," she answered. "I overslept."

Ben turned to a young man behind him. "City folks," he said with a grin, folding his arms in a way that made his thick, muscle-toned carpenter's arms strain against the sleeves of his T-shirt.

Jill leaned against the door.

"This is Kyle," Ben said, then looked back at Jill. "My number one helper."

She wondered if Kyle would be as irritating as his boss. "Nice to meet you, Kyle."

The young man nodded.

Ben tipped the brim of his baseball cap. "Do you think we could come in?"

"Oh," she said, stepping away from the door. "I guess I'm not awake."

"No problem," Ben replied as he bent down and hoisted a wooden box of tools. "We're going to be in the basement, so we'll be out of your way. I'd say you could go back to sleep, but I'm afraid we'll make too much racket."

"Whatever," she said. She didn't care about the details of his work: she only wanted it over, finished, so she could get back to her life, if she still had one, if Christopher hadn't dropped off the face of the earth, or if she didn't kill him first. She only knew that right now she needed a shower, and that she was damned if she was going to call him again and endure the humiliation of his voice-mail message. "I'll be upstairs," she said, then left the men—and their muscles—to their tasks, whatever they might entail.

After her shower, Jill sat at the kitchen table amid the cartons and trash bags of last night's work. She stared into a mug of black coffee, trying not to think about the hammering going on in the basement or the silence of the phone in the hall. Maybe Christopher had never made it to Boston: maybe the small plane had crashed into the sound. Or maybe there had been an accident in the city: a taxicab sprint across town to the Copley colliding with a transit bus. Would anyone know how to reach her? Addie had probably called him yesterday on his cell phone. Had Jill remembered to give Addie the number here?

"Mom?" Jeff called from the hall.

She sat up and took a swallow of coffee as her son rounded the doorway into the kitchen.

"Did you call the phone company yet? I've got to get on-line."

She stood, carried her mug to the counter, and splashed the dark liquid into the yellowed enamel sink. "I'll try them now. There are leftover muffins for breakfast."

Sidestepping boxes, Jeff moved to the counter and opened the bag of muffins. "Hey, where's that jelly you had out yesterday?"

Going to the phone, Jill shook her head. Her mother's beach plum jelly had been a hit with her son. She wondered if Florence Randall would have shown any enthusiasm. "In the refrigerator," she called back, then pulled the directory from the small drawer of the phone stand and proceeded to attempt to get Jeff connected with the rest of the world.

The operator left her on hold for what seemed like an hour.

"Is there a jack?" the woman asked when she finally returned.

"There's an extension in the upstairs hall," Jill answered, then remembered that Florence had balked at that: she'd felt that one phone per house was quite enough. "I doubt if there's one in the room."

"In that case, we'll have to send an installer. You'll have to make an appointment."

"Fine," Jill said. "Just tell me when."

"We have an opening on the twenty-third."

"The twenty-third? Of August?"

"That's right."

"Mom," Jeff's voice whined from the kitchen, "I can't wait until then."

He appeared beside her, pain in his eyes and a trace of beach plum jelly at the corner of his mouth.

"Look," Jill said into the mouthpiece, "we can't wait that long. This phone line is for Jill McPhearson. I'm vacationing on the Vineyard, and I need the line for business."

There was a pause at the other end. "Well," the operator said, "perhaps we could squeeze you in . . ."

"I don't care how much it costs," Jill said, winking at Jeff.

"How about Wednesday. Six P.M.?"

"This Wednesday?"

"Yes."

"That's fine." She quickly hung up and high-fived Jeff. "Consider yourself on-line," she said, pleased at the power of her very own name, the name Jill *McPhearson*, not Randall.

His smile widened. "Thanks, Mom. You're the greatest."

Suddenly the phone rang. She jumped. It had been a long time since she'd heard the sound of an old-fashioned bell; a long time since electronic tones had eliminated rings.

"Oh, no," Jeff groaned. "They changed their minds."

She picked up the receiver.

"Jill?" It was Christopher's voice. "I've been trying to reach you. The line's been busy."

She waved Jeff away, then laced her fingers through the coils of the long black cord. "I thought you were dead," she said.

"Dead? Why?"

"You said you'd call last night. After your meeting with Fischer."

"I did? Oh. Sorry. The meeting ran late. Then Addie and I spent a few hours hashing out the options."

The curling of her muscles around her stomach could have been jealousy. But, she reminded herself, he'd been with Addie, not Lizette French.

"What options?" she asked, trying to sound calm, collected, unhurt.

"Well, it's not definite, but he mentioned that a show like ours has potential for national syndication."

She sat up straight. Her eyes widened. "Oh, Christopher. Was he serious?"

"It's still early, honey. I expect he's just testing the waters as they say in mediaville."

A national show. Syndication. Her eyes darted around the faded flowers on the walls of the house of her past.

"We'd probably have to leave Boston, though. RueCom is based in Atlanta, so maybe there. Maybe New York. Or," he added, "L.A."

"L.A.?" she asked, suddenly unsure if the land of celluloid and trials-of-the-century was her idea of home. "When will we know?"

Christopher paused. "I'm not sure. He did make one comment that bothers me. He's concerned about the scope of our stories." He hesitated again. "But I told him it's nothing to worry about. That you can handle it."

Her neck tightened. "Handle what, Christopher?"

He sighed.

She gripped the receiver.

"Fischer thinks your stories are too local-sounding. He's afraid you don't have the experience to deliver national stuff."

Her face began to burn. "You're kidding, right?"

"No."

"My God, Christopher. I've been in television nearly twenty years."

"In Boston. Not nationally."

"Big deal! I know what I'm doing."

"I know that, honey."

Her words came out in short, little breaths. "What about you? This is your first real show."

"I guess he thinks my baseball commentary counts

for something. Between that and pitching, my Q-ratings are strong."

Q-ratings, Jill thought. Those infernal numbers that declared the popularity of a personality. "And I have no national Q-rating."

"Right."

She crossed her legs and shook her foot. "Then I guess I'll just have to prove it to the old bastard."

Christopher laughed. "That's my girl. But don't worry. He wants to wait for the next Nielsens. To be sure we're not a novelty."

"November," Jill said.

"Maybe what he really wants is to wait until after the wedding, to be certain you and I are a sure thing."

She tried to smile. "Is that a joke?"

"I never joke about a lifetime commitment."

"Mr. Edwards," she spoke softly, twirling the cord again, "are you only marrying me for my ratings?"

"Ask me that again the next time I wake up with you on top of me naked."

A tingle surged through her. "I think I'd better hang up now," she said. "Or this call will be billed as a 900 number."

Christopher laughed. "Yeah, well, one of us has to get to work if we're going to be famous. I'll call you tonight and let you know if *Good Night, Boston* survived without you."

"You do that." She laughed. "I love you."

"I love you, too," he said.

She hung up the phone, pulled back her hair, and felt her smile tighten. Lizette French, no doubt, already had a strong Q, with national exposure solidly under the belt of her spandex bodysuit. Jill pressed her fingers against her temples and wondered what she would need to do to prove to Maurice Fischer that she, too, was Q-rating material.

By noon, Ben had worked up the kind of sweat that he loved—soaking through his T-shirt, running down his brow—the feel-good kind of sweat that told him he'd worked hard, he'd done good. He'd never been sure which he enjoyed more: designing and thinking through the perfect renovation, or actually getting his hands dirty, making it become reality. Whatever it was, it sure beat what he had to do tonight: face the zoning board and try to get them to approve the plans for Menemsha House. But he was ready.

He set down his tools on the basement floor, picked up his towel, and wiped his face. "Come on, Kyle, let's get out of this hellhole and grab some lunch." As they passed through the backyard, Ben noticed a small figure stretched across a beach towel on the back lawn. Dark hair cascaded around headphones. "That must be Jill's daughter."

Kyle moved beside him and followed his eyes. "Not bad."

Ben shot him a glance. "Don't get any ideas. She's too young, and she's not your kind."

Kyle smiled.

They walked to Main Street, then around the back of a bookstore to Suzie's Luncheonette, where tourists rarely went because of its size—small—and its smell—grease. Ben clutched his stomach and blessed the fact that Carol Ann was nowhere around.

They ordered quickly—two burgers and fries for Kyle, a chicken salad sandwich and cup of minestrone for Ben—then grabbed two Cokes from the self-serve cooler and sat on wobbly chairs at a just-cleaned table. Ben picked up a napkin and dried the surface.

"So tonight's the big night," Kyle said, popping the top of his Coke.

"Yeah," Ben answered. "It ought to be interesting." Getting the variance would enable him to run a "commercial" venture on the property, though, for the life of him, Ben didn't understand why Menemsha House needed to be called "commercial." He'd already decided that after maintenance, taxes, and utilities, the balance of admission fees would be given back to the town. He'd thought it would stave off any opposition. But since the threat from Ashenbach—or whoever the hell sent it—Ben realized he couldn't be sure of anything. "Are you coming to the meeting?"

"For a little while. I've got a date though, so I hope they don't drag it on too long."

Ben nodded. He'd become accustomed to Kyle's dates, Kyle's girls. "I'd appreciate it if you could be there. It might help to have an islander on my side."

Kyle laughed. "You're forgetting I was born in Worcester."

"Born there, maybe. But your roots are here. Your name is here."

The waitress delivered their sandwiches. Ben plucked another napkin from the black metal container and set it in his lap.

"You've lived here almost as long as I have," Kyle said.

"Don't tell that to the town fathers. They still think I'm a tourist who forgot to go home." He picked up his spoon and tasted the soup. No matter how warm the day, Ben loved soup. He savored the flavors now, thinking how much he missed Louise's home cooking, Louise's home cleaning, Louise. It was true—they had first come to the island as tourists, vacationers, trying to escape their increasingly hectic life in Baltimore. Ben's high-pressure job as a junior architect with one of the city's most prestigious firms; Louise's equally chaotic schedule of teaching and caring for six-year-old Carol Ann. He had just completed the plans for some restorations at historic Williamsburg, and his boss had allowed him a much-needed week off. At first, Ben had hesitated. His drawings were completed, they had all been approved. Technically, his work was done, but for some reason, Ben felt that it wasn't.

Louise packed their things and they headed for Martha's Vineyard, for their first real vacation in the seven years they'd been married.

Once on the island, surrounded by history, enraptured by the unspoiled beauty of the Vineyard homes, Ben realized why he'd felt incomplete in Baltimore: he realized he not only wanted to draw the plans, he wanted to execute them, too. He wanted to be the one to shore up the old beams, to restore the hand-carved woodworking. He wanted to be the one to carefully replace the bubble-glass windowpanes, to carefully fix the wide floorboards, to recapture the pride of the original craftsmen. He wanted to re-create their art.

Thankfully, Louise understood. She left Ben on the island to scout for a home and returned to Baltimore where she called the movers. Neither of them had ever regretted it.

"Any more notes?" Kyle asked quietly, interrupting Ben from peaceful memory.

Ben shook his head, wishing Kyle hadn't been there when he'd opened his mail. There was no sense in both of them looking over their shoulders. He pushed aside the cup, examined the sandwich, and took a bite—homemade chicken salad, without the little bit of pickle that Louise had always added. He chewed slowly, then swallowed past that damn little lump. "The plans and the duplicates are done. The hands-on workshop looks great."

"What about liability?"

Ben groaned. "I'll make it safe. Honest."

Kyle laughed. "Don't yell at me. I'm only trying to second-guess what the board will say."

"Thanks, but no thanks. I'll get plenty of insurance. There are other hands-on programs—there's one at Woods Hole. A few dull adzes can't be any more dangerous than kids sticking their hands into live fish tanks with crabs and God knows what else."

"Well, I'm on your side, you know that."

"Thanks, Kyle. Menemsha House is a dream. But," he added with greater detachment than he felt, "if it's not meant to happen, then so be it. I can sell the property. Pretend it never happened."

"Hey," Kyle added as he bit into his second burger, "my mother could always list it. God knows she could use the money."

There was only one way she could come up with twenty grand. Fast. And Rita knew she'd have to move quickly.

She sat in her rattling Toyota on Main Street in Vineyard Haven, waiting for some white-haired old lady who could barely see over the steering wheel to squeeze her Town Car into a slot in front of the string of shops. Rita drummed her red polished fingernails with the well-bitten cuticles on the dusty dashboard.

"Move your buns, lady," she seethed. "Get your fat ass off the street."

Finally, the white-hair made it. Rita sped past and flipped her off. At least the old lady had held up the line long enough so there was clear sailing to West Chop. She fumbled in her purse for her spray cologne, aimed it at her neck, and stepped on the accelerator.

"Like it or not, Joe Geissel, you're going to sell your house."

.   .   .

He'd told her to come by at two o'clock. At ten minutes 'til, Rita pulled off the road, passed the fortress rows of tall, thick hedges, and drove up the long, circular drive. *Madam*'s Mercedes was nowhere to be seen—she'd obviously left on the six-fifteen last night. Right on schedule.

Parking in front of the house, Rita killed the engine and took a quick, last check in the rearview mirror. The crimson lipstick, she knew, was a little bright with her red hair. As she got out of the car, she also realized that, chances were, Joe's wife never owned a white knit top quite as tight as hers or a red denim miniskirt that looked even shorter when she stood on the gravel driveway in her canvas platform shoes. She probably did, however, own more gold than the trio of chains draped around Rita's neck. But what the hell, Joe hadn't given Rita the perks of being a wife. Now, it was time he paid up. Her way.

Standing in front of the grand house, Rita scoped the view: two massive floors—nearly ten thousand square feet, she'd bet—complete with picture windows front and back, enabling her to see straight through the house to the expanse of salt water beyond.

"Two million six," she whispered with a smile. "He'll settle for two. Even." She nodded in confirmation, then crossed the lawn and, as instructed, went around to the back door. The servants entrance.

He opened the door with a smile on his face, a white terry robe tied across his wide middle and, Rita figured, nothing but a hard-on underneath.

"You're early," Joe said.

She slouched on one hip, letting the hem of her skirt rise even higher, then arched her back, thrusting her small, but damn perky titties toward his eager leer. "I was hot," she said.

Joe laughed and stepped from the doorway. "I have just the thing to cool you down."

She paraded past him into the house. On the way, she grabbed his groin. She was right. He was hard. She quickly remembered what her mother used to say: *Men only want one thing, Rita. Everything else they do is foreplay.* Well, Rita Blair could play with the best.

"Can I have a lemonade?" she asked.

"Vodka?"

"No. Straight. I'm a working girl." And Joe had no idea just how much work she intended to accomplish this afternoon.

While he fussed with the glasses she cruised the kitchen. It was a little out-of-date, with sixties kind of knotty pine cabinets and shiny Formica counters. The appliances, however, looked in decent shape, though they were that god-awful copper-colored shit that invaded the island when the parents of the baby boomers had dug up enough money for a second home. She wondered if she could convince the Martins that knotty pine and brown appliances were back in style.

Strolling to the breakfast area, Rita quickly decided this is where she would focus the Martins' attention. The round alcove was walled with windows: the ocean panorama was right out of a tour book. Thank God, madam had hung no curtains, nothing that would block the view that would bring the big bucks for this otherwise aging, oversized shithole.

Joe appeared beside her. "Your cocktail, my dear."

She took the cobalt-blue glass—probably something right out of the Tiffany's catalog—and smiled through her crimson lips. "Thanks."

"It's a funny word, isn't it? Cocktail?" He was leering again, moving his eyes from her breasts to her crotch. "Think about it. Cock. Tail. I give you cock. You give me tail." He laughed.

Rita didn't. She ran her finger around the thick rim of the glass, leaned against the glass-top dining table, and braced herself. "You can give me something besides your cock, Joe," she said, stifling a cringe at the word.

He moved against her, brushing his rock against her thigh. "What do you have in mind?"

She sipped her lemonade. It was too sweet. Sickish. She smiled. "I want this house."

Joe laughed. "Baby, it's all yours. Whenever you want. Monday through Friday." He took a drink. "Except, of course, Tuesdays. Tuesdays are golf days."

She winced a little, but forced a smile. "Don't get nervous," she said, "I'm not planning to move in." She set her glass on the table and pulled off her top. She stood, naked from the waist up, framed by the wall of windows that overlooked the sea. "Suck my tits, Joe," she commanded. "Suck them hard and make me come."

He stepped forward, and set his glass beside hers, his hand trembling, his penis now poking through the opening of his robe.

Rita arched her back again as he bent his mouth to her. The chill of his drink made her nipple stiffen. She moaned, then tried to regain control. If her plan was going to work, she had to keep her senses.

"Two million six," she whispered as she reached to stroke his throbbing penis.

Joe kept sucking.

"Two million six for this house. What did you pay for it, Joe? A hundred thousand?"

"Ninety-five," he murmured as he switched breasts. "Back in '68."

His cool tongue was getting warmer. Hotter. Firmer.

She stroked him.

"That's a hell of a profit, Joe. Think of what you could do with two million six."

"I can't think of anything but what I'm doing right now." He reached between her legs and pushed her nylon panties down. No matter how hard she tried to focus, Rita was wet.

Then the IRS notice flashed into her mind. She tightened her grasp around him. "You know you want to sell this place, Joe. Let me do it for you. Let me help."

"All I want to do is fuck you, baby," he said as he raised his head and lifted her ass onto the table. He spread her legs and pushed his penis into her. It swiftly tunneled into her waiting heat. "As for this house," he said as her hips responded to his thrust, "fuck it. I'm not selling. There's no way I'm leaving this island and giving you up."

Rita bit her lip and sighed, then let him fuck her good.

Ben stood in the back of the Town Hall meeting room, clutching his blueprints, wishing Carol Ann were there. Sixty or seventy folding chairs were crammed together, all occupied, none by his daughter and her husband and their kids, his grandchildren. Maybe Carol Ann was more concerned about keeping her job than showing support for her father.

Terry Clarkson sat at the long table facing the audience, centered between the American flag and the seal of the State of Massachusetts. He was taking motions on Zac Lambert's request to designate the ten acres behind his property as wetlands.

"Now, more than ever, we've got to protect our environment," Zac said.

Ben felt his confidence sliding out the door.

"I second the motion," an old woman in a gray cardigan bellowed.

"Here, here!" another islander shouted.

Terry Clarkson banged his gavel. "Motion passed," he declared. "Next, Ben Niles. Ben, you here?" Clarkson craned his neck around the room.

Ben hesitated a beat too long and blew his chance to escape.

"Back here," he called, raising the blueprints of Menemsha House high in the air.

The sixty or seventy heads turned toward the back. He knew the redness that crept up his neck would ease if he saw just one friendly face, one face that didn't look as though it wanted to run him out of town.

"Come forward, Ben, where we all can see you."

On watery legs he couldn't quite believe were his, Ben walked down the aisle. It wasn't until he reached the front row that he spotted Dave Ashenbach. Ashenbach was not smiling. *Men do not always share the same passions,* Noepe's words came into his mind.

Ben averted his eyes and faced Terry Clarkson. "These are my plans to restore my property in Menemsha," he said.

Clarkson nodded, allowing Ben to continue.

Clearing his throat, Ben unrolled his plans. The crinkle of the paper knifed through the silence. Quickly he glanced at the sheet. Staring back at him was the layout—and the hands-on workshop for the kids. Noepe's words came again: *If you feel you are right . . . do not relinquish your dream.* Ben smiled. His legs grew sturdy; the redness washed from his neck.

"The house is an eyesore," he began with confidence. "I purchased it that way. Now I want to restore it into something the town—in fact, all of the island—can be proud of."

Still, silence loomed behind him.

He cleared his throat again. "When I first thought of Menemsha House, I thought what a wonderful place it would be for the children. Island children, not just tourist children. I wanted to create a place for them to come and to learn their heritage." He glanced around. "It might help if I could hold up the plans, let everyone have a look."

Clarkson nodded and gestured to two board members. The men rose and walked to the front of the table. Ben stepped to Clarkson's side and handed the blueprint to the men. They held it up. Ben stepped aside and pointed as he spoke, indicating where the workshop would be and how the features of the Vineyard's architectural history would be incorporated into the house.

"Menemsha House is a living museum," he concluded, "that will add value to the property and increased tax revenue to the town." The tension within him eased. He turned to face the audience. At the back of the room he saw Carol Ann, arms folded, a noncommittal look on her face. Still, she was there. "I'd be happy to answer any questions."

"Are you going to charge admission?" someone asked.

Ben shifted on one foot. "Yes. But after the taxes, utilities, and maintenance, the profits will go to the town."

"What about our kids?" asked the woman in the gray cardigan. "It doesn't seem right that they'd have to pay."

He hesitated. "Well, that's something I'd have to look into."

"Are you going to advertise it?"

"Well, yes. I'd have to. So people would know . . ." *Advertise it?* His hopes faded again. *Did they think he wouldn't advertise it?*

A man Ben recognized but did not know stood and narrowed his eyes. "I'm not sure about this. It would mean a lot of traffic."

"There's plenty of room on the grounds for parking," Ben answered.

"Menemsha's a fishing village. We don't want parking lots." It was Dave Ashenbach. "If you want this mu-u-u-seum so bad, why not put it in Oak Bluffs, where you live?"

Ben felt his pulse begin to beat inside his fists. "Because the property is in Menemsha. I bought it for the setting, for the view. I thought it was best for a museum of such historic value to be situated away from the crowds."

"Only going to move the crowds to Menemsha, as I see it," Ashenbach retorted.

The air in the room tightened.

"It's for the children," Ben responded.

Murmurs filled the room. The pitch quickly swelled.

Clarkson banged the gavel. "I think you'd better go back to the drawing board, Ben. See if you can give us some options. We can't grant any variance without more substance."

Ben turned and looked at Clarkson. *Substance? What the hell is that supposed to mean?* The redness crawled up his neck again.

Clarkson shifted his gaze to the papers on the table before him. "Next," he said firmly. "Stan Drake. You want to build a bay to store your boat?"

Ben stood numbly a moment, facing the islanders, facing those people who would never believe he was one of them. Stan Drake moved down the aisle toward the table. Ben pulled the blueprints from the men, quickly rolled them, and headed, chin raised, toward the back of the room, toward Carol Ann.

· · ·

Outside, Ben tossed the plans into the Buick. "Those sons of bitches blew me off," he said.

"Dad, I tried to warn you . . ."

"*Give us some substance? We need more options?* They knew what they were going to do before I even came tonight. Ashenbach got to them. I should have saved my breath." He got into the car, slammed the door, and backed away, forgetting to say good-bye to Carol Ann, forgetting to thank her for showing up after all.

Chapter 8

He drove the power saw through the beam, visualizing Dave Ashenbach's neck. Ben had come to Jill's house early this morning, set up the sawhorses in the backyard, and didn't much care if his noise woke them up. This was just a job, another job, a task to be done. It was hardly the work that would fulfill his dreams.

Kyle shouted toward Ben as he came around the corner by the back fence. "Didn't know we were starting before eight."

Through the plastic haze of his safety goggles, Ben glanced at Kyle's clean T-shirt, his open denim vest. Unlike the boy, Ben already had a layer of sweat around the rim of his cap. He shrugged and went back to his work.

Kyle drifted over and stood by the pile of already cut beams. Ben hoisted one on his shoulder to take to the cellar.

"I'll give you a hand," Kyle said, stepping forward.

"I got it," Ben replied, walking toward the bulkhead, wincing at the strain in his shoulder. He'd been hoisting beams for years. When had it become so difficult? *Age,* he thought, *is a bitch.*

He angled his way down the concrete steps, into

the dim, damp cellar. Setting down the beam, he pulled off his hat and goggles and wiped his forehead, thinking that maybe he'd feel better if he hadn't stayed up until three. But there had been work to do. When he'd arrived home after the zoning board meeting, Ben had shoved the blueprints into the corner and gone on a manic sweep of his kitchen, cleaning up clutter, heaving out trash, all the while berating himself for the work he'd let slide while wasting his time on that damn Menemsha House. There were dozens of calls he'd yet to return—the congressman who'd purchased an estate in Osterville over on the Cape, the columnist who wanted his Nantucket beach house refurbished, the duchess who wanted God-only-knew-what done to the stables on her Chatham property. His work was *wanted,* damnit. He was in demand. And people were willing to pay, big time. He kicked himself now for screwing around with a job as small as Jill McPhearson's house. That's what he got for thinking that staying on the island in August would pave the way for Menemsha House. That's what he got for believing in dreams.

He sat down on the beam now and admitted to himself that it had all been a waste of time.

"Ben?" Kyle's voice called from the bulkhead. "Are you all right?"

The boy's tall frame moved down the steps, silhouetted against the August sunlight, lean and firm, with a thick head of hair, not unlike what Ben once had, back when he could tote a beam a mile and a half and never have to stop to catch his breath.

"I'm sorry I didn't get to the meeting last night," Kyle said.

"You didn't miss much."

"They turned you down?"

Ben laughed. "They barely listened. It was bullshit."

"God. That's awful. . . ."

"Hey, you win some, you lose some. We've got enough to keep us busy with real work." He eyed the crumbling brick foundation. "Remind me to call the mason at lunchtime. We've got to get him over here to start this repointing."

"Sure, Ben."

"This job must be done by Labor Day," he said, then walked past Kyle, up the stairs, into the bright sun.

"Ben?" Kyle was behind him now. "Isn't there anything you can do? To save Menemsha House?"

Ben lifted one end of another beam. Kyle quickly bent and raised the other.

"Something tells me no matter what I come up with, it's a dead issue." They moved the beam, set it down on the horses.

"But if you don't restore the house, what are you going to do? Sell it?"

Ben leaned against the horse and rubbed his shoulder. "Jesus," he said, shaking his head, "Christ. I don't know yet." A thought flashed through Ben's mind that Kyle's curiosity may be self-serving—that he was once again laying the groundwork for his mother to get the listing, to score the commission. He picked up the saw, crouched, and lined up the position of the blade across the beam. What the hell, he figured, at least Kyle was trying to take care of family—something that too damn few people in the world did anymore. So what if Kyle was interested in finding out if there was anything in it for him.

He adjusted his goggles and flipped the switch on the saw. It revved a second, then Ben began to guide it carefully across the beam, fine chips of wood spewing into the air. Suddenly he knew what the problem had been: nobody felt that Menemsha House had anything "in it for them."

They hadn't cared that it would be an educational

facility as well as a museum. They hadn't cared about the increased taxes. Hell, he owned the property and had to pay taxes anyway. The slight increase would hardly be noticed. The promise of profits hadn't worked, either—probably because they didn't trust him to be honest about it. Islanders, after all, only trusted their own.

The blade ripped through the end of the beam. Ben turned off the switch and stared at the two pieces of wood, remembering the one woman who had said the island children shouldn't have to pay. Even if he agreed, he doubted it would be enough to satisfy the people. He had to think of something else . . . something more.

"You want me to move these beams to the basement?" Kyle asked.

Ben lifted his head. "What? Oh. Yeah. Sure."

He pulled off his cap and goggles. Why hadn't he realized it before? He had to think of something to really whet their appetites . . . something that was in it for them. He rubbed the sweat on his brow and stared off across the backyard, his gaze landing on the ferry . . . the slow, steady Chappy ferry that provided dependable transportation, year in, year out. Reliable transportation was a necessity, yet a luxury on the Vineyard, where prices were steep and gas even steeper.

Transportation.

The idea came so quickly he couldn't believe he hadn't thought of it before.

Transportation.

Kids.

School.

School bus!

That's it, he thought with sudden clarity. He'd buy school buses—one for each of the five school districts, one for the regional high school, maybe two. If they didn't want them, he'd offer something else—computers, maybe—anything to show them he cared, that he was committed to the island, that he was one of them.

Then, there'd be no way they'd turn him down.

He smiled and plunked his cap back on his head, wondering if he could pull it off and thinking that Louise would have been proud.

Jill lay in bed, squinting through the sheer canopy at the ceiling, one arm bent over her forehead, trying to deaden the ache that bored into her brain with the screech of the saw. Apparently, the Ben Niles code of adhering to authenticity precluded power saws. She must have been crazy to think she could stand living here for a month amid all this commotion.

Closing her eyes, she realized that this house had probably never heard such noise: except for her mother's bursts of dementia, it was always so placid, so unchaotic, with George off at the tavern, Florence wordlessly working through her daily chores, and Jill just trying to stay out of the way.

She pulled the covers over her head, knowing she must get up, take a shower, see what the kids were doing. Jeff was probably at his computer, making do until he could get on-line. Amy, however, would be twitching. And though Jill knew she should keep cleaning, keep weeding out her parents' things, she didn't think she could stand the noise of the workmen. Maybe she should get out of this house and Edgartown all together, drive Amy to Oak Bluffs and give her a chance to buy something special for the photo shoot.

She closed her eyes again, drew in a long, slow breath, and wished she were back in Boston, back to the fast-paced predictability of her days, where she never had to worry about finding things to do, or if she would have the energy to try.

Amy probably would have preferred to go into Oak Bluffs without her mother, but shopping was shopping, and next to boys, clothes were a major priority at fourteen.

Jill poked through a rack of dresses at one of the nicer shops along Circuit Avenue, the kind of shop where she and Rita used to gaze longingly into the windows, Rita wishing she could afford to buy something, Jill wishing her mother would allow it.

While waiting for Amy to emerge from the small dressing room in the back, Jill noticed that the store was crowded with mothers, daughters, and mothers with daughters. Most were absorbed in the back-to-school selections—jeans and Ivy League tops, long cotton skirts and baggy vests, and, of course, miniskirts, the rack from which Jill had quickly steered Amy away.

"Mom?" Amy stood in front of a makeshift curtain dressed in an outfit that Jill had picked out—pink shorts and a top, trimmed with embroidered butterflies. With her mounds of black hair contrasting with the pastel colors, she looked adorable.

"That's cute," Jill said.

Amy rolled her eyes. "It's queer, Mom. I wouldn't be caught dead in it." She turned on one heel and disappeared behind the curtain again.

Jill returned to the rack, realizing that Amy had now passed the age when her mother's opinion mattered, when Jill could run to Filene's or Jordan Marsh on her lunch hour, pick out a few outfits for her daughter, and know they'd be fine.

Shopping with Amy was something else. It was one more thing Jill didn't know "how" to do, one more of life's seemingly natural experiences that Jill had never had with her own mother.

Then she remembered the diary, remembered her

mother's entry about putting together a trousseau. She wondered if Florence and her mother—Jill's grandmother—had shopped for it together.

She clenched her jaw and continued her prowl through the dresses.

A clerk appeared beside her. "May I help?"

Jill half smiled. "Only if you can tell me how to bridge the generation gap."

The woman's island-weathered skin crinkled into deep folds from the corners of her mouth to her gray-haired hairline. "I'm not sure that's possible. Is she looking for something special?"

"I'm looking for something decent," Amy said from behind them. She now wore a denim jumper and a navy-and-white-striped top—another of Jill's selections.

"I look like a geek. I can't possibly be in *Lifestyles* dressed like this."

The clerk turned back to Jill, seemingly undaunted by Amy's last remark. "Perhaps a skort? It looks like a miniskirt, but really is shorts."

Jill looked at Amy and realized that her daughter, indeed, looked like a geek. Not unlike the way Jill had looked when she'd lived on the island—bell-bottom-less in a bell-bottom world.

"Let's see what you have," Jill said, and followed the woman to another rack, with Amy in close pursuit.

As they skimmed through the section of Junior size threes, the woman kept her eyes on the rack. "Aren't you Jill Randall?" she asked.

Jill swallowed. She'd hoped Oak Bluffs was safe, that no one would have known her here. She wondered if she could say no. Then she remembered that if Amy decided on anything, Jill would use a credit card. The card might say "McPhearson" not "Randall," but her first name would give her away. She pulled out a seafoam-colored skort and held it up. "Actually it's McPhearson now. Jill McPhearson."

The woman nodded and picked out a white tank to go with the skort.

"I'm not sure about a tank," Jill said, "they're so form-fitting. Amy's a little young . . ."

Silently, the woman held up a matching long vest.

"Well . . ." Jill said.

"That's cool, Mom. Let me try it. Please?"

Jill nodded. Amy grabbed the clothes and returned to the dressing room.

The woman toyed with her glasses that dangled from a long cord draped around her neck. "I knew your mother," she said. "Florence."

Jill tried not to show any reaction.

"We went to the same church."

"In Edgartown?" she asked, knowing perfectly well that's where Florence had gone to church.

"I live in Edgartown. I'm Hattie Phillips."

Quickly Jill searched through her memory. The name Hattie Phillips was vaguely familiar. "Yes," she said, "how are you, Mrs. Phillips?"

"That's Miss Phillips. Never did marry."

"Oh," Jill answered, not sure whether or not she should say she was sorry.

"Too bad about your mother. I helped with the memorial service."

The air-conditioning in the shop seemed to have been turned up. Or down. Whichever direction it took to turn the place into an igloo. Jill rubbed the coolness on her arms. "Yes. Well, I was in Russia. Thank you. . . ."

Hattie Phillips waved a hand. "No thanks necessary. Florence was one of a kind. A real special lady. We miss her."

Jill didn't know how to respond. One of a kind? A real special lady? She pictured her mother in her neatly pressed apron, standing at the stove, her jaw rigidly squared as she focused her need for perfection on a pot of simmering beef stew. Braced, Jill realized, always braced for something to go wrong. Then she thought about the woman who had written in the diary—a joyous young woman with hopes and dreams and expectations. She wondered which Florence Randall was the woman Hattie Phillips had known.

Thankfully, Amy came out of the dressing room. "It's cool, Mom. I want it."

Jill eyed her daughter. The tank was, indeed, form-fitting, hugging Amy's svelte frame, showing off curves that Jill thought she was much too young to have—let alone show off. The skort was short— but it was split. The vest, however, was the saving grace, smoothing the edges of Amy's womanhood enough to safeguard her youth. Besides, Jill thought, right about now she'd do anything to get out of here.

"Okay," she said. "We'll take it."

Amy squealed and returned to the dressing room, while Jill dug in her purse.

"We've all been wondering about the house," Hattie said as she processed the credit card. "Are you going to keep it?"

Jill had a sudden image of the old church ladies, sitting around their circle, contemplating the fate of that one-of-a-kind Florence Randall's hearth and home. "Well," she answered in a stumble of words, "I'm not around here very much. I thought it would be best to sell. . . ."

Hattie rang up the outfit without saying that was too bad, or we'll be sorry to see you leave, or even "How long did your family own the house?" Instead of these things, Hattie said nothing, which, in Jill's mind, was even worse, making her feel like the ungrateful daughter that surely she had always been, and that surely all the island ladies had always known.

Amy didn't want to stop for lunch. "I'll get fat, Mom," she replied. "I'll have some melon when we get back."

When we get back, Jill noted, not *when we get home.* The house on Water Street was, after all, no more of a home to Amy than it was to Jill. It was a house, that was all. A house to sell. A house to get rid of. Once the infernal sawing and banging and hammering ceased. If that ever happened.

As she started to pull into the narrow driveway, Jill jammed on the brakes. A red Porsche convertible was parked in her way.

"Cool car," Amy said.

Jill sat back and eased the tension of her seat belt. "Maybe. But it almost killed us." Backing up the Range Rover and angling it onto the street, she wondered who belonged to the car and why it was in her driveway.

She squeezed the vehicle behind Ben's Buick, wishing he weren't still there, that he had gone for the day, that he was done. *No such luck,* she whispered to herself as they got out of the car and walked to the back of the house.

The yard was a litter of wood and tools, with a small cement mixer and wheelbarrow poised by the bulkhead—a mess that would have driven Florence Randall into her kitchen for weeks. But what was more surprising was the presence of a bleached blond young girl who leaned against one of the saw-horses, a picnic basket at her feet, a red-lipped grin on her wide mouth. She wore short jeans and an open white shirt that did little to cover the full breasts protruding from her too small bikini top. Neither Ben nor his helper was there.

"Hi," the blonde said, with unflinching certainty that it was perfectly acceptable to make herself at home in someone else's backyard. "You must be Jill. I'm Carrie."

There had been few times in her life when Jill had taken an instant dislike to someone. This was one of them. "Is that your car in my driveway?"

"Oh, yeah." The girl tipped her chin. "My birthday present. From Daddy."

"Cool car," Amy said again.

Jill shot her a look, then turned back to Carrie. "Perhaps Daddy never explained the difficulty of parking on the Vineyard."

"Oh," Carrie answered with a slight pout that looked as practiced as the one Amy frequently wore. "Sorry. I didn't know anyone would be using the driveway."

Jill sighed. "Well, never mind. I found a space." She started toward the back door, then turned around. "Is there something I can help you with, Carrie?"

The girl shook her head and kicked her toe at the picnic basket. "No. I'm waiting for Kyle. I brought him lunch."

"How nice," Jill replied. She looked at Amy. "Come on, honey, let's get your clothes on hangers."

"You've been shopping?" Carrie asked as she moved from her post at the sawhorse and sashayed toward Amy. "Can I see what you bought?"

Amy looked at Jill, then Carrie. "Sure." She opened her bag and began taking out her new outfit. "My picture's going to be in *Lifestyles*," she beamed as she held up the pieces for Carrie to examine.

Jill shook her head and went in the back door, wondering what her mother's island-church lady friends would think once word got around that a photo crew from *Lifestyles* was going to be at the Randall house, and what a shame it was that the old place was going to be sold.

. . . .

A few moments later Addie called.

"The photo shoot will be next Wednesday," she told Jill.

A thrill rushed through her. *Work!* she thought. *Thank God for work.*

"We'll arrive Tuesday afternoon," Addie continued. "The crew will be in later that night. I've booked them at The Daggett House."

Only Addie could manage to get rooms at The Daggett House in August on short notice. "Good. It's only a few doors down."

"I assume you have a guest room for me?"

Jill thought about the small sewing room across from the kitchen. It was one room she'd yet to investigate; she had no idea how much work it would entail. There used to be a twin bed in there, usually hidden by bolts of fabric. And, of course, the hi-fi.

"Yes," she said. "Of course you'll stay here." Then she remembered Ben, and the mess and the noise. She stretched the cord as she walked to the hall window and looked into the backyard. Amy was still standing with Carrie. Amy was laughing. Jill frowned and said into the phone, "You know, Addie, I'm not sure how this is going to work. The house is a mess with the workers. . . ."

"Get rid of them."

Jill looked at the lawn, at the ruts she knew the sawhorses were making. *Well,* she thought, *that's Addie's problem.* It was all her idea—Ben Niles, the photo shoot on the Vineyard—let her figure out how to make it work. "Is there anything special you want me to do?"

"Yes. Look your best. Wear one of those hideous cotton dresses—you know the type—with the high waist and little flowers and a hemline that brushes your ankles."

Jill knew the dresses. She owned none. "I really don't think . . ."

"It will make you look motherly. Homey."

Homely, was more like it, she thought. "I thought I was supposed to look like a celebrity."

"Don't worry. You will. Get a floppy straw hat, too. And canvas sandals that lace up the calf. I'll make sure there are plenty of fresh flowers around. And berries. Are there any berries in season? We want everything to look country, cozy, *au naturale*."

Jill thought of the beach plums. She resisted suggesting that she stand at the stove making jelly.

"As for the kids—make sure they look like real kids."

Jill winced. "They are real kids, Addie. I'm sure that won't be a problem."

Addie laughed. "Just have them in real clothes. Not too much makeup on Amy. We don't want her looking older than her mother."

Jill glanced out the window again. She wondered how long she was going to be able to keep Amy from growing up too quickly, from looking older than her mother—or worse—as old as Carrie whoever-she-was.

The annoying beep of Addie's call waiting cut through the line. "I'll see you next week. Gotta run." She quickly hung up.

Returning to the hall table, Jill replaced the receiver as Ben came up the basement stairs.

"Is it okay if I wash up for lunch?" he asked.

"Sure," she responded. "Oh, and, Ben? Next Tuesday and Wednesday, you can't be here working."

He hesitated in the doorway, then nodded and moved into the kitchen.

She went back to the window and looked out at her daughter, who seemed to be mesmerized by the way Ben's helper, Kyle, was joking with Carrie, and by the way the young couple picked up the picnic basket, waved good-bye, and headed off toward the Chappy ferry, his hand firmly planted on her ass.

It was then that Jill realized Addie had never even thanked her for agreeing to the *Lifestyles* spread, and for subjecting her kids to the media world against her better judgment.

Kyle would have shit if he'd seen the lunch tab. Rita filled in twenty dollars in the tip area of the American Express receipt and said a quick prayer that it had been worth it: blowing more money on vodka gimlets and cracked crab salads for the Martins than she made in a week at the tavern would pay off if she could get them to make an offer on Joe Geissel's house. For, no matter what Joe claimed, Rita knew money talked. And nothing talked louder than a firm offer.

"Are we going to see the house now?" the missus asked as she waddled back from the Captain Webber's white and gold ladies room.

Rita smiled at the melon-flowered, caftan-draped woman, who apparently thought Captain Webber's was deserving of her finest Vineyard attire. "Why don't we go in one car?" she suggested, certain that her Toyota would be uncomfortable for the two oversized Martins. Not to mention the fact that the last thing she wanted was for her car to be spotted anywhere near Joe's. Even though it was Tuesday— the day of his weekly golf game—one could never be sure who was watching the estate.

"I'll drive," the mister said quickly.

Rita smiled and stood up. "Then let's go."

"It's incredible," Mrs. Martin said in an almost-whisper as they stood in the backyard, overlooking the sound.

"Yes," Rita agreed. "Of course, it needs some updating . . ." No sense in making them think she was too eager.

"How much updating?" Mr. Martin asked, shielding his gimlet-clouded eyes from the bright sun.

Rita walked toward the patio. "Not a lot. What it really needs is a decorator's touch. Someone with taste such as yours, Mrs. Martin." She didn't need to turn around: she knew they would have followed her to the round wall of windows that encased the breakfast nook. The breakfast nook, and the glass-topped dining table where Joe had told her he wasn't going to leave the island and give her up.

She walked right up to the windows and beckoned the Martins closer.

They looked at each other, hesitating.

"No one's home," Rita said. "They were called out of town unexpectedly. Otherwise, I'd have the key."

They inched their way forward. When they finally pressed their faces against the glass, Rita knew that what they were seeing was just what they wanted.

"Oh, my," Mrs. Martin exclaimed. "It's such a large house."

"With plenty of space for those grandchildren," Rita commented.

"Plenty of space for them not to get in the way," Mr. Martin added.

She quickly moved them around to the side, to the carriage house that had a converted apartment on the second floor. "There's a great apartment up there," she said. "Perfect for guests."

Mr. Martin nodded. Mrs. Martin positively glowed.

"Is there a gardener?" she asked. "The grounds are so lovely."

Rita stepped to a yellow rosebush that regally

clung to a freshly painted trellis up the side of the
carriage house. "Do you enjoy flowers, Mrs. Martin?"

"Oh, my, yes."

Personally, the thought of gardening made Rita
gag. Slathering oneself in bug repellent, then wreck-
ing a perfectly good manicure was not her idea of a
good time. "Roses love the sea air here," she commented, having no idea if what she was saying was a
lie or not. "They bloom without any trouble at
all . . . very naturally." She reached up and
plucked two healthy blossoms from the bush,
handed one to the missus, kept one for herself.

"Well," Mr. Martin harrumphed as he looked
back to the house, "this certainly is quite a place."

"As I mentioned," Rita said, gently sniffing the
rose fragrance and hoping she wouldn't sneeze, "it's
not officially on the market yet. The owners are hoping to make a deal before they have to go through all
that—you know, all that nonsense and bother of a
multiple listing."

The missus nodded as though she knew what Rita
meant.

"So if you're interested, you should consider making an offer. I think they'd be inclined to sell quickly,
and you could get yourself quite a deal."

The mister nodded.

"Oh, there's one other thing," Rita added as she
purposely strolled back toward the view, "I'm not
the only agent who knows the owners are considering selling. You, of course, are the only people I've
brought out here. But I can't speak for anyone else. I
have to be honest with you. For all I know, a deal
has already been made." Good, she thought. The
bait is out.

"Well," Mr. Martin said, puffing out his chest,
"of course, we'd want to actually get inside. See the
rest."

Rita raised an eyebrow. "You could make a tentative offer," she suggested. "With a contingency on approval of the interior." She couldn't believe she was saying this. She couldn't believe anyone would be stupid enough to think this kind of tactic was anything more than bullshit. Then again, this was Martha's Vineyard, where premium properties often enticed eccentric buyers.

Mrs. Martin rocked on her sensible, seashell-colored pumps. Mr. Martin rubbed his hundred-dollar cracked-crab-salad-full stomach.

"I'll tell you what, Miss Blair," he said. "I'll give you a call tonight. Can I reach you at home?"

"If I'm not there, just leave a message on my machine," Rita said coolly as she led the way back to the front of the house, to the circular driveway, trying not to rip off her SurfSide Realty blazer and shout "Holy Shit" to the world.

Later that night, as Rita sat by the phone, the call came.

"Miss Blair," the gravelly voice said into her answering machine, "this is Mr. Martin."

She leaned forward on the edge of the thirty-something-year-old sofa, her heart pounding wildly in her throat.

"We've talked it over and decided to make an offer. Two million dollars. Flat. No negotiating."

She leaped from the sofa and screamed "Yes!" Then she quickly sat down again, as though Mr. Martin could hear her reaction, as though he might find out how important this was.

"Of course, as you mentioned," he continued, "the offer's contingent on our approval of the interior." He paused. Rita stared at the machine.

"But I'm sure that won't be a problem," he said. "Give us a call when you have an answer."

He hung up the phone, and Rita beamed. She was going to sell Joe's house; she was really going to sell Joe's house. She could pay off the IRS before they took her away. And, almost as good, she could tell Charlie that she was done at the tavern. Then she'd never have to worry about running into Jill or facing that bitch again.

She leaned back against the sofa and realized that tears were pouring down her cheeks.

Chapter 9

 Jill had managed to drag Jeff from his computer for dinner; Amy, incredibly, had agreed to eat.

They sat at a table by the window at the Wharf, Jeff devouring fish and chips, Amy picking at chicken Caesar salad. Jill nibbled on scallops and decided this was better than staying in that house, better than cooking in that kitchen . . . the kitchen that once belonged to Florence Randall, that one-of-a-kind, real special lady.

"Mom, you're not going to believe who Carrie's father is," Amy chattered. "Sam Wilkins. Sam *Wilkins*, the rock star. Do you believe it?"

Jill sipped her iced tea. "I'm surprised you know who he is. He's from my generation."

"He's a *legend*, Mom. *Everybody* knows Sam Wilkins."

"Who's Sam Wilkins?" Jeff asked.

"Mom," Amy said, turning her head from Jeff, "tell him to shut up."

Jill sighed and returned to her scallops. "Cut it out, both of you."

Amy tossed back her hair. "It's really cool, Mom. Carrie lives in L.A. and everything."

L.A. A picture of Lizette French sprung to Jill's

mind, followed by a vision of Sam Wilkins's daughter in her abbreviated clothes. Carrie was well suited for L.A. She started to tell the kids that they might be living in L.A., too, but quickly changed her mind. There would be plenty of time for that later, *if* they struck a deal with Maurice Fischer, *if* RueCom was serious, if Jill could prove she was capable of doing national stories.

Suddenly Jeff bolted from his seat. Jill looked over at his empty basket of dinner. "I'm going to the men's room," he said and quickly disappeared.

"Can't you do something about him?" Amy asked once Jeff was gone.

Jill tried not to smile. "Your brother is your brother, Amy. Someday you'll appreciate each other."

Amy rolled her eyes. "But, Mother, he's so juvenile."

"He's sixteen. All sixteen-year-old boys act that way until they get their license."

"Carrie has her license."

And a shiny new Porsche, Jill wanted to add.

"She invited me to her house tomorrow. They live on the beach. In Gay Head."

Jill shook her head. "She's a lot older than you, Amy."

"She's only eighteen, Mom. That's not so old."

"I don't want you driving with her. You're too young." She noticed Amy's jaw tighten.

"What if you drive me there?"

"As I said," Jill replied, "you're too young to be hanging around with eighteen-year-olds."

"Great," Amy whined. "And just what do you expect me to do for the next three and a half weeks on this stupid island? I don't have any friends here. I'm not like my geeky brother who stays in his room and plays with his computer." The pitch of her voice changed to anger. "You won't let me go to the beach alone. You won't let me have any friends. You barely let me *breathe*, Mom."

Jill sipped from her water glass, deciding to ignore Amy's comment. Her daughter, after all, had no idea what it was like to be imprisoned by a mother, entrapped in emotional shackles since the day she'd been born. She glanced at Amy, at the lowered dark eyes so strikingly Florence's, and wondered if, when Amy turned eighteen, she would follow in Jill's footsteps and leave home.

"Hey, Mom," Jeff called as he reappeared at the table. "There's a sign in the hall for volleyball. It's every morning on the State Beach. Can I go?"

She set down her fork. "I didn't know you play volleyball."

"I'm on the intramural team at school."

Jill signaled for the check, realizing that perhaps she knew as little about her own children as she had about her mother. "Well, I guess . . ."

Amy stood up. Her chair flew from under her. "Oh, great. That's just great. He can do anything. I can't do shit." She stormed out of the crowded restaurant and through the front door.

They had driven back to Water Street in silence. Amy had closed herself in her bedroom; Jeff had returned to his computer. Jill stood in the middle of the kitchen, wondering which boxes to pack next, certain that Amy hated her as much as she, at fourteen, had hated her own mother. Hopefully, Amy would grow out of it. The way Jill never quite had.

She opened one cabinet and saw exactly what she expected to see: the dark blue enamel lobster pot. She hauled it out: nested inside were varying sizes of stew and soup pots. Slowly, she examined them. The smallest was aluminum: Florence only used it for homemade chicken broth. Next came the turnip pot for Thanksgiving, the cast-iron clam chowder pot, the battered beef stew pot. She sat back on her heels and studied the array of Florence's kitchen essentials. Then, she ran her hand around the top of the beef stew pot, remembering snowy winter nights, when she'd walked home from school in the almost-dark, and felt, upon opening the door, almost happy, almost safe, when greeted by the aroma of the simmering stew.

Closing her eyes now, she could almost smell the aroma.

"Great stew," she could hear her father say. It was always "great stew," or "great chowdah," or "great casserole." And each evening, Florence gave a tight little nod in response, never a "thank you," never an acknowledgment, as though she didn't really care if he liked it or not.

But once, he had forgotten to compliment her. Halfway through the meal, she'd thrown down her spoon, burst into tears, and fled to the sewing room.

Jill stared at her father who sat, motionless, one hand gripping a chunk of half-eaten cornbread. It wasn't until the sounds of Benny Goodman filtered into the dining room that George—and Jill—resumed their meal in silence, as though nothing had happened, nothing had changed.

She bent her head now, pulled back her hair, and tried to smell inside the pot. But no comforting aromas lingered: only the distant scent of cleanser, dulled by years of unuse.

Staring into the pot, Jill wondered why she was putting herself through this, and why she felt as though she were going to cry.

Quickly she shook her head and stood up. Renesting the pots, she grabbed a carton and lifted the stack inside, then closed the lid and zipped a strip of tape across the opening. She grabbed a felt marker, scrawled "Pots" on the side of the brown box, and underlined it with an angry black streak.

She rested back on her heels and wondered why she had done that. Why had she packed the pots as if she were moving them, taking them . . . where? Home? Did she want these Florence Randall reminders in her kitchen? Did she really want the long-ago aromas to follow her back to Boston? Or to L.A.?

"The church women," she said aloud. She pushed the carton against the wall and knew what she would do. She would donate all of Florence's things to the ladies of the church. Surely they still had a rummage sale or whatever they called them today. Surely the ladies would enjoy picking through Florence's things, helping themselves to whatever they wanted, raising money for their cause with the remnants.

Jill put her hands on her hips, pleased with her decision. Oddly, she knew it was what Florence would have wanted. To leave her legacy to those who would appreciate it; to those who knew what a very special lady she had been.

The only problem was, Jill would have to face them.

She stared at the cartons, knowing she couldn't face Hattie Phillips. She couldn't face her mother's blue-white-haired friends. There had to be another way.

Shoving the carton aside, Jill almost laughed. The ladies would have loved this stuff, though. They would have loved pawing through it and arguing over it all—even the hideous vase in the widow's walk.

Then, she remembered the diary. Should she throw it away? Should she give it away?

Forty years from now, would she want Amy to give hers away, if Jill had ever kept one, if Amy still despised her?

After packing several more cartons, Jill went to bed. Her back ached from unfamiliar chores, her head ached from God knew what, and her mind whirled with jumbled thoughts of Amy, of her mother. As she lay in bed staring up at the canopy, willing the sleep that would not come, she knew she agreed with Amy on one thing: three and a half weeks on this stupid island was too much to ask of any of them.

She squeezed her eyes closed and wondered how her mother had endured so many decades here. Well, she reasoned, the how was apparent. It was apparent by the soup pans and stew pots, and, of course, the beach plum jelly pot hidden in the basement. It was apparent by the songs of Benny Goodman, still embedded in Jill's brain.

Yes, the how was apparent. But what about the "why"? Why had Florence been so content to be sequestered here?

Slowly, her mind drifted to the diary, to the small part she had read, written by a young woman with dreams, with hopes, with excitement about the future.

It was so hard to believe it had been written by her mother.

She rolled onto one side, pulled the musty sheet more tightly around her. She'd known that Florence was raised in New York City. She'd known she had a sister named Myrna. And she'd known that Florence and Myrna had "breeding," from the times she'd heard her mother chastise Rita, Jill's one and only friend. "That girl has no breeding," Florence said on more than one occasion. "She's a bad influence on you."

Jill flipped onto her stomach and pushed her face into the pillow. If Florence had such breeding, why did she ever come here? Why did she ever stay here?

And had she thought that proper "breeding" meant raising your daughter to be miserable?

Slowly, Jill pulled herself up and sat on the edge of the bed. There had to be more to Florence Randall than pots and pans and proper breeding. There had to be something . . . something Jill's father had seen in her, long ago. Or had it been nothing more than a ruse?

Without stopping to reconsider, Jill got out of bed, pulled on her robe, slipped into her slippers— her apricot satin city slippers—and left the bedroom, heading for the hall, heading for the widow's walk.

Sun. Sept. 23, 1945

Jill took a long breath and stared at the page. She curled her feet in under her and pulled the hand-made quilt around her legs. Then, slowly, she began to read.

I met him in the park today. His name is George. He has just returned from England; on his way home to Martha's Vineyard. He looks so handsome in his uniform. He asked to take me to the cinema tonight—I said yes! Mother will never approve.

Jill smiled, then read on.

Mon. Sept. 24, 1945
George Randall is wonderful! He brought me flowers today . . . white carnations. He is taking me to the park this afternoon. Is this the man I've waited for?

Thurs. Sept. 27, 1945
He kissed me! In under the bridge in Central Park, he stopped rowing the boat. He stood up.

The boat rocked, and I was so scared my heart started to beat really fast. At first I didn't know what he was doing. Then he leaned over and kissed me. His lips tasted like pipe tobacco, warm and smoky. He rested his strong hand against my cheek—I worried he'd feel how flushed I'd become. But then, he kissed me again. Oh, God! I think I shall never see that bridge or a rowboat or orange autumn leaves again and not remember that I was kissed by a handsome man in uniform . . . a son of a tavern owner. Wouldn't Mother just die if she knew?

Sun. Sept. 30, 1945

He holds my hand at the most wonderful times. Today we stood at the counter at Romano's Deli, ordering bread and cheese and grapes for our picnic lunch, when, suddenly, George reached out and took my hand. He squeezed it so gently I thought I was going to melt right then and there, all over the floor.

I wonder if Daddy ever held Mother's hand. It's hard to picture her letting him do that—it might have mussed her manicure! Holding hands, to her, was probably a pointless thing, something she couldn't have been bothered to let him do.

It's hard to remember Daddy, he's been dead for so long. One time I told Myrna that Mother must have killed him, with all her demands and her need to always be in charge of everything. Myrna punched me and told me to shut up.

Jill tucked her hair behind her ears and wondered what it would have been like to have a brother or a sister—someone to tell you to shut up the way Amy did to Jeff. She bit her lip and forced herself to focus on her mother, to keep reading on.

Wed. Oct. 10, 1945
George's papers have come through. He leaves for home tomorrow. I knew that this would happen, but I didn't want to believe it. I never wanted our fairy tale to end. He promises to write, but I don't know if he will. I think that I will go to bed now. I think that I will cry.

Wed. Oct. 17, 1945
I can't believe I did this. I went to George's rooming house this morning, I went to help him pack. He closed the door behind us. He took me in his arms and told me that he loves me. It felt so good to have him close to me. It felt so good for someone to love me. I kissed him back a thousand times—those soft, warm, tobacco-y lips. And then we laid down on the bed—the squeaky, springy, thin-mattressed bed. I can't believe I did this. It didn't hurt— George would never hurt me. He loves me. Oh, God, I hope he loves me.

Jill blinked. Quickly she reread the last entry. *And then we laid down on the bed.* Did it mean they'd made love? Did her mother . . . her proper, well-bred mother . . . actually make love to a soldier in a rooming house?

She tried to picture what Florence must have looked like when she was young. Like Amy, perhaps, with that elegant black hair, that peachy, creamy skin. Jill realized that she had never seen a photograph of her mother in her youth. She wondered if that was unusual, then remembered that Rita's mother had pictures of herself everywhere—from grade school through motherhood—set in awkward, plastic frames scattered throughout their house.

There were no such photos of Florence Randall.

Jill's stomach ached. She wanted to close the book, she wanted to go back to bed and pretend she'd never seen this. Instead, she turned the page.

Thurs. Jan. 31, 1946
I have to pinch myself. I look into the mirror, and I can't believe that I'm a married woman. I wonder if I look different. George says I'm radiant. Even the Justice of the Peace said I looked radiant. And he doesn't know our secret! George found work down on the docks and says he doesn't mind living in New York City. Mother still won't come to our apartment. She says there won't be room for her to visit in one room with a bath down the hall. But I don't care how small it is. It is ours, and I love my husband so very much. I'm going to do everything to be a good wife. And to be a good mother. Gosh! I can't believe I'm going to be a mother!

Jill gasped. A *mother?* She shot her gaze back to the top of the page: *Jan. 31, 1946.* 1946? Jill wasn't born until 1953.

Her thoughts raced. Did her parents *have to get married?* If Florence had been pregnant, it wasn't with her.

"My God," she said quietly. "My God." With halfhearted hesitation, she slowly turned the page again. Then, a piece of something slid from the book.

Jill looked into her lap. There, upon the antique quilt, rested a tiny lock of golden hair. She picked it up and held it gently, as though it might shatter, as though it wasn't real. Her hand began to tremble.

Fri. July 12, 1946
We have a precious baby boy. His name is
Robbie—Robert, after George's grandfather. I
have never known such happiness.

The lock of hair fell from her hand. Jill stared at
it, as it lay on the open book. Her heart ached, her
temples pounded. She lifted her head, felt the tears
that stained her cheeks. The thought that her mother
had kept such a secret . . . the thought that her
mother . . . Florence Randall . . . could have had
such emotion . . . *any* emotion . . . was beyond
Jill's comprehension.

Florence Randall had been cold.

Florence Randall had been a bitch.

Florence Randall had not been the sort of woman
to . . . to *love* a baby.

But a baby *boy*? Had there really been a baby
boy? A son for Florence? A . . . *brother* for Jill?

She looked out the window, out toward the sea.
The morning sky was turning pink, the lazy harbor
tide slowly slapped the shore. And Jill felt the tug of
the past trying to pull her back, trying to suck her
down into its chasm, as though her mother's hand
had reached up from the grave to lure her back to
the misery of her youth.

Quickly Jill slammed the book. "No," she said
firmly. Brother or no brother, Florence Randall was
dead. And she did not have the power to screw up
Jill's life again.

Chapter 10

At seven-thirty, Jill was seated at the small rolltop desk in the music room, scrawling out notes, pouring her sleepless adrenaline energy into the one thing she could count on: her work. Christopher had said Maurice Fischer wasn't sure she could deliver stories of national scope. Right now, proving herself was much more important than dwelling on things over which she had no control. Besides, working was the only way to forget about her mother, forget the damn diary, and forget some unknown brother named Robbie.

She stared at the paper in front of her, trying to concentrate. It had been easier to come up with ideas when she'd been a street reporter. News would happen—a murder, a fire, a gang-related drug war. It had been easy to create spin-off stories when the initial seed had been planted: talk to the victim's co-workers, share the plight of three families left homeless, interview the mother of the gang leader. The main story led to others. It was simple.

Developing her own fresh ideas was something else, something she'd shined at with *Good Night, Boston*. But knowing how to take that to a national level somehow seemed elusive.

She looked over her notes. An update with an O.J.

juror two years later? An in-depth look into the life of a Las Vegas blackjack dealer? A where-are-they-now series on high school graduates voted the most likely to succeed?

Jill squeezed her eyes tightly, dropped the pen, and rubbed the back of her neck. Everything, it seemed, had been done. Done, overdone. And most of it hadn't turned out to be "good news"—the types of stories that made *Good Night, Boston* unique.

The sound of a car door slamming jolted her. She opened her eyes and saw Ben Niles emerge from the old, shiny car. Leaning her back against the rungs of the Windsor chair, Jill watched the man's slow, deliberate movements as he opened the trunk, hoisted out a toolbox, set it down, and massaged his shoulder. She smiled, glad she wasn't the only one to have aches in her over-forty muscles.

Ben adjusted the Red Sox cap on his head, then, with those disturbingly strong-looking arms, he picked up the box and made his way toward the backyard. As he passed the living-room window he paused and gave a small wave to Jill. It startled her. She hadn't realized he'd seen her. Quickly she blinked, ran a hand through her uncombed hair, and returned the wave. Annoying as he was, she supposed it wouldn't hurt to pretend to be friendly.

As she picked up her pen again, Jill tried to refocus on her work. But she sat, distracted, unable to continue. *Who is Ben Niles?* she wondered. *Who is this man with this solid, sought-after reputation? A man who certainly can afford more than an ancient car and a beat-up baseball cap?*

Her thoughts began to gel. Beneath his blue-collar exterior, there must be a story there, she reasoned, a story that would intrigue TV viewers. Surely a man held in such regard for the work he performed—the *art*, as Addie called it—must have some explanation for sequestering himself on this godforsaken island when he could probably command a huge business of international renown. A story on Ben Niles might be just what she needed. Ben Niles, house renovator to the stars.

While swirling doodles in the margin of her page, Jill thought about Ben. How had he learned his craft? What made him different? Why was he in such demand by people willing to pay outrageous fees?

And what about Ben, the man? Did he have children? Was he married? How old was he?

Suddenly her pen stopped. *How old was he?* He looked to be older than Jill by several years. Could Robbie be the same age as Ben . . . if Robbie were still alive?

She gripped her pen, trying to stop her thoughts. Then, the need for sleep crawled through her body, just as, from the backyard, the power saw roared to life.

The morning heated quickly, and by eleven-thirty Ben was ready to break for lunch. Maybe busting his ass was the best way to take his mind off his problems, but it wouldn't do much good if he dropped dead from sweating in the blistering sun. Besides, he suspected that Jill McPhearson wouldn't even appreciate it.

"Lunch plans today?" Ben called over to Kyle, who stood by the cement mixer, helping Dan Ellis— the island's best mason—mix another batch.

"Yeah," Kyle responded with a grin. "Sorry."

Ben shook his head. "No problem." He pulled off his cap and T-shirt and mopped the dampness from his chest. Looking down at the mass of curly gray hairs that carpeted his softened flesh, Ben thought about the kind of sex Kyle must be having with Carrie—young, uninhibited sex that probably generated more heat that any steamy August morning. He wondered if he would ever make love with a woman again; he wondered if he would ever want to. In the two years since Louise had died, he'd hardly thought about it, as though grief had shut down his manhood, stripped him of his libido.

Not that he hadn't had opportunity. There were at least a dozen casserole-toting, over-forty women who had appeared at his door more than once since Louise died. Women like Rachel Bowen, the never-married neighbor with island-scrubbed skin, long, gathered skirts, and a soft smile that tried to hint she would make a fine wife. But even her best macaroni and cheese could not create a stir below his belt.

Still . . . he thought, tugging the damp shirt over his head once again . . . the idea of a body as firm and lust-filled as Carrie's . . .

"Shit," he said aloud and shook his head quickly. The heat must really be getting to him. The only thing this body was good for now was staying alive, keeping his shit together, and trying to make at least one dream come true. As long as Kyle was busy for lunch, he might as well drive cross-island to Barbara Jean's coffee shop for a tuna sandwich, and see if Dave Ashenbach was around. It was time Ben Niles confronted his enemy one-on-one. What the hell, things couldn't get any hotter than they already were.

Barbara Jean's was another hole-in-the-wall diner the tourists avoided, which was fine with Barbara Jean and with the couple of dozen locals who depended on its five A.M. opening for their breakfast, and on being able to grab a sandwich from eleven to two.

Inside the linoleum-floored, Formica-shiny restaurant, only two of the eight chrome-and-vinyl stools were vacant. As Ben made himself comfortable on one, he noticed that Dave Ashenbach—that beer-bellied son of a town father—was holding court at the corner table, where he'd probably been since 1953.

"Afternoon, Ben," Barbara Jean said, her white apron stained from the grill, her pencil poised over a small pad. "What'll it be?"

Barbara Jean Rogers had been one of the few "available" ladies who had not pursued Ben after Louise's death. But then, she probably had her fill of island men day in and day out.

"Tuna on white toast," Ben said. "And coffee."

"Soup?"

Boisterous laughter came from Ashenbach's table. Ben wondered if the man was talking about him. His stomach tightened. "No," he answered. "The sandwich is fine."

Barbara Jean ripped off the page and clipped it on the circular metal stand that stood at a window that opened into the kitchen. Ben took off his cap and set it on the counter. Then he swiveled on the stool, stood up, and walked to where Ashenbach sat.

If the man saw him coming, he didn't acknowledge him.

"Dave," Ben said as he reached the table for four.

The man took a bite of a thick burger. Its juice ran down his fingers to his wrist. "Yeah?" he asked between chews.

Ben stiffened at the knees. "I'd like to talk to you about Menemsha House."

Ashenbach laughed. A piece of burger shot from his mouth onto his ragged beard. He didn't bother to brush it away. "You talked to the zoning board," he said, his eyes fixed on the man who sat across from him. "You heard what they said."

"I heard the runaround. I've come up with some options, but there's no point in going forward with them if you're going to fight me."

The beer-belly grinned. "What makes you think I'm going to fight you?"

"Because someone wants to stop me. I assumed it was you."

Ashenbach pushed back his chair and looked at Ben. "Look, Niles, I don't really give a shit what you do with that house. As long as you stay the hell off my land." He turned around and sunk his teeth into his burger again.

"Sandwich is up," Barbara Jean called to Ben.

Ben turned to her. "Wrap it, please. I've got to get back to work."

She had on the sexiest thing she owned: a fitted white tank dress with a neckline down to there and hemline up to here. Rita apprised herself in the full-length mirror behind her bathroom door and smiled. She knew she didn't look forty-three. Hell, in this outfit, she barely looked thirty. Still, it was a good thing Kyle was at work: she'd rather not have him see how decidedly trampy she looked. There were some things a mother just shouldn't reveal.

Clipping on two-inch gold earrings, she fluffed her red curls and touched up her eyeliner. Joe Geissel would squirm. The only thing she hadn't decided was if she'd let him screw her before or after she told him about the Martins' offer. The two-million-dollar offer that was going to change her life.

But she had to move fast. The Martins were returning to Brookline on Sunday. It was already Wednesday, and Rita had to finalize things before then. She didn't want them going home, thinking it over, changing their minds.

She grabbed her purse from the vanity and went down the slanted stairs of the old saltbox. As she opened the front door, the phone rang. She sighed a moment, wondering if she should answer it. It could be the Martins. It could be the IRS. More than likely, it was some pushy telemarketer calling to say she'd won some stupid prize.

She shrugged and went out the door, letting her answering machine deal with whoever the hell it was.

The best part about Wednesdays was that Joe was rested from his golf game on Tuesday, unpressured with "family" obligations until Friday, and horny as hell. *Hump Day*, was what they'd called Wednesday when Rita was a school kid. She laughed as she maneuvered the car onto the road toward West Chop. Little had Rita and Jill known then that Rita would have taken that meaning literally.

A slow ache crawled through her belly as she thought of Jill again. Thankfully, the distraction of fighting for her life had left little time for Rita to think about her long-lost friend. And Kyle had been seeing so much of his girlfriend that Rita had been spared listening to an elaborate narration of how wonderful Jill McPhearson was, what a gorgeous house she had, and what an exciting life she led. Kyle, the common laborer, had hopefully not attracted Jill's attention. And hopefully, Jill had not learned that Rita was his mother.

As she wove her way through the snaillike traffic, Rita wondered when she and Jill had each changed so much, why the friendship that Rita had cherished since kindergarten had grown uncomfortable, then distant, then disintegrated altogether.

She thought about the sixth-grade talent show that Jill had talked her into doing. Rita's mother had made them costumes—black tights and jackets covered with sequins and glitter. They had wobbled on stage together—Jill loving the attention, Rita trying to camouflage her inner terror.

Me and My Shadow. Together they had crackled out the song, in tune with their clumsy dance steps, waving their canes and tipping the top hats that Rita's mother had made from plastic milk jugs covered with black felt. They'd worn red lipstick and rouge, and looked quite terrific. But when Rita, the "shadow," got too close to Jill's cane, she tripped and fell to her knees. The music abruptly stopped; silence hung in the small auditorium. Pain shot through Rita's legs. She glanced up at Jill. Her best friend looked panic-stricken. Slowly, Rita pulled herself up, pasted a smile on her face, and bowed. Their teacher, Miss Topor, proudly stood and led the applause in the small auditorium.

Me and My Shadow.

She should have known then that Jill was destined for greatness, that Rita would forever be in the background, trying to pull herself up. But had that meant they could not be friends? What had really happened? Rita wondered as she turned down the road toward Joe's estate. Why did best friends lose what they had?

Since Jill, Rita had never let herself become close to another female, not, in fact, close to anyone. She supposed that Jill had made another best friend, someone with smarts more like her own, someone who wasn't satisfied with life as it was, making penuche for shut-ins and scraping by to make a buck. A woman someone very much unlike Rita, who needed to do whatever it took to protect her secret, to protect her son, and had been dumb enough to get into trouble with the IRS.

She parked the Toyota and sat for a moment, trying to refocus on why she was here. Joe. The money. The Martins' offer. The chance to quit that god-awful job at the tavern and keep Jill Randall McPhearson where she belonged—in the back of her mind, along with the rest of her past.

She took a deep breath and summoned every cell of courage that swam within her island blood. Then Rita got out of the car and walked toward the back of the house. As her high heels crunched on the gravel driveway, she prayed that Joe would agree to the offer, and that she hadn't worn the world's sexiest dress for nothing.

Reaching the back door, she smiled. Joe tried so hard to be macho, the way he always waited for her to ring the bell, for him to politely answer the door, as though he hadn't been expecting her, as though he hadn't been waiting, drooling, watching out an upstairs window for her arrival.

From behind the door, Rita heard footsteps. She straightened her dress, smoothed it across her breasts. She shook back her red curls and readied her eager smile.

The door opened. Rita smiled. Then her face froze. Joe was not standing in the doorway, an erection under his robe, a leer in his eyes. The person in front of her was not Joe at all. It was a woman. A goddamn woman dressed in beige linen shorts and a sleeveless silk shirt. A woman with perfect revitalizing makeup right out of the ads in *Vanity Fair*; a woman with soft-colored hair and what Rita would bet were real diamonds on her ears.

The woman must be *Madam*.

"Yes?" the woman asked. "May I help you?" Even the tone of her voice was subdued, confident, moneyed. Like someone who didn't have to work for a living or be bothered to talk to anyone who did.

Rita forced her face to move. "Actually," she said, "I'm not sure." Which, of course, was not a lie, for Rita had no idea what to do next.

The woman folded her hands across her narrow waist. Rita was suddenly conscious of her hookerlike dress. She moved her large canvas bag in front of her, trying to hide everything that the dress clearly didn't, trying to not feel inferior to this woman whose class so resembled what she had seen in Jill the other night. Jill McPhearson. The best friend who became too good for lowly Rita Blair.

Anger heated her skin. Rita tossed back her curls again. She removed her bag from in front of herself. *Bitch*, she thought. *No one is better than Rita*, she said to herself. *No one. Especially the wife of the man she was screwing.*

"My name is Rita Blair," she said boldly. "I'm the owner of SurfSide Realty." She wished she looked more professional; she wished she'd worn her damn blazer.

The woman squinted in the sunlight. Rita had hoped there would be more crow's-feet around her eyes. She cleared her throat.

"I'll come right to the point, Mrs. . . . is it Mrs. Geissel?"

Madam nodded.

"I have a party who is extremely interested in buying this property," Rita said, wondering where the hell Joe was and why he was hiding when he probably knew damn well she was standing here with egg on her face and her spike heel in her mouth. "They've made a very substantial offer, and I wondered if you and your husband might be willing to speak with me a few minutes."

Madam smiled. "Someone wants to buy this house?" she said with a hint of condescension.

"It's a lovely property," Rita squeaked. "But given the weak market today, I'm sure you'll agree that my clients have made an astounding offer."

Madam smiled again. "Well, Ms. Blair, our house is not for sale."

Rita smiled back. "Oh, surely, Mrs. Geissel, everything is for sale when one hears what someone else has to offer. Perhaps if you talked it over with your husband . . ."

"Sorry," Madam said as she began to close the door. "As I said, our house is not for sale."

She closed the door. Rita stood mute, the sixth-grader embarrassed by what she had done, the scene she had caused, the obviously second-class person that she was.

Jeff had called to say he'd made friends with a couple of boys who played volleyball on the beach: a summer kid and a townie, who were going to teach him to windsail—something certainly healthier for him than staying tied to his computer. As she dug window cleaner and furniture polish from the utility closet, Jill realized he hadn't even asked what time the phone man was coming to hook up the additional line.

Amy rounded the corner with a towel in one hand and a pout on her face. "What are you doing?" she asked Jill.

"I've got to clean the spare bedroom for Addie next week."

"Can't you pay someone to do that?"

Jill laughed and shook her head. Her kids *definitely* weren't island kids. Her kids *definitely* weren't Florence Randall's. An unexpected knot formed in Jill's stomach.

"I'm going out back to get some sun," Amy said. "If that's all right with you."

The sarcasm was evident, but Jill would not acknowledge it. She rubbed her stomach and tried to smile. "Of course it is, honey. Just stay out of the way of the workmen."

Amy strutted out the back door.

Jill gathered the cleaning tools and headed for the room at the back of the house. As she opened the door, a thick haze of dust enveloped her. She coughed and rubbed her eyes. In the darkness, she saw only shadows. Crossing toward the windows, she pulled up the shades. Sunlight strained to permeate the film of age covering the glass, casting an eerie sepia tone over stacks of old magazines on the small twin bed, atop a cherry bureau, and across the hi-fi. But as Jill looked around, her eyes rested on the black Singer sewing machine that stood in the corner and was coated with a thick white layer of unuse. This was where Florence had sewn so many of Jill's clothes: shapeless plaid jumpers for the first day of school, straight wool skirts and blouses with bows. Clothes that never quite looked like the ones in the shops on Circuit Avenue.

She wondered if Florence had ever made clothes for Robbie.

Quickly turning back to the window, she sprayed a heavy mist of cleaner, ripped off several paper towels, and began to scrub, thinking of how much she'd hated those clothes, how ordinary they had made her feel, and how sick she had become each time she was upstairs in her room and could hear the quiet hum of the Singer below. It always meant she'd have to thank her mother for making her a new outfit, to pretend as though it were something special. She never dared to tell her mother how she'd really felt: it wouldn't have been right.

Right? she thought now. What was right? Was it right that Jill had a brother and no one had told her? Was it right that she had no idea who he was, where he was, if he was?

Stop it, she commanded herself. *Stop thinking about them. Stop thinking about him.*

The telephone rang. Jill dropped the paper towels and whisked from the room, grateful for the well-timed distraction.

It was Christopher.

"Hi. I just wanted you to know I'm thinking of you."

"How nice. Are you having a busy day?" She slid onto the cane-seated chair by the phone stand and curled her hair around her finger. She wanted to tell him about the diary, and about Robbie. But the words stuck in her throat, unable to rise to the surface, as though speaking them would make it . . . real.

It was easier to talk about work. "I came up with an idea for a story. One that Fischer should like." Quickly she told him her concept about Ben. "Imagine," she ended, "the home renovator to the stars, sequestered away on Martha's Vineyard." She waited for him to respond.

"Well, it might work," he said finally.

Might?

"Do you know anything more about him?"

Her hopes that he would lighten her mood began to slide. "Not yet. I wanted to run it by you first." That, of course, wasn't true. Jill had rarely found the need to review her ideas with Christopher. After all, she was the reporter, not him. He was the baseball player who happened to have the Q-rating.

"Let me talk to Addie about it," he said.

She shifted on the cane seat and stared at the old black phone.

"What are the kids up to today?" he asked, changing the subject in a flash.

She pulled her eyes away and hesitated, then decided it was pointless to argue over the phone. "Jeff is learning to windsail," she said flatly. She looked out the window toward Amy who was stretched on a towel at the far end of the yard, her Walkman stuck to her ears. "Amy is annoyed at me again."

"What now?"

"She met a girl I don't want her to hang out with." She turned from the window. "The girl is eighteen. She's also Sam Wilkins's daughter."

"Sam Wilkins? As in Grammy-winning Sam Wilkins?"

"The one and only."

"Jesus. I didn't know he had a place on the Vineyard."

"He probably came here to escape the scandal."

"That was a long time ago."

"Well, word has it from his daughter that he's planning a comeback." She wondered why they were talking about Sam Wilkins when she'd rather be telling him about the way her head ached, the way her heart ached. She'd thought that doing a story on Ben Niles would help take up her time, take up her mind, take her thoughts off that damn diary and her mysterious brother. Maybe she should just tell Christopher and get it over with.

"Hey, I've got an idea," he said.

Jill winced at the abruptness of his voice.

"Maybe you could do a story on Sam."

"He doesn't give interviews, Christopher." Anyone—everyone—in the business knew that. She stifled her annoyance at his ignorance—him, the one with the Q-rating.

"He will if he's planning a comeback. It has national appeal, Jill. It would make Fischer a lot happier than a story about some builder."

A story about some builder? Jill grasped the receiver more tightly.

"You've got to think big, Jill. You've got to take risks. That's what RueCom expects."

Her irritation grew. "What are you suggesting? That I walk up to his house, knock on his door, and say 'Hi. You don't know me, but if you give me an interview, it surely would make Maurice Fischer happy'?"

"Honey . . ."

"We do stories about *real* people, Christopher.

Sam Wilkins is fluff entertainment. We don't do fluff."

"The way he destroyed his career was hardly entertaining."

"Sensational crap, Christopher. Another thing that *Good Night, Boston* isn't," Jill bristled. "What's wrong with my idea on Ben? I'm sure I could turn it into something of 'national' interest. *Good* news, remember?"

"Fischer wouldn't see it that way. Besides, you couldn't have a better connection to get to Sam Wilkins if you paid for it."

"What are you talking about?"

"Amy. If you let her hang out with Sam's daughter, it would be a perfect cover."

Jill turned back to the window and gazed out at her daughter. She knew that Amy was miserable. She knew that Amy hated her again. She also knew that Amy was only fourteen. "Absolutely not," Jill answered, then said she really had to get back to work and that maybe she'd call him later.

"I won't be home until late," he said, with only the slightest hesitation. "Lizette is having a few friends to her hotel suite for dinner."

Chapter 11

She wasn't going to think about it. She wasn't going to think about the fact that she was stuck here on this island while her fiancé was cocktailing it up with the blond bimbo of the year. The blond bimbo who happened to work for Maurice Fischer and who no doubt knew her national stuff.

After hanging up the phone, Jill went into the kitchen, poured herself a glass of iced tea, and wondered what she should do.

You've got to think big, Christopher had said. But was she capable of it? She had thought "big" in the past—first, when she knew there was a bigger life for her off the Vineyard, then when she went after a bigger job, moving from reporter to anchor. And *Good Night, Boston* had been a risk: the show could have failed; Jill could have been unemployed.

She took a big gulp of tea and realized she resented Christopher for telling her she had to take risks. Since leaving the island, every day of her life had been a risk.

Then again, Christopher had no way of knowing. She hadn't really told him. Had she?

Setting the glass on the counter, Jill knew she hadn't shared her pain for many reasons: most importantly, because she was intimidated by his past—one of four boisterous kids, raised by loving parents in a huge, always-active home, destined for stardom from his high school baseball days through to his television career. She hadn't told Christopher about the pain of her struggle, because she'd been embarrassed by it. Embarrassed that she'd had to work so hard to be happy and successful, when it all came so naturally to him.

But now, she needed to measure up to his standards. She needed to prove that she could.

She looked out the window toward Amy again. Would there be any harm in letting her visit Carrie Wilkins? They'd only be here a few more weeks. Carrie was too old for her, true, but maybe a visit or two might be what Amy needed to perk her up, and make her not hate her mother quite as much.

Maybe Jill would get the story on Sam Wilkins.

Maybe Maurice Fischer would be pleased.

And maybe—just maybe—Christopher would be so impressed that he'd realize he loved her enough to keep his hands off Lizette French.

But was it worth sacrificing her daughter?

You never let me breathe, Mom. Amy's words echoed in her thoughts.

Perhaps it was time to let go: let go of her old ways of writing her stories, her old ways of trying to be a good mother. As long as she was here to let go of the past, she might as well keep going. She might as well try to establish a better relationship with her daughter than she'd had with Florence; she might as well stop thinking of her mother.

And Robbie, she thought. *Whoever he was.*

The future, after all, was what mattered now.

Before she knew it, Jill walked out the back door, past the mess of sawhorses and lumber, past the thick clumps of hydrangea, past the past.

"Amy?" she asked as she approached her daughter. "I need your help."

As old New England as the Randall home was, Sam Wilkins's house was California moved east. It hadn't been difficult to find: Carrie had told Amy they lived off Lighthouse Road, and the sleek silver mailbox on the edge of the street had boldly read "Wilkins" as though it belonged to no one important, as though it marked the estate of someone named "Johnson" or "Brown" or "Adams," not *the* Sam Wilkins of international—and infamous—fame.

Jill aimed the Range Rover toward the sprawling, glass, hilltop mansion fully aware that she was about to break the Vineyard's unwritten code as a place where you could display your name without worrying about encroachers or nosy neighbors or media people intent on invading your privacy for the sake of a story. For the sake of their career.

The small seed of guilt that grew within her Jill quickly dispersed. Carrie, after all, had invited Amy. It wasn't Jill's fault that Amy's mother just happened to work for the media. Besides, Sam Wilkins might not even be home.

She parked the vehicle and they got out.

"Why don't you see if Carrie's around? I'll wait here."

Amy skipped up the flagstone walk toward the huge double doors. Jill leaned against the Range Rover and took in the view of the ocean, so much more grand here than at the small harbor in Edgartown, so much more turquoise, so much more peaceful.

"Hi," Jill heard Amy say. "I'm Amy McPhearson, Carrie's friend. She told me to come over. Is she here?"

Jill turned and looked toward the door. Standing

inside, looking at Amy, was Sam Wilkins himself—older than she remembered seeing him, silver-haired now, but still Sam Wilkins. Lanky, charismatic Sam Wilkins, with the sultry looks that carved his fame; the larger-than-life publicity icon; the difference between local and national interest.

She wondered if she should walk over and introduce herself.

"She's down on the beach," she heard Sam say. He stepped out the door. "I'll show you how to get there."

Jill stood up straight, wishing she'd taken the time to change her clothes and that she had pulled her hair from this juvenile ponytail. Addie would be appalled.

Sam guided Amy toward the side of the house, in Jill's direction.

"Amy?" Jill called.

"Oh," Amy said. "That's my mom." She smiled at Jill with a budding PR smile that hinted she was capable of following in her mother's career footsteps. "Mom, is it okay if I go down to the beach?"

Jill braced a hand against the side mirror. "I'll wait here to make sure you find Carrie."

"Down those stairs," Sam said, pointing to a wooden-railed stairway tucked in the dunes. "Just listen for loud music."

Jill stepped forward. "If you want to stay awhile, that's all right. I'll pick up your brother, then come back and get you. Just let me know."

Amy waved and trotted down the stairs, out of sight.

Sam walked over to Jill. "Hi," he said, extending his hand. "Sam Wilkins."

"Jill McPhearson," she answered, shaking his hand, making a mental note of its large size, its softened skin.

A broad smile spread across his face. "Christopher Edwards," he said.

"What?"

"Christopher Edwards. That's where I've seen your face. In pictures with him."

She laughed. "We're getting married."

He released his grasp. "Congratulations."

"Thanks." She flicked her gaze across the expanse of land. "This is quite a place you've got here."

"Care for the fifty-cent tour?"

"Sure."

They walked to the edge of the dunes. Beneath them, the sea kissed a long strip of white sand. Off to the left, Jill could see the cliffs of Gay Head; to the right was another hill, marked by another enormous house, though this one appeared to be an old, Vineyard-style home. "You have an incredible view," she said.

"It's even better inside," Sam said. "Follow me."

She fell in behind him. They circled back to the front and went through the huge double doors of the house. Straight ahead, one massive, wide-sweeping room had a windowed, two-story wall.

"I love the sea," Sam said. "Pacific. Atlantic. Makes no difference."

"Do you sail?" Jill asked.

He shook his head. "I love looking at it. Not being on it. The sea's like a woman. Fickle."

Jill looked at him.

He laughed. "Sorry. No offense intended."

"None taken," Jill answered, and wondered why his words had come so quickly, and what the real story was that lay behind them—the real story, not the one beleaguered by the tabloids. "My daughter tells me you're thinking of making a comeback."

He looked out the windows. "Thinking, yes. Doing is another story. I'm working on it."

"I'd better warn you," Jill said, having learned

long ago that directness was one thing a man appreciated, and that, coming from a woman, it usually took them off guard. "I'm in television. Entertainment type of news. *Good* news."

He kept his gaze fixed on the sea. "I know that."

Embarrassed, Jill didn't know what to say.

"Would you like to see the rest of the house?"

She nodded. "Very much."

The kitchen was a huge V-shape, at the center of which was a low table, in which was carved a barbecue pit. Jill wondered if this was an L.A. trend, if Lizette French had one, and if she and Christopher would if they had to move there, if RueCom offered them a deal, if Maurice Fischer thought Jill was good enough.

They moved through the house, room upon room, all airy and light, all decorated in southwestern-style pastels and clay pots, except for the enormous music studio, the walls and the ceiling of which were covered in black foam, the floor with thick charcoal carpeting. Upstairs, the master bedroom suite was incredible, with a fireplace that overlooked the sea. The second floor was molded against the slope of the dunes, with a walk-out deck that held an enormous hot tub.

"I'd show you the other bedrooms, but I'm sure Carrie's is a mess. And I have guests in the others."

"Well," Jill said, "I wouldn't want to disturb anyone."

Sam nodded and led the way back to the first floor. As they entered the kitchen, a small man in a white robe and headpiece swept past them carrying a glass of orange juice. Jill sensed Sam stiffen. "Can I get you anything, Isham?" he asked the man.

The man grinned. "I am fine," he said with a thick Arabic accent uncommon to the Vineyard. His eyes fixed on Jill.

"This is Jill McPhearson," Sam said. "Her daughter is a friend of Carrie's."

The man nodded and left the room. Jill thought that for a house guest, Isham, whoever he was, certainly didn't seem to be a close friend of Sam's.

Just then the front door opened. "Mom?" Amy's voice called into the hallway.

Jill walked toward the door.

"I found Carrie. Is it okay if I stay?"

"For a little while," Jill answered. "I'll be back to get you." Amy raced out of view, and Jill turned to Sam. "I hope it's no trouble having Amy here."

Sam shrugged. "I'm only sorry you have to leave."

Jill smiled, amazed at the possibility that the plan was going to work. She had made a good impression on the unreachable Sam Wilkins, and she just might get the story that Christopher wanted. But first, she would give Sam a little time to get to trust her. Then, the story would be hers. And Maurice Fischer would be thrilled.

After Jill picked up Jeff, she returned to Edgartown. She reasoned that she would never be able to think "big enough" if she didn't overcome her fears: letting Amy spend a little more time with Carrie seemed like a good place to begin. Besides, she thought as they pulled into the driveway, it might help Sam get used to having a McPhearson around.

She only hoped she'd get as enthused about his story as she did with the ones that were her own ideas. She only wished she could have been doing this some place other than here. It was difficult being Jill McPhearson, the television star, while surrounded by the memories of Jill Randall, the dejected child.

As they stepped from the Range Rover, a telephone company van pulled up in front of the house.

"Cool!" Jeff, sun-pinked and happy, called, racing to the man and letting him in the front door.

Jill decided to walk around the back of the house, to go to the harbor and watch the boats. It might help her formulate an angle for the Sam Wilkins story; it might help spark her creativity, stimulate her interest.

As she went through the backyard, Ben Niles was sitting on the sawhorse, a glass of water pressed against his brow.

"Hot day," Jill said.

"August," Ben answered. "Either this one's the hottest in years, or it was easier to take when I was a kid."

Jill smiled and kept walking. Then she stopped and looked down at her feet. *When I was a kid.* When had Ben been a kid? A chill cut through the heat and went to her heart. *Whose kid was he?* Jill stopped walking. She knew it was impossible. She knew it was crazy. Maybe the heat had fried her brain.

A shiver shook through her. She turned back to Ben. "I remember plenty of hot summers," she said with what she hoped was a lighthearted laugh. "But then, I was born in 1953."

"Well, I've got seven years on you."

Seven years. She quickly subtracted, then caught her breath.

1946. The same year Robbie was born. She squeezed her eyes against the white-hot sun, then forced her people-pleasing smile. "Were you born on the Vineyard?"

"Nope," he answered brusquely, as he rose and set down his glass. "I was a city boy."

City boy? *New York* City? Her heart began to thump as she tried to remember if she knew what year her parents had come here. She could not.

"New York?" she asked, her voice coming out in a rushed, quiet breath.

"Baltimore," he answered.

Her racing heart began to ease. She frowned. Then Jill remembered her mother had never told her about Robbie. It was possible Florence had lied about other things, about anything. She and George could have lived in Baltimore. . . .

She really was going crazy.

She started to speak. Her mouth was dry. She cleared her throat, then asked, "Do you come from a large family?"

Ben laughed. "What is this, twenty questions?"

She brought her hand to her mouth. "Sorry," she said. "Can't help myself. Reporter's instincts."

"Well, I didn't come from a large family. I was an only child. My father was a dentist. My mother was a teacher."

The edge in his voice cut through her hope. Ben wasn't Robbie. Ben wasn't the brother she'd known nothing about. *Of course he's not Robbie, you fool,* she said to herself. Then, another thought jarred her: Ben wasn't Robbie . . . but maybe he knew who Robbie was. If he had been raised on the island, maybe he remembered her brother.

"Have you been on the island long? Did you go to school here?"

Ben spread a blueprint on the ground and studied it. "I've been here twenty years," he answered. "And counting." He turned to a stack of tiles piled beside the blueprints. He picked them up. "Of course, according to folks here, I'm still just visiting. Now if you'll excuse me, I want to replace that downstairs bathroom ceiling."

"Oh," she replied, trying to mask her frustration. "Of course. I didn't mean to keep you."

Ben steadied his eyes on hers. "What with our two days off next week. . . ."

A seagull shrieked in the distance. Jill fought to regain her composure. "I'm sorry about that," she said. "I hope it doesn't interfere with your schedule."

"I said I'd try to have your house done by Labor Day," he answered. "We'll do our best, but two days is a lot of time to lose."

She cleared her throat. "Some people will be here from the media. They'll be taking photographs. . . ."

He waved her off. "No problem. I've got a client over on Nantucket who needs some work. I could use a couple of days to get the plans laid out." He turned to the house. "Kyle," he called, "give me a hand with these ceiling tiles." Jill watched Ben's helper—Carrie's boyfriend—emerge from the bulkhead, sweat shimmering off his youthful chest, a broad grin on his face.

"Yes, Master," he joked.

Ben swatted Kyle on the arm, and the two of them disappeared into the house.

She turned and resumed her walk toward the harbor, where white sails softly glided across the quiet water. Off to her left, she saw the lighthouse. The place where she and Rita used to go, to think, to talk, to share their deepest hopes and dreams and secrets. Not that they'd known what secrets were. Not secrets like long-lost brothers. She stood at the edge of the water and tried to stop the gnawing in her stomach. The gnawing, the wondering. If Ben didn't know anything about her brother, Robbie, was there someone else on the island who did? Someone she could learn something from?

She could always go back to the diary. Jill shuddered. *No.* She did not want to read one more word of her mother's . . . *confession.* She did not want to see her mother's handwriting, feel her mother's feelings, or touch that damn silky lock of baby's hair.

But, goddamnit, she wanted to *know*.

Then it hit her. The tavern. The 1802 Tavern, her father's business. His father's before that, and before that, and before that. Charlie Rollins had bought the tavern from Florence after Jill's father had died. Maybe Charlie knew something about Robbie. Charlie was older than Jill . . . maybe he knew something. . . .

Rita pulled the white dress over her head and threw it on the floor. As she walked toward the bedroom, she checked her watch and wondered if she should bother to dress for work . . . if she should bother to go to the tavern at all. Taking the risk that she'd run into Jill was something she couldn't handle. She'd had enough failure for one day.

On her way past the end table, she flicked the red button of her answering machine.

"Hi, baby," came Joe Geissel's voice.

She grabbed the cotton robe from the back of the bathroom door and wondered why the sound of his voice now made her feel like vomiting.

"I sure hope you're not on your way over here," he whispered heavily. "My wife just arrived. Jesus. Just what I fucking need."

As Joe paused on the tape, Rita glared at the machine. "Christ," she muttered, realizing it must have been Joe calling when she was running out the door, primed to win him over, ready to seal her big deal.

"I don't know why she's here in the middle of the goddamn week," Joe went on. "Don't know if she's staying through to Sunday or not. You'd better not call me, babe. I'll let you know when she's gone."

He made kissing sounds into the phone, then hung up.

Rita moved into the living room, plunked in the Boston rocker beside the fireplace, stared at the yellowed wallpaper, and wondered why her life had become so pathetic. Joe Geissel was just one more in a long line of married men who offered sex . . . and safety. It had been years since Rita had slept with anyone who was morally, technically, or legally "available"; years since she'd even slept with an island man. Men—boys they had been then—like Buck Winthrop and Don Reilly and even Charlie Rollins who, though now her boss, thankfully seemed to have forgotten that he and Rita had once professed their "love" in the secret room of the 1802.

Buck, Don, Charlie—Rita remembered them all. The sex had been fun, the consequences, steep. But now, surviving nine months at a crack without a roll in the sack had become less painful than getting involved with someone who knew every move you made, had ever made, and every move your family ever made.

She hadn't minded, until Kyle. Since then, she'd steered clear. There was no way her kid was going to be raised with the kind of mother Rita had, the kind of mother that Hazel was, the kind Jill knew nothing about.

Jill had seen only the good parts of Hazel: she did not know how the woman cried at night, scared to be alone. Jill did not know that it had been Rita who parented her mother, not the other way around; Rita who massaged her mother's neck when the tension took its toll; Rita who made her own meals from the time she was five, and did the laundry and cleaned the house, because her mother was too busy working, or too hungover.

Jill had never seen these things. She had not seen them because Rita hadn't wanted her to know. Any more than Rita had ever told Jill about the nights—

so many nights—when Rita lay awake, listening to the sounds of thumping and pumping in the room next to hers, or the times she'd found her mother, bare-ass naked, giving some guy a blow job in the backseat of a car parked under the streetlight in front of the house.

To Jill, Hazel Blair had been wonderful, free, accepting. To Rita, she had been a responsibility. It still amazed Rita that Hazel had finally found a man who loved her, a tourist who took her from the island, married her, and safely tucked her in financial security in a mobile home in Sarasota.

Yes, Rita thought now, she'd been right to have stuck to married men, to not have to fear that islanders would talk about her, the way she'd suspected they'd talked about her mother. Islanders like Florence Randall, who wanted nothing to do with Rita's mother and made it clear from her coldness that she wasn't crazy about Rita and Jill being friends.

But though Rita might have a life of hard work and few rewards, she would never become the subject of island gossip. She would never do that to Kyle. Maybe someday God would make it worth her while—maybe someday she, too, would find a man who would take her loneliness away.

Yeah, she thought to herself, *and maybe someday I'll win the fucking lottery.*

She rose from the chair and quickly erased the message on the answering machine. No sense in Kyle hearing Joe Geissel's garbage.

She went into the kitchen, opened the cabinet under the sink, and took out the bottle of scotch. "Shit," she said as she held the bottle to the light. Only about an eighth inch of the amber liquid swirled around the bottom. And she'd forgotten to pick up more.

Unscrewing the cap and swigging the residue, Rita tossed the bottle in the plastic wastebasket by the back door and stared out the window over the sink. What she needed was a drink. A decent, stiff drink. Maybe she should get dressed after all. Maybe she should go to the tavern early, sneak a bottle into the secret room, and have herself a ball. Let Charlie worry about it if she was too smashed to work.

It was past the hour for the lingering lunch tourists; too early for the cocktails and dinner crowd. Jill hoped it would be a good time to talk with Charlie, to use her interviewing skills to discreetly uncover what she wanted to know. As she stepped through the old oak tavern door, she decided she'd approach him the same way she would any unsuspecting target: praise him first, admire his accomplishments, then let him think he was going to help her solve a problem. It was a technique that worked every time.

An elderly couple sat at one table, an island map spread in front of them. At one end of the bar were two thirty-something women, sipping from wineglasses, their heads close in conversation.

Jill walked past the tables to the opposite end of the bar. She slowly pulled back a tall wooden chair and sat down. For Jill, the child, it had once been a high climb to reach the top of the chair. She wondered if she had ever sat in this very chair . . . while waiting for her father . . . while procrastinating about going home. She quickly pushed away the flashback and flicked her eyes around the room, reminding herself of her mission.

In a moment that seemed like an hour, Charlie Rollins appeared from what Jill knew was the kitchen, toting a tray filled with glasses. He hadn't seemed to age—he still looked like the same jovial, dirty blond-haired teenager who had a love of surfing and an eye for Rita. Charlie had never been the greatest-looking of the boys, but there was an assuredness about him, a kind of big brother sense. *Big brother*, Jill thought, and tried to calm the butterflies that fluttered inside her.

Charlie glanced at Jill and smiled beneath his now filled-out mustache. He set the tray by the sink, then blinked and looked at Jill once more.

"Hey," he said with a genuine grin, "Jill Randall. God, I heard you were back in town."

"Long time, no see, Charlie."

He wiped his hands on his clean white apron and moved toward her. "Wow, you look terrific. The city has been kind to you."

"You don't look so bad yourself. I'm glad to see this place hasn't killed you."

His eyes swept the tavern. "This place? Not a chance."

She followed his gaze. "You've done a wonderful job. It looks exactly as it always did. My father would have appreciated that."

"Well," he said, laughing, "it's not the easiest place to maintain." His eyes moved over the room. "Had the plumbing replaced, and the wiring. And I had termites whose ancestors must have moved in back in the eighteenth century."

"I'm having some work done at the old house now," Jill said. "Did Ben Niles do your restoration?"

"Ben?" Charlie laughed. "He only works for summer people. People with the big bucks."

"Oh," Jill said quickly, then changed the subject. "Well, business here certainly seems to be booming. I was in the other night with my family . . ."

Charlie nodded. "So I heard. I was upstairs doing the books."

"Is your office upstairs?"

He laughed. "Hell, my whole house is. I live there."

Jill remembered that her father had rented the

apartment over the tavern, though she'd never been up there. "Well," she continued, "my kids got a kick out of seeing their roots."

"I'll bet," he said, shifting his gaze to the women at the other end, then back to Jill. "Hey, can I get you something? Wine? A beer?"

Jill settled back against the rungs of the chair. "Sure," she said, "I'll have a beer."

"Draft?"

"Sure," she answered, wondering how many years it had been since she'd had a beer, if, in fact, she'd had even one since leaving the island. "Do you have a family, Charlie?"

Charlie held a tall glass up to the tap and pulled the lever. Dark golden liquid gushed forth. "Me? Nah." He set the foamy glass on a paper coaster in front of Jill. "I almost got married once. Her name was Betty. Came here with her folks one summer back in, I don't know, somewhere in the early seventies. Anyway, Betty hated it here. Wanted to live in the city." Charlie winked. "But I guess you know the feeling."

Jill smiled. She wanted to ask him if he knew what had ever happened to Rita, but reminded herself that was not why she was here. "Do you miss having children?"

"Me? Between this place and being a town selectman, I hardly have time. There were six kids in my family. I've got eleven nieces and nephews now— plenty of family to go around."

She congratulated herself for the way she got him to open the door to what she wanted to know. "Big families must be nice," she said. "I always hated being an only child."

"That's right," he said. "You didn't have any brothers or sisters, did you?"

Clearing her throat, she sipped of the dark beer.

The taste bit into her tongue. "Actually, I did have an older brother."

Charlie scowled. "You did?"

A sinking feeling drowned her butterflies. "You don't remember him?"

Charlie shook his head. "Nope."

"He was seven years older than me. You don't remember hearing my father talk about him?"

"What was his name?"

"Robert. Robbie."

Charlie looked up to the beamed ceiling. "Robbie. Robbie Randall." He shook his head again. "Nope, don't remember. Where's he at now?"

Just then the women at the end of the bar pushed back their chairs and stood up. "Thank you," one of them said as she peeled off some bills and set them on the bar.

"My pleasure," Charlie answered, and walked toward them. "Come back again."

The women giggled and left. Jill took another sip of her beer, then stood up, too. There was no reason to stay. "I've got to run, too, Charlie," she said, pulling a five-dollar bill from her bag.

Charlie held up his hand. "No charge. And," he added with a smile, "I don't think you're going anywhere."

She scowled at him, then realized his gaze had veered to one side, toward the front door.

"Look who's here," Charlie said.

Jill turned quickly and looked squarely into the frozen face of her best friend, Rita Blair.

Why me, God? Rita wanted to shout as she stopped in her tracks and stared at Jill.

"Rita!" Jill exclaimed. She opened her arms as if she expected Rita to rush into them, tell her how wonderful she looked, and say what a fucking great thing it was to see her.

Rita stepped back and fluffed her curls. "Jill."

Jill's arms dropped quickly to her sides. "Gosh, it's so good to see you. How are you?"

Rita shrugged. "Older. Wiser." She moved to one side of Jill, hoping the pounding of her heart wasn't visible on her neck. "Charlie," she said, "I've got to talk to you. Right now." She turned back to Jill. "Will you excuse us?"

Jill looked at her queerly. "Sure. Sure, Rita." She clutched her bag. Her obviously several-hundred-dollar, designer asshole bag. "Stop by and see me, okay? I'm at the house. . . ."

"Sure," Rita responded, then motioned to Charlie. "Come on in the back. This is important."

Rita hadn't realized until that moment just how important coming here had been. She now knew she was going to tell Charlie she was quitting her job: IRS or not, there was no way Rita could work at the tavern, as long as Jill lived two short goddamn blocks away, as long as there was any chance in fucking hell that Jill knew the truth about Kyle.

Chapter 12

 Jill went in the front door and stepped over the drop cloths that covered the foyer floor. Ben and Kyle were in the dining room replacing the rotted window casings. She waved without speaking and went directly upstairs.

Once there, she picked up the phone from the hall table and dragged the cord into the bedroom. She closed the door and called Christopher. She was finally ready to talk; she finally needed to share her pain.

His voice mail clicked on.

"Damn," Jill said. She almost hung up, then waited for the beep. "Hi. It's me," she said quietly. "I really need to talk to you." She hung up, set the phone on the floor, and flopped on the bed, trying not to envision him with Lizette. Just as her eyes closed, the phone rang.

It was him.

"Oh, thank God," Jill said. "I was afraid you were out on a story or something."

"I'm in the studio. Have you forgotten we do a run-through from four to five?" His voice sounded busy—the tone of an energetic man with a productive life. Suddenly Christopher, Boston, and Jill's entire world seemed a million miles away. She felt her need slide beneath the layer of her soul.

"So what's up?" he asked.

"Oh, lots of things."

"Honey, I love you, but I've got makeup in ten minutes."

"Oh. Right." She toyed with the phone cord, stretching its coil, watching it spring back. She wanted to tell him about her mother's diary. She wanted to tell him about her brother. But, once again, the words that came from her mouth were different. "I met Sam Wilkins today."

Christopher paused. "And?"

"And I met him. That's all." *And I have a brother I never knew about*, she wanted to add, but pulled at the phone cord instead.

"Hey, that's terrific."

"It's a beginning. I'm still not sure if it's right for Amy. . . ."

"Jill. Let her grow up."

She let go of the cord. It bounced on the floor.

"Is there anything else? I've got to get into makeup."

She wanted to tell him about Rita. She wanted to tell him her best friend had snubbed her only moments ago. But picturing Christopher standing in the studio, watching the giant clock on the wall, Jill realized it was foolish to waste his time on mother stories and schoolgirl hurts. "No," she answered, "I guess not. I miss you. I can't wait until next week. Even though the place will be crawling with people, at least we'll be together."

"Oh, that reminds me," he said, "there's been a slight change in plans. Addie will be there Tuesday, but I won't fly in until Wednesday morning."

"Maurice Fischer again?"

"I'm having dinner with him."

Jill didn't respond.

"Does that bother you?"

"That you're meeting him again—without me? Of course it bothers me." *And it bothers me that I have a brother and that I've lost my best friend.*

"I told you not to worry. RueCom is still in the preliminary talk stage. I've got to go now. I'm being paged."

"Christopher?" Jill asked quickly before he hung up.

"What?" His voice was edgy now, impatient.

"Don't tell him about Sam Wilkins yet, okay? Until I'm sure I can get the story."

Christopher sighed. "Okay. I won't."

She said good-bye and stared at the ceiling, wondering if being here—in this house, on this island—was, indeed, making her crazy.

Then she thought about her father. George Randall had been tall and lean like Jill, and, she suspected, smart. Very smart. He was handsome enough with his closely cropped mustache and beard, and full head of thick, gray-then-white hair. He had warm blue eyes—eyes like Christopher's—and an outgoing personality that was the antithesis of her mother's. George was well liked at the tavern, well liked on the island.

A thought struck her. Her eyes flashed open. *If George Randall was such a great guy, what the hell had he been doing with her mother?* Her mother—a woman who barely spoke unless to criticize, a woman who had a son of whom no one ever spoke.

Suddenly Jill had an idea: How would she handle this if it were a story? Where would she begin?

She would, she knew, begin at the beginning. She would distance herself, she would be objective, divest herself of any emotional connection. The way any good reporter would.

And there was only one place to begin.

She closed her eyes and took a deep breath. *It's*

just another story, she told herself. *Another story, waiting to be told.*

And she could do it.

She could do it.

Before she could change her mind, Jill jumped from the bed and rushed into the hall, dizzy from the quick movement. She ripped open the door to the widow's walk as Jeff stuck his head from his room.

"Mom? Aren't you going to pick up Amy?"

"Not now," Jill barked as she flew up the winding stairs, two at a time, in search of the answers, in search of the truth.

Sun. Aug. 24, 1947

Robbie took his first steps today! He wobbled at first, then his chubby little legs moved forward, one, two, three steps! Then he fell—kerplunk!—on his well-padded bottom. Oh, how I love this child. I wish my mother would come to visit. I wish she could have been here to see Robbie's first steps. I wonder if she had been as excited when she saw me take mine. And if so, when all that had changed. I guess it was when I married George. She once said she didn't know what to tell her friends about him. I guess she decided it's easier not to tell them anything than to tell them his background, to tell them he works on the piers.

If only she wouldn't be that way. If only she could see George as the loving, wonderful husband he is. If only she could have seen Robbie—her grandson—take his first steps.

The air in the room grew still. Up here in the widow's walk, higher than the sounds of the workmen, above the world of reality, Jill saw a tear drop onto the page. She blotted it slowly, then felt a small ache when she saw the ink smear.

She turned the page.

Thurs. Sept. 30, 1948

It is so hard for George to live in the city. He hates the crowds and the noise and the "hideous traffic" he always calls it. I know he stays here only for me, but why do I want to stay? My mother and sister barely speak to me. Mother didn't even come for Robbie's birthday. I suppose she would have if Robbie were Myrna's boy, if he belonged to the daughter who did everything right, like marry a Charlton and live on Park Avenue, three blocks down from her. I suppose it's not fair to make George stay here. After all, he has parents who love him, and a home where he's welcome. Where we're both welcome. Robbie, too.

I liked Martha's Vineyard all right when we visited there last month. But live there? With no theater or nice restaurants? Of course, it's not like we can afford to go anywhere in the city right now. But, still, maybe someday we will. I wish George would let me get a job. As much as I'd hate to be away from Robbie, the money would help. I wonder what I could do.

Tues. Dec. 28, 1948

George thinks I saved up the money from his pay envelope to buy the Christmas presents— the tool set for him, the red wagon for Robbie. If only he knew I'm a working girl! Mondays and Wednesdays, from nine a.m. until two p.m., I'm actually a seamstress on Seventh Avenue! Of course, it's only temporary, until the spring line is ready. It's strange to be there in the back room, where everyone shouts and

*where the hum of sewing machines is so loud
you can't hear yourself think. I remember going
to the showings with my mother and Myrna,
wearing my hat and my gloves and my shoul-
der-padded suits. We'd preview the collection
and watch Mother make notes on her small yellow pad. Then the chauffeur would drive us to
the Plaza for tea.*

*Ah! The back room of fashion is a long way
from the Plaza . . . a long way from the audience I used to be a part of out front. I wonder if
Mother and Myrna will come this spring. I
wonder what they would do if they knew I was
back here, stitching and sewing, making the
dresses that Mother might mark on her pad.*

*I have a nice baby-sitter for Robbie. Mrs.
Donnelly. She lives around the corner from the
shop. It's easy for Robbie and I to leave after
George has gone to work, then catch the cross-
town bus. Robbie loves the big bus, but I told
him it's our little secret. I hope he doesn't spill
the beans to George. It would hurt his pride
too much, finding out I have a job. And I could
never, ever hurt George. I love him so much.*

Jill rubbed her eyes. She didn't know how much
more she could take. The inside of her mouth was
dry, her lower lip sore from biting. Still, she could
not stop. She could not stop long enough to digest
the words—and their meaning. She could not stop,
for she feared if she did, she would never pick up the
diary again.

Mon. April 4, 1949
  *They want to keep me! "Your work is ex-
traordinary," JD, my boss, said today. I wish I
could share this with George! Maybe soon I
will have the courage. I'd better hurry, though,*

because Robbie is talking more and more these days, and I'm so afraid he's going to let on about the bus and about Mrs. Donnelly. Oh! I might as well tell George. What will he do? Will he be angry? Will he forbid me to work? Oh, I hope not. It's such fun to think I've come such a long way from making Red Cross bandages. Maybe tomorrow I'll stop on the way home and buy a nice leg of lamb with my pay. Lamb in the middle of the week! That ought to put him in a good mood!

The next page of the diary was blank. Then, writing appeared again.

March 21, 1951

Jill rubbed her eyes again and stared at the date. *1951?* She turned back and realized that two years had passed. She studied the writing. It looked different, somehow. Fainter, less structured, as though it had been penned by a different hand.

March 21, 1951
    I never thought I'd write in this book again. But then, for a long, long time, I never thought I'd think again, feel again, breathe again.
    Mother Randall is being so nice to me, I can't imagine why. I don't even mind living on the island now. It doesn't matter where I live, the pain doesn't seem to stop. And George is happier here, so I guess that's good.
    As nice as they are, sometimes I think I can hear them whispering. I cannot hear their words, but I know what they must be saying: If it weren't for me, Robbie would not be dead.

A shadow passed over the widow's walk; the air grew thick with silence. Jill held her hand to her throat and forced herself to read on.

> *There. I said it. Robbie is dead. My son. My life. It's been almost two years since the accident. Since we were leaving Mrs. Donnelly's, since he got so excited about the "big bus" that he broke from my hand and ran into the street, since that battered yellow taxicab sped around the corner . . .*
>
> *George says it wasn't my fault. He says he still loves me. But I know he must hate me. Hate me for taking that job he knew nothing about, hate me for thinking I had to make money because his job wasn't good enough, hate me for being the reason his son is dead.*
>
> *Oh, God, will this pain never stop?*
>
> *He wants to have another child. I cannot bear the thought. No child could ever be as wonderful as my Robbie.*

Jill grasped the edge of the brittle page. A small piece crumbled in her fingertips. She turned to the beginning of the book, to the small lock of golden hair that lay tucked between the pages. She held it up, felt its silkiness. "Oh, God," she said. "Oh, God."

She dropped the hair back in its place; the book slid to the floor. Slowly Jill rose, her eyes fixed on the book. "Oh, God," she said again, then turned toward the doorway and fled down the stairs, down to the second floor, down to the first, and out the front door—the front door of Florence and George Randall's house, where Jill had never been wanted.

She walked. Tears stained her cheeks; she clutched her stomach, held her heart, as though her insides were going to fracture, as though her soul were going to break apart and spill onto the sidewalk.

She moved past shoppers, languid tourists wearing smiles and leather sandals. She kept moving, kept walking, not caring if anyone recognized her, for she didn't recognize herself.

By the time she reached the end of Water Street, Jill realized where she had come. The lighthouse stood before her. The lighthouse where she'd spent so many hours, months, years, with Rita, thinking, dreaming, hoping.

She climbed down the dunes and found the path that led to their special place. Perhaps she'd find an answer here, perhaps she'd find some understanding as to what she had just read.

On the rocks, under the pier, what she found, instead, was Rita.

Jill stared at the back of the curly red hair. On the ground beside Rita stood a half-empty bottle of scotch. The ache in Jill's heart began to quiet, soothed by the comforting presence of her best friend—her once, a long time ago, best friend. She brushed her tears away and took another step.

"Care to share that bottle with an old friend?" she asked.

Rita's head didn't turn toward Jill. Instead, she remained rigid, motionless, her face kept fixed toward the sea. "Did you follow me here?"

"No." The crunch of footsteps on shells made Jill look around. A group of tourists wandered near the lighthouse. She stepped closer to where Rita sat. "May I join you?"

Rita shrugged. "Last time I checked, it was still a free country."

Jill hesitated a moment. She didn't need Rita's caustic coldness right now. What she needed was a friend. She looked off across the harbor, at the small white sails that floated against the sky, at the soothing tide that gently licked the shore. *Low tide,* Jill thought. *Low tide. Best time for quahogs.*

She looked down at Rita. "Remember quahogging?" she asked. "You always got the best ones. I don't know how you did it."

"Survival," Rita answered. "They were dinner."

A pang of guilt resonated through Jill; guilt that she had always had so much more than Rita, guilt that she had been the lucky one. Or so it had seemed.

She hesitated a moment, then stooped beside her friend. "I thought maybe you'd be glad to see me."

Rita laughed. "Sorry. I was just too darned busy to roll out the red carpet."

Jill settled against a rock and faced Rita, noticing that her eyes were still bright and unlined, though Rita had always deplored sunglasses, unless, of course, they were used as a disguise. As if anything could hide that wild red hair.

"Are you still angry at me for leaving the island?" Jill asked.

Rita stared off toward Chappy. "If I remember correctly, I left before you did."

Summer memories returned. Jill thought about the loss of her friend, remembered the unanswered questions. Suddenly Jill's mother—and Robbie—seemed less important. They were gone. Rita was here. And Jill needed Rita more than ever.

"Where did you go, Rita? Why did you leave?"

Picking up the bottle of scotch, Rita took a swig. She held it a moment, then passed it to Jill without making eye contact, without changing the guarded expression on her face. "Why did it surprise you that I left? You were the one who always said what a shithole this place was. You were the one who couldn't wait to get out of here."

Jill looked down the long neck of the bottle, then raised it to her lips. The scotch burned her throat, cauterizing her pain. "But you were the one who wanted to stay."

Rita shrugged again. "Shit happens."

She handed the bottle back to Rita. "I've missed you."

A look of doubt bounced from Rita to Jill. "How long has it been? Twenty-five years?"

"Twenty-six."

"Yeah, well, you missed me so much I never even got a Christmas card."

"My mother never told me you'd come back."

"That's no surprise. You should have guessed, though. You always thought I was destined to rot in this place."

Reaching out, Jill touched Rita's arm. Rita pulled away.

Jill took back her hand and rested it in her lap. "I was trying to make a new life for myself."

"And a fine job you did. So what is it now, Jill? Are you going to be another of the island's famous celebrities who graces us with your presence once a year?"

"No. I'm selling the house."

Rita laughed. "See what I mean? You don't care about it here. You don't care about any of us. You never did."

A small wave lapped the shore. "Is that what you think?"

"You always thought I'd wind up like my mother. Well, in a lot of ways I guess I did. That should make you happy."

"Rita . . . I never meant . . ."

Rita's voice was slow, deliberate. "Yes you did. You were smarter than me, Jill. Prettier. More ambitious. I guess that's not a crime."

"It is if I hurt you that badly."

"You didn't hurt me, Jill. Pissed me off, maybe. But, no, you didn't hurt me."

Jill remembered Rita's laughter, Rita's toughness, and that Rita had always used these defenses to hide her insecurities, to hide her feelings that she wasn't as good as the kids who lived in the houses with mothers and fathers, the kids with dinner waiting on the table and clean, pressed clothes in their closets.

The heat of the sun warmed her face. "Life doesn't always go the way we want," she said. "No matter how hard we try."

Rita pulled her knees to her chest. "No shit."

The sound of a motorboat approached. They both turned to watch as it shot through the water, white foam splashing, leaving a deep "V" of a wake.

"I can't believe you still come here," Jill said.

"Not many other places to think around here," Rita answered. "Especially in August." She hugged her knees and looked at Jill. "I was real sorry about your parents. Your dad. Your mother."

"Thanks."

"I went to the service. For your mother."

Jill flicked her gaze back to the lighthouse, to the tourists. "I was in Russia," she said, aware that her words sounded weak, because Rita would know the real reason Jill hadn't returned had nothing to do with Russia. "Is your mother still . . ."

"Hazel?" Rita laughed. "Nothing's going to kill her. Found herself a man a few years ago. They live in Sarasota now."

Jill nodded. "That's nice. She's such a great person."

Rita plucked the bottle again and took another drink. "Yeah, well, she's different."

Closing her eyes, Jill let the sun soothe her skin, let herself find comfort in the sound of Rita's voice, in the way her words danced with a spirit all their own—a familiar, safe dance that Jill had missed for so long. "I've never had another best friend, Rita," she said, her eyes still closed to the sun, her heart opening to her friend.

Rita didn't reply.

Jill sat up and checked her watch. "I'd love to have you meet my kids," she said. "In fact, I have to pick up my daughter now." She hesitated a moment, then heard herself add, "Would you like to come?"

Rita paused for a heartbeat, or maybe it was two. "What time is it?"

"Five-thirty."

"I've got to start work at six. I tried to quit, but Charlie wouldn't let me. I'm a waitress there. At the tavern. Like my mother was."

"Tell Charlie he can live without you for one night," Jill said. "Come with me, Rita. Please."

Rita seemed to think about it. "What the hell," she finally said. "Why not."

The sun seemed to smile; the world seemed to come back into focus. "Great," Jill said as she rose to her feet. "We've got so much to catch up on. First, though, we have to go back to my house and get the car. Amy's out at Gay Head."

"The car?" Rita asked.

Jill brushed off her shorts. "Hopefully, the work-men or any of their friends haven't boxed me in. I'm having some work done on the house and it's a power-saw nightmare."

"I'll tell you what," Rita said as she screwed the cap on the bottle. "You get the car. I'll wait here."

Jill didn't understand why Rita didn't want to come to the house, but, then, Rita was Rita, and she always was independent. "Don't go away," she said as she waved good-bye and headed toward the road, realizing then that she hadn't asked Rita if she had ever married, or if she had any kids.

.   .   .   .   .

She was in the clear. At least about Kyle, Rita was in the clear.

She stared across the water and hugged her arms around herself. Jill had never known why Rita had left the Vineyard; she'd never known that Rita had been pregnant. Her secret was safe now, safe forever. And Jesus, it felt good to have a friend again.

Chapter 13

After Jill picked her up, they swung by the tavern where Rita broke the news to Charlie. "I'm not punching in tonight. Got something important to do," she said quickly and rejoined Jill in the monstrous white Range Rover, not caring that Charlie had a look on his face that said he could kill. Wednesday night or not, August was no time to ditch work.

On the way out to Gay Head, Rita tapped her fingernails on the dash and hummed to the sound of the radio.

"I think Charlie's still a little in love with you," Jill said.

Rita laughed. "Charlie Rollins? God, Jill, you're dreaming." She turned her eyes to the side window so Jill wouldn't see her face.

"He was a nice guy, though. Still is."

"He's an upstanding citizen is what he is. He doesn't only own your father's tavern, he's a town selectman now."

"He told me. He also said he never married."

"Guess not," Rita replied, then looked back to Jill. She hadn't seen her in over twenty-five years, and didn't feel like talking about Charlie Rollins. "And you're about to do it for the second time."

"Do what?"

"Get married." The words stuck in Rita's throat. She didn't know why. But even from here, she could see the sun shoot shards of color off the bowling-ball diamond on Jill's finger.

"Yes. But this time I'm getting married for the right reasons."

Rita nodded but didn't feel the need to respond. Jill, after all, had always done everything for the "right" reasons. *Her* right reasons, anyway.

"You haven't told me if you ever married, Rita."

There. Well, Jill had spoken the words, asked, in her own way, the question. Rita shifted on the leather seat, reached up, and curled a lock of hair. "Yeah, well, sure," she lied, wondering if Jill would still be able to see through her lies. "It was a long time ago, though."

"Who was it? Anyone I know?"

She pulled her feet onto the dash, studied the pink-tipped toenails that poked through her sandals and needed another coat of polish. "No. A guy from Worcester. He went to Vietnam and never came back." It had been a long time since Rita had needed to tell the lie. She hoped Jill didn't pressure her for the details.

"Oh, God. That's terrible."

"Like I said," Rita continued, dropping her feet to the floor once again, "it was a long time ago. Another life." She looked out the window as they wove around the curve toward Lighthouse Road. "I've got a kid."

"Rita! Why didn't you tell me?"

Rita shrugged.

"A girl?"

She shook her head. "Boy."

"How old is he?"

She hesitated, then blinked. "Twenty-five."

"Twenty-five? My God, you've got a twenty-five-year-old son?"

A picture of Kyle came into Rita's mind. Strong, handsome Kyle. Her son. Her kid. "Yeah." She turned to Jill. "Imagine that. I could be a grandmother even."

"A grandmother? God, Rita . . ."

"Well, I'm not. At least not that I know of."

Jill laughed. "God, this is exciting. I can't believe you have a son. What's his name? What does he do?"

"Funny you should ask. His name is Kyle, he works for a guy named Ben Niles, and right now I do believe he's busy at Jill McPhearson's house—getting it ready to sell so she can leave me again."

He wasn't going to let Ashenbach win. Ben pushed his supper dishes aside and set the calculator on the kitchen table. On his way home he'd stopped at O'Briens' and had them write up a quote for school buses—he could, he knew, buy them cheaper off-island.

But Ben was determined to do everything it took to play the game. In fairness, the fact that he'd never felt like he'd been accepted on the Vineyard was probably as much his fault as theirs. He'd spent so much time and effort with summer people, had received so much publicity about his work on the lavish homes and mega-million-dollar estates on the Cape and Islands, it should be no surprise that no one thought he'd ever put down roots here.

But he had, damnit. He'd raised a family here, buried his wife here. Christ, his grandchildren were *born* here. The Vineyard was his home, and he was damn well going to let everyone know it. Starting with the zoning board, and ending, if it came to that, with Dave Ashenbach's ass plunked squarely on the next ferry out of here. Dave Ashenbach, or whoever the hell his enemy was.

He did a rough estimate on bus insurance, maintenance, gas, and drivers' wages. He studied the total: the annual cost would be staggering. But hell, the ridiculous fees he was paid had to mean something, something more worthwhile than another stack of savings bonds in his safe deposit box. There was plenty there already for the grandkids . . . now it was Ben's turn, Ben's time.

The gentle sounds of Shumann's *The Merry Peasant* drifted from the CD in the living room. Ben smiled, knowing he was finally merry, and that he was a far cry from a peasant. And no matter what Carol Ann thought, Louise would have been proud that he'd stuck to his guns and worked out a plan. He thought of his wife a moment, then realized that the pain inside his gut was not as bad as it had been last month, or the month before. And that little lump in his throat seemed to have eased. Perhaps the grief was lifting. Perhaps Ben Niles would survive without his wife—his love, his support, his greatest companion. Perhaps he would survive without her after all.

Suddenly the doorbell rang. Ben sighed and rubbed his hand across his hairline that was ever-so-slowly creeping toward oblivion. He glanced at the teak-carved clock over the refrigerator: eight-fifteen. Too late for Rachel Bowen and her casserole-of-the-week.

He rose from the chair and went to the back door. Through the white café curtains he saw a figure standing in the dusk, a female, her head turned from his view. Well, he thought, he was right about one thing. It certainly wasn't Rachel Bowen. He turned the knob and opened the door.

"Well," he said with all the poise that he could muster, "what brings you to Oak Bluffs, Carrie?"

The girl snapped around and flashed a huge, full-lipped smile. "Hi, Ben. Can I talk to you for a minute?"

He tried not to notice that she wore short shorts and a white T-shirt with no bra. He kept his gaze fixed on hers, but the image of her young, firm thighs did not escape his eye. He folded his arms and leaned against the doorjamb. "What can I do for you?"

She swept a lock of hair from her face. "Do you mind if I come in?"

Did he mind if she came in? *God,* he moaned somewhere deep inside. "Sorry, Carrie, but the house is a mess. I'm working." Was he really saying these words? Was Ben Niles really forgoing the chance to be alone with the one piece of female flesh who had stirred his groin for the first time in two years?

"Please?" she asked in a whisper so low he could hardly hear it.

Across the way, a lamp went out in Rachel Bowen's kitchen. Ben watched a silhouette move across the Cape Cod, ball-fringed curtains: a silhouette of a woman, the best offer he'd had. Until now. He shifted on one foot. "No date with Kyle tonight?"

Carrie pouted. "Kyle's filling in for his mother at the tavern. She took the night off or something."

He nodded.

She swept back that hair again, then looked down to her chest and brushed a nonexistent bug or a piece of lint from the dark nipple that poked against her tight T-shirt—the nipple that Kyle, most likely, knew so well.

Ben slipped his hands into the pockets of his pants. "Can you make this quick, Carrie? I'm working."

"It's too late to be working," she said with a smile. "What you need is a break."

What I need is a cold shower, he thought, but answered, "No breaks tonight. I'm too far behind."

Carrie pouted again. "I really wanted to talk to you about Menemsha House."

He raised his eyebrows. "What do you know about Menemsha House?"

She grinned. "Let me in, and I'll tell you."

His misguided lust gave way to anger. "Stop playing games, Carrie. What do you know?"

The corners of her mouth tightened. "I know you need zoning board approval."

"So?"

"So I came to tell you if there's anything I can do to help . . . or my father . . ." Her grin vanished altogether. "But seeing as how you're such an asshole, forget it."

Ben laughed. "Thanks anyway, but I'm all set."

"Don't be so sure."

"Then let's just say I have a plan they won't be able to refuse."

Carrie dropped her gaze to the step on which she stood. "Be careful, Ben. I'd hate to see Kyle lose his job because his boss did something stupid." She lifted her eyes again, then backed down the steps. Without another word, she sprinted toward the red, red Porsche, jumped inside, and gunned the engine—emitting the unmistakable, unmatchable rumble-hum-rumble that only a Porsche can have.

Ben stayed in the doorway after she'd left, wondering why in the hell she had really come, and what in the hell she had meant.

It was almost as though they'd never been apart. Jill and Rita went shopping together, had lunch together, romped through the dunes, barefoot together, as if they were twelve again, as if they had never not been best friends. On Sunday afternoon they went to the beach and sipped a pitcherful of daiquiris that Rita had whipped up in the blender at home. Jill coated her face with more sunscreen and turned down the volume on Rita's portable radio.

"You've done such a great job with Kyle, Rita," she said. "You are to be congratulated."

Rita laughed and rolled onto her back. "I won't be doing such a great job if I don't get back to work soon. I should be showing houses today, not hanging out."

"From the sounds of your life you haven't hung out since we were kids. Maybe it's time."

"I barely had time to hang out then."

Jill scanned the beach. Across from them were two teenage girls, giggling. Jill wondered if they were best friends, and hoped they would never drift apart. For even though she and Rita were reunited, Jill still hadn't mustered the strength to tell her about the diary. It was too private, too painful. So painful she was not able to tell the one person to whom she had once been able to tell everything.

"I thought boys would be harder to bring up than girls," Jill said, brushing sand from her leg. "But Jeff seems to be doing just fine. It's Amy I'm having trouble with."

"She's a beautiful girl."

Jill laughed. "Too beautiful for fourteen. That makes me nervous. I feel so . . . inexperienced."

"Hey," Rita said as she sat up and took another sip from the thermos. "Our mothers didn't have any experience either. And we turned out all right."

Scooping a fistful of sand, Jill sifted it through her fingers. It was the perfect time to tell Rita about the diary. And if she didn't tell someone soon, Jill felt as though she might burst. She opened her mouth to speak, just as Rita laughed.

"Then again," Rita said, "our mothers probably never worried about how we'd turn out. Back in the dark ages when we were kids, they just kept going and expected we'd be fine. I think everyone analyzes things too much today. I think everyone should spend less time dwelling on shit and just live."

"Maybe you're right," Jill answered. Maybe she was dwelling too much on the diary. Maybe she should give it up, let it go. Like everything else. There was nothing she could do to change it, or no one she could learn more from. Her mother's sister, Myrna, may still be alive, somewhere. But Jill had never met the woman, had no idea where she lived. What's done was, apparently, very done. The way her mother had wanted it.

"Living is tough enough without making more out of it than we need to," Rita continued.

Jill looked toward the teenagers again. When she and Rita had been that age, they could never have dreamed that their lives would have turned out the way they had. She turned back to Rita. "Are you okay, Rita? I mean, are you really okay? Emotionally? Financially?"

"Sure, kid. I'm fine."

"I'm going to list the house with you, you know."

Rita lay back down on the blanket. "Thanks," she said. "I think it'll be an easy sell."

Jill pulled her knees to her chest. "I hope so. I'm really excited about marrying Christopher. I'm excited about our new life." It was too soon to tell her about the RueCom deal. It was too soon to tell her about L.A. She didn't want to alienate Rita again, make her feel that Jill thought she was better than her.

"I've got a couple of hot buyers on my heels right now," Rita said.

"For my house?"

"No. One over in West Chop. The only trouble is, the owner doesn't want to sell. Neither does his wife."

Jill laughed. "Leave it to you."

Rita sat up again. "Well, shit, it's a two-million-dollar deal. They've made an offer without even seeing the inside. I really want to pull it off."

"If I know you, you'll think of a way."

"I've been sleeping with the guy all summer. That hasn't worked."

"Rita! You've been sleeping with someone because you want to sell his house?"

Rita smirked and looked at Jill. "Hey, a girl's got to do what a girl's got to do."

Jill slapped the edge of Rita's arm. "I don't believe you!"

"Believe it, kid. It hasn't been all work, though. He's a pretty good lay."

"God!" Jill moaned and flopped against the blanket.

"Hey, what's the difference? You're sleeping with the guy who's going to move your career forward."

"I'm not just sleeping with him, Rita, I'm going to marry him."

"And you didn't sleep with him before he proposed?"

Jill laughed. "Okay, okay. But he wasn't married."

Rita shrugged. "Semantics," she said.

Jill sat up again and took another sip of her daiquiri. "There must be other two million-dollar houses you can sell."

"Not with hot buyers."

"Well, what are you going to do?"

"I don't know. Got any ideas?"

"You're the one who always had the ideas, Rita. Besides, you've never been one to take no for an answer."

"I think I could get Joe to come around. His wife's another story."

"Then come up with a way to convince her."

"I'm not going to sleep with her, too."

"God, Rita, you are incorrigible. You know what you need? You need a real life."

"I have a real life, thank you."

"No. I mean you need exposure to other things in this world. Other people besides . . ."

"Besides islanders? Are we back to that? Jill wanting to escape from the Vineyard? Rita staying behind?"

Jill turned to her. "Look, I've got an idea. *Lifestyles* magazine will be here Wednesday for a photo shoot of us. Christopher will be here, too. Why don't you come over and watch? I'm not crazy about the whole thing, and I'd feel a lot better if you were there."

"And maybe I could meet some people from the real world?"

Jill smiled.

"Tell you what, kid. I'll put in an appearance if you come with me later that night."

"Come where?"

"To Oak Bluffs. Wednesday is Illumination Night."

Jill groaned. She'd forgotten about the Vineyard tradition—the lighting of the Japanese lanterns in the gingerbread houses that surrounded the Tabernacle in the Methodist campgrounds.

"It'll be like the good old days," Rita said with a wink. "We can look for boys."

Jill shook her head, but managed to grin, as she wondered just how much more of the good old days she could stand.

Rita decided to fight fire with fire. Jill was right about one thing: Rita Blair never liked taking no for an answer. Joe Geissel and his country-club wife should be no exception.

Though Jill had tried to talk her into having pizza with her and the kids, Rita said she'd blown the whole day screwing around with Jill and that some of us had to work for a living. What Jill didn't know as Rita waved good-bye was that she had no intention of working at the tavern tonight: she had, instead, finally come up with a plan to assure her the sale of the Geissel's house, the solvency of SurfSide Realty, and the IRS away from her door.

After leaving Jill's, Rita drove home and changed into jeans, sneakers, and a lightweight sweater, then grabbed one of the tickets from her investment that had paid off after all.

Maneuvering her car toward Vineyard Haven, she wished she'd thought to bring her yellow slicker. Clouds were rolling in, and there was nothing worse than being stuck in a heavy mist on the top deck of a ferry.

Once on the pier, Rita flashed her resident's ID and her precious Sunday night ticket. Thankfully, they gave her no flack.

She quickly crossed the pavement and climbed up the steep stairs of the passenger entrance, hoping beyond hope that Joe's wife had not changed her schedule again, that she would, as usual, be booked on the six-fifteen. Rita never understood why the woman didn't fly back and forth to Boston, but then she'd learned long ago not to question the motives of tourists.

Moving quickly to the upper deck, she pressed her way through the people and stood by the rail. There was no need to search for Joe's wife yet: there would be plenty of time once they were under way, and no chance of Joe spotting Rita among the crowd, in case he'd come to see his darling wife off. He would, after all, never expect to see Rita here: he would assume she was doing her islander duties of serving up hamburgers and curly fries, staying out of the way of those more fortunate.

"This time," she whispered into the wind, "you're wrong."

Without turning around, she sensed the crowd behind her swell. The level of laughter and talking rose; the sounds of feet shuffling and cameras clicking were all around her. She gripped the rail and waited for the engines to roll over, hoping, beyond hope, that she would not puke. For someone brought up by the sea, it always amazed her that seasickness seemed welded into her genes. She reassured herself that as long as she stayed topside, she'd be fine.

The engines, at last, rumbled. A veil of smoke spewed from below. Rita closed her eyes and counted to ten, trying to remember to look off to the horizon, to not look down, to not panic. She took a deep breath, just as she felt the floor beneath her move. She gripped the rail harder.

"Rita?" came a voice from behind her.

She quickly opened her eyes and turned around. The air around her swirled. Facing her were the Martins.

"We tried to call you," the missus said. "You weren't home."

Rita touched her churning stomach, then forced a smile and tried not to think about the dizzying air. "No," she said, "I'm not home. I have to make an emergency trip to Falmouth." She looked over their shoulders, scanning the other passengers. Joe's wife was not among them.

"When we didn't hear from you we assumed . . ."

"I can't tell you more, other than that my trip has to do with locking up your deal." She looked off to the right. Still, no one who resembled Joe's wife.

"Oh, how wonderful! We were afraid . . ."

Rita held her hand to her lips. "There's nothing to be afraid of. It's just taking a little longer than I hoped. Can you come back next weekend?"

"We hadn't planned . . ." Mr. Martin said.

"I'll pick up your tab," Rita said quickly. "A room at the Charter House, complete with ferry tickets." If she'd been a Catholic she'd have said a quick "Hail, Mary," with the hopes that the owners of the Charter House remembered how many times when real estate was flourishing, Rita had thrown business their way.

"Well, if it would mean we could see the house. . . ."

"I'll call you," Rita said. "I promise. Now, if you'll excuse me, I must go below and tend to business. I'll be in touch in a day or two, okay?"

"Well . . ."

"I promise," she repeated as she slipped away and headed for the stairs. Puking or not, she'd have to look for Joe's wife on the lower deck.

Grabbing hold of the railing Rita gingerly made her way down the stairs. When she opened the door to the enclosed lounge, she knew her search was over: Joe's wife sat on a bench, her aristocratic snot nose buried in a book.

Rita took another deep breath and looked out the window toward the horizon. If only she could see land, it might make it easier. But the fog was building; no land could be seen, no reassurance that solid ground would soon be beneath her feet.

Then she reminded herself that if she didn't close this deal, she'd see more than land. She'd see a courtroom and cell bars and an IRS agent impounding her house. She moved to the bench. A college-age boy sat beside Joe's wife, headphones glued to his ears, his ratty-looking sneakers marking the beat.

Rita tapped him on the shoulder. "Would you mind if I sat here?" She kept her gaze averted from

Joe's wife. "I'm not feeling well and I need to sit down."

The boy looked perplexed.

Rita plucked an earphone from his ear. "Get up," she commanded. "Or I'm going to throw up."

The boy quickly rose and disappeared in the crowd.

Rita sat next to Joe's wife and stared straight ahead. From the corner of her eye, she saw the woman set down her book.

"That was quite a tactic," Joe's wife said. "What other lengths do you go to to sell a house?"

Rita swallowed, surprised that the woman remembered her. But then, her damn hair was always a dead giveaway. There was simply no hiding for Rita Blair.

"What makes you think that's why I'm here?" she answered. Hell, if this broad could be bold, so could she.

Joe's wife laughed. "I own a marketing firm, Miss Blair. I deal with salespeople every day."

Rita refused to act surprised that Joe's wife had remembered her name.

"You're not his first wife, are you?" Rita asked.

"What?"

"I said, you're not Joe's first wife. What are you? Number three? Four?"

The woman was silent.

"Why would you turn down a cool two million when it will only make it easier to split when it comes time for the divorce? The fact that you only come to the Vineyard on weekends tells me you really aren't in love with the place. Or, perhaps, with your husband, either."

Joe's wife stood up. "Excuse me," she said, and tried to squeeze past Rita.

Rita reached out and touched the wife's arm. "You do know that while you're in the city each week, your husband is very busy conducting his own business on the island, don't you? His own, very personal business?"

The woman stiffened. "Look, you," she said, pointing a sharp fingernail at Rita. "My husband, and my life, are none of your business. And if, for one minute, you think I'd do business with you, you're wrong."

Rita sighed. "Two million dollars. Cash. My bet is you could get it all if you played your cards right. Even though adultery is no longer grounds for divorce in the state of Massachusetts, I do believe Joe is from the old school. I'd take the cash if I were you, lady. And I'd take it fast."

The woman wrenched her arm from Rita's claws. Rita quickly stuffed a card in the pages of her book. "Think about it," she said. "The market is bad. This is no time to walk away from a hot offer." She folded her hands in her lap. "Call me by Tuesday, or the buyers are gone."

As Joe's wife stormed down the aisle, Rita stifled a swell of nausea and prayed that she'd gotten her point across, and that this damn boat would quickly find land.

Suddenly the bitch stopped and turned back. When she reached Rita, she leaned down and breathed into her face. "For what it's worth," she seethed, "I don't know where you get your information, but I am my husband's first and only wife. We have been married thirty-four years." With a puff of her cheeks, she marched away, leaving Rita to feel like the stupid ass that she was for believing that bastard's lies.

Chapter 14

Monday morning Jill dug through the mess in her mother's sewing room, changed the bed, polished, and cleaned. She almost looked forward to Addie's arrival tomorrow. It was time this house had some life, some people in it, other than tentative families and noisy workmen.

"You'd hate every minute of this, Mother," she said as she took the bed pillows outside to air in the sun. But curiously, Jill no longer cared what her mother would think. Finally, she was beginning to see herself as her own person, undefined by Florence Randall, unrestricted by her mother's expectations. It was while she was picking hydrangea blossoms to brighten Addie's room that Jill realized the cloud of her mother had lifted, as though being with Rita had confirmed Jill's sense of inner worth. With Rita's no-nonsense attitude and free-spirited soul, her friend had the gift to make others feel special, to make them less troubled about themselves, about life. Whether Florence Randall had liked it or not, Rita was a good person. And so, for that matter, was Jill.

She went back into the house and found a vase for the flowers, feeling sad that she'd had a brother she would never know, feeling sad, somehow, for Florence, the woman who clearly blamed herself for his death. But was the death of one child any reason not to want another? And, once the second child had come, was that any reason to . . . to what? What had her mother thought of Jill? Had she never been able to love her, the way she'd loved Robbie?

She put the flowers in the guest room and decided she needed to know. Maybe now—when Jill was feeling good about herself—maybe now she had the strength to learn more.

She took a deep breath and went up the stairs, back to the widow's walk, back to the past.

Sept. 14, 1953

My stomach is so huge I can hardly stand it. I don't remember being this uncomfortable with Robbie. It's so hot here on the island, so hot in our room upstairs. I can't sleep at night. Sometimes I come outside and sit here on the lawn, and pray for this to be over soon, pray that I will have this baby and get it over with.

I'd prayed for a miscarriage, too. But that didn't work either.

Jill bit her lip and wondered how Rita would react if she were sitting beside her now.

"Holy shit," Rita would probably say. Imagining those words gave Jill the courage to read on.

Nov. 4, 1953

Well, I did it. I had a daughter last night. George is elated. He sat by my hospital bed and held my hand the whole time, though I've no idea why.

His parents are thrilled, too. As for me, I just want them all to leave me alone. I just want to sleep. I just want to sleep.

Feb. 17, 1954

Mother Randall is a much better mother than me. She knows how to hold the baby so she won't cry; she knows how to sing to her, how to rock her. I don't know why I can't do these things. I think I did them with Robbie. It's so hard to remember now. It was all so long ago. He would have been eight years old this summer. I wonder what he would look like. I wonder what he would think of his baby sister.

We call her Jill. She is rather pretty, and I guess she's a good baby. But every time I look at her I can only see Robbie. I am glad Mother Randall doesn't feel the same way. She tells me I'll feel better in the spring, when I can get out of the house and walk Jill in the carriage. But I don't want to walk her in the carriage. I don't want to ever leave the house with her, the two of us alone. I can't be trusted to do that. Maybe Mother Randall will walk her, if I ask her nicely.

July 12, 1954

Today is Robbie's birthday. No one seems to remember but me. Mother Randall took Jill to the church fair today. I'm glad she loves my baby so much.

George's father died in April, and taking care of Jill gives Mother Randall something to do. It is best, for both of them, if I don't interfere.

I think I will make chicken soup today. I wish the beach plums would hurry and ripen so I can get started on the jelly Mother Randall showed me how to make.

Jill shut the book and closed her eyes. Slowly, she rose and went to the windows overlooking the town. She tried to remember her grandmother. She did not. Looking off toward the white-steepled church, Jill only remembered being very young, standing in a church pew, with Mother on one side, Daddy on the other. She remembered holding Daddy's hand. She remembered organ music and the strong scent of flowers and the dim lights and the sounds of crying. Somehow, Jill knew it was her grandmother's funeral. But she had no recollection of the woman who had loved her so much, had cared for her when her own mother was unable.

She folded her arms and stared out over the town. Tears ran down her cheeks. *Unable*, she thought. Florence Randall had not loved her daughter because she had been unable.

But a woman had loved Jill. A woman had taken care of her; nurtured her, loved her. The grandmother who had gone too soon to have been more than a memory of death.

Jill sucked in her breath and wondered why no one had helped her mother, why no one had known she needed help. Why hadn't her grandmother done something? Why hadn't her father?

It was the 1950s, Rita would rationalize in her pragmatic way. *It was the 1950s and no one knew about stuff like that.*

Sadly, Jill knew that Rita would be right.

She brushed away her tears, knowing she had read all she could read for one day, feeling her strength diminished, her good mood deflated. Setting the diary back in the trunk, she stared at it a moment, then rose and crossed to the stairs, leaving the widow's walk behind.

At the foot of the steps, voices came from Amy's room.

"Trust me, Amy," Jill heard Carrie say. "The

photo shoot will be great. I've done a million of them."

Jill paused, hung her head, and resolved to be a better mother to Amy, to let her daughter know that she was truly loved. She never wanted her daughter to wonder why she had been born, or who she could turn to in a moment of need.

Rounding the corner, she walked down the stairs. All she wanted now was some fresh air and some peace. She'd give anything to get back to work.

It had been awkward as hell working with Kyle today and not telling him about Carrie's visit last night and that maybe Kyle should consider dating a girl a little less . . . friendly. Rather than have to keep facing the kid, Ben had sent Kyle over to Menemsha House to pick up a couple gallons of the wood sealant he was storing there.

Standing in the backyard at Jill's house now, eyeing samples of windowsills, he wondered why the hell he felt guilty. He hadn't, after all, succumbed to Carrie. Exciting as it might have been, he would have had to face himself in the mirror in the morning when he shaved.

He picked up a sill with a deeper ledge and decided it would be best for Jill's house. The authentic ones were nothing more than a casing, and people today liked to have a place to put white candles in their windows at Christmas. He could save the real thing for Menemsha House, if it ever happened. And when Kyle returned, he could send him off again—this time to buy the rest of the sills.

He chuckled to himself as he set down the casing, took out his notebook, and calculated the number that needed replacing, wondering how many errands it would take before he could look at Kyle eye-to-eye again. Hopefully, after the zoning board meeting tonight, Ben's thoughts would be pleasantly diverted, despite Carrie's come-on, despite Carrie's warning.

The sound of the screen door closing made him turn his head. Jill stood on the back step, looking past him, looking deep in thought. She was dressed like an islander today—denim shorts that made her long, lean legs glow in the sunlight, a pale yellow T-shirt that showed the outline of a lacy bra underneath. Ben felt a slow heat rise in his loins. He quickly turned his gaze back to his notebook.

"No sawing today?" Jill's voice called out.

"Trying to find a stopping place so we'll leave you alone for a couple of days." God, he thought, he must be losing his mind. It wasn't hard to remember that was what happened when your dick started ruling your brain.

She moved off the steps and walked toward him. "I'm really sorry for the inconvenience."

He tried to smile. "You're the boss."

She peeked down at his notebook. "How did you get into this? Restoring old houses?"

His eyes caught the look of those soft, smooth hands. He gripped his pen. "Twenty questions again?" His nostrils filled with a light, refreshing scent, as though she'd bathed in something called "Spring Mist" or "Morning Dew."

"Sorry. It is curious, though. There are so many home remodelers and contractors, but I get the feeling that what you do is different."

"I restore. Authentically. For the most part."

"For the most part?"

Ben stood. "Take these windowsills of yours." He breathed deeply to clear his head, then quickly explained why he'd chosen the more up-to-date version.

"I suppose it makes sense. So what I'm getting is a Ben Niles watered-down version."

Staring at the sills, Ben wondered why he'd forgotten that women could be so . . . infuriating. "What you're getting is Ben Niles for the nineties," he answered sharply, not bothering to add that the work would still have the Ben Niles imprint; that it would still mean something, totally authentic or not. He shoved his notebook into his pocket. "As soon as we're done here, there's a place on Nantucket we'll be doing—everything authentic, from the nails we'll be hammering to the tools we'll be using. Hand-wrought adzes. Wood chisels. That sort of thing."

"No power saws?"

"Nope. Not a one."

She brushed back her hair. A thin line of perspiration lined her brow. "It's too bad I can't do a story on you," she said.

Ben laughed. "I get enough publicity, thanks."

"I could have before, but I guess we're changing our format a little."

He had no idea what she was talking about. Nor did he care. He only wished she would leave.

"Of course," she added with a grin, "if you were to shoot someone, our producers might reconsider."

He laughed again. "I think I'll pass."

"If you change your mind, let me know. But right now, I guess I'd better let you get back to work. I'll see you Thursday, right?"

"Thursday," he confirmed. "Have a good photo shoot."

She turned and headed for the water. As Ben watched her leave, watched the easy gait of her steps, the slight sway of her back, he couldn't stop himself from wondering what he would have done if instead of Carrie at his door last night, it had been Jill.

He bundled up the plans along with his proposal for the school buses and checked the clock over the refrigerator. Eight-fifteen. Forty-five minutes to kill until the zoning board would begin hearing proposals.

Ben let out a sigh and decided to go out to the workshop and putter around until it was time to leave. He'd never been one for sitting still, especially when there was something to be nervous about. As he went out the back door into the dusk, he wondered if Carol Ann would show up at the meeting. He hadn't told her he was going back: no doubt, however, she'd seen his name on the agenda. If they'd bothered to add it to the list.

In the dimness of the workshop, Ben picked up the antique wood chisel, feeling the coolness against his palm, the smooth curve of the wood handle, the familiarity of the tool that had most likely spent more time in his hand than in its original nineteenth-century owner's. Running his finger along the tip, he felt its dullness, then walked to the sharpening table.

The late-summer sun cast a comfortable dimness across the small room. Slowly, Ben drew the tip along the bench stone, the way it had once been done, the way he still did it. Early tools, early methods. It was what he loved most, what made him an artisan instead of a builder. He half wished Jill McPhearson wasn't leaving the island: he might have been able to convince her to do a story after all—not on Ben Niles, but on Menemsha House.

Apparently, though, in order to get that he'd have to shoot someone. Dave Ashenbach.

"No problem," he said with a grin, and realized how pathetic the media had become.

Menemsha House would be genuinely newsworthy: young people studying the craft of their ancestors, learning that the best of everything did not necessarily come from an electrical outlet and was accomplished in record time. It was something Kyle was only now beginning to realize: Ben could see it in the boy's sensitivity and in his dependable performance.

He turned the tip of the chisel over, drew it several times against the stone, and wished, once again, that Kyle had been his son, that he and Louise had had more children. In Baltimore, there hadn't been time. With his long hours of training, Louise's teaching schedule, and Carol Ann to take care of, the weeks, months, and years had too quickly slipped by.

When they settled on the Vineyard, Carol Ann was already six, nearly seven. By the time Ben's business was under way, Carol Ann was almost ten, an age, they'd decided, that was too late to bring another child into the family. Louise, Ben suspected, had regretted it, too. But at the time she was trying to please him, and in truth, at the time, it was his work that pleased him most. His freedom to do what was so right for him, his opportunity to fine-tune his talents.

So there had been no other children besides Carol Ann. And she was a good daughter, despite the fact they didn't always agree.

Ben smiled as he gently touched the tip of the now razor-sharp chisel and realized that sometimes he just liked to get Carol Ann going, liked to watch her cheeks turn pink, her muscles tense. It was the one time he could see himself in her, the one time that besides her looks, he was assured she was his child, too, not just Louise's.

Just as Ben moved to replace the chisel in his wooden tool box, the door to the workshop creaked opened. He turned quickly, half expecting to see Carol Ann. Instead, a dark figure loomed in the shadow of dusk. A dark figure, wearing a ski mask.

"What the hell . . ." Ben muttered.

The figure thrust its arm toward Ben and locked around his throat. Ben jerked; the wood chisel slipped from his hand. He jabbed his elbow into the figure's stomach. The figure groaned, spun Ben around, and shoved him against the workbench. Ben snapped up his knee and nailed him in the groin. They fell to the floor, pulling the Menemsha House plans down with them. Ben landed on his arm. Pain shot through him. Wood shavings stung into his eyes.

Know your enemies, came Noepe's words. Ben struggled to raise his hand, fought to pull at the ski mask. Just then he saw the figure grab for the chisel. Ben rolled onto his side as another pain shot through him, this time through his shoulder. He reached up and felt the warm, sticky blood. His blood. Next to the blood was the chisel, sticking straight up from his flesh. He tried to rip it out; the figure quickly rose and ran from the workshop, the door slapped shut.

Ben lay on the floor, unable to move. The pain crept through his neck, up to his head, down his arm.

"Jesus Christ," he said quietly, as finally the chisel let go and clattered to the floor. Another pain shot through Ben's arm. He closed his eyes and tried to catch his breath. Wood shavings touched his tongue. "Jesus Christ," he muttered again.

The last thing he saw before everything went dark were the plans for Menemsha House, coated with his blood.

Chapter 15

 Tuesday morning, Joe Geissel banged on Rita's front door. She peered at him from the upstairs window, wondering if she should go downstairs.

"Mom?" Kyle called from the bedroom next door. "Someone's at the door."

Shit, Rita thought as the banging persisted. If she didn't go downstairs, Kyle would. And there was no need for him to know about Joe—no reason to know how desperate his mother had become in order to protect their lives. It was just her dumb luck again that Kyle was home this morning, that he had the next two days off work at Jill's. She pulled on her thin cotton robe, ran her hands through her curls, and went downstairs to face the wrath of the man who only last week had told her she was the best thing that ever happened to him.

"What the fuck do you think you're doing?" he screamed as she opened the door.

Rita stepped outside and closed the door behind her. "My son is inside," she said. "Please keep it down."

"I don't care if the pope is inside. I want to know what the fuck you're doing, and I want to know now." His cheeks were puffed and red with rage, his eyes like little slits in the sunlight. As he shouted, his jowls flopped up and down against the collar of his plaid, short-sleeved shirt.

Rita folded her arms and leaned against the door. She hadn't realized how old Joe was, how ugly. "I'm not going to speak to you until you calm down," she said quietly.

He puffed his cheeks again, then dug his hands into the pockets of his chinos. Rita wondered how long it had been since she'd seen him in clothes, then was embarrassed for herself, that her life had been reduced to this.

"What are you doing, babe?" he asked. "Why'd you do this to me?" The redness began to fade from his cheeks.

"I'm just a working girl trying to make a living," she said. "I thought you wanted to sell your house."

"I hadn't planned on getting a divorce in the process."

Rita hid her inward smile. Sparks must have been flying over the line between Boston and West Chop yesterday. For that, it had been worth her little trip. For that, it had been worth staying up half of Sunday night puking. She looked out to the street, at Joe's big Mercedes parked crooked on the dirt shoulder, and wondered if the neighbors wondered what a Mercedes was doing in their neighborhood, and if Rita had finally hit it big. "Maybe you should have thought of that before you slept with me," she replied.

He steadied his slit eyes on her again. "I guess I should be more careful in my choice of partners. I thought I could trust you."

She sneered. "You never planned to leave her, did you? Well, I've got news for you. I never thought you would. In fact, if you had, I wouldn't have taken you. You're just a used-up piece of shit scumbag, Joe. If you think for one minute I fell for your bullshit, you're wrong. Dead wrong." She wished her insides would stop squeezing together; she wished her head felt as confident as her words sounded.

"I told you I needed more time."

"You told me a lot of things. Like this was the fourth Mrs. Joe Geissel. And that I was only welcome in your home from Monday through Friday. Do you think I'm stupid, Joe? Is that it?"

"Why did you go to her?"

"Maybe I wanted to see what she has that makes her better than me. Well, you know what? She has shit, Joe. She's got a face like a truck and if her nose were any higher in the air, she'd take flight."

He stared at her, his slit eyes opened wide now. The redness had come back to his cheeks.

Rita took a short breath and continued, before she lost her nerve. "I had a buyer for your house, you asshole. A two-million-dollar deal. But you know what? I wouldn't sell it now if it were the last house on the Vineyard. I wouldn't sell it if I was down to digging quahogs for dinner again. I don't need your fucking money, and I surely don't need you. Rita Blair will make it just fine without you." She put her hands on her hips and turned to the door. "Now get the hell off my property before I call the cops."

With that, she went inside, slammed the door behind her, stood in the middle of the fraying, braided rug, and started to shake all over.

"Mom?"

Rita clutched the tie of her robe. "It's okay, honey," she called up the stairs. "It was just business." She quickly tried to wipe the tears from her cheeks, but Kyle's footsteps down the stairs beat her to it.

"Jesus," he said as he looked at his mother, then darted to the front door. He ripped it open just as

Rita heard the gravel spit from beneath the tires of Joe's Mercedes. "What's going on?" Kyle asked.

She kept her back to him and went into the kitchen. She stood at the sink a moment, then reached for the coffee maker. "I told you, Kyle. It was just business." Her words sounded strong, her words sounded confident. She only wished her hands would stop shaking. Taking the coffee can from the refrigerator, she tried to scoop out the grounds. Half the tablespoon spilled out; brown granules skittered across the counter, then pinged onto the tired linoleum. "Shit," she said as she dropped the measuring spoon into the sink and started to sob.

Kyle's arm was suddenly around her. "Mom. God, are you okay? Who was that creep?"

"Just a sale gone bad. It's not the first time."

"It's the first time you've reacted like this."

An image of the IRS office came into her mind, followed by the scent of stale jailhouse air, the sound of a cell door slamming. "Oh, Kyle," she cried, "I do believe your sainted mother has screwed up."

He guided her to the table. "Sit down," he ordered. "And tell me everything that happened."

She sat. "Make some coffee," she said. "Please."

"Only if you promise to tell me the truth."

Rita nodded and tried to collect her thoughts. She listened as Kyle poured water in the coffee maker, dug fresh grounds from the can. He deserved more than this for a mother, she thought for the thousandth time. He deserved a mother he could depend on, no matter how old he got, no matter what. In her selfish need to keep him from worrying the way she had always done with Hazel, Rita had gotten in over her head, bitten off more than she could chew, counted her chickens before they hatched. There was a reason, she realized now, that those old sayings were ever written in the first place.

But what had she done that was so wrong? She

had only wanted to own her own business. When Franklin had gotten sick her opportunity was there—Rita Blair's one chance to be somebody. Sure, she could have gone to work for one of the agencies on the island—it would have been easier. But this was her big break, her very own *Good Night, Boston.* SurfSide Realty was supposed to turn her life around.

Then the real money problems began.

She tapped her fingernail on the edge of the table and was amazed that she'd been too stupid to know that the one Peter you didn't borrow from to pay Paul was the IRS.

Kyle set a steamy mug in front of her. Rita ran her thumb over the handle, looked into the dark liquid, and wondered how coffee would taste out of a tin cup.

Her son sat down and looked at her. "Well?"

She picked up the mug, took a short sip. "Well," she said slowly, "I think I'm going to go to jail." She set down the mug and kept her eyes fixed on it. She could not look at Kyle, she could not look at the son she'd tried so hard to protect.

"Mom, get real. You said you'd tell me the truth."

"It is the truth."

Kyle didn't move. "Does this have anything to do with the IRS?"

She jerked up her head. "What do you know about the IRS?"

"When I came home the other day, I saw you cram something in your briefcase. You were upset. When you went upstairs to change for the tavern, I looked inside. I read the letter."

Tears formed at the corners of her eyes. She opened her mouth and looked away. "Well, then, Mr. Smart-Ass, I don't have to tell you what's wrong."

"You owe them over twenty grand."

She held her coffee mug steady with both hands. "Remind me to kill the teacher who taught you to read."

"Jesus Christ," Kyle muttered. "What happened?"

Taking another long gulp, Rita realized the time had come to level with Kyle. Though she'd wanted to protect him from this—from everything—facts were facts. She might as well prepare him now for the inevitable. She set down the mug and told him the story. She told him how each week she'd barely been able to write out the net paychecks for her two secretaries, let alone think about the money she was "holding back" for payroll taxes. The truth was, there had been no more money in the checking account to "hold back." "I didn't do it on purpose," she said at the end.

He leaned back in his chair. "So you owe the IRS twenty grand. I can get the money."

"How? I already mortgaged the house to buy the business. I'm broke, Kyle. I've been buying groceries and paying the utilities out of the money I make at the tavern."

"I said, I can get it."

"You're not selling your truck. You worked too hard to get it. And you're not going to borrow it from anyone."

"My boss is rich."

"No. I hardly know him. I got myself into this. I'll figure a way out."

"No offense, Mom, but you don't seem to be doing that too well."

"I tried."

"I know."

"I'm sorry."

"I know."

She took another sip of coffee.

"Can you call Grandma Blair?"

Rita shook her head. "I'm too old to go running to Mommy, Kyle. Besides, I'm not going to screw up your grandmother's life."

"What about Charlie Rollins?"

"No."

"Well, what then? You can't go to jail, Mom. That's ridiculous."

"Maybe I'll sell a house."

"How many have you sold this summer?"

"None. But it's still only August." Rita knew, though, that it was probably pointless. She'd run the scenario over and over in her mind too many times. Joe Geissel had been her one hope.

Kyle grabbed his keys from the counter.

"Where are you going?" Rita asked.

"If you insist on doing this yourself, you need all the energy you can get," he said. "I'm going out to get us some breakfast. I figure four big, fat eclairs ought to do it."

He went out the door. Rita wondered how she had, at least, been blessed with having such an incredible kid. An incredible kid, that's what Jill had called him. Jill. Rita's mind kicked back into gear. Jill was the one person who might be willing to help. If only Rita could find the nerve to ask.

"I don't suppose this old house is air conditioned," Addie bristled, moving to the windows in the sewing room, then snapping the shades from Florence's half-way-up-and-no-higher position all the way to the top. She pulled off her large-brimmed hat and fanned her round cheeks. She'd been bitching about the heat since she'd waddled off the plane.

"No." Jill leaned against the Singer and wondered why she always felt small in Addie's presence. She suspected it wasn't the difference in their girth. "I can get you a fan. . . ."

"Better make it two. I need to have my wits about me for tomorrow." She plopped on the bed, her camellia-flowered, apricot tent dress billowing over the midlife bulges it was supposed to conceal, then settling on the yellowed George Washington bedspread. She began extracting bottles and jars from her Louis Vuitton bag. "I checked with the weather station. Tomorrow will be sunny. We'll do most of the shooting outside. As planned."

Apparently, even God wouldn't have dared to thwart Addie's agenda.

"Christopher mentioned he's having dinner with Maurice Fischer again," Jill said.

Addie pulled out a small mirror and a tube of bright pink lipstick. She pursed her thin lips at the glass and slowly outlined them. "Everything will be fine, as long as Christopher follows my instructions."

Shifting on one foot, Jill wished Christopher had told her more, wished she didn't feel as though she didn't count, as though this deal wouldn't affect her life, and her career, as well as his. Sometimes, Addie seemed to forget that, too. "What instructions?"

Addie flicked her a glance. "At this stage?" She turned back to the mirror and blotted her lips with a tissue. "He only needs to act as though he'll do anything Maurice wants."

Jill wished Addie had said he should act as though *they* would do anything Maurice Fischer wanted. "Did he tell you about the Sam Wilkins story?"

"Of course. It's brilliant. Can you do it?"

"I'll do my best. But even if Sam agrees, there's no guarantee I'll be able to shape it into our 'good news' format."

"Anything with Sam Wilkins will be good news to Fischer. Right now, he's more important than your audience."

Jill didn't mask her surprise. "But isn't our format

what makes *Good Night, Boston* so successful? Isn't it why Fischer was interested in the first place?"

Addie tossed her lipstick and makeup back into her bag. "Don't be naive, Jill. If this show goes national, there will be more than one change."

"What other changes?"

"There's no need to bother about that until the time comes." Addie stood up. "Did you get a dress for the shoot?"

Jill knew when a subject had been dismissed. She drew in a deep breath and decided she'd let Christopher deal with Addie tomorrow. "I went into town this morning and picked up a couple of earth-mother things. You can choose the one you like best."

Addie nodded. "Good. But right now, I'm starving. Where does a person get a decent meal on this hotter-than-hell island?"

"There's a nice place for fresh fish in Oak Bluffs," she said. "I thought we could take the kids."

"I hate fish," Addie said with a snort. "And I'm really too tired to deal with children tonight. Besides, we need to talk about tomorrow. I'm sure the children would be bored."

Jill forced a smile. "You're probably right." She moved toward the doorway. "We can run down to the tavern. I'll call Charlie and have him reserve us a quiet table." Then she went into the hall, slouched against the wall, and wondered if, wherever they moved, Addie would be moving there, too.

She awakened to the feel of something warm against her skin. Lying on her side, Jill opened her eyes and looked down at the arm draped over her, at the hand that caressed her breast. She smiled. "You're early," she murmured. "Or I'm waking up late."

"A little of both," Christopher answered, pressing his nakedness against her back.

His hardness stirred against her as it grazed her buttocks. Below her waist, she began to tingle. "I'm glad you're here."

He pulled her back closer to him. "Me, too."

"I must have overslept because the power saw isn't going today."

"Addie's outside with the photo crew. Give her a minute and she'll make more noise than a power saw."

"Oh," Jill groaned and moved closer against him. "She gives me a headache sometimes."

Christopher laughed. "I know, honey, but . . ."

"But she's only got our best interests at heart."

"And her fifteen percent," he added.

Jill turned to face him. She took him in her hand and began to stroke. "Speaking of being realistic," she whispered, "Addie told me I was naive to think *Good Night, Boston* wouldn't change. What did she mean? Oh, and how was your dinner?"

He took a lock of Jill's hair, entwined it in his fingers. "Dinner was wonderful, but I missed you terribly."

"Did you dazzle him?"

"You would have dazzled him more." He lowered his head and sucked her nipple.

"You didn't tell him about Sam, did you?"

"I told him you were working on a piece that would knock the socks off the world."

She grinned. "Well, that certainly puts the pressure on."

He slid his hand between her legs. "I don't think we need to talk about this right now."

"But what about the changes, Christopher? What did he say?"

"Just a couple of minor things, including that there will be a big emphasis on promotion."

"Well, I'd expect they'd promote it."

"Not them. Us. I get the feeling we'll have to do a lot. But don't worry, honey," he said as he probed his finger around her vagina, then thrust it into her warmth. "I'm sure Addie will handle all that."

She moved with the rhythm of his finger, but her thoughts were on Addie—on how the woman had already handled their promotion, including the use of Jeff and Amy—the same children the woman had been "too tired to deal with" last night.

"What kind of promotion? More *Lifestyles* layouts?"

Christopher's finger stopped. "Jill. Please. I'm trying to make love to you, not conduct a meeting."

"Sorry," she said. "I'm only concerned about our future. I wasn't the one at dinner with Fischer, remember?"

His penis grew soft. She slid her hand away.

Christopher rolled onto his back and sighed. "Okay, you win," he said without humor. "He talked about product endorsements. Plus, appearances at film premiers and charity events. They'll want us to be seen." He paused. "There. Are you happy now?"

Ignoring his sarcasm, Jill thought of her calendar that was already too packed with work, with her life. "Are they forgetting we'll have a show to do Monday through Friday?"

He sat up, drew up his knees, and folded his hands on top of them. "That's another one of the changes. We'll still be on every day, but the workload won't be as demanding."

"We'll be doing national stuff. How can he say the workload won't be as demanding?"

He tented his fingers in an upside-down "V." "Because we won't have to write the stories."

She thought she must have heard him wrong. "What?"

"We'll have a staff to do the writing. And the producing. All we have to do is sit behind the desk and look impressive."

"You're kidding, right?"

"No."

The warmth he had generated now turned to a chill. "So we'll be nothing more than talking heads."

"Hey, if talking heads is what they want, count me in. For a three-year contract at a million five apiece, I'll talk my head off."

She yanked back the sheet and got out of bed. "That may be fine for you, you were a baseball player. But, God, Christopher, I'm a journalist. Journalists research. They write. They produce their own stories."

"Does Barbara Walters do her own research?"

"I wouldn't know."

"She has a staff, Jill. I keep telling you that you've got to think of the big picture. Besides, Fischer isn't talking Boston. He's talking Hollywood. L.A."

Jill threw on her robe and went to the window. She moved the thin sheer drape and looked outside. A small army of blue-jeaned-clad people—women with short hair, men with ponytails—swarmed over the lawn, setting up tripods and umbrellas. Close by, watching them intently, stood Amy. "So, it's L.A.? Not New York? Or Atlanta?"

She heard the familiar rattle of Christopher's belt buckle as he pulled on his pants. "A little Hollywood life might be exciting. If you think you can manage to let yourself get excited."

"Just what Amy needs," she said quietly, "life in L.A." She looked down at the life below her, listened to the fervor of voices, felt the pulse of activity. Then she glanced over to her mother's hydrangea bushes and thought about their predictability, the fact that year after year, they had blossomed there, would continue to blossom there. They were island flowers, rooted in the land. They flourished in the salt air and grew colorful in the limy soil. But Jill Randall had not flourished on this island. She had been an unwanted child, whose roots had never quite taken hold. She had needed something, somewhere different. She had needed to find somewhere where she felt she belonged. Yet even still, deep within her, lay the seeds of the hydrangea, in the soil of the Vineyard.

She turned to Christopher; he was putting on his shirt. She went to him and straightened his collar. "I'm sorry," she said, and she meant it. For Jill knew her life was about to change, about to become everything she had ever dreamed of and more. She couldn't let the doubts of her childhood ruin it now.

"No problem," he answered. "I'll see you outside."

As Jill watched him go, she decided that later tonight, when they were safely alone in bed, she would make it up to him. They would make long, wonderful love, and then she would read to him from the pages of her mother's diary. She would share her pain with the man she loved. Maybe then the ache inside her would subside. Maybe then, once and for all, she could move on.

Chapter 16

The backyard looked like the spring flower show at the National Gardens. How Addie had come up with the pots and pots of daisies and sweet williams and nasturtiums that were now tucked between Florence's rows of blossoms, Jill had no idea. She also had no idea how long it would be before the flowers—and the people—would wither in the August heat. Addie kept splashing her face and throat with water from the outside spigot, and though she seemed to be perspiring more than the rest, Jill suspected Addie Becker would be the last to cry uncle.

Jeff had been the first.

"Mom," he wailed long after noon as he flopped beside her on the stairs between takes. "Do we have to do any more? They've already taken a billion pictures."

They had photographed the four of them—the family of the new millennium—having a simulated picnic by the water, packing their bikes as though they were about to set out on an island exploration, and sitting on the back steps. They had photographed Christopher playing volleyball with the kids while a smiling Jill looked on; they had photographed Jill and Amy clipping fresh flowers supposedly for the family dinner table. Jill did not mention her failed family brunch, or the fact that the only time they ate together was when they were out.

Thankfully, Addie had quickly dismissed her thought to shoot at the tavern ("Too dark, too dreary," she'd remarked) as well as Christopher's suggestion to use the Chappy ferry for a backdrop ("Quite tasteless and inappropriate"); Jill, in turn, had refused to let her recruit a neighbor's golden retriever to "round out" the all-American look of the family.

"Hang in a little longer," Jill said to Jeff now. The back of her neck was baked from the sun, her cheek muscles were sore from smiling, and in her heart she agreed with her son that enough was enough. She looked across the yard at her daughter, who was having her makeup replenished by Carrie—a visitor to the "set." Amy, at least, was enjoying the day.

She shifted her gaze back to the cameras, where Christopher stood with Addie, their mouths moving, their heads nodding, conspiring about the next setup.

Just then the sound of a truck in the driveway drew Jill's attention. It was a white van, with black letters that read "White Glove Catering" emblazoned on the side. It was, she realized, another part of Addie's grand plan.

"Break for lunch!" Addie shouted to the crew of nine, ten, eleven, Jill had counted.

All activity predictably ceased. Jill had been on enough photo shoots to know that when food arrived, nothing else mattered. It wasn't that way in journalism. When there was a story to get, the story was gotten, no matter how long it took, no matter how many lunch breaks were missed. The story was the only thing that mattered—the story, and the deadline. She wondered how long it would take her to accept that journalism wasn't Hollywood, and that once the RueCom deal was sealed, she'd never have to worry about that sort of thing again.

Addie instructed the crew to clear the two long tables set up on the lawn, then directed the caterers to spread them with white tablecloths. In moments, the tables were covered with a plethora of plates and bowls of salads and vegetables and fruits, plus a heaping array of colorful butter cookies and what appeared to be brownies with huge chocolate chunks. As her eyes grazed the table, Jill realized she had no appetite at all.

"It's too hot to eat," she said, though she noticed Addie's plate was filled. Christopher seemed satisfied with a spoonful of red potato salad and a slice of steamship round.

"Try to eat something, honey," he said. "We've got a long way to go this afternoon."

She wanted to protest, but quickly remembered that when the cameras were on you, and your future was at stake, you smiled and did what you were told. You grinned and you bore it. The way the Lizette Frenches of the world surely did. She ladled some fruit into a dish and went to sit on the back steps. Christopher followed.

"It wouldn't be so bad if it weren't for the heat," he said as he settled in beside her.

Jill pushed the spoon around the fruit, selected a ripe strawberry, and raised it to her mouth. "I can't imagine how many more shots they want." She wished the sun would go down, she wished the crew would leave, she wished she were alone in bed with Christopher. Alone, to share the diary.

"Addie says they have enough out here," he said as he took a mouthful of salad.

"Out here? I thought this was the only place she wanted them to shoot."

"She changed her mind. She wants one in the living room."

"Inside the house?"

"Yeah." He said, smiling. "Beside the fireplace."

"The fireplace? Oh, no. Don't tell me . . ."

He laughed. "You got it. She wants a roaring fire."

Jill groaned. "Are you sure this is the way to L.A.?"

"You can take it," he said as he playfully poked her shoulder.

She winced from the sunburn that had penetrated her shirt and wondered what made him think she was so tough. Was it because—except for this morning—she adapted to him so easily in bed? Did he think her physical needs and her needs for success were more important than her emotional ones? Tasting another strawberry, she wondered if he'd think she was so tough once he heard excerpts from the diary, once he learned about the real Jill Randall McPhearson—the Jill underneath the makeup, far from the camera lens, the Jill who had been hurt so much.

"This doesn't look like such hard work to me," came a voice from the side of the yard.

Jill turned to see Rita, standing, one hand shielding the sun's glare, her eyes surveying the elegant luncheon buffet.

"Rita!" Jill cried and stood to greet her. "I'm so glad you came!"

If Jill didn't know better, she'd say that Rita held back a little, as though she were shy, as though she were intimidated. "Rita," Jill said as Christopher stood, "this is my main man. Christopher Edwards. Christopher, I'd like you to meet Rita Blair. My best friend."

The two shook hands; Jill looked for approval on Rita's face. She could not tell if it was there.

"Well, you're going to have your hands full with this one," Rita joked.

"That probably works both ways," he answered. Jill smiled, but wondered if he really believed it.

Rita laughed and turned to Jill. "So how's it going? They get enough pictures of you yet?"

"No," she answered, "Christopher keeps breaking the camera."

"Just remember our deal. Tonight's Illumination Night. I'm here, so you owe me."

Illumination Night. Jill had forgotten. She wanted to say no to Rita. She wanted to be with Christopher. Alone. But she could not say no, not to Rita, not to her best friend. "You're right," she said, tucking her arm through Christopher's, "and Christopher is going to love it." Thankfully, Rita didn't remark that having him along would "cramp their style."

"Sorry, honey," Christopher said. "I forgot to tell you. I have to go back to the city tonight. I've got to do that story on that new Red Sox pitcher."

Jill frowned. Yes, she remembered the story: it had been Addie's idea—the life of a major league hotshot compared with the life of a little leaguer. It was going to be poignant and appeal to the male audience. Christopher, of course, was perfect to handle it. "Right," she said, "that will be a great story." She turned and told Rita about the concept, trying to mask her disappointment that he would not be there for Illumination Night, to hold her later in bed and to listen as she read the pages of her past.

The chisel had nearly severed an artery. On top of that, his arm was broken, and the doctor had told him he was lucky to be alive. If Carol Ann hadn't found him, Ben could have bled to death.

He stared at the IV bag that dangled from the metal pole and counted the drips down the snakelike tube. It was a pointless exercise, he knew, but the distraction kept his mind off the pain, if not off the realization that someone had actually tried to kill him.

The worst part was, he didn't believe Dave Ashenbach was behind it. Dave was a loudmouth: the sort of man who gets his satisfaction by trying to prove he is louder than everyone else. But was he a murderer? Ben just didn't buy it. Even though, in the dim light, he hadn't had a good look at his assailant, Ben was certain the man didn't have Ashenbach's jiggling hulk. And he was hard-pressed to believe that Dave could have convinced anyone else to do the job over a strip of abutting land that no one but him would give a damn about.

On the seventy-ninth drip, Ben realized he had no idea who had done this to him, or why, or what he was going to do next. He had not told the police about the threat over Menemsha House. He preferred to believe the attack had nothing to do with it; that it was the work of a lone vandal, looking only to steal something. After all, the ski-masked figure hadn't brought a weapon. It's not as though trying to kill Ben was premeditated.

Then again, he reminded himself as he squeezed his eyes shut against the pain, the Vineyard had little crime. It was one of the reasons he and Louise had loved it so much. There was little crime, simply because there was nowhere to run, nowhere to hide. It wasn't as though someone could knock off a bank and beat feet to the next county. Not without a plane or a boat.

The door to his hospital room opened and Carol Ann walked in, carrying his lunch tray. She was dressed in an off-white shirtdress that made her skin seem even creamier, her copper hair more vivid.

"Hi, Daddy."

Ben smiled. It had been a long time since she'd called him Daddy.

She set the tray on the tall table and swung it over the bed. "Did you get much sleep?"

He reached for the bed control and pressed the button, raising his head, causing his shoulder to throb, and making him wonder if the damn pain medication was ever going to kick in. "A little," he answered. "Shouldn't you be at work?"

She pulled a chair close to the bed, in strictest adherence to hospital regulations: Carol Ann would never have dared to sit on the edge of the bed. "The doctor said you can go home today. The nurse will be here soon to take out the IV."

Ben nodded and, with his tube-attached hand, raised the silver dome on the tray. A gray-white lump of what he supposed was fish jeered back at him. Beside that lay a sad clump of mashed potatoes and a pile of limp-looking carrots. He replaced the dome and reached for the cup of juice. Carol Ann quickly moved forward and peeled back the lid.

"How long will this damn cast be on?" He looked down at his right arm, plastered white from his forearm to above his elbow, and tried not to think about what would have happened if Carol Ann hadn't gone to the zoning board meeting, if she hadn't been alarmed by his absence, and if she hadn't had the daughterly need to check on her father.

"Three or four weeks. It depends on how quickly you heal." She stuck a straw in the cup and moved it closer to him. Ben leaned down and sipped like a helpless child.

"Great. I'm sure Jill McPhearson will be delighted to hear that."

"It's not your fault, Dad. You didn't plan this."

"It *is* my fault, Carol Ann. Your mother always told me I was too independent. If I'd hired more people, the work could still get done if anything happened to me."

"So why didn't you?" Carol Ann asked with a slight smile curving her lightly glossed lips.

"Because I never thought anything would happen."

Carol Ann sighed. "Drink your juice, Dad. We've got to talk about something."

He drank his juice.

"You're coming home with me," she said. "You can't take care of yourself."

Her words sliced through him more than the pain. "I can take care of myself."

"Dad, you can't. You can't use your right arm. Never mind working, you won't be able to dress yourself. You won't be able to cook for yourself."

He smiled. "I'm sure Rachel Bowen will be glad to help."

"Dad, I'm serious."

With his left hand, Ben shoved the tray aside. "So am I. I'm not a cripple, Carol Ann. I can manage."

Tears swelled in her eyes. "Dad, someone tried to kill you. If they tried once, they'll try again."

"No they won't. I think it was an accident. I don't think they thought anyone was there."

"I disagree. I think it was about Menemsha House. Dad, please give it up. Please. I lost Mother. I can't bear the thought of losing you, too."

He wanted to come back with some flip remark like "we all have to go sometime." He wanted to tell Carol Ann he had no intention of going anywhere. But the pain in his shoulder and the tears in her eyes told him that maybe she was right. Maybe he should give up.

"Are you coming home with me?" she asked.

He looked down at the cast. "Might as well. I can't even drive my car. Leave it to me to have a stick shift. Leave it to me to break my right arm."

"Good," she replied and rose from the chair. "I'll check back with the doctor and see when you'll be released. Tonight is Illumination Night. If you feel up to it later, we can take the kids over to the campgrounds."

Yes, maybe Carol Ann was right. Maybe it was time he started acting less like a rebel and more like a grandfather. The truth was, it would be fun to spend time with the kids tonight. And he'd always loved the tradition of Illumination Night—years ago, he and Louise decked their house as well, though it was a distance from the Tabernacle. In recent years, however, Ben had grown to dislike the commercial slant it had taken: the tourist attraction, complete with merchandising carts whose attendants hawked those eerie fluorescent light sticks that the kids waved in each other's faces. Somehow, it had taken the charm off the old custom; but Illumination Night was an island tradition, and whether anyone believed it or not, Ben Niles was an islander, through and through.

"Mother, this island is so queer," Amy said as she sat in the passenger seat of the Range Rover, pouting.

"Illumination Night is fun, Amy. You'll see."

Amy grunted something unintelligible, turned her head from Jill, and stared out toward the sea.

The truth was, Jill hadn't been too crazy about the idea, either. But Rita had suggested they meet at the bandstand—the way they had done as teenagers—and Jill had decided to put aside her reservations for the sake of their friendship. It wouldn't be the first time she'd done that. Like the time Rita got her hands on two fake IDs, and they tried to get served at a tourist café in Oak Bluffs; or when Rita convinced her they should ride their bikes out to Gay Head, sneak down to the water at the base of the cliffs, and make moaning sounds of Wampanoag ghosts into the wind to rattle the tour bus people above. That was a prank they'd done more than once.

Jill smiled now, looking forward to the evening with Rita, relieved that the *Lifestyles* ordeal was behind her, even though Christopher had returned to Boston. "We're meeting Rita there," she said.

Amy did not respond.

"She's coming with Kyle. You like Kyle, don't you?"

"He's Carrie's boyfriend, Mom."

"I didn't mean like that. I meant, he's a nice boy, isn't he?"

"He's not a boy, Mother. He's practically old enough to be my father."

Jill laughed and wondered what Kyle—or Rita—would think of Amy's assessment of the twenty-five-year-old.

"I'll bet Carrie won't be there," Amy said.

"Don't be so sure. You might think it's queer, but most people on the island actually like Illumination Night."

"Only because there's nothing else to do."

Jill fell silent and kept her eyes on the road. She couldn't, after all, argue with that.

They were late, something Rita always hated. But by the time she'd finished the paperwork for the new listing of the Fullam house that was in a terrible neighborhood, needed many repairs, and would take forever to sell, she'd called Jill and told her to go ahead without her, that she'd hitch a ride with Kyle and meet her there. What Rita hadn't known was that Kyle was going to drive out to Gay Head first and pick up his girlfriend, Carrie, daughter of Sam Wilkins.

Rita leaned against the window of the pickup now, pinned between the door handle and the girl of

Kyle's dreams. She tried not to notice the long, tanned legs that rested against her stubby, freckled ones. She tried not to notice the short shorts or the fact that the girl had on nothing under her white halter top. She tried not to think about what her son did with this girl when the lights were out.

She'd thought about not coming tonight, but Charlie had assured her that business at the tavern would be slow, what with everyone headed for Oak Bluffs. She tuned out the foreplay chatter of the two young people now, rested her head against the vibrating glass, and remembered why she'd decided to come after all: maybe the night would bring up fond memories for Jill, put her in a good mood, and pave the emotional way for Rita to hit her up for a loan. Twenty thousand, to be exact.

"Grandpa, will you buy me a stick?" John Jr. cried above the cacophony of music that rose from the crowd and the band and the laughter that engulfed the darkness in Trinity Park.

Ben looked down into his grandson's huge blue eyes, amazed that at four years old the boy was clever enough to know what he wanted and bold enough to ask. "If you really want one," Ben answered, succumbing to modern society with only slightly less hesitation than an Amish grandfather whose grandson just announced he wanted to go away to college.

John Jr. pulled his warm little hand from Ben's grasp, leaving Ben with an odd sense of loss. "Yes, yes! I want a green one!"

"A green one it is, then," Ben said, using his left hand to grope for his wallet.

"I'll get it, Dad," Carol Ann said as she pushed the stroller up to his side. Ben glanced down at the baby, Emily, and wondered how any kid could sleep through the racket.

He started to say he had a broken arm, he was not helpless, then he looked at his wallet and wasn't quite sure how he'd get at his money using only one hand. "Take it out of here," he said, handing the wallet to his daughter. "And buy a balloon for Emily's stroller."

Carol Ann took the wallet and went to the concession. Her husband moved next to Ben.

"I think I'd go out of my mind if I broke my arm," John said.

Ben stared at him. "Yes, well, that's an option I'm considering."

John laughed. "What are you going to do about your work? Is your helper going to be able to handle it?"

"Some of it. I've been trying to think through the details. He's going to earn his keep, that's for sure."

Carol Ann returned with the kids, John Jr. waving his light stick, and the small family followed the crowd toward the Tabernacle. Ben was beginning to wish he hadn't come; he was tired and he hurt, but he hadn't wanted to disappoint Carol Ann; he hadn't wanted to disappoint John Jr.

They reached the Tabernacle just as the lantern was brought onstage and lit. Cheers roared from the crowd. Ben started to applaud, then realized he couldn't. *What is the sound of one hand clapping?* he remembered hearing somewhere, sometime. Well, he thought now as he watched the revelry around him, apparently the sound is nil. He shifted on one foot and felt slightly foolish for not being able to join in. He wondered how one man could be fifty one day, and two days later feel ninety-five.

Suddenly the night air began to glow. He turned and saw the Japanese lanterns shimmering from the campground houses that encircled them. Reds and yellows and oranges and greens cast their festive colors around the park. John Jr. waved his stick and whooped.

Just then an arm nudged Ben's left side, his good side. "Fall off a ladder, Niles?"

In the rainbow glow of the night, Dave Ashenbach stood beside him, laughing. He carried an orange light stick.

"Something like that," Ben responded.

"You really ought to be more careful. I'm sure those grandkids of yours wouldn't want to see you hurt worse." With that, Ashenbach waved his light stick and ambled off through the crowd.

Ben stared after him, wondering what the hell he had meant. He hadn't seemed surprised to see Ben's arm in a cast. Then again, he hadn't seemed surprised to see Ben at all. If he'd been behind the assault, he might have expected Ben was dead.

He felt a tug on his pocket. "Grandpa? Can we go look at the houses now?"

Ben pulled his eyes from Ashenbach. "Sure, John Jr.," he said, taking his grandson's hand in his left, and beginning the route through the campground.

At the fourth house, Ben spotted Jill. She was standing beside a woman with red curly hair, who looked a lot like Kyle's mother, whom Ben had only seen once or twice.

Jill must have felt his eyes on her, for suddenly she turned around. "Hello, Ben," she said, then noticed the sling. "Good heavens! What happened to you?"

He smiled. The expression on her face seemed genuine. "An unhappy customer."

"I doubt that," Jill replied. "Is your arm broken?"

"Just a small break."

She pointed to the thick bandage that must be showing through the neck of his crew shirt. "Your shoulder's hurt, too."

"Yep. But I'll be on the job tomorrow. What I can't manage, Kyle will."

The redheaded woman turned around. "Did I hear my son's . . . oh, my God, what the hell happened?"

Ben laughed. "You're Rita Blair, aren't you? Well, Kyle doesn't even know about this, but he's in for a lot of bullwork in the next few weeks."

Rita scanned the crowd. "He's around here somewhere. Just look for that floosie girlfriend of his . . ."

"And my daughter," Jill added. "Amy is with them . . ."

"Don't tell me," Ben said, "your son stayed home with his computer."

Jill smiled. "Actually, he's with some friends he met playing volleyball. I think everyone on the island is here."

Ben thought about Dave Ashenbach. "Yep. Apparently there's no way to keep anyone out."

His pocket tugged again. "Grandpa? Can we go now?"

Ben looked down. "In a minute." He glanced back at Jill. "This is my grandson, John Jr."

"He's adorable."

"Thanks. How did your work go?"

"My work? Oh. The photo shoot." She nodded. "It was fine. Hot. Tiring."

"Good. Well, I guess we'd better get moving. I'll be at the house tomorrow, and don't worry about this arm, we'll find a way to meet your deadline."

"Forget about my deadline, Ben. Just make sure you get yourself well."

Ben tipped his baseball cap and went on to the

next group of houses with John Jr., thinking that Jill McPhearson was not at all like most of the celebrities he'd done business with, and that it was nice to have a woman like her be concerned about him.

It was also a little unnerving.

Chapter 17

Jill wandered through the crowd, stopping when people recognized her, pausing when Rita saw someone she knew. In the glow of the lanterns, an odd familiar feeling had surfaced: a feeling that she was home. Her feet were tired, her head buzzed from the tide of voices that ebbed and swelled from the crowd: still, Jill realized she was smiling, and that there was, indeed, something to be said about the comfort of familiarity.

Then she saw Amy cross between the pews of the Tabernacle and head toward her, her face radiant in the light. Amy had, however, removed her vest. Jill winced at the sight of her daughter's young breasts, firm and revealing in the chill of the night.

"Mom, can I go now? Please?" Amy asked as she reached her mother.

"Put your vest on, honey. That tank top is too tight."

Amy sighed and slipped the vest over herself. "Yes, Mother. Anything you say, Mother. Now, can I go?"

"I'm not ready to leave, honey."

"Kyle said he'd take me home. Please, Mom," she continued with a roll of her eyes. "This is so boring."

"I thought you'd have a good time with Carrie."

"I was. We were. But she and Kyle had a fight. She left with somebody else."

Rita appeared at Jill's side. "Let the kids go, Jill. I can catch a ride home with you."

"Well," she hesitated, feeling that no one seemed to understand Amy was only fourteen, yet wanting very badly to let her daughter breathe.

"My kid's responsible," Rita joked. "Honest."

Jill smiled. "Okay," she agreed. "I'll see you at home later."

The look on Amy's face was one of genuine thanks.

"Is it okay if we stop for ice cream?" Kyle asked.

"Frozen yogurt," Amy chided.

"Okay, okay," Kyle said with a laugh. "Frozen yogurt."

"Fat free."

Jill slipped her hands in the pockets of her linen pants and decided that the sparks she saw between them were nothing more than a mother's overactive imagination. "Only if you get chocolate," she answered.

"Great. See ya, Mom."

"Amy?" Jill called after her.

Amy turned around.

"Didn't you get a light stick?"

Amy flipped back her hair, waved, and walked away. It could have been worse, Jill supposed. Amy could have ignored her completely.

"She'll be fine," Rita said, taking Jill's elbow and guiding her toward the Tabernacle. "Look," she said, pointing toward the side of the building. "There's Jesse Parker. Remember him? He works at the post office now."

Jill squinted and saw a group of several men. She couldn't pick out Jesse Parker.

"The guy in the blue T-shirt," Rita said. "I want

to go talk to him. His mother's in a nursing home. I promised to bring her some fudge."

Jill studied the tall, thin man with the high-blood-pressure red face. He looked to be twenty years older than she and Rita; not as though they had grown up together, gone to school together. "You go ahead," Jill said. "I'll wait by the tree over there." She walked to a large oak while Rita went to mingle with the boys.

Settling on the ground at the base of the tree, Jill surveyed the people. Her mind drifted back to the Illumination Nights of years ago—how she and Rita had combed the crowds, how Rita's mother had told them it was the perfect place to find boys, because women always look more beautiful in candlelight.

But the only boys they had ever seen were the boys they saw all year in school, or the boys who belonged to the tourists and weren't interested in the island girls. She smiled now as she thought of Amy's remark earlier tonight. *God, Mom,* her daughter had said, *this is so queer.*

It had not been queer to Jill and Rita when they were fourteen—it had been a very special island event, like the annual regatta or the beach plum festival at the church. It had been something to look forward to, something to do.

Jill wondered if Amy would have felt the same way if she'd grown up on the island, if Illumination Night had been a part of her youth. She picked a brown oak leaf from the ground, and thought about those August nights when she was very young and the lanterns had looked like a thousand fireflies, glowing with magic, sparkling with excitement. She remembered holding her father's hand, walking through the crowds, whispering to him, as though real voices would break the spell.

Once, her mother had come with them. Jill thought she must have been around seven or eight.

Florence packed a picnic basket with cold chicken and deviled eggs, cole slaw and watermelon. Just before dusk they spread a blanket on the beach across from Ocean Park: Mother had not wanted to eat where the other families were clustered together sharing sandwiches and laughter and jugs filled with Kool-Aid. Still, Mother had come.

Jill tried to pull up the memories of the rest of that night, tried to remember what her mother had been like, what her mother had said, what her mother had done.

"Wipe your fingers," Florence said when Jill finished eating her chicken. "Wrap the bones in a towel. Don't throw them in the bag."

Jill dutifully obeyed.

"Can we go to the park now?" she asked, carefully tucking in the ends of the paper towel, the way Mother instructed, so the bones wouldn't fall out.

"Not until the music starts," was the answer.

She remembered sitting very still on the blanket, pretending to watch the surf, yet straining to listen to her parents' conversation, waiting for her mother to say they could go. She was afraid if they didn't hurry, the fireflies would be gone before they got there.

She did not remember the rest of that night, only that it hadn't been as much fun as when she and Daddy had gone alone, as though the magic had vanished.

"It's only because you're growing up," Daddy said the next morning. "Things look different when you're a grown-up."

Jill brushed a few dead leaves from the back of her legs now and wondered why she had been so quick to believe her father. Perhaps it was because she had feared they had not had a good time because of her, because of something she'd said, because of something she'd done. Somehow, she must not have tried hard enough, or surely, her mother would have been happy, their Illumination Night outing more fun.

Jill watched the crowds begin to thin and stayed quietly in her place, as still as a firefly whose light had gone out. She thought about the last excerpt of her mother's diary, about the knowledge she now had of her mother's inner torment, her belief that she was not, did not know how to be, a good mother. It was, in fact, true. But Jill now knew it had not been her fault. Nor had it been her mother's.

Most incredible of all was Jill's father. George Randall must have been a man of great patience, a man with a deeper kind of love for Florence than Jill had been capable of understanding. A kind of love Jill still did not know. If that kind of love could even exist in the bizarre, self-serving world of today.

"Come on, kid," Rita's voice called out. "Let's get out of here. I've had as much folksiness as I can take for one day."

Jill pulled herself from the ground. "Rita," she said as they walked toward the park, toward the Range Rover. "Can we go somewhere and talk? There's something I want to tell you about." She'd decided to tell Rita about the diary. Maybe she'd even show it to Rita. Maybe she could help her deal with this. Maybe Rita, her best friend, could help.

"Sure," Rita answered. "I've got a great idea. Charlie probably closed up early. I know where he stashed a great bottle of single malt scotch. There's something I want to talk to you about, too."

The tavern was dark, the front door locked.

"No problem," Rita said. "I know how to get in the back."

"Break in?"

"Not exactly break," Rita said as she motioned for Jill to follow her. "More like pry."

"Oh, Rita, I don't know . . ."

"Charlie won't care. He loves me, remember?"

Jill got in step behind her and they started toward the alley. The night was as dark as the campgrounds before the lanterns were lit, the path was narrow.

Suddenly a can rattled. Jill stopped. Her heart raced. "Shit," Rita said. "Me and my big feet."

"God, Rita, don't do that again. You scared me to death."

They started walking again, Jill gingerly looking down, as though she could see her feet in the dark. She thought about the few times she'd come down this alley—tagging along behind her father. Then, Jill had known nothing would happen to her. No matter how dark or scary the alley was, she knew her father would protect her. Walking down here had been an adventure then; something to do that was much better than staying in the house, the stuffy, tension-filled house.

As they made their way around back, a shadow fell across the Dumpster. Jill looked up: the back light was on, the way her father had always left it. She almost expected him to be there, too.

Rita went behind the Dumpster and emerged with a crowbar. "Don't look so shocked," she said. "All I have to do is pry off the padlock. There's a hammer we can put it back on with when we leave."

"Charlie never gave you a key?" Jill whispered, then wondered why she was whispering. If Rita wasn't afraid to break in, why was she? After all, it wasn't as though the Edgartown police cruised the back alleys. Besides, if they were caught by the police, Charlie Rollins would never press charges.

"The key was lost years ago. Besides, the lock's all rusted now."

"Isn't there a regular lock? A dead bolt or something?"

"Why? This works fine. Besides, it's not like

there's a high crime rate on the island, remember?"
Rita moved toward the door with the crowbar.

Jill turned her back to Rita and shifted her eyes
around the area, the lookout sentry. She had to admit it was fun being with Rita again, letting herself
fold into Rita's own special brand of mischief.

"Holy shit," Rita whispered, "looks like someone
beat us to it."

Jill turned around. "What are you talking about?"
Her eyes fell to the lock that dangled from the door.

"Someone got here before us."

"Someone broke in!" Jill exclaimed, as though
that wasn't exactly what they were doing.

"Well, hell," Rita said as she started to open the
door, "then I guess this means we're not breaking
and entering."

"But what if someone's in there?"

"Look in the window. Do you see any lights on?"

Jill groaned. A picture of the tabloid headlines
flashed into her mind: *TV personality arrested for
burglary*. She wondered how Addie would get her
out of that one.

"Come on," Rita said. "Don't be such a chicken."

How many times had Rita said those words to
Jill? Jill shook her head. "Okay, okay," she answered, and stepped into the darkness behind Rita.

Rita snapped a switch. Light flooded the kitchen,
awakening a scent of pine cleaner and ammonia.
Shiny aluminum pots hung from poles stretched
across the ceiling; the long, stainless-steel counter
gleamed, the huge cast-iron stove was scrubbed and
tidy, standing in wait for another day, another flurry
of tourists. It did not, in fact, look much different
than thirty, forty years ago, when it was Jill's father
who owned it and Rita's mother who was the waitress.

"See?" Rita asked. "No villains."

Jill shivered.

"Come on. The single malt's in the secret room."

Just as they started toward the pantry closet, toward the hidden door that led to the room, laughter rang out.

They stopped. Rita looked at Jill.

"What?" Jill started to ask.

Rita put her finger to her lips. "Ssh," she whispered. "I think it came from the dining room."

Jill grabbed her arm and motioned to the back door. "I told you . . ."

Rita shook her off and headed for the dining-room door. "If someone's in here," she whispered, "I've got to call the cops."

"Isn't Charlie upstairs?"

"If he is, he must be asleep. Or he would have heard this by now. Follow me."

Jill held her breath, then let it out. Rita was nuts. Rita was crazy. But Jill couldn't let Rita go in there alone. She tiptoed to the dining-room door and looked over Rita's shoulder.

The door opened slowly without a creak. She peeked into the darkness. No one was there.

Laughter sounded again. High-pitched laughter.

Rita put her finger to her lips again, then waved for Jill to follow. They went into the dining room, maneuvering their way through the tables that stood empty, the chairs neatly stacked on top. From outside, the streetlamp cast an eerie glow into the room. Rita pointed to the bookcase beside the fireplace—the other entrance to the secret room.

Slowly, Jill stepped beside her. They pressed their ears to the row of books; from within came the sounds of voices, muffled through the wall. Rita raised the crowbar over her head and signaled Jill to push back the bookcase. Jill hesitated a moment. Rita shot her a look of impatience. Quickly Jill grabbed the third shelf down, the one with the reprints of Dickens, the one she remembered was the trick door.

She pulled back the bookcase as Rita cocked the crowbar. The opening was exposed, as were the intruders.

Jill caught her breath.

"Holy shit, what the hell's going on here?" Rita asked, lowering the crowbar.

But she needn't have asked. It was perfectly evident what was going on. Kyle sat on a table, one hand holding a bottle, the other hand positioned on top of someone's head: someone who was kneeling on the floor in front of him, her mouth deftly sucking his erect penis. That someone, Jill realized as a shock of ice knifed through her body, was Amy.

"Get away from her!" Jill screamed at Kyle as she lunged toward Amy and grabbed her arm, yanking her upright. "Get away from her or I'll kill you!"

"Mom," Amy wailed, the booze on her breath souring Jill's stomach. "Leave me alone."

Kyle zipped his pants and slid from the table. He held up his hands. "No contest," he said.

"Jesus Christ, Kyle," Rita mumbled.

Her face flaming, her heart about to leap from her chest, Jill pushed Amy through the doorway of the secret room. With a firm grasp on her daughter's elbow, she kept pushing—through the dining room, through the kitchen, out the back door. By the time they stepped outside, Jill could not catch her breath.

Amy shook free her arm. "I can't believe how you just humiliated me."

"*You? You* can't believe how *I* just humiliated *you?*"

Amy tucked a wad of hair behind one ear. Jill stepped forward and slapped her across the face. The sound of the sting echoed in the stillness of the night.

Amy's hand flew to her cheek. Her dark eyes—Florence's eyes—turned to steel.

"Leave me alone, you bitch," Amy hissed, and took off through the alley, running.

A tremor tore through Jill's body, engulfing her every muscle, her every nerve. She raised her shaking hands to her face that was now wet with her tears. "God, God," she cried into the darkness. Never had she struck her children. Never. Never. Not with all the problems, not with all the arguments. She had wanted her children to know no violence. She had wanted them to be happy, she had wanted them to feel safe in their home. Yet now she had undone all that. She had become no different from the abusive parents she once reported on, on the streets of Boston, in the houses you'd least expect. She had done it because she had been trying so hard to trust her daughter. She had been trying so hard to stop being so protective, to stop being so smothering, so judgmental, the way her mother had always been with her.

She had tried. But, like Florence Randall, she had failed.

Her thoughts scattered in a million directions, each disconnecting from everything she'd ever believed, from every hope she'd ever dreamed. Nothing made sense. Nothing at all.

"Jill?" It was Rita's voice. "Jill, are you all right?"

Slowly Jill turned and faced her best friend. The friend whose son had just violated her daughter, and subsequently, herself. She wiped the tears from her face and slipped her hands into the pockets. "Get out of my life, Rita," she said quietly, then turned and went back down the alley, her heart filled with a heaviness that she had never known.

Chapter 18

Thankfully, Carol Ann's Nissan was an automatic. Ben balanced the bulk of his right arm as he parked at the Gay Head lighthouse and emerged from the small car. He looked up into the sky: its indigo background was swabbed with its familiar streak of pink; a few gentle, gray gulls glided across it, calling out to awaken their senses, readying their lives for another day.

On the ancient cliffs, Noepe sat, silhouetted against the dawn.

"My friend," Noepe said into the wind, without turning to know it was Ben.

"Noepe," Ben replied, then walked to the old man and squatted beside him. "There has been trouble."

Noepe nodded. "It was expected."

Ben stared off toward the Elizabeth Islands. "I no longer think Dave Ashenbach's the one trying to stop me."

"Do your plans interfere with his land?"

"Not interfere. Just abut it. I don't think even Ashenbach is stupid enough to try to kill me over that."

Noepe folded his arms and closed his eyes, the lines of his face curving toward his long, white ponytail, the bronze patina of age soft on his cheeks.

"You do not sound like a man who is going to give up."

Ben sat on the ground and kicked a small piece of shale from the cliff. "I've thought about it."

"But?"

"But I'm not sure that the attack on me was connected."

"Where did it happen?"

"In my workshop. At home."

"Have you been attacked there before?"

He laughed. "No. Of course not."

Noepe opened his eyes, his gaze fixed on the horizon. "Great books have many thoughts on the theory of coincidence. That there is no such thing. That it is part of the greater plan."

"Do you agree?"

A small smile crept across his salt-white lips. "The question is, do you?"

A lone gull landed on the clay-colored cliffs. It pecked at a sliver of stone and raised its head, its tiny black eyes connecting, for a moment, with Ben's. Then it took flight once again.

"What emptiness inside you are you trying to fill, Ben Niles? Is it the loss of your wife? Are you still trying to replace her being?"

Ben looked at Noepe in disbelief. He had never thought he was creating Menemsha House to replace Louise. He had don it to pass the time. He had done it to do something for the kids. Not to replace Louise.

He quickly blinked and gazed out to sea again, wondering why he felt as though he wanted to cry. He wanted to answer Noepe, but the lump in his throat dared him not to.

"I am sorry if my words upset you," Noepe continued. "But has there been no woman for you since your wife? Has Menemsha House become your woman? These are questions you must answer only to yourself. Only then will you be able to determine if it is worthy of your death."

Ben remained silent, letting Noepe's words linger in the air, float into his thoughts. Perhaps, he realized, that was exactly what he had done: tried to harness a dream to fill his soul, to prove to himself that it had been Louise, not him, who had died. Somewhere along the line his grief had subsided, but Menemsha House had taken on a spirit of its own, tapping into his rebellious nature, rousing his anger to a dangerous place, fueled by his, yes, his emptiness, his loneliness.

"I must leave you now," Noepe said, rising from the rocks and drawing in a deep sea air breath. "The new day has begun." He smiled. "I must again become a boring accountant."

Ben smiled back but did not respond. He listened to the soft sounds of Noepe's moccasins as they tread across the cliffs, moving, without effort, from one world to another. But Ben remained seated, studying the sea, until the sun had climbed in the sky, and the ache in his gut had calmed.

When he arrived to work at Jill's, Ben was surprised that Kyle's truck wasn't in the yard. He'd stayed at the cliffs longer than he'd planned: it was now eight-twenty, and the only vehicle around was that god-awful white Range Rover that looked like it belonged on a safari, ready to hunt down big game, bigger, certainly, than the skunks and raccoons that called the island home.

City people, he muttered under his breath, then remembered how nice Jill had been to him last night, how uncelebrity-like, how civilized. Slipping the car into a space on the street, Ben realized that he missed his old Buick, with its obstinate steering and weighty bulk: a car that you could depend on in a world that had become undependable. He walked around to the back: the house was quiet; Kyle was nowhere around.

Pulling off his baseball cap, Ben scratched his head. Maybe Kyle's mother had told him about the broken arm. Maybe Kyle thought if Ben couldn't work, he wouldn't be needed.

"Damn," he sputtered, and hated the fact he was sputtering like an old man. But if this job was ever going to be finished by Labor Day, Kyle had better get over here. Fast. And it looked as though the only way that was going to happen was if Ben called him.

He went onto the back porch and peeked in the window. Jill sat at the table, a lacy robe around her, her hair uncombed. A mug sat in front of her, which she appeared to be ignoring. Instead, she stared into space, much the same way Ben himself had just done out at the cliffs. He wondered if her problems were as grave as his, and if her dreams—or her life—were at stake.

He hesitated a moment, then raised his good hand and rapped on the window.

She snapped her head up, startled from wherever her thoughts had been. Seeing him, she rose from the table on what looked like wobbly legs, then shuffled toward the door and opened it.

"Good morning," she said, but the day-old mascara encrusted on her lashes and the red webbing that threaded through the whites of her eyes told Ben that her morning definitely was not good.

"Sorry to bother you, but could I trouble you to use the phone?"

"No trouble," she said, stepping away from the door. "Come in. You know where it is."

He nodded and went into the hallway. "I can't figure out why Kyle's not here yet. I thought I made it clear to his mother last night that my broken arm can't hold things up. The show must go on," he said with a chuckle, hoping to ease whatever was on Jill's mind. She was far too nice—and far too pretty, even in her obvious state of disarray—to have such heaviness on her mind.

He picked up the receiver as Jill stepped into the hall.

"Hang up the phone," her voice said, its "good morning" pleasantry now gone.

"Pardon me?"

"I said hang up the phone."

He did not ask her to repeat it again. He'd heard her. Loud and clear. He put the receiver back in the cradle. "Is something wrong?"

"Look, Ben, this is nothing against you. But if the only way you can finish the work here is to have Kyle do it, then I'll have to fire you. That boy will not step foot on my property again."

Ben stared at her. He could not imagine what had happened. He could not imagine why she didn't want Kyle around. Had he ruined something? Stolen something?

"Look, Jill, Kyle's worked for me for a long time. If something has happened . . ."

She folded her arms across the tie of her robe. "It's none of your concern."

"Excuse me, but Kyle is my employee. If one of my employers is upset over something he's said or done, then it damn well is my concern."

Jill was quiet a moment. Then she moved back into the kitchen. "Please," she said so quietly Ben had to strain to hear her, "just go away and leave us alone. I'll see that you're paid in full."

He took off his cap and rubbed the brim between his fingers. "I don't take money for a job not done. And I don't leave a job until it's finished."

He watched as she picked up her coffee mug and pretended to drink from it. She clutched it so hard, her knuckles paled. Coffee spilled over the rim.

Quickly he reached out with his left hand. "God, Jill, you're shaking." He took the mug from her grasp and set it on the table. "What's going on? And what does it have to do with Kyle?"

She looked into his eyes, took a deep breath, then let it out slowly, painfully. "Walk with me down to the water," she said at last. "I'll tell you everything."

Ben wanted to kill him. This was the kid he had spent so much time training, this was the kid he wished had been his son. Now, all he wanted to do was tear him apart, limb by limb, starting with the thing that Kyle hadn't been able to keep in his pants.

He stepped on the accelerator of the Nissan and aimed it toward Beauford Terrace. His heart ached for Jill—a frightened mother, who had witnessed her daughter's innocence crash down around her, shattered in the centuries-old darkness of the 1802 where the ghosts of her ancestors still roamed.

The worst part was, it was Ben's fault. If he'd never allowed Carrie to hang around Jill's while Kyle was working, Amy wouldn't have met her, wouldn't have tried so hard to be like her. It was his fault, goddamnit.

He ripped the Nissan onto the shoulder in front of Kyle's house, got out of the car, stomped up the walk, and pounded on the door. Within seconds, Rita opened it.

"Let me talk to Kyle," Ben seethed, fighting to keep his voice under control and his temples from exploding.

"He's asleep."

Ben pushed past her into the house. "Then I'll damn well go and wake him."

"Hold it right there, mister," she said, grabbing the sling on his arm. "You have no right busting in here. . . ."

"It's okay, Mom," came Kyle's voice from the top of the stairs. "Send him up."

Rita yanked her hand away, exhaled her anger, and disappeared into the kitchen.

Ben tromped up the stairs, his arm throbbing under the white plaster cast, his shoulder pounding where the chisel had been rammed.

In the doorway of one of the bedrooms stood Kyle, wearing pajamas and a pitiful look. Among other things, he was obviously hungover.

"Why, Kyle? That's all I want to know. Why?"

"I'm sorry, Ben. I know I let you down."

"Let me down? Are you crazy? The girl is fourteen, Kyle. *Fourteen*. There are laws against this. Is that what you want? To spend the best years of your life behind bars?"

"She said she was sixteen. Almost seventeen."

Ben banged his hand against the yellowed wall. Plaster crumbled to the floor.

"I was only trying to make Carrie jealous. We had a fight . . ."

Ben snorted. "A fight? You had a fight with your girlfriend so you were trying to show her you didn't need her? Is that how it went, Kyle?"

"Carrie . . ." Kyle began, then shook his head. "Never mind. We had a fight, that's all."

Ben bored his eyes into Kyle. "I can't believe how stupid you are. I can't believe how stupid *I* was for trusting you."

"I didn't fuck her, Ben."

He raised his fist in front of Kyle's face. "Only because you were interrupted."

Kyle shook his head. "That's not true."

"Of course it's true. I wasn't born yesterday." He stared at the boy, his rage still pumping. But Ben didn't know what to do next.

"I suppose this means I'm fired," Kyle said calmly.

He quickly thought about all the work that lay

ahead. Jill's house. The estate on Nantucket. The others. Then he remembered the look on Jill's face. The look of shame, the look of hopelessness. "Yes," he answered before he let himself think any longer. "You're fired, Kyle. Don't bother to come to my house. I'll put your check in the mail."

With that, he spun around, marched down the stairs and out the front door, knowing he had done the right thing, and hoping to hell the pain in his gut would go away.

Rita leaned against the counter in the kitchen, wishing she had a drink, wishing she'd never been born, and wondering if she and her only child would be imprisoned in the same jail.

Jill wanted to go back to Boston.

"You can't," Christopher said when she called him that morning.

"I have to," she answered. She was lying on the bed of her parents' room, the phone cord stretched from the hall, the door closed. Slowly, she told him what had happened. When she finished, he was silent. "I have to get off this island," she said.

"Look, honey, I know this is upsetting, but it's not the end of the world."

"Not the end of the world? Christopher, she's fourteen."

"Kids are faster today. Their world is faster."

"Well I think it stinks."

"So do I. But you have teenagers, Jill. You were going to have to face this sooner or later."

She wove her fingers through the black coils of the cord. "I would have preferred later."

Christopher sighed. "Listen, honey, Labor Day

weekend is only a couple of weeks away. Can you hold out until then?"

"No. I want to leave today."

"It's not that easy. I've made some plans. . . ."

"What plans?"

"With Maurice Fischer. I promised him a weekend on the Vineyard."

Jill squeezed her eyes closed. "I wish you'd talked to me about it first."

"I didn't think it mattered. You knew I was coming for the long weekend. You're coming home with me, remember?"

She opened her eyes and looked past the Boston rocker in the corner, toward the white curtains adrift in the morning breeze.

"Besides," he continued, "won't you need more time to work with Sam Wilkins?"

Sam Wilkins. Her stomach rolled. "If it weren't for Sam Wilkins, Amy wouldn't be in this mess. If I'd never driven her over there to see Carrie—to make *friends* with Carrie, for God's sake—it never would have happened."

"Jill, that's ridiculous."

"Is it? It's because of my damn work that this happened. I sacrificed my daughter for the sake of a story." She didn't add that the story had been his idea. "This is all happening too fast, Christopher. I have a responsibility to my kids. I probably never should have agreed to the *Lifestyles* spread. And I'm not altogether sure L.A. is the right place for them. Certainly not Amy." It wasn't until she said it that Jill realized how much this had been on her mind.

"Wait a minute, Jill. You're overreacting."

His words stabbed her.

"Amy had a small escapade with some island boy," he continued. "Are you going to let that ruin the rest of our lives?"

Her head ached, her mind felt as though it had left her body, her breathing became shallow, painful, labored. *Overreacting?* He thought she was overreacting? It was the same thing he'd said when Jill was upset over Amy's too-mini-miniskirt. Would he feel she was overreacting if Amy were *his* daughter?

"I'm sorry if that sounds a little strong," he continued. "But you've got to think about reality."

Up from her heart, tears rose. "The reality is I want to get off this damn island. I want to come home. I want to go back to work."

"Your work right now is there. I suggest you take a shower, clean up, and track down Sam Wilkins. You need to get your mind on something else, something productive. If you can pull the story together by Labor Day, it will impress the hell out of Fischer."

She didn't answer because she was afraid she would scream.

"Have you talked with Amy since last night?"

"No. She hasn't come out of her room."

"Go easy on her, Jill. This is a tough age for her. And she's facing a lot of changes. Us included."

Jill wondered if there was any age that wasn't tough, forty-three included.

"Now pack up your notebook and go to Sam Wilkins. It will give both you and Amy a chance to cool down."

She turned on her back and stared up at the canopy ceiling.

"Okay?" he asked.

She pressed her hand to her forehead. "Sure," she answered, "I guess."

"It's for the best, honey. Everything will be fine."

They said good-bye, and Jill hung up the phone. She sat on the edge of the bed, rocked back and forth slowly, and realized that even if she wanted to leave today, she couldn't. She hadn't finished weeding out her parents' things, and now there was the problem of making sure the work around here would be done.

The Sam Wilkins story, however, could wait. Right now the most important thing Jill could do was to try to talk to Amy, try to get this out in the open—face the problem, then move past it—the way Florence Randall never would have done.

But first, she had to figure out what the hell she was supposed to say.

She didn't blame Jill for wanting her out of her life. Rita parked her car, walked to the front door of the nursing home, and wondered if oral sex could be considered rape. She had no idea if Jill would press charges, and the worst part was, Rita wouldn't blame her for that, either.

Walking down the long corridor toward Mrs. Parker's room, Rita realized the only person to blame was herself. She was to blame for setting a bad example for Kyle, for being no better role model than her own mother had been, for allowing him to think that screwing the tourists was fine, as long as it got you what you wanted.

She clutched the small box of fudge and knocked on the door of Room 114, not knowing whether Mrs. Parker or Rita was the one who needed cheering up.

"Come in," came a faint whisper.

Rita straightened the front of her short lavender T-dress and went into the room.

The first thing that struck her was how dark it was in there. Dark and stale, with, thankfully, no nursing home urine smell.

"Mrs. Parker? It's me. Rita Blair."

The shadowy bump on the bed responded. "Rita Blair? Oh, my, what a surprise."

Rita navigated around the clutter of chairs and tables. "I brought you some fudge. Penuche."

"How sweet you are, Rita," Mrs. Parker said as the motor of the bed whirred, elevating her head. "I've always said what a sweet girl you are."

A lump rose in Rita's throat. "I hope I didn't wake you."

"Not at all. I was daydreaming. It helps to pass the time."

Rita remembered when the term "passing the time" horrified her, as though people were eager to make the minutes, hours, years fly by, as though they were excited about growing old. Looking at the frail woman in the grayed light now, she supposed that no matter what anyone did, time was damn sure going to pass anyway. Might as well daydream if it took the edge off your problems; might as well stay up all night making fudge.

"Would you like me to open the drapes?" Rita asked. "It's a beautiful day." She set the box on the tray table and walked to the window.

"That would be nice. How is your mother?"

"Fine," she answered, pulling the cord to the traverse rod. Light flooded into the room. She reached over and cranked the window, letting in a gentle, warm breeze.

"I had so many good times with Hazel. Remember the summers you spent with us? Two or three, wasn't it?"

"Three summers," Rita said. She looked at the garden of get well cards thumbtacked to the small bulletin board across from the bed, then sat in a black vinyl chair. "I was seven, ten, and twelve." The Parkers' house had been the one summer retreat she'd enjoyed: Mrs. Parker baked cookies and pies and taught Rita how to make fudge—how to "pass the time," until Rita and her mother could go home.

"I miss your mother," the old woman said.

Rita lowered her eyes to her lap. Two tears spilled out, tiny dark spots of sorrow staining her dress.

Mrs. Parker stretched a blue-veined hand toward her. "What's the trouble, dear?"

Rita shook her head. "No trouble. I guess I miss my mother, too." Until that moment, Rita hadn't known just how much she did miss Hazel—missed having her to talk to, even missed taking care of her. She could have talked to her mother about Kyle and Amy; she could have talked to her about the IRS, about Joe Geissel, about his pain-in-the-ass wife. But somehow, these weren't the kinds of conversations you had by way of Ma Bell. She wondered if that had been the real reason she'd come today: because she'd needed to connect with an older woman, a mother's love.

"I still miss my own mother," Mrs. Parker said.

Rita looked up. "You do?"

She nodded, her pink scalp peeking through her thinning hair. "Imagine that. I'll be eighty-two this year, and I still miss my mother. She's been gone thirty years. Nearly thirty-one." She sighed a shallow, small-lunged sigh.

"Thirty-one years . . ." Rita said.

"Sometimes, when I have problems, I close my eyes and talk to her. She always listens, and I always hear what she tells me to do."

Rita's gaze fell back to her lap.

"What would your mother tell you now?" Mrs. Parker asked.

Raising her head, she smiled. "My mother would tell me I should visit Mrs. Parker more often."

The woman nodded again. "Have a piece of your penuche, dear. It will make you feel better."

.   .   .

Three pieces of fudge and an hour later, Rita walked into the sunlight of the parking lot and knew what she had to do. It was too late to change what had happened between Kyle and Amy, but maybe it wasn't too late to help herself. She would begin by putting an end to the lies.

Chapter 19

The door of the tavern was unlocked: Charlie, thankfully, had come in early.

"Hey, Rita. I didn't expect you until six," he said, wiping his hands on a towel behind the bar. "The damnedest thing happened last night. Someone pried the lock off the back door. I thought maybe someone had broken in. But nothing seems to be missing."

Rita sighed and slid onto a bar stool. "Charlie, we've known each other all our lives, haven't we?"

He frowned. "What's wrong, Rita?"

She closed her eyes and wished that things were different now, that things could have been different years ago. "I need your help." She opened her eyes to see his reaction.

Setting down the towel, Charlie leaned toward her. "Anything. You know that."

The furrows on her brow deepened. "It's about Kyle," she began. "He brought Jill's daughter here last night. We caught them in the act in the secret room."

Charlie's eyebrows raised. "Here?"

She winced and gestured toward the bookcase. "There." She hoped he wouldn't comment that it wasn't the first time the room had been used for such purposes. But Charlie said nothing, as she should have known. He was, after all, a gentleman—something Rita had too little experience with. She squirmed on the stool and wrapped her feet around the legs. "Jill's daughter is only fourteen."

Charlie whistled. "No shit."

"I'm afraid there might be some consequences."

"Jesus," he said with a shake of his head. "What was he thinking?"

"He was thinking about himself. The way most men do." If her words hurt his feelings, he didn't show it. Anyway, Rita reassured herself, he probably knew it was true. "But that's not the point," she continued. "The point is, I'm . . ." Her words choked out, squeezed by the sudden constriction in her chest . . . "I'm scared, Charlie. I don't want my kid to go to jail."

"How can I help? Should I talk to Jill?"

She shook her head. "No. I'm the only one who can help Kyle. But in order to do that, I've got to get my own act together."

Charlie smiled. "I always thought you've been in control of things."

Rita snickered. Mrs. Parker thought she was sweet. Charlie thought she was in control. She rubbed her hand across the shiny mahogany and wondered if anyone ever really knew anyone else. "I'm hardly in control, Charlie. I'm surprised the Vineyard 'grapevine' hasn't learned that yet."

"I don't listen to gossip, Rita."

She narrowed her eyes and studied him. "No, I don't suppose you do. Well, the truth is, Charlie, the IRS is banging on my door, and I haven't got a pot to piss in."

"The IRS? Jesus, Rita. Do you have any more good news this morning?"

"Please, Charlie. This isn't easy for me to ask."

He softened his tone, lowered his voice. "Do you need money, Rita? How much?"

"I was wondering if we could consider it an advance against my pay . . ."

"How much, Rita? I'll do what I can . . ."

"Twenty grand," she said quickly, before she lost her nerve.

Charlie looked like he'd swallowed a quahog, shell and all. "Twenty grand?"

She slid off the stool. "Never mind," she said, "I shouldn't have come." She turned to walk away.

"Rita, get your ass back here."

Rita stopped. She couldn't believe that gentleman-Charlie-Rollins had spoken to her that way. She turned with a half smile. "Get my ass back there?"

He grinned. "Yeah. If you get your ass back here I'll give you the twenty grand. You can pay me back a hundred years from now. I don't care."

Slowly, she edged back toward the bar. "Charlie, do you mean that?"

"Of course I mean it, you idiot. You think I don't give a shit what happens to you?"

Rita swallowed hard. *No,* she wanted to say. *I never thought you gave a shit what happened to me.* Then Jill's words came back to her mind. *I think Charlie is still a little in love with you.*

She ran her hand through her short red curls and wondered if there was any chance that Jill had been right.

It was almost noon before Jill knocked on the door to Amy's room. There was no answer.

She turned the knob and pushed against the door. It didn't open. There was, she knew, no lock on the door: this, after all, had been her room, and Florence would never have allowed it.

"Amy, I don't know what you have in front of the door, but move it. I want to come in. We have to talk."

Silence.

She shoved the door again. It opened only a couple of inches, enough for Jill to see that the solid cherry bureau was wedged against it, that no one lay on the rumpled bed, and that the window was wide open. Beyond the window stretched the arms of an oak tree—limbs close enough, sturdy enough to provide swift escape.

"God," Jill moaned, and pressed her forehead against the door. "Amy. Amy. Where are you?"

She sucked in her breath and gave another heave on the door. The bureau moved enough for her to see the entire room. The entire, empty room.

"No!" she wailed. "Oh, God, no."

Without stopping to summon Jeff's help, Jill bolted from the doorway, bounded down the stairs, and raced out the front door to the Range Rover. Her thoughts whirled. If Amy had run away, she must have gone to Kyle—the boy she probably felt was in love with her, the boy who'd probably insisted she "prove" her love for him.

Jill's stomach rolled over again and again. She snapped on the ignition, punched the shift into reverse, and backed out of the driveway without looking.

Brakes squealed. A horn blasted.

She ignored the car on the road and stepped on the accelerator.

With one fist in her mouth and tears streaking her face, Jill wound the vehicle through the small, one-way streets, out toward Edgartown Center, out toward Rita's house. She had no idea how long Amy had been gone—she could have left right after they got home last night. But wouldn't Rita have called?

Wouldn't Rita have let Jill know her daughter was safe?

"Damn you, Rita Blair," she cried as the traffic toward the center grew more congested and the little patience she had shortened.

At Main Street, she turned right and headed for West Tisbury Road.

It was there that she saw her: among the clutter of tourists walked Amy, her sneakers padding along the brick sidewalk, a duffel bag slung over one shoulder. Her head was bent; her hair was pulled back in a ponytail. She looked much younger than her fourteen years.

Jill jammed on the Range Rover's brakes in the middle of the road. She blew the horn. Amy paid no attention.

Jill ripped open the door and jumped from the vehicle.

"Amy!" she shouted. "Amy, come back here."

Amy stopped, turned around, and stared at her mother.

"Lady, move your car," someone shouted.

"Get out of the way," another driver ordered.

She marched up to Amy and stopped herself from grabbing her arm. "Where are you going?"

"None of your business." Her defiant eyes locked on Jill's. But she did not attempt to walk away.

"Amy, honey, please," Jill managed to say. "Please, don't do this."

Another horn blew.

"Please tell me where you're going."

"I'm going somewhere where I'm wanted."

Where I'm wanted. Her daughter's words plunged to her heart. Why didn't Amy know she was wanted? *Jill* had been the daughter who had not been wanted. Jill, not Amy.

"You're holding up traffic, Mother."

Jill bit her lip. "Please come home, honey. We need to talk."

"There's nothing to talk about."

"There's everything to talk about. I'm sorry I slapped you."

Amy reached up and brushed her hand across her cheek.

"Please, get in the truck. We don't have to go home. I know a place we can talk. If you want to leave after that, you're free to go." Jill had no idea where those words were coming from. Was she telling Amy it was all right for her to leave? Was she setting her fourteen-year-old daughter loose on the street with her permission?

A shiver ran through her as another car blasted its horn.

"Lady, come on!"

Amy glanced over to the car. "Okay. We'll talk. But don't expect me to change my mind."

"Were you going to Kyle's?" Jill asked as they sat on the rocks under the pier, out at the Edgartown Lighthouse.

"No."

"To Carrie's?"

Amy didn't answer. She lifted her eyes. They were glazed with tears. "I had nowhere to go, Mom. I was too embarrassed to go to Carrie's. And Kyle doesn't want me."

Jill picked up a shell. With its ragged edge, she carved lines in the sand. "I want you, honey. I have always wanted you, even before you were born." She wished she could tell Amy about her mother's diary; she wished she could share that Jill had been the unwanted child. But no matter what growing up Amy had done last night, she was still a child, and should not have to deal with her mother's problems, her mother's insecurities. The way Jill had been forced to do, without even realizing it.

"He gave me vodka, Mom. That's the only reason I did that."

"You didn't have to drink it, Amy. I'd hoped you'd respect yourself more than that."

Amy crunched her knees to her chest, folded her arms on them, and buried her face. "Carrie had some. They were drinking all night at the Tabernacle."

"And you wanted to be like Carrie."

"They had a fight. Carrie took off. Kyle was pissed, Mom. Then he got really drunk."

Jill sighed, half wishing she had some of Rita's scotch now, something to soothe her own pain. "This isn't about Kyle. This is about you, Amy. About us. I'm really sorry I slapped you. I was so shocked. I guess I just don't want you growing up too fast."

"Maybe you don't want me to grow up at all."

"I don't know," she answered, trying to be as honest as she could, trying not to be evasive, the way her mother surely would have been. "Maybe you're right."

A seagull landed on a nearby rock. "Are you okay, honey?" Jill asked.

Amy shook her head. "It all happened so fast, Mom," she whispered without looking up. "Kyle said he had something better than ice cream. He said he knew where we could go. . . ."

Jill clenched her jaw. It was difficult not to interrupt Amy, to restrain herself from jumping up and screaming that she wanted to kill the son of a bitch.

Then, Amy's tears flowed. "I was scared, Mom. Part of me wanted to do it, but part of me was so scared."

Jill reached out and put her arm around her, biting back her own tears, holding in her own pain. "It's okay, honey. It'll be fine."

"I get so confused, Mom. I hate being fourteen."

"The only thing that matters is that you don't hate yourself."

"I hate Kyle."

Jill pulled her daughter close to her. "It's not right to hate anyone, Amy. I'm sure Kyle has his own problems." She wanted to bite off her words before she'd said them. "All that matters is that you're okay." She stroked her daughter's long hair, her thick, dark hair, Florence's hair, and wondered if her own mother had ever held her, had ever tried to heal her wounds.

"I'm not okay," Amy sniffed and raised her head. "I'm beat. I was awake all night."

Jill tilted her head down so it touched Amy's. "Me, too, honey. You should have come to my room." She rocked her daughter slowly. "No," Jill added, "that's not right. I should have come to yours."

They sat by the lighthouse a few moments longer, perched on the rocks in a delicate mother-daughter balance.

"Maybe I'll give Ben a hand," Jeff said.

Jill had finished fixing him lunch—a lunch that had been strangely silent, with Amy asleep, at last, upstairs, and Jill moving about in weak, post-crisis exhaustion. She was not sure if Jeff knew what had happened last night: she only knew that they had returned to find the bureau had been mysteriously removed from the doorway to Amy's room, set, once again, against the wall where it belonged.

She looked out the kitchen window at Ben, who stood at the sawhorse with an adze, trying to smooth the surface of a replacement living-room beam.

"Honey, that's a nice idea, but I'm not sure there's much you can do."

Jeff scraped the chair against the wood floor and stood. "Maybe I can learn," he said brightly. "Maybe he'll teach me." He walked to Jill and kissed her cheek. "I'm a computer whiz, Mom. How hard can a little manual labor be?" He smiled and went out the door, the screen smacking behind him.

Jill touched her face where her son had just kissed her. The kiss said it all: that he knew what had happened, that he was trying to make up for the pain his sister had caused Jill.

She wondered if her life would have been easier if her brother had lived; if he could have been there for her mother when she and Jill had difficult times. Then she wondered how Florence would have been different if Robbie had not been killed, and if Jill would never have been born, or conceived, at all.

She looked out the window at her son now, who was holding the antique tool the way Ben was showing him, who was trying so hard to make everything right. She was so lucky, she knew. So lucky that her life had not been as empty as her mother's.

Cleaning up the dishes, Jill decided she would not go visit Sam Wilkins today. The thought of seeing Carrie was too much: she might be tempted to tell her to keep her sex-starved boyfriend to herself.

Tomorrow, or the next day, would be soon enough to start the story. She could certainly put off Christopher until then, maybe tell him Sam was off-island for a few days. She switched off the coffeepot, took a last look through the window at Jeff, and decided there was only one thing she wanted to do today, only one person she wanted to share her pain with. Maybe if she learned more about her mother, she would not feel so alone. Jill turned from the kitchen, went into the hall, and climbed the stairs to the widow's walk.

September 6, 1959

It's hard to believe my daughter has started school. I didn't want her to go. George didn't ask if I wanted to walk her: he knew what my answer would be. It was hard, to see them set off together, her little hand in his. She knew she was safe, though. She knows she'll always be safe with her father. She would not be safe with me. Never with me. Maybe today I'll make her a new dress. I'll use the dark green wool plaid: she looks so pretty in green. It matches her eyes.

Jill ran her palm over the page, wishing she could remember the dark green wool plaid, thinking that life had been easier then, when people simply lived day to day, and did their best to get by. Even Florence hadn't seemed to realize her behavior was sick; it was as though she accepted the situation as it was, accepted that she could never feel close to her daughter. And yet, there was the dress, and all the dresses that came after that, those ugly, homemade dresses that Jill had detested so.

She held up the diary and pressed it to her breast. "Mother," she whispered, "I am so sorry for you."

It was several moments before she could continue, before she could regain her composure, before she could harness her emotions and put some objectivity between herself and the diary. When she did, the world of her youth cracked open, viewed not from her memory, but from . . . the other side.

Sept. 17, 1960

I was so nervous today. I needed to pick beach plums—their time is growing short. But George had to work, of course, and with Mother Randall gone . . . I didn't know what to do with her, with Jill.

George told me to take her with me. I didn't think I could. What if something happened? He said nothing would. He said I had to try.

So I tried. I gave Jill her own basket, and we walked down to the lighthouse. The beach plums aren't as good there as they are in Tisbury, where I usually go. But I couldn't travel too far from home, not with Jill along.

We only picked two baskets, because I didn't want to be gone too long. It isn't nearly enough for all the jelly I need to make. But the best part was that George was right. Nothing happened. I think Jill had a good time. I'm not sure if I did—I was too nervous to think about that, I was too nervous when I realized this was the first time we've been alone together, out of the house, where things can happen.

Maybe we'll go back tomorrow.

They had, Jill remembered, gone back the next day. And every weekend until the berries passed their time. She remembered feeling clumsy, not knowing what her mother had expected her to do, not knowing what to say, afraid she would say something wrong, or pick the wrong berries, and her mother would never let her go again.

She remembered she kept very quiet and tried very hard to pick the best.

She did not know if she'd done a good job—she didn't recall that Florence ever said. She only knew that each year, at the end of August, when the berries replaced the blossoms, they began their weekly ritual—mother and daughter, their baskets in tow, working side by side in awkward silence.

Jill looked down at her fingers now and remembered the sharp sting of the thorns of the beach plum branches and that she had never dared complain.

Nov. 25, 1963

    We had a fight today. I try so hard to never raise my voice to Jill, but today she gave me no choice.

    Today was President Kennedy's funeral. Schools were closed—everything was closed— and Jill wanted to watch it on television. I would not let her. She is only ten years old. Too young to see such misery, too young to know of death.

    "If you don't let me watch it I'll hold my breath until I turn blue," Jill shouted at me.

    I was so taken back I didn't know what to say. I didn't know what to do. In my mind I pictured Robbie, bleeding on the sidewalk, his little cheeks, his little mouth, slowly turning blue.

    It wasn't fair. It wasn't fair for her to say that. It wasn't fair and it made me even angrier.

    I went into the sewing room and got my big pinking shears. Then I went back into the living room, walked behind the television, and cut the electrical cord.

    After I put the shears away I decided to make pea soup and corn bread for dinner. George said he was taking Jill for a walk. I have no idea if they went to someone else's house to watch the funeral, and I don't want to know.

    When I heard them go out the front door, I sat down at my kitchen table and cried. I cried and cried, hoping the hurt would go away. It did not.

    I don't know if what I did was right; I never know if what I'm doing is right.

Jill lifted her head, remembering the argument. George had taken Jill to the tavern, where they'd watched the funeral on the black-and-white television with the small, round screen that he kept in the secret room. He made Jill promise she wouldn't tell, so her mother wouldn't get upset.

She sunk her teeth into her lower lip and forced herself to remember going home that day. There had been no visible tears that stained her mother's cheeks—only her mother, who, as usual, stood at the stove, her head bent in concentration.

If Jill had seen her cry, perhaps life would have been much different.

But Florence could not let that happen, for Florence was trying to be a good mother, the only way that she knew how, the same way Jill was trying now: mother and daughter, daughter and mother, caught in different times, bound by different rules.

She felt her anger toward her mother slowly begin to lift. Florence Randall no longer seemed to be the tension-riddled, overprotective, critical mother. She now was Florence Randall, the woman, the person. The woman who had cried after George and Jill left the house that day—because she had not wanted her daughter to witness the pain of death.

With hurt in her heart, Jill forced herself to return to the diary. The excerpts were spotty—often months passed before another passage was written; each time, it had to do with Jill. Page after page, she continued the journey, lost in the world of her mother, lost in another generation when intimacies were left unsaid, and showing love was never done.

And then, the mood shifted.

February 8, 1965
Jill brought her friend Rita home from school today.

Rita. Jill stopped a moment and caught her breath. Rita. Had it really been Rita's fault that Kyle and Amy had done what they'd done? Had she really told Rita to get out of her life?

She shook off her thoughts and went back to reading.

> *Rita is an odd girl, with tasteless red curls all over her head. She laughs very loudly, not the way I was taught to laugh. I've heard so many things about her mother. I wonder if Rita will turn out like her. Or if she already is. I really wish Jill would find someone more suitable to be her friend. The kids today grow up so much faster than when I was a girl. I hope Rita doesn't get Jill into any trouble.*

Jill sighed and wondered if she should call Rita. She was her best friend. Had been. Always would be, whether or not they talked. She tried to picture Rita's reaction if she let her read the diary, if she saw her mother's description of her. But Jill wasn't sure what Florence had meant by the lines "I've heard so many things about her mother. I wonder if she'll turn out like her." Had something been wrong with Hazel Blair? Or had Florence only been referring to the fact that she had to raise a child alone and had to work to earn a living?

She pushed her thoughts aside and turned the page. The excerpts continued—references to Jill's school years, the time she played Mary Magdalene in the church play, the first date she ever had.

> *She is so smart in school,* one excerpt read. *She made a wonderful science project about volcanoes. I don't know how she figured it out.*
> *Sometimes I wish we lived in New York again,* another commented. *I would take Jill to the fashion shows. She is much more beautiful than any model I've ever seen. Mother would*

*be jealous. Myrna would be, too, that my
daughter is the most beautiful. The smartest.
And the sweetest.*

Suddenly Jill realized she was reading all the
things her mother never told her: that she was
pleased, that she was proud, and that . . . and that
she loved her.

And then the warm feelings melded into guilt.

January 30, 1970
   *Jill came home from school tonight and an-
nounced she wants to go to college. Boston
University. At first I didn't like the idea. The
city is unsafe, but she doesn't know that yet.
Then, the more I thought about it, I changed
my mind. I am glad she wants to leave here. I
want her to have a full life, a good life. I want
her to be happy. I don't want her to end up
with a life like mine. I don't want her to end up
like me.*

A soft little moan crept from Jill's throat. She
turned the page and read on through the tears that
now flowed freely.

July 22, 1970
   *I knew that girl would be nothing but trou-
ble.*

Jill blinked. She rubbed the wetness from her eyes.
She frowned. *Trouble?* Quickly she scanned the
page. Then she forced herself to begin again, to start
at the top. She forced herself to read the words
slowly, carefully. Because she couldn't believe what
she had just read.

*I'm sure George never expected me to find
out. How often do I go to the tavern? But I
needed money to pay the window cleaner, and
he had forgotten . . .*

*I don't think anything has hurt this much
since my Robbie was killed. I would never have
believed it, but I saw it with my own two eyes,
and heard it with my own two ears.*

*They were inside the secret room, but he'd
left the door from the kitchen open.*

*"If you're going to have a baby, you're going
to need some money," he said, clear as day.
"Two thousand dollars should be enough."*

*My heart stopped beating. Two thousand
dollars? Why was he giving away two thousand
dollars? And who was going to have a baby?*

*I was glad no one else was in the kitchen. I
would have been so humiliated if anyone else
heard.*

*Then I heard a small, familiar voice say,
"Thank you," then I stepped back into the pantry so I wouldn't be seen.*

*That's when she came out. The one who is
going to have the baby. The one who my
George just gave two thousand dollars to. Rita
Blair. With the horrible hair and the trailer-
park laugh. Rita Blair has taken two thousand
dollars from my husband. Because she is going
to have his baby.*

I hope she dies.

Jill slammed the diary closed. Her pulse raced.
Her father? Rita? No, she thought, it couldn't be
true. She opened the book again and looked at the
date. July, 1970.

The summer of 1970. The summer after high
school graduation.

Nausea flooded through her. Her hands grew

damp, her heart numbed. That was why Rita had lef the island! She had been pregnant, pregnant with . . . Kyle?

The boy who had just had sex with Amy? The boy who, apparently, had been conceived by Jill's own father?

Conceived by Jill's father.

White heat of reality flashed on her cheeks.

Her mouth dropped open.

She tipped her head back and wailed.

Then she leaped from the floor, grabbed a half-filled trash bag, and vomited into it, retching out the sour bile, heaving up the sickening betrayal that meant Kyle Blair was her half-brother.

Chapter 20

She had to get to work.

She could not stay in the house a minute longer, a second longer.

Jill quickly brushed her teeth, scrubbing the truth from her soul, erasing the disgust.

With shaking hands, she tried to put on makeup. Blush smeared pink across her face: she slammed the brush into the sink and rubbed the color off.

She looked at herself in the full-length mirror. *Linen crop top and capri pants,* was all her mind could deal with among her tossed and disoriented thoughts.

Quickly she changed her clothes. If she was going to see Sam Wilkins, she had to look her best.

She grabbed her sandals. Her heart pounded so hard she had to sit on the edge of the bed to lace them.

Suddenly she stopped.

I can't do this, she thought. *I will have a nervous breakdown at his front door. I will explode into tears. I cannot go on as though everything is all right.*

MY BEST FRIEND SLEPT WITH MY FATHER.

She closed her eyes and panted, trying not to picture her father and Rita . . . where? She jumped from the bed and stared at the mattress. There? There, on the bed where he and Florence slept?

MAYBE IT WAS IN THE SECRET ROOM.

"No!" she shouted, burying her hands in her face. "No, I will not think about it. I can't. I can't."

She tore her hands away. Her eyes darted around the room. Her notebook was downstairs. At the rolltop desk. In the living room.

She hurried into the hall, raced down the stairs, and flew into the living room.

She stopped. Jeff stood there, on a ladder, helping a man she'd never seen before hoist a beam into place.

"Jill," Ben asked, from where he stood beneath them. "Is everything all right?"

She nodded quickly and bent to finish lacing her sandal. "I'll be at Sam Wilkins's," she announced without looking up.

Then she grabbed for her notebook. "I'm going to do some work."

The ride to Gay Head was erratic as Jill alternated between frenzied accelerating and hypnotic steering. Somewhere along West Tisbury Road, her thoughts began to settle. She looked off toward the beach and noticed a magnificent osprey nest: a home of twigs atop a high pole, alone in its quest for life, alone, but surviving.

It was then that Jill realized she no longer was alone, the way she had been as a child. She had Christopher, she had the children. She had a wonderful career ahead of her—as long as she didn't fight it, as long as she didn't let the past become her trap.

She decided now that it shouldn't matter what had happened, or what was going to happen. She had trusted her father, she had trusted Amy, she had trusted Rita. In less than twenty-four hours, all that trust had been shattered. Florence had felt that nowhere was safe. No matter how much she had tried to protect Jill—had tried to protect herself—nowhere had been safe.

But Jill was luckier than that. She knew what was safe.

As she gripped the wheel and kept going straight, she vowed to herself that nothing would screw up her life, that no one—not her daughter, her best friend, or her father's memory—was going to change that.

And if it meant getting the best damned story that would spin Maurice Fischer's head and blow Lizette French off her four-inch heels, then that was exactly what Jill was going to do.

"Jill McPhearson," Sam said as he greeted her at the door. "What a pleasant surprise."

She forced her muscles to ooze with her audience smile, her camera glow. "Hello, Sam. I'm sorry to stop by without calling, but I need your help." *Your daughter's boyfriend violated my daughter, and you owe me,* she'd wanted to say. But Jill had decided there would be time for that later, if Sam didn't comply . . . time for the media to twist his comeback into a scandal wracked with illicit adventures and statutory rape—a scandal in which Jill would find a way to dump Sam squarely in the middle.

The media has power, she reminded herself. *And I am the media.*

"In fact," she added as she shook back her hair and looked directly into his rock-star blue eyes, "I think we can help each other."

He leaned against the door frame and folded his burly arms across his still-taut stomach. "Tell me more," he said with a grin.

She cleared her throat and held up her notebook. "I want to do a story on you. If you're serious about making a comeback, you'll see this as your golden opportunity."

"I don't give interviews anymore."

"I understand that. I also think we both know enough about the business to know that without some positive publicity, you can kiss your chances good-bye." If she'd learned one thing from Addie, surely it was that.

"Not necessarily. I used to have an agent who said, 'It doesn't matter what they're saying about you, as long as they're talking about you.'"

"And has that theory helped you over the past few years?"

His slow smile broadened. "Touché. But I really don't think that exposure in the Boston market will exactly make my star soar again."

"What if it's more than Boston? What if it's national?"

His eyebrows raised. "Are you making a career move?"

"Perhaps."

"And my story will help you get there?"

"As I said, I think we can help each other."

He studied her face. His eyes drifted over her body. Jill was determined to stay relaxed, to not flinch. She arched her back slightly, in a not-so-innocent flirtation. If that's what it would take, she'd let him think it would work.

"You're a persistent woman, Jill," Sam said. "Doing my story must be important to you."

"It is."

"Perhaps it wouldn't have to be strictly business."

"It would."

"For sure?"

"For sure."

His eyes narrowed. "Too bad."

"I'm sure that's my loss," she replied, carefully blinking her eyes, tossing another lure.

He laughed, then stepped out of the doorway. "Okay, Jill, we might as well get started."

"Do you mean it?"

"We can walk down to the beach. I don't want to disturb my guests."

Jill remembered Isham and wondered if he was still here with his entourage of strangely attired friends.

"Do you have an angle in mind?" he asked as they crossed the dune toward the narrow wood stairs that led down to the beach.

"Absolutely," Jill answered. "I want to start by exposing the truth. Did you kill your wife?"

Sam didn't respond until they reached the base of the long stairs, until they stepped onto the beach. "Do you have a conscience, Jill? Or have your edges been sharpened by your career?"

Of course I have a conscience, she wanted to reply. *It's Rita who doesn't seem to have one.* She shook out the sand that sifted into her sandals. "What kind of a question is that?"

"A straightforward one. Like the one you asked."

"I'm the reporter. I'm the one who's supposed to ask the questions."

They stood for a moment, Sam looking at the sea, Jill looking at him, wondering if there was any way that this was going to work. "Let's go to the left," she said. "Toward the cliffs."

"It's rocky there."

"But there aren't many people." She started to move ahead, then stopped. "Have you ever been there?"

"I've always said, why walk on rocks when you can glide on sand?"

She laughed and urged him to follow. "Come on. It's beautiful there. I haven't done this in years." But as she started moving toward the cliffs, Jill wished she could change her mind. This was, after all, a favorite place that once she and Rita had. She squeezed her eyes against the sun, against her pain. She stumbled on a rock.

Sam's arm quickly righted her. "See?" he said. "It's too rocky. Let's go the other way."

Jill looked at the water's edge: it was far enough out. There would be plenty of time to walk to the point, before the tide came in. She loved the cliffs; the view of the lighthouse from below. She was not going to let memories of Rita ruin it for her. She was not going to let Rita ruin her future, the way it had ruined her mother's.

And right now, Sam Wilkins was her future. In order to get his story, she needed to show strength. She needed to prove she could take risks.

"I thought you were a risk taker," she said with a smile.

He returned her grin, then stepped forward. She fell into stride beside him, navigating the rocks.

"Have you ever lost everything, Jill?" he asked suddenly.

She looked down at her feet, hugging each rock around her toes. "I thought I did when my ex-husband left. Then I realized I had my children. And I had myself."

"Ah," Sam said as he reached down and picked up a small dark stone. A perfect band of white was ringed around the top. Jill wanted to tell him it was a "lucky stone"—an ancient Indian omen. But she didn't want to interrupt his thoughts. He studied the stone, then drew back his arm and tossed it into the waves. It skipped across the water, then disappeared from sight.

"When my wife had the accident," he said, his

eyes fixed on the spot where the stone had sunk, "Carrie tried to kill herself."

Jill was glad she was walking beside him, so he couldn't see the stunned expression on her face. Her instincts told her she should open her notebook and take out her pen. Instead, she kept walking.

"My daughter was a crack addict," Sam continued.

Again, Jill hesitated. "I didn't know that. I'm sorry."

He stretched his arms, to equalize his weight among the rocks. "She'd run away. I hired an investigator to find her. He called late one night to say that Carrie was in a crack house outside of L.A."

The breeze grew stronger as they neared the point. Jill paused a moment, and reclipped the hair at the nape of her neck.

"My wife didn't know anything until she took the call. She jumped in her car and sped down the highway."

Jill caught up to him again. "So your wife wasn't tearing off after an argument with you, as the tabloids reported." She didn't add that they'd also said there was a chance that Sam had tampered with her brakes.

"There had been no argument. I wasn't home."

"How long ago was this?"

"Almost seven years," his voice said with the slightest break. "Carrie was twelve."

She stopped. Even the image of Sam's reckless daughter and the hurt that she had caused did not make this right, did not make this fair. She had been twelve. Just a little girl. "Oh, God, Sam, how awful."

He slipped his hands in the pockets of his jeans and continued moving forward.

"Why didn't you tell the truth?" she asked.

"Surely it would have ended the speculation. Your career wouldn't have collapsed . . ."

"I had to protect my daughter."

As Florence had tried to protect her. As she had tried to protect Amy. "So you lost everything."

"Nearly."

"But now you're planning a comeback . . . a world tour. That will cost millions, won't it?"

"Of course. I have backers for that. But I'm not talking about money. What I really lost, Jill, was something inside myself. Something in here." He clutched his fist to his chest. "I've written many songs about it. We'll go into the studio when I return to L.A. The tour will begin after the first of the year." He bent and picked up a piece of shell, then tossed it into the sea.

Jill cleared her throat, trying to hold back her enthusiasm, trying to hold back the excitement that she, indeed, had herself one hell of a story. "You just threw out a perfectly good piece of wampum, Mr. Wilkins."

He turned to her and smiled. "Excuse me?"

"Wampum. The Indians used it as money. The purple and white shred of the inside of an oyster shell."

"Would it have bought back my career?"

She grinned. "Maybe. On the island, maybe."

They rounded a curve. Ahead loomed the cliffs, as tall as a three-, maybe four-story building, majestic with their striations of black and white and rust, their marbleized facade staring across the water, as they had done for centuries.

"Incredible, aren't they?" Jill asked.

Sam shrugged. "You've seen one rock, you've seen them all."

She laughed. "The Gay Head cliffs aren't rock, Sam. They're soft. They're clay."

He scowled.

"Come on. I'm an old hand at this." She climbed over several boulders, gingerly stepping from one rock to another, not caring about the demise of her two-hundred-dollar sandals. And then, she touched the cliff. "Look," she said, bending down to touch the red clay. "Have you ever seen anything more magnificent?"

"No," Sam replied into the wind. But he wasn't looking at the cliff before him; he was looking at Jill.

She ran her finger over the smooth, supple finish of the clay, trying to ignore his look. "The Wampanoags own the face of the cliffs," she said. "It is their heritage."

He reached out and touched her arm. "Did we come here for a history lesson or an interview?"

She kept her eyes fixed on the clay. "We are all products of history, Sam. This is a part of mine." Then she turned to him abruptly. "Why are you willing to tell the world about Carrie now? Do you no longer need to protect her?"

He touched the cliff where her hand had been. "Carrie wants this for me."

Jill suspected Carrie wanted it for herself. She suspected his daughter would forever love the publicity. She watched his hand as it probed the clay, as it unearthed a sparkling vein.

"Fool's gold," she said. "The cliffs are loaded with it."

"All that glitters?" Sam asked.

She smiled, then looked to the top. "There's the lighthouse," she said. The deep rust-colored lighthouse blended with the shades of the clay, standing, as it had for nearly two centuries, overlooking the water, a watchtower for those at sea, flashing one red beacon, one white.

"And around the next bend the tourists are lined up at the telescopes."

"So you are an islander."

"Enough. Do you think they can see us?"

"No. It's too steep."

"Look," he said, "more fool's gold." He stepped over the rocks to a hollow in the cliffs, a shallow cave sculpted by nature within the clay.

Jill followed. When she reached him, he pulled her inside, his face close to hers, hers, to his. "You haven't asked where I was that night," he whispered. "You haven't asked why I wasn't home."

"Does the world need to know?"

"I need to tell it. I had been at the studio. A late-night session. About the time my wife's car went off the road, I was making love to a beautiful young girl. Since then, the guilt has been overwhelming. Until now."

He leaned down. His mouth found hers. She tasted his lips—their fullness, the salt, the sea air. His hand rested cool against the warmth of her midriff, beneath her top. Suddenly she ducked from his grasp and held up her hand.

"Do you see this diamond, Sam? Don't be confused. This is not fool's gold."

Sam smiled. "You are a beautiful woman, Jill."

She looked toward the waves. They moved closer against the rocks. "Tide's coming in," she said. "We'd better head back. Let's take the long way, up through the dunes. If you're lucky, I'll treat you to some sassafras root."

As she traversed the rocks and headed toward the dunes, Jill's excitement was difficult to restrain. She had all the makings of a dynamic story—the kind Maurice Fischer would love, the kind that would seal the RueCom deal.

She only wondered what the cost would be to Carrie, and then wondered why she should care.

.   .   .

Later that night when she talked to Christopher, Jill refused to tell him the details. "It's going great," was all she said. "And there's something else—Sam is having a huge Labor Day picnic. We're invited."

"Maurice will be with us."

"Maurice, too."

She hung up the phone and slept better than she'd ever imagined she could.

Chapter 21

The Wednesday before Labor Day weekend, Jill sat at the desk in the living room, trying to ignore the strong scent of fresh paint and the sounds of sweeping brushes coming from the dining room. After several meetings with Sam, she finally had enough for a story. She compiled her notes now and roughed out the visuals. It would be Fischer's decision whether the segment should appear on *Good Night, Boston* or be saved for their syndicated show. Jill thought it would be a smash for their premier—proof that Christopher Edwards and Jill McPhearson would be viable competition on the national scene.

And though her years of training told her she should get an all-important confirmation of Sam's "confession," she then remembered she was no longer a street reporter, bound by street reporters' rules.

As she chewed the tip of her pen, her gaze drifted to the ceiling. The new beams were in place, looking every bit like the original ones. Incapacitated or not, Ben Niles had made sure the work on the house was perfect and, thankfully, almost complete. Jill knew that Jeff had been a big help to Ben, and for that she was grateful. It was wonderful to see at least one of her children with a focus, a purpose, unlike Amy who went to the beach alone every day, and sat in somber unhappiness each night at dinner. For both the kids' sakes, Jill was eager for them to return to their schools, their normal lives. As if anything would ever be normal again.

She still, however, had to decide what to do about the contents of the house. Any lingering thought that she might call the church women was now impossible. What if they had known about her brother? What if they knew the truth about Kyle?

Rita may have known someone who could take care of the house, but she could not call her either. Jill's stomach still felt sick at the thought of her friend, and of her friend's son, her father's son.

She pushed the thoughts from her mind and looked around the room, at the antique furniture, the scrimshaw humidor, the curio table filled with her great-great-grandfather's whaling hook, his tavern record book, the inkwell and quill pen, the gold pocket watch. Jill knew these things were more than memorabilia of an era gone by—they were valuable, but not to her. She knew that all she had to do was look up an estate liquidator in the yellow pages; still, she procrastinated. Anyone she called would probably have known her parents, and the less contact she had with islanders now, the better.

"When we're done here we only have to put the whale in place," Ben's voice drifted from the dining room. "Would you like to do that for me, Jeff?"

"Sure," Jill heard her son reply. "Where does it go?"

"In the glass over the front door. We'll replace the block that's there."

Jill bent her head and returned to her notes. The house was almost complete; her reason for being here nearly over. Christopher and Maurice Fischer would be here Friday, and Monday they would load up the Range Rover and get back to her real life, where no mothers or brothers or halfbrothers were lurking, and no diaries existed.

All she had to do was find someone to come in and clean out the junk. She wished there was someone she could trust to ask.

"I couldn't have done this without you, Jeff," Ben's voice drifted again from the next room.

Jill sat up straight. Ben Niles. Why hadn't she thought of him before? She rose from the desk and went to the doorway of the dining room. "Ben?" she asked. "I have a problem you might be able to help me with."

He had a wooden stick in a can of paint and stirred with his left hand in an awkward, spastic motion.

"I will if I can," he said as he looked up at Jill, his soft gray eyes set in a smile.

"You've seen everything in the house. I'd like to turn it over to someone—an estate liquidator or someone. But I don't know anyone appropriate on the island."

He paused. "You're going to get rid of everything?"

"Yes."

"You don't want to sell it furnished?"

Jill frowned. She hadn't thought of that. "Well, I suppose . . . I don't know. Surely the next owners wouldn't want the personal things. Pots, pans, the sewing machine . . ."

"I can ask around."

She hesitated. "No. There's no need. I just thought maybe you knew someone . . ."

"Tell you what. I'm going to Nantucket tomorrow. I've got to try and put off my next job until this damn arm is healed. It's quite a cottage, and I know the people are into antiques. Maybe they'd be interested in some of the things."

This wasn't exactly what Jill wanted. She didn't want to sell things piecemeal: she wanted to dump it all quickly, in one place. She wanted to sever her responsibility—and her ties to the Vineyard—in one swoop.

"I don't know. . . ." she said.

"Would you like to come with me?" he asked suddenly.

"What?"

He moved a drop cloth with his foot. "Maybe if you talked with the people, you might be able to strike a deal. Get rid of the whole lot, if you're sure that's what you want."

"Oh, it's what I want all right. You're going tomorrow?"

"We'll wrap up here today."

Jill turned to Jeff. "Would you mind if I went to Nantucket?" What she'd really wanted to ask was if he minded staying here to watch over Amy. Hopefully, Jeff would know that.

"I don't care, Mom. Maybe I'll go to the beach with Amy. Play some volleyball."

She said a silent prayer of thanks again for her brilliant son. "What time are you leaving?"

"I'm catching a nine o'clock flight."

"Not the ferry?"

"The ferry is for tourists who have two hours and fifteen minutes each way to kill."

"Right," Jill replied, not wanting to admit that in her nearly eighteen years of living on the Vineyard, she had not once gone to Nantucket, not even for the famous inter-high school football games. Her mother had not allowed it. "Shall I meet you at the airport?"

The flight over was smooth, but cramped. Jill was grateful that the loud engine of the tiny plane hampered conversation: she did not want to talk about

Amy; she did not want to talk about Kyle. She suspected Ben knew that, and she was glad he understood.

A silver limousine waited for them at the airport. Jill did not hide her surprise. "Your reputation must certainly precede you," she said to Ben with a smile.

"They must have sensed that the beautiful Jill McPhearson would be accompanying me," he replied as they stepped inside the leather interior.

Jill sat down and tried not to show her surprise that Ben took this all so lightly, and that he had called her beautiful. "This doesn't impress you, does it?" she said, once they were under way.

"What? The limo?" He laughed. "I think it's fairly ridiculous. But if it makes my clients feel better to have the hired hand picked up in a stretch, hey, who am I to take their fun away?"

She began to wonder once again what the real story was behind Ben Niles, and was irritated that Christopher had not felt it could be worthy of *Good Night, Boston.* As they rode along the narrow streets that were cluttered with bicycles and bordered by too-close-to-the-road white houses and shops, Jill thought there must be many people who lived on the Cape and Islands with lives like Ben Niles—content in their crafts, superior at their work, yet, aside from big paychecks, were largely unrecognized.

"The *Yankee* article certainly impressed my publicist," she commented.

"It was a fluke." He laughed again, his dimple sinking into his right cheek. "A friend of one of my neighbor's is a writer. She was on the Vineyard last summer, and I guess she was bored."

Jill smiled, and wondered if he'd had a relationship with the woman, then wondered why she was wondering that. "Addie said it was a fine article."

"It was embarrassing."

She thought about the upcoming *Lifestyles*

spread. Until then, until the kids were involved, Jill had not minded publicity. She'd always felt it was part of the job. "Yes, well," she said quietly, "the media can be embarrassing."

Ben laughed but said nothing.

The "cottage" owned by Ben's clients turned out to be an expansive, gray-shingled home set amid acres of rolling green lawn, stone walls, with several chestnut mares grazing against the cloudless sky. Jill sat quietly in the airy sun porch that overlooked the harbor, sipping tea from a bone china cup. The wicker furniture held bright floral cushions; the island breeze created a symphony of melodic wind chimes that hung from the wood-slatted ceiling. The elderly couple—Mr. and Mrs. Sherman—talked with Ben, while Jill's eyes roamed the area, thinking what a wonderful location this would be for a photo shoot. At one point, Ben rose.

"I'd like to look at the stables now," he said. "Perhaps you would take me, Mr. Sherman? Then Jill and your wife could talk business."

The woman, indeed, was an antiques dealer. "Not the flea market kind, my dear," the sweet woman spoke softly as she peered over bifocals at Jill. "Only exclusive materials. They must be authentic."

"Oh," Jill reassured her, "believe me, they're authentic. They've been in my family forever, I think."

The woman frowned. "It's a shame you have to let them go."

"I don't have to." Jill found herself defensive. "I want to. I've no need for them. My fiancé and I will be moving to the West Coast." She quickly described the larger pieces—the rolltop desk, the Victorian settees, the four-poster beds. "There are other things as well. A sewing machine, pots and pans . . ."

Mrs. Sherman nodded, making notes on a small

pad decorated with a border of violets. "I don't get over to the Vineyard often," she said, "but my daughter can do the legwork. Perhaps you know her. Misha Sherman?"

Jill shook her head, grateful she'd never heard of her.

"Misha is our eldest," Mrs. Sherman continued. "We adopted her when she was eleven—just before Israel gained their independence in 1948."

"You adopted her?"

"My husband was in international finance. His work took us all over the world, but we made Nantucket our home. We raised nine adopted children here—all from different countries. All orphans of war."

Jill smiled. It was difficult to believe this frail, seemingly private New Englander had a life so rich, and had done deeds so philanthropic in an era when so many—like Florence Randall—had sequestered themselves from the world and lived only for themselves, and their own flesh and blood.

"You never had children of your own?" she asked gently.

"Oh, my yes. Four. All boys, God bless them. But there was always room at our table for more. Would you like to see their pictures?"

Jill nodded and followed Mrs. Sherman's slow steps into the house, into a large, sunny living room resplendent with color, antiques, and warmth. An ebony baby grand filled one corner, its top protected by a crocheted shawl that was lovingly covered with a multitude of picture frames.

She listened carefully as Mrs. Sherman pointed out each of their children and each of their grandchildren—a happy blend of light- and dark-skinned faces, blonds and brunettes, thin children, chubby children, short and tall—their laughter singing through the small squares of glass set in the neat little frames. Jill thought of the photo-less house in which she'd grown up and felt a pang of loss for things she'd never known.

"It looks like the United Nations," she said with a smile.

"Oh, my dear, it's nothing so politically noble. Just one big family, making the best of our world: two doctors, three teachers, a lawyer, and . . . oh, my, I believe I've lost track."

Jill's eyes moved over the pictures again. She realized there was quite a story here. Not a sensational Sam Wilkins story, but a good story. A story with soul.

It was after one when Ben returned with Mr. Sherman.

"You must stay for lunch," Mrs. Sherman announced. "We have fresh cod cakes today."

"Jill," Ben asked, "would that create a problem for you?"

She thought about the Shermans, about the kind of life they'd had. She thought about her need to find out more. It may never be a story that would make national airwaves, but her curiosity would not let it go. "No," she replied with a smile. "No problem at all."

After lunch, they strolled the grounds, surveying the beach plum crop just coming into picking season. Jill found herself longing to turn back the clock, longing to carry the large wicker basket, to walk alongside her mother, in the one thing they had shared. She found herself wishing she had known then how much those outings had meant to her mother.

By midafternoon, heavy clouds enveloped the sky. When Ben mentioned they must get back to the Vineyard, the Shermans seemed genuinely sorry to see them leave.

So was Jill.

The limo dropped them at the airport, and Jill stood at the chain-link fence, while Ben went to check on the gate. She studied the cluster of small planes and wondered how many of these people had stories: people like the Shermans, wealthy, salty islanders, who had done good for the world, yet remained unnoticed. Their lives had purpose—still had purpose, even in their elder years. Jill silently wished Christopher could see the depth of such stories. "You have to think bigger than that, Jill," she could almost hear him say. "No one cares about some old people on Nantucket." Maurice Fischer, she knew, would agree.

"I hope you aren't in a hurry to get back," Ben said as he came back to where she stood. "Fog's rolling into the Vineyard, and the plane's not taking off."

"Oh," Jill said, hoping she sounded disappointed.

"We can just about make it to the ferry, if you don't mind the long trip."

"Two hours and fifteen minutes with tourists?" she asked with a smile.

"And their bikes," he groaned.

"I think I can handle it."

They took a cab to the docks and scooted onto the Hi-Line boat just before it backed away from the pier. It was not, Jill noted, as large as the Woods Hole ferry.

"Passengers only," Ben remarked as they scanned the deck in search of seats, all of which seemed to be taken by weary-looking travelers with sunburns.

"Let's stand by the rail," she said. "I love to watch the water."

They pushed their way to the rail and found a space big enough for the two of them. The boat began to roll and chug toward the open sea. Then, the skies began to drizzle.

"I'd say we should go below," Ben said, "but you can be sure it's packed down there."

She tilted her face to the rain. "It's okay. I love the rain," she answered. "I'd forgotten how much." She licked a drop off her upper lip and turned to Ben. "I hope your wife won't be holding dinner for you."

"I have no wife, Jill. I'm a widower." He said the word as though it were a foreign, unknown land, like Siberia or Mars.

"I'm sorry."

"Me, too." He tipped the brim of his cap as though trying to shield his eyes.

"How's the arm?" she asked, trying to change the subject.

"The cast should come off next week. I'll be back in my house and back in my car."

"Your car is unique."

"It's dependable."

"It suits you."

He smiled.

She shifted against the rail. "You did a remarkable job getting my house done."

With his gray eyes steady on the water, Ben nodded. "Like I said, I don't leave a job unfinished."

Jill brushed back her hair. Raindrops coated her forehead.

"I feel responsible, Jill," he continued. "For what happened between Kyle and your daughter."

She flinched. "You? Why?"

"Because I should have made it more clear to Kyle what was expected of him. And what wasn't."

"It wasn't your fault, Ben. Kyle is . . ." She choked on the sound of his name. "Kyle is a grown man. He should have known better, even if Amy didn't."

"I shouldn't have allowed that girl to hang around

your house. She was a bad influence on your daughter."

Jill folded her hands on the rail. "I encouraged it, Ben. I encouraged their friendship so I could get Sam Wilkins's story."

"And did you?" he asked. "Did you get what you wanted?"

Suddenly Jill felt as though tears were going to drown her eyes. She thought about Amy, Kyle, and Rita. She thought about her mother's diary, and wished she felt confident to keep moving ahead. "I'm not sure," she answered. "Do any of us ever really get what we want?"

Ben shook his head. "I've been trying to restore a house in Menemsha. To turn it into a hands-on museum. Looks like I'll never get that."

"Why not?"

"Politics. Personalities. Greed, you name it."

"Tell me more."

"Twenty questions?"

Jill smiled.

So he told her. He told her how unique Menemsha House was going to be, from its place atop the dunes where Gay Head meets his land.

Jill remembered the big old Vineyard house next to Sam's. "I've seen the house," she said quietly, "from Sam Wilkins's."

He nodded and continued his story. When he reached the part about how his arm was broken, Jill was horrified. "All over a museum?"

"A museum to me, who knows what it represents to whoever tried to kill me. A friend of mine says that men have different passions."

She wondered if that friend was a woman, but decided it was best not to ask. "Ben, isn't there something that can be done?"

"I tried. They don't want money, but I suspect you already know that about islanders. I came up with a plan to provide school buses, too. But I never got to present it. Not that it would have made a difference. They have their own agendas, and don't care about anything else."

"Except their privacy." Jill laughed. "They despise having their privacy intruded upon, their dirty laundry aired."

Ben scowled. "It's strange, isn't it? Generation after generation, it remains the same." He stood up straight and looked at Jill. "But sometimes we get what we want. Take you for instance. You want to sell your house. That will happen."

She turned to him. "That bothers you, doesn't it? That I'm going to sell the house?"

"It's your house. But it's such a classic. The architecture is incredible. I just hate to see a fine old place like that one be turned over to some family who doesn't appreciate its value, or who will turn it into one of those god-awful Bed and Breakfasts." He shuddered.

Jill laughed. "But don't you think that life is cyclical? That sooner or later, everything must change?"

"No. Not unless people force it. Look at the 1802 Tavern. How many years was that in your family?"

She winced. "Since it opened. Until my father died."

"You've never mentioned your parents," he said. "You left the island early, so I assumed you couldn't wait to get away."

"I didn't really know my parents," she heard herself say. And then, whether it was because of the slow, dreamlike rolling of the boat beneath her feet, the hypnotic rise and fall of the ocean, or the fact that she had held the pain of the last few weeks in too long, Jill said, "I found my mother's diary. In the widow's walk. I learned some things I wished I hadn't known. I learned I had a brother. I learned my mother didn't want me."

With her words, the irony struck her. "It's odd, isn't it? That I have made a career out of delving into other people's stories, but I never examined my own until now?"

Ben placed his hand over Jill's. "I'm sorry, Jill. I didn't mean to pry. Please, this is none of my business."

At least he didn't tell her she was overreacting. "I need it to be someone's business," she said quietly. "I can't keep this inside me any longer."

"Well," Ben said as he looked out to sea, "I'm a good listener. For a tourist."

She held back a moment, then spilled out each detail, bit by bit, as page after page of her mother's diary flashed into her mind. When she neared the end, she told him about Rita. About Kyle.

"All these years, I'd felt I abandoned my father, that I let him down by leaving him alone with my mother." She gave a short laugh. "Apparently, I needn't have been so concerned about him." Her words trailed off as their sound resonated the pain.

Ben did not speak: he simply slipped his arm around her—his one good arm, his strong carpenter's arm. She dropped her head against his shoulder and wept with the soothing rain, feeling foolish that she had bared so much, and wishing there were some way she could thank him for listening.

Chapter 22

 "Where the hell have you been?" Christopher greeted her at the door. "Look at you, you're all wet. You're a mess for chrissakes. Go upstairs and dry off before Fischer sees you looking like that."

Jill stood in the front hall and stared at him in disbelief. "I thought you weren't coming until tomorrow."

Christopher glowered. "The weather is supposed to be bad tomorrow. I didn't want to take a chance on not getting in. I tried to call, but it seems you were spending the day on Nantucket. With that builder." Anger shot from his eyes.

"Christopher . . ."

"Just get upstairs and change, Jill. Fischer's in the guest room getting ready for dinner. I thought we'd take him to the tavern."

She thought of Rita and quickly said, "No. Not the tavern. Let's go to Gay Head. To The Outermost Inn." She'd seen it on her trips out to Sam's; he'd told her the cuisine was spectacular.

He chewed his lower lip. "Just change. Please. And hurry. This is not making a great first impression."

Jill went upstairs, thinking that she'd meant to

have fresh hydrangea in the guest room, that she'd not even taken the time yet to lay out clean towels for Maurice Fischer, and that Christopher had quickly managed to break her finally relaxed mood.

Dinner was polite. Jill had dressed in her shimmer bouclé shell and short skirt, even though it was too formal for the island. She remained on her best behavior, the model of sophistication, of Q-rating material, as she smiled across the table at the white-haired man with the neatly trimmed mustache and California tan. She raved about the grilled yellow fin tuna, and tried not to think about the fact she'd had a better time standing in the rain with Ben. Yet Ben's presence stayed with her, in a way that even the comfortable dining room and cozy fire had not been able to quiet.

Maurice seemed entranced by the tableside view of the dunes, the food, and the inn itself, especially the photos of Bill Clinton's visit that adorned the downstairs. Apparently, the president's "Q" was sufficient testimony that The Outermost Inn was superior.

Over homemade ice cream and espresso, Christopher proposed a toast.

"To Jill," he said, his demitasse cup raised high. "Who has managed to become the only living soul to be granted an interview with the one and only Sam Wilkins."

Fischer's eyebrows jumped. He looked at Jill. "Is this true?"

She bypassed the ice cream and sipped her espresso. "Well, yes," she said quietly. "He has given me an interview. I'm still working on piecing it together."

Fischer laughed. "We have reporters to do that, Jill. This is incredible. How did you do it?"

She glanced over at Christopher, not knowing how to answer.

"She's a lady who knows how to land the big stories, that's all," Christopher said with a wink.

Fischer merely nodded and took a long swig of his coffee. "Lizette tried to interview him last year," he said. "She struck out."

Jill wanted to smile, but didn't dare.

"Not only that," Christopher added, "but we have an invitation to his Labor Day weekend party. When is that, honey?"

The party seemed unimportant now. The party, the fluff, the story. She set the demitasse in the small china saucer. "Saturday," she replied.

Fischer nodded again but did not reveal his emotions—a true politician, a pure corporate executive. However, Jill knew he must be elated: schmoozing with Sam Wilkins would not only be a coup on the West Coast, it would also look good to the RueCom board.

Later that night, when they had arrived home and settled into bed, Jill lay awake, listening to the foghorns and the clang of the buoy bells, thinking about her day with Ben and about standing in the rain on the deck of the ferry. Ben had said that sometimes we get what we want: Jill tried to decide if that was true, and if so, how long it took. Then her thoughts drifted to her mother, and she wondered if Florence ever found that kind of peace.

When she was certain Christopher was asleep, Jill quietly crept from the room and up the widow's walk stairs.

August 30, 1970
  My daughter is gone. She left the island to-day, just as the beach plums have begun to

ripen. I fear she will never return, nor will ever know the empty hole inside of me that she left behind. When she stood on the top deck of the ferry and waved good-bye, I tried to smile and show her I was happy for her. But when we returned home I was sick to my stomach. I feel as though I have let another child down. I feel as though I have failed.

Jill thought back to the day she left for college. She remembered standing on that deck, remembered waving to her parents. She'd felt a little sad at leaving her father, but she'd felt as though her mother had been glad to see her go. She had no idea her mother had become sick over it. She had no idea her mother had ever cared that much.

May 17, 1974

Jill has graduated from college. She called today to tell us she was staying on in Boston, that she has a job at a television station there. I suppose I will never see her again. Perhaps it is best for her. I have only ever wanted what is best for her. And it is best for her to remain away. I heard that Rita Blair is home again. Home—with her small boy. She's telling everyone she married, and that her husband died. I know differently. George knows differently. But I cannot tell him that I know. I just can't.

The ache in Jill's chest grew heavy. She forced herself to turn the page, forced herself to read on. Entry after entry mentioned the church fairs, making beach plum jelly, shelling quahogs. There was no further mention of Rita; no further mention of Jill, as though they had ceased existing, as though they had never been. Then came 1978.

April 12, 1978
Jill got married. She never even called to say she was going to. She just did it. His name is Richard McPhearson, and I guess he has a lot of money. I don't know why she did not invite George and me to the wedding. I wonder if my mother felt so odd, when she was not invited to ours. Perhaps God is paying me back for being a bad daughter myself.

"What are you doing up here?" Christopher's heavy whisper jolted her from the diary.

Jill quickly closed the book and set it in the carton. "I couldn't sleep," she said. "I came up to go through some things."

"I saw the light under the door," he said as he looked around. "It doesn't look as though you've made much progress. Are you sure you're ready to leave on Monday?"

Jill nodded. "I have a woman who's going to take care of everything. That's why I was on Nantucket today."

He ran his hand through his sleep-tousled hair. "Oh," he replied, "well, I really didn't think you were off having a romantic tryst with the builder."

Jill smiled and stood up. "He's not a builder, Christopher. He's an artist. And a good one. He would have made a good story."

Christopher rolled his eyes. "Come back to bed, honey. The sooner I get you off this island, the happier we'll both be."

The sooner Jill left the island, the happier Rita would be. Kyle had barely come out of his room for the two weeks since they'd caught him with Amy and Ben had fired him. And Rita could not stand working at the tavern every night with one eye on her customers and one on the door. Though she doubted Jill would ever want to see the inside of the tavern again, Rita knew she'd breathe a lot easier once Labor Day had come and gone, once Jill had returned to her world and left Rita the hell alone in hers.

She tossed her SurfSide blazer on top of last night's clothes that lay in a heap on the chair of her bedroom. Even though it had poured, it hadn't been a bad day, Rita realized as she sifted through the clean clothes piled on the bed, in search of her waitress uniform. She'd listed two properties for the "hurry up and get rid of it before winter" tourists, and at the post office, Jesse had handed her the best news of all—the return receipt that assured Rita the IRS had their money, paid in full. As soon as she changed, she was going to tell Kyle. Maybe it would pick up his spirits, maybe it would take some pressure off him, now that he didn't have a job.

As she pulled the uniform over her head and stood at the mirror, trying to assess if she could get away without ironing it, the rumble of a sports car rose from the street below. She crossed to the window just as Carrie Wilkins emerged from a whore's-red Porsche.

Kyle must have heard it, too, for his footsteps zipped past the hall outside Rita's room and clomped down the stairs. Rita held her breath and wondered if she should intervene.

Stay out of it, her better senses warned her. *Kyle's a big boy. He can take care of himself.*

She stood in the middle of the floor, put her hands on her hips, then walked to the door and opened it just wide enough for listening.

"You lost your job," Carrie's voice announced.

"Word travels fast."

"Can I come in, Kyle? It's raining, in case you didn't notice."

"I noticed."

Silence. Then, "I thought we had an understanding, Kyle."

"You're the one who walked away."

"Only because you were being stupid."

"I didn't think so."

Silence. Rita leaned closer to the hall.

Finally, Carrie spoke again. "It's not too late for us to patch things up."

"I'm not what you think I am."

"A child molester?"

"You told me she was almost seventeen."

Carrie laughed. "I lied."

"What else have you lied about?"

"Nothing, Kyle. I guess I was testing you."

"I guess I flunked."

Silence again.

"Come on, Kyle. We need each other."

He didn't respond.

"Will you think about it?"

"I already did."

"You had a job then. Maybe it's time to reconsider."

Rita heard the jingle of keys.

"My father's having a picnic tomorrow," Carrie went on. "He likes you, Kyle. He'd like to see you succeed."

The front door closed. Rita quickly closed hers, then slouched against it, trying to figure out what the conversation had meant, and if her son was about to leave the island and move to L.A.

Ben had picked up his mail, driven the Nissan back to Carol Ann's, and reminded himself to tell his daughter to get the windshield wiper fixed, once the August lines at the service stations were gone. He was grateful that there were only a few more days of summer madness left, that after Monday, the level of traffic would be bearable once more, and that next week he'd be driving his Buick again and be back home where he belonged.

He sat on the wicker glider on the small porch of his daughter's Cape now, enjoying the sweet, fresh scent of the rain and sifting through the envelopes. Like most things, it was not easy to do with one hand.

"Grandpa, Mommy said to ask you if I can help."

Ben looked up at John Jr.

"I'm real good at opening mail."

"I'll bet you are," Ben said, and patted a space beside him on the awning-striped cushion. "Come on up here and give me a hand."

John Jr. slid onto the chair. Ben adjusted his sling and handed him an envelope off the top. "If it's a bill, I don't want to know," he said with a smile.

"Grandpa! I can't read, yet!" the boy exclaimed.

"Do you know numbers from letters?"

The boy thought for a moment. "Yes."

"Good. Then anything with numbers, throw on the floor."

"Oh, Grandpa." John Jr. giggled, then as he positioned the tip of his tongue firmly between his lips, his small, chubby hands unsealed the first envelope. He pulled out an ad. "This one has numbers," he announced and tossed it to the floor.

Ben glanced down. "It has numbers, all right. It says I may have won ten million dollars."

"Is that a lot of dollars?"

"Nah," he replied, then handed him the next envelope. It was small and square and white, and had been hand-addressed. Ben assumed it was another get well card, probably from Rachel Bowen, who had already sent three.

John Jr. peeled back the flap and removed the card. Ben glanced over his grandson's shoulder and saw the words "You're Invited" scripted on the front.

"Open the card," he said. John Jr. complied.

The calligraphied message was simple:

Labor Day Picnic
Sam Wilkins
Lighthouse Road—Gay Head
Saturday—Four p.m.

Ben read it again. Sam Wilkins? Why was Sam Wilkins inviting him to his Labor Day picnic? An unwelcome thought flashed through his mind. Carrie was Sam Wilkins's daughter. Did this have something to do with Kyle? Were they going to try to convince him to hire Kyle back?

But what the hell would they care about Kyle Blair? Surely they'd be returning to the West Coast after this weekend.

"Grandpa? Should I throw this on the floor?"

Ben shook his head. "No. Put that one aside. I need to think about it." He handed John Jr. the next envelope, then wondered if Sam Wilkins needed some work done on his house. Maybe Jill had recommended Ben . . . his mind stopped in midthought. Jill. Would she be at the picnic?

He turned his gaze back to the rain, remembering how it had looked on her face, how it clung to her lashes, how it beaded on her brow like tiny jewels that sparkled with every word she spoke.

Then he remembered the jewel on her hand, and its icy reality of the life that was hers.

Dressed in yellow slickers that Jill had found on the back of the pantry door, they had taken Maurice Fischer on a drive around the island, stopping in antique shops, sidestepping puddles, and pointing out one sight after another. Mostly he was interested in where the celebrities lived: Carly Simon, Mike Wallace, Spike Lee.

By dinnertime, Jill could no longer stand the wet rubber smell of their coats or the humidity that kept fogging the windows inside the Range Rover. But when they returned to the house, one more thing caught Fischer's eye.

"Is that the Chappaquiddick ferry?" he asked when they pulled into the driveway.

Jill shot a look at Christopher. He grinned. "Yes," he answered, "the one and only."

"Well, I suppose no trip to Martha's Vineyard would be complete without a ride on it."

Jill felt her insides groan. "I suppose not," she said, with diminishing cheeriness in her voice.

Christopher backed out of the driveway and maneuvered the vehicle down the road toward the ramp. Thankfully, they were third in line and wouldn't have to wait forever to cross.

They drove out to Cemetery Road, past the Lawrence cottage where the infamous party had been held, then to the Dyke Bridge, which had long ago been replaced. Jill kept up a running commentary to Maurice, who sat with rapt attention, staring out the window, as though witnessing the Grand Canyon for the first time. Or Disney World. Once in a while, he shook his head.

"Imagine," he said, "you lived right here when it all happened. Did you realize it would be captured in the history books?"

"Not really," Jill said, directing Christopher back toward the ferry. "I was just a kid. I was more fascinated by the way the world reacted. Did you know tourists actually took pieces off the bridge as souvenirs?"

Fischer shook his head again.

They returned to the ferry in silence, Jill hoping that, at last, Maurice had his fill of sightseeing, antiques, and Chappaquiddick. As they rolled onto the small, raftlike ferry and began to bump across the channel, Jill thought back to that year, to the impact it had had, not only on her life, but on all the islanders. Unlike her, once the inquest was over, the islanders shrunk into their protective skins, covering their bruises with their centuries-old pods, carrying on as though nothing had happened. It was, after all, the New Englanders' way—shielding their privacy no matter what.

Privacy, Jill suddenly thought. It was the most important thing to islanders. She thought of Ben Niles. Privacy was the one thing he hadn't considered in his goal to build Menemsha House.

As the little ferry chugged to the Edgartown side, Jill smiled. For she now knew how she could repay Ben for having been so kind to her.

Chapter 23

"I'm working on a story about the island," Jill said as she stood on the front steps of Terry Clarkson's home Saturday morning. With her research wiles and the Vineyard phone book, she'd quickly learned that Clarkson was the man to see. Telling Christopher she had something important to take care of, she'd left him alone to entertain Maurice before the picnic this afternoon. As exciting as the future was, the present seemed more important right now.

The door frame Clarkson leaned against was still damp from yesterday's rain. He squinted in the early sun and folded his arms in disinterest. "You need to speak with the Chamber of Commerce. Not me."

"No," Jill said firmly. "You're definitely the one I want. Are you familiar with the TV show *Good Night, Boston*?"

"Just because we live on the island doesn't mean we're hicks. I know who you are, Ms. McPhearson."

"Do you know I was raised in Edgartown?"

"Doesn't everyone?"

Jill took out her notebook and clicked her pen, ignoring his comment. "My story isn't about Edgartown. It's about how small towns stifle progress."

Clarkson didn't flinch.

"I'm talking about Ben Niles, Mr. Clarkson. His plans for Menemsha House. Can you tell me specifically what the problem is?"

Clarkson stared at her a moment. "There's no problem. Mr. Niles simply hasn't met the board's criteria."

"What criteria is that?" Jill asked, jotting nonsensical notes on her pad, a reporter's trick of intimidation.

"Look, I don't know what you're doing, but I suggest you talk with Mr. Niles. He's the one who hasn't complied with us. Not the other way around." He started to close the door. Jill stuck her foot inside.

"I have spoken with Mr. Niles," she said. "He's made several changes. Are you aware that he plans to provide the school department with much-needed buses—at his expense?"

"No. But as I'm sure you know bribery doesn't wash on the island. Mr. Niles is not a native. Perhaps he doesn't realize that."

As she'd expected, the buses wouldn't have made a difference. "He doesn't see it as bribery, Mr. Clarkson. He sees it as a way of helping the island kids while bettering their education. What does the zoning board have against that?"

Clarkson sneered. "Menemsha is a fishing village. Mr. Niles wants to transform it into an entertainment center. The two do not mix. Now if you'll excuse me . . ."

"One more question, please," Jill said quickly. "Is the town prepared to handle the fallout of negative publicity?"

He frowned.

"Oh, and by the way," Jill added, "I forgot to mention that my show will be going into syndication soon. The story won't air until then—until it can receive national attention."

The lines of his forehead deepened.

"Menemsha House may not be important to you, Mr. Clarkson, but I'm sure people all across the country will be interested in hearing that Martha's Vineyard dislikes providing new learning opportunities for their children and for the tourists' children. I'm thinking of titling it 'Martha's Vineyard— Drowning in Backwater Thinking.' Kind of catchy, don't you think?"

Clarkson's jaw went rigid. "Ms. McPhearson, what exactly are you trying to do?"

"I am merely trying to help a friend. I am fortunate enough to have the power of the media behind me. We both know that approving Menemsha House is not going to send the Vineyard into turmoil. My theory is that if Ben Niles had been born here, his proposal would have been approved without question. I think it's time we exposed that little bit of narrow-mindedness to the world."

She folded her notebook and returned it to her purse. "But don't worry, Mr. Clarkson, I'm sure the island can handle it. After all, it can't be much worse than Chappaquiddick."

Clarkson's face reddened.

"Of course," Jill said with a laugh, "Chappy helped the economy, didn't it? All it cost was having our privacy invaded." She shrugged. "Perhaps that means the Vineyard is not adverse to progress, after all." She turned and headed down the walk. "Well, thanks for your time. If I don't hear from you before I leave Monday, I'll assume the board has decided I should go ahead with my story."

She went down the walk, climbed into the Range Rover, and turned over the ignition with a smile of satisfaction.

• • •

Carol Ann was helping Ben button his shirt when the phone rang. He'd not had any idea what to wear to Sam Wilkins's picnic: his daughter suggested the navy short-sleeved shirt and tan, lightweight denim pants—the ones with the pleats that she'd bought him last Christmas, the ones he hadn't removed from the drawer until now, until she'd insisted on coming to his house to be sure he was properly attired.

"People who matter will be there," she'd said. "It could mean more work for you. Lots of work."

Surveying himself in the mirror while Carol Ann went to answer the phone, he decided that if he owned a pair of Dock-Sides, he could easily be mistaken for a tourist.

"Dad?" Carol Ann said when she returned to the bedroom. "It's for you."

"Well, now," he said with a smile, "I suppose we should have expected that, seeing as how this is where I live."

Carol Ann's look told him she was annoyed. Two weeks of having her father under her roof must be trying her patience. He damn well knew it was trying his.

"Ben?" a strange voice asked when he picked up the receiver in the kitchen. "This is Terry Clarkson."

Ben frowned. "What can I do for you?"

"The board would like to speak with you about your alternative plan. It's my understanding you are willing to buy school buses."

Ben was stumped. How the hell did Clarkson find out? Then he remembered. He'd gone to O'Briens' for quotes. On this island, nothing—including business deals—was sacred. "I priced out the possibility," he replied, "then decided it wasn't worth the effort. I figured your minds were made up, no matter what I did."

Clarkson laughed. "Well, you figured wrong. Of course, we'll need to meet with you to iron out the details, but if you're serious about the buses, we've decided to give you the go-ahead."

The shock Ben felt was equaled only by the bolt of excitement that charged through him. "What?"

Clarkson spoke clearly. "Menemsha House. The museum. It's yours if you still want it."

He scratched his head, not knowing how to respond. Half of him cautioned himself to be wary of zoning board chairpersons bearing good news. The other half chuckled to himself and said, "This is wonderful news, Clarkson. No one will be disappointed. You have my word."

"We'd like to get together next week. At your convenience, of course."

Ben hesitated. Telling Clarkson he would be tied up on Nantucket next week working for the internationally renowned Hubert Sherman would probably not bode well with his newfound acceptance into the Vineyard fold. Sherman, after all, had his face on *Time* magazine last year—another celebrity, another beach plum thorn in the zoning board's side. On the other hand, Sherman was a class act. Ben knew he would understand if the job was delayed a few more days. "Next week is fine, Terry. How about Tuesday?"

"Seven o'clock. Bring the plans."

"Of course," Ben said and hung up the phone.

"Dad?" Carol Ann had moved beside him. "Was that Terry Clarkson?"

"That," he said as he turned and kissed his daughter's cheek, "was one call I never expected. I don't know what happened, but something did. They've given me the go-ahead for Menemsha House."

Carol Ann frowned. "Why?"

"Why? Who knows? Maybe they took a look at their books and realized I could help move them into the asset column."

"I don't like it, Dad."

"Come on, honey. Don't rain on my parade."

She shook her well-meaning head. "I'm not trying to, Dad. It's just that I know Terry Clarkson. I work with all those people, remember? Something's up, and I don't like it."

"You still think Dave Ashenbach is out to get me?"

"I don't know."

"Why don't you let me worry about that. Whatever—or whoever—wanted to stop me has obviously been overruled. Now let me comb what's left of my hair so I can get out of here. It's not every day a poor islander like me gets invited to a party at Sam Wilkins'."

But as Ben brushed past her and went into the bathroom, trepidation crept in. He decided that tomorrow morning he'd go out to the cliffs. Maybe Noepe would have some inside knowledge as to what in the hell was really going on.

A yellow-and-white-striped canopy framed with overflowing pots of white bleeding hearts was stretched above the wide lawn, bordered by dunes and overlooking the water. Beneath the canvas stood linen-covered tables accented with crystal bowls of yellow roses; in one corner a stringed quartet played a selection that Jill recognized as Vivaldi.

She stood between Christopher and Maurice Fischer in her white crepe sundress and matching calf sandals, holding the top of her white straw hat with one hand and musing that this was no ordinary Labor Day weekend picnic on the island. But then, she reminded herself, Sam Wilkins was no ordinary tourist, and it was probably part of his plan to emerge with great vigor and an attitude that breathed confidence in his impending rebirth.

From behind her sunglasses, Jill let her eyes explore the two hundred plus guests who had gathered: from the long-robed Arab house guest and his entourage to a cluster of T-shirted men holding beer cans—most of the men were occupied ogling the *Penthouse*-looking blondes who apparently had been imported from the West Coast, wore few clothes and tans that were much too dark. Maurice was no exception.

"This is quite a summer place," he said, motioning toward the house with the hand that held his flute of champagne. "It's not what I expected to see on the Vineyard."

Jill smiled at the way his language had slipped into calling the island "the Vineyard" with the familiarity of a well-seasoned tourist. "It's the new Vineyard," Jill responded. "New blood."

Fischer nodded.

"Would you like to meet our host now?" Christopher asked, then turned to Jill. "Honey? Do you think you could round up Sam?"

She glanced through the maze of people, the sun glinting off their gold and their jewels. "I'm sure he's around somewhere. Don't go away." She started off through the crowd, brushing shoulders with people she didn't know, smiling her Jill McPhearson, TV-host smile. "Have you seen Sam?" she asked one young couple who resembled Haight-Ashbury holdovers frozen by time. The long-haired, beaded man pointed down toward the beach.

"Tending the lobster bake," he said.

She made her way to the stairs—the stairs where Amy had gone the day Jill had brought her out here, three weeks ago, a lifetime ago. Amy had not even pouted when Jill told her where they were going today; she had merely retreated to her room, the safest place she seemed to be able to find these days.

At the foot of the stairs, more people were strewn along the beach, laughing, talking, drinking. A volleyball game was in full force; a huge tarp billowed across the lobster pit—where, Jill sensed by the long-ago familiar aroma, lobsters and mussels, linguine and corn, were simmering under layers of seaweed. Long grills had been set up near the tarp—it was there that Jill spotted Sam. He was wearing a white apron and chef's hat and holding a long fork.

As she walked toward him, an arm reached out from the crowd and stopped her.

"Jill," said the voice she had hoped wouldn't be here.

"Hello, Carrie," she answered, her eyes fixed straight ahead.

"Jill," Carrie repeated, "I wanted to stop over, but I was afraid I wouldn't be welcome."

She had hoped that Carrie hadn't found out; she had prayed it had not become island gossip.

"Kyle told me," Carrie continued. "He called me that night, after . . ."

Jill looked down at the red-painted fingernails that gripped her arm. "Please take your hand off me."

Carrie released her grasp. "I guess I was right. About not being welcome."

"I think it's for the best."

"How is she? How is Amy?"

"She's fine, thank you. She is home packing. We're going home Monday."

"So are we. Would you tell her . . . would you tell her I said good-bye? And that I'm sorry?"

"You didn't do anything, Carrie. It was my fault for thinking she was mature enough to have an eighteen-year-old as a friend. An eighteen-year-old with a twenty-five-year-old boyfriend. Now if you'll excuse me, I was on my way to see your father." She walked quickly away, aware that the sand was stinging between her toes through her sandals, and that the sun was much hotter down here on the beach.

Sam didn't see her approach. His back was to her; he was blocking her view, but Jill could hear the man's words.

"What can I say? I did the best I could. We did the best we could."

"You didn't try hard enough," Sam said. "I had your word."

The steaks sizzled. Jill felt as though she should leave, that she shouldn't interrupt. But the thought of returning through the crowd and facing Carrie alone again left her standing in the sand, immobile.

Suddenly Sam turned around. "Jill! I didn't know you'd arrived."

Her smile quickly vanished when she realized who the man talking with Sam was: it was Terry Clarkson, head of the zoning board. "I see you've invited half the town," Jill said, averting her eyes from Clarkson's cold stare.

"Oh, sure," Sam said with a sweep of the barbecue fork. "Everyone's welcome at Sam Wilkins's. Be sure to include that in your story."

"By all means," Jill responded. "And when you have a minute, there's someone up by the tent who's very eager to meet you. Maurice Fischer."

Sam's eyebrows shot up. "RueCom?"

Jill nodded.

He handed the fork to Clarkson, plucked off the chef's hat, and pulled the apron over his head. "Come on, lady," he said, slipping an arm around her waist, "let's go pave the way to our futures."

They crossed the beach and mounted the stairs. Jill kept her eyes focused on her footsteps: if Carrie would stay below on the beach, perhaps she could get through this party, perhaps she could keep her mind on the reasons she was here. At least Kyle didn't seem to be around. Perhaps things had ended between Kyle and Carrie. She wondered if Rita would be pleased.

At the top of the stairs, Jill noticed a man in navy and tan, one arm in a sling, a familiar smile set on his face.

She followed his gaze toward the house that stood on the next hilltop—then she realized why she had not recognized him: he must have left his Red Sox cap at home. "Ben," she said quickly, "I didn't know you'd be here."

"Ben Niles?" Sam asked as he extended his hand. "Sam Wilkins."

Ben shook his hand, then looked at Jill. "It's not every day the island has a bash such as this."

"I'm glad you could make it," Sam said. "I thought you might be too busy finalizing the plans for—what is it?—a museum?"

Ben smiled. "Menemsha House," he said, pointing across the dunes, then looking back to Jill. "It's going to happen," he said. "They gave me the approval an hour ago."

"Oh, Ben, that's wonderful," Jill said with what she hoped sounded like surprise. "Really," she added, "that's wonderful."

Ben nodded, his dimple set with his grin. "I thought you'd be pleased."

"I am. I'm very happy for you."

"Well," Sam said as he grasped Jill's elbow again, "it was nice to meet you, Ben. Enjoy the party." Quickly he steered Jill toward the tent, but not before Jill had a chance to turn back and look, just in time to see Ben give her a nod.

Rita stared at the dried-up frozen dinner and wondered if she would be alone, eating these, for the rest of her life. The scents of grilled hamburgers mingled with the sounds of life that drifted through her kitchen window—Labor Day picnics, Labor Day laughter. The island always reached a higher pitch on this long-awaited weekend, the way people on airplanes begin talking more loudly just before the landing wheels lock down, as though it was safe now to be yourself, for you'd never have to see these people again.

But Rita would see these people again, just as she'd seen them for so many years. Charlie Rollins, Jesse Parker, Jesse's mother. Island people. Her people.

She picked up her fork and moved around the brown lump that was supposed to be chicken, thinking about the biggest picnic of all—the one at Sam Wilkins's house. She wondered if Kyle had decided to go, and if Jill and her boyfriend had been invited.

Then she set down her fork and wondered why she gave a shit.

"Not even Barbara Walters was able to interview me." Sam laughed as he tasted the strawberry short-cake in front of him and raised his fork in a mock toast to Jill. "I'll tell you something, Maurice, this little lady is incorrigible."

They were seated under the canopy, where they had been served an enormous feast. Dusk was beginning to soothe the crowd; the strains of Vivaldi had been replaced by a trio from Sam's former backup group who subtly interspersed his most popular recordings with a blend of contemporary songs.

Jill had felt they were monopolizing Sam's time, but the host didn't seem to mind. And if Maurice knew he was being courted, he didn't seem bothered, either.

"I've known all along that Jill was special," Maurice said, "which brings me to something I've been wanting to mention. I planned to wait until later, but it would be more fun if everyone here was part of it."

Jill's heart began to race. She dared not look at Christopher. She took a sip from her glass. The flattened champagne bubbles fluttered down her throat.

"Sam?" Maurice asked. "Do you think your little band would mind if I borrowed their microphone?"

Sam pushed back his folding chair. "Not at all."

Jill moved forward on the edge of her seat as she watched Sam escort the RueCom king to the area where the music played. Christopher took her hand.

"This is it, honey."

She stole a glance at him. He smiled.

"Ladies and gentlemen," Maurice began, the microphone in one hand, the other hand high in the air. "May I have your attention, please."

The crowd murmurs dwindled, then ceased. "Most of you may not know my face, but hopefully you know my name. I'm Maurice Fischer, and I am the president of RueCom International. Hopefully, this island has cable access."

A ripple of laughter floated under the tent.

"Like all of you, I came here today as a guest of Sam Wilkins." He looked to Sam, who nodded and waved. A smattering of applause followed quickly.

"Aside from the great party he's put on, Sam and I have something else in common. We've become friends with one of your natives, Jill McPhearson."

Jill wanted to shrink from sight. Her eyes darted quickly around. She did not see Carrie. But she did see Ben Niles. He smiled.

"Jill thinks I only came to the Vineyard for a weekend away," Maurice continued. "What she doesn't know is that I have actually come bearing good news. Good news, the kind of stuff she and Christopher Edwards have brought back into vogue with their enormously successful television show."

There was more light applause. Jill wondered if it was coming from the out-of-town guests or from the islanders, but didn't want to look around to find out.

"The good news is simple. RueCom thinks that Christopher Edwards and Jill McPhearson make a damn great team. So great, in fact, that my company has made the decision to syndicate their show. As of October first, they will no longer be saying 'Good Night' to Boston, but to all of America."

Jill's hand tightened around her glass. She felt Christopher's arm slide around her shoulders. He leaned down and kissed her cheek.

"Hey, that's terrific," Sam said, stepping up to the microphone. "Let's hear it for Jill and Christopher!"

The drummer played a flourish; the crowd cheered. Jill glanced over at Ben, who stood by one of the canopy poles, a tentative smile directed toward her.

"Are you happy, honey?" Christopher whispered in her ear.

Jill blinked. Her thoughts blurred together. Despite all the talk these past few weeks, she realized now that she'd never really believed it would happen, never believed it could happen to Jill Randall, the stringy-haired girl who'd stood outside of the Duke's County Courthouse dreaming of the day when the world would be hers. Suddenly her mind began to spin with images of elaborate sets and elegant wardrobes and the name "Jill McPhearson" on the small screens in kitchens and living rooms and the multiscreens in television stores across the nation. She wondered if they would meet the president. "My God," was all she could manage to say.

"We'll have to finish out September in Boston." Christopher's words sounded like a faraway echo in her ears. "Then it's off to L.A., Hollywood, here we come."

The band started to play again as Maurice and Sam made their way back to the table.

"I guess you won't be getting rid of me as a neighbor, just because you're selling the house here," Sam added.

Her smile vanished. The house. The Vineyard. *It will, at last*, she thought, *be over. It will at last be behind me, behind that other person, Jill Randall, who will be gone forever.*

She let Sam refill her champagne glass, then half-listened to their chatter about concepts and television and Hollywood. She smiled and nodded, but it was all so dizzying, as though they were talking about someone else, some other person not connected with her. Every so often Christopher gave her a wink or squeezed her hand, pressing the cool, pear-shaped diamond against her flesh, sealing her future. At last.

Suddenly the haze of the champagne, the headiness of the laughter, and the beat of the music were pierced by a shout. A fierce, desperate shout.

"Fire!"

Jill snapped her head in the direction of the sound.

"Fire!" the voice yelled again.

Footsteps began running. Guests began screaming, shrieking, "Fire? Where?"

"Fire!" the voice shouted again. "Over on the ridge!"

Jill turned with the crowd, looking toward the next hill, where all she could see were sharp orange flames, bright yellow sparks, and Ben's dream silhouetted against a black cloud of smoke.

Chapter 24

Ben ripped off the cloth sling and took off across the dunes. Around him people ran, shouted, slammed car doors, gunned engines. People—island people. Not the celebrities, not the tourists.

"Ben! Ride with us!"

"Come on, Ben!"

But he didn't take the time to stop. He didn't want to slow the adrenaline pumping through his veins. He wanted to run. So he ran. And he ran, stumbling in the sand, yanking off his sneakers, tossing them into the dunes. He ran, his eyes focused straight ahead, up on the hill, up toward Menemsha House.

Halfway there, he fell. Grit dug into his hands, his mouth. He spat. He cursed the fact that he was fifty years old. He cursed the cast on his right arm that screwed up his balance. He cursed, then he righted himself and ran again.

The closer he got, the more engulfed the structure became. As he reached the last dune, heat blasted toward him.

"Jesus," he cried, then raced up the slope.

A hundred yards from the house it happened. The explosion was so quick, so intense, it knocked him backward. He looked up in time to see the huge mushroom of blue-white heat, the orange and black cloud burst across the summer sky. The paint thinner. The primer. The tubs of wood sealant. *And God, the bottled gas.*

He fell to his knees. "Jesus," he cried again as the shriek of sirens wailed up the road, muffled only by the sharp cracks of wood igniting, splintering, caving in, and by the shock of pain bouncing from his mind to his heart.

He stayed on his knees, he could not move. Rubber-coated firemen jumped from trucks, hauling hoses and unleashing the tanker. They shouted back and forth; Ben could not hear their words. His senses were numb, his thoughts paralyzed. Suddenly one man appeared at his side.

"Ben!" he yelled. "Ben! Who's inside?"

Ben looked up at the sweat-streaked face. "What?"

"We need to know if someone's in there. There's a truck parked beside the garage."

Ben stared at the man. "Jesus," was all he could say.

It was over an hour before the fire was under control enough to allow anyone to enter what was left of the house. It would have been worse, they said, if the gas tanks had been filled. It would have all been gone. Leveled.

By now, the sun had set; darkness had covered the land, the way the sun rises, the sun sets, no matter what has happened on earth, no matter what man has endured, or not endured. In the still-glowing embers, framed by the now blackened sky, Ben stood by the ambulance and watched and waited. Then a yellow-coated fireman emerged from the remnants with a body draped over his shoulder. Ben didn't have to look to know it was Kyle.

"Ben?" a thin voice wept. "Ben? Are you there?"

Ben swallowed back bile and leaned toward Kyle. The boy's face was charred, his eyes half-open and dazed. "I'm here, kid."

"Ben," he said in a voice so small, so weak, "Ben, I'm sorry." His chest rose. His chest fell. "I'm sorry," he whimpered. "I never meant to hurt you." Then his eyes closed, and his head dropped.

"He's still breathing," the paramedic announced as he tore the seal off a needle and started an IV.

As they worked on Kyle, Ben turned his head back to the embers, wishing he could vomit the ache in his gut, praying that Kyle was strong enough to survive, wondering what Kyle had meant. Had he set the blaze? Had he sent the threat? And had—oh, Jesus—had Kyle been the one who attacked him? The questions made him feel sicker, as the answers seemed grievously clear.

"Ben?" came Terry Clarkson's voice from beside him. "There's nothing else to be done here. Do you want a ride home?"

He shook his head. Behind him, he heard the gurney being hoisted into the ambulance, he heard the heavy doors slam. He lifted his head to the smoky sky, tears threatening to sting the corners of his eyes. "I'm going to walk back to Wilkins's and get my car. Thanks anyway."

He started down the road, his head bent, his arm throbbing. The ambulance passed him. He did not look up. As if in a funeral procession, more vehicles began to go by, descending the hill, in mourning for the boy whose life or death was uncertain, in mourning, Ben thought, for the grizzly aftermath of reality, in which fire depletes the soul and reminds us that we are only human, here for a moment, a flash in time. We are dispensable, our worlds destructible.

He walked along the road, avoiding the dunes. Cinders poked through his socks, but the pain on the soles of his feet was nothing compared with the pain he felt within. Kyle. His trusted helper. Kyle, the man Ben had wanted for his son. The man who had violated a fourteen-year-old girl and destroyed himself while attempting to destroy the one man in his life who had cared about him.

When he reached the top of Sam Wilkins's driveway, Ben looked around. The yellow-and-white-striped canopy stood alone: the music had died, the laughter had ceased. The cars that had been parked helter-skelter all over the lawn were nowhere to be seen. Only Carol Ann's small gray Nissan remained, a single reminder that people had been here, a party had happened.

He sighed and lumbered toward the car. Just then a shadow stepped from the darkness.

"Ben?" It was Jill McPhearson's voice.

He turned and watched as she moved closer, her white dress flowing around her like the robe of an angel.

"I sent Christopher back to the house," she said. "I thought you might come back for your car."

He nodded, but said nothing.

"Are you all right?"

He bit his lip. "Yeah. Sure."

"You lost your shoes."

He looked down at his feet. He noticed that his tan pants—the ones Carol Ann loved—were now streaked with thick black smudges of soot.

"And your sling," Jill added.

They stood in silence.

"Is the house . . . gone?" she asked.

Ben dug the car keys from his pocket and examined them carefully, as though he needed to study the small silver keys to determine which one would start the car, which one would make this all go away. "It might as well be," he said, then added, "Kyle was hurt."

He thought he heard Jill take a breath. "I know," she answered. "Someone came back and told us."

He stared at his socks. They were coated with sand, crusted with grit. "He's hurt bad. It's amazing he's still alive."

Jill stepped forward. "If you'd like to go to the hospital, I'd be glad to go with you."

He frowned. "Why?"

She lowered her eyes. "Because you're my friend. And Kyle is Rita's son. Rita is my friend, too."

She did not add that Kyle was her brother, her half brother by blood. But Ben could see the anguish in her eyes.

He opened the door and stood back. "Maybe you'd better drive," he said. "I'm not sure I'd get us there in one piece."

You'd think if they wanted people to be comfortable they'd do something about the goddamn air-conditioning, Rita thought as she sat on the gray vinyl chair in the emergency room waiting area freezing to death. Her feet, crossed at the ankles, barely touched the floor; she clutched her stomach around her bare midriff, wishing to hell she'd thrown on a sweater over her halter top and shorts. A nice warm sweater, one of Kyle's. A sweater that would make her feel close to him, close to his scent, his smile, his life.

She stuffed a fist in her mouth to prevent a cry from escaping. Then she swung her feet back and forth beneath the chair, wondering what was taking so goddamn long and why they wouldn't let her in to see him. He was her only child, for chrissakes. Her kid.

A harried woman in white pants and a tunic

trimmed in pink marched into the waiting area, studying the clipboard she held in her hand. Rita sat up straight. Her heart stopped beating.

The nurse flipped a page on the clipboard, then looked up. "MacElby?" she asked.

Rita stared a moment, then took as deep a breath as she could muster and rubbed the back of her neck. Across the room a fat old man in plaid Bermudas hauled himself from his seat. "That's me," he said. "Is my wife okay?"

"Follow me," the nurse ordered, and he waddled behind her down the hall, through the swinging doors behind which, somewhere, somewhere, Kyle was lying now, alone, without his mother.

Rita closed her eyes and wondered for the hundredth time since the phone call why Kyle had not been at the Wilkins's picnic, why he had been at Menemsha House, why, why, why.

They'd told her he was badly burned. His face, his chest, his arms. Her beautiful son. Burned. Charred. Rita had heard there was no other smell like it. Fried flesh. Her son's flesh. Blistered. Raw. Gone.

She clutched her stomach more tightly. She could not stop her head from bobbing, as it marked time in rhythmic sync with the swinging of her feet.

There was no one she could call.

Her mother was too far away.

She had no other friends. No one to sit beside her and wait. And talk. And listen. And just shut up and be there.

There was no one, because she'd wanted it that way. It had seemed too great a risk—the fear that if anyone got too close, if anyone uncorked her, her secrets would bubble over, her sins would spill out. If that had ever happened, Kyle would have hated her.

So now there was no one.

No one except Jill.

But she couldn't call Jill. Jill would never come. Why would she? Their worlds were too far apart. And Kyle had "spoiled" her daughter, ruined her for life. But they had been friends. First, for so many years. Then, friends again, in the way that only women can be for other women, without the constant dance of foreplay and the never-ending pressure of expectations, the way men and women seemed to be.

Get out of my life, Jill's last words to Rita had been.

Rita chewed the inside of her mouth and wished to God she had a drink.

They didn't speak on the drive to the hospital. Jill kept her hands clutched on the steering wheel, afraid to let go, afraid to lose control of her thoughts, her focus, herself.

She had told Ben that Rita was her friend. But was she? Did she really even know Rita any longer? Once, they shared their lives. Once, they shared their dreams. Once, they shared their deepest secrets.

Over and over the thoughts tumbled in her mind, as Jill tried to make sense of that summer of 1970. When had Rita been with Jill's father? Why hadn't Jill known? They'd rarely been around him. Rita had hardly known him. Or so Jill had thought.

As she turned at the blue and white hospital sign, Jill reminded herself that Rita had barely known her own father, either, that the only males in Rita's life had been one boyfriend after another. Boys. Not men. Not fathers of friends. Not that Jill had known.

"Swing right for the emergency room," Ben said.

Parking the car, Jill wondered if she'd ever really known Rita at all, the way she hadn't known her mother, the way she hadn't known her father. Then she wondered if she had come to the hospital for Rita's sake, for Kyle's, or for Ben's.

She turned off the ignition and lowered her head. "I'll wait here."

Ben nodded and got out of the car.

The minutes ticked slowly. Rita stared at the huge white clock with the black numerals that hung over the doorway—a jeering reminder of the long emergency room wait. She'd been here close to an hour already, with probably half the night to wait.

She glanced at a table overflowing with magazines. *Might as well read,* she thought. *Sooner or later they're going to come out and tell me Kyle's okay.* She rose from her chair and walked to the table. Leaning over, she shuffled through the magazines—old, tourist-rumpled magazines, but something, at least, to do. She picked up one that looked as though it had lots of recipes—maybe she'd start cooking again, the way she'd done when Kyle was little. She stood by the table and fanned through the pages, looking for the perfect foods that Kyle loved. He might be home recuperating for quite a while. She might as well start planning now.

Instead of returning to her chair, Rita paced the room, glancing at the color photos of pastas and tortes and fruit-layered compotes. But Kyle was an eclair man, Rita thought. Meat, potatoes, and eclairs. She threw the magazine back on the table just as Ben Niles stepped into the room.

"Rita?" he asked.

She stared at him a moment. He was filthy and disheveled and he wasn't wearing shoes. The arm with the cast stood frozen in place without its sling. It was smeared with black soot. She wondered if he'd been in the fire with Kyle. Then she remembered that the fire was at his house, on his property, and that it was his fault Kyle was now in the room he was in, with God-only-knew-what being done to him.

She folded her arms and turned away.

"Rita," his voice said from behind her. "I'm so sorry."

She stared at the painted white wall, at the tacky oil painting of a sunset over the ocean.

"Has there been any word?" he asked. "Do you know how he's doing?"

She balled her hands into fists and clenched them to her stomach. "Why?" she asked flatly. "Are you afraid we're going to sue?"

Ben didn't answer. The clock ticked off another minute. The orange circle on the canvas seemed to disappear beneath the horizon.

"I didn't know he was going to be there," Ben said. "I was next door at Sam Wilkins's . . ."

"Which is where Kyle should have been," Rita said. Quickly she turned on her heel. "Why wasn't he, Ben? Why wasn't he at that party instead of at your house?" Her head was pounding now; a lump had crawled into her chest.

"I don't know. I just don't know."

The nurse in white-trimmed-in-pink came into the room. "Mrs. Blair? The doctor would like to speak with you now."

Rita looked at her. Fear drenched her body. *The doctor would like to speak with you now.* Not "You can see your son now," or "Kyle is asking for you." None of those words. Simply *the doctor would like to speak with you now.*

She shot a glance back to Ben. He stepped forward and took her arm. "I'll go with you," he said.

Rita wanted to pull her arm away. She wanted to punch his gut, slap his face. But the touch of his hand softened the steel in her heart. She sucked her cheeks between her teeth and let him guide her down the hall.

• • •

"Please, Mrs. Blair, sit down," the doctor who looked no older than Kyle said when they entered the small cubicle with his name on the door. "Robert Palmer, M.D.," the plaque read. Rita sat in another gray vinyl, waiting-room-like chair. Ben stood beside her.

Young Dr. Palmer leaned against a desk that was buried in file folders. He took off his glasses and held them in both hands. "I'm afraid the news isn't good."

Ben put his hand on her shoulder.

"Your son has third-degree burns over sixty percent of his body."

She heard Ben let out a groan, but Rita sat silent, as rigid as the arm under Ben's cast.

"We're doing everything we can, but the prognosis is not good. Right now, he's hanging on."

Rita lifted her chin. *How long do you think he'll be in the hospital?* she thought, wondering if there would be time to recheck those recipes, to go to the grocery store.

The doctor looked at Ben, then back to Rita. "If the situation were less critical, we'd airlift him to Boston."

"Kyle hates flying."

"In any event, we've ruled out that possibility."

Rita nodded. "Good," she responded. She studied her manicure. The tips of two fingers were chipped. She really must get home and redo them before she showed any houses tomorrow.

"Apparently you don't understand," the doctor said so softly she had to strain to hear.

She raised her head again and watched as he mouthed the words: "Your son's chances of survival are slim."

The air in the room was a vacuum that sucked the oxygen from her brain. The file folders, the desk, the doctor, began to blur, began to sway. Rita gripped the edges of her chair. "Could you speak a little louder?" she asked. "I seem to be having trouble with my ears."

The doctor repeated what he'd said.

Ben stepped closer to her chair.

Rita's eyes dropped to the glasses the doctor held in his hands. They were brown-framed, thick-lensed. *What the fuck does he know about Kyle?* she asked herself. *The guy is half-blind.* She looked back into his half-blind eyes. "When can I see him?"

"It will be a while. They're still working on him."

She closed her eyes, floating with the dizziness of the room. She did not want to think about what they were doing to her son. To her beautiful, handsome, strong, healthy son. She did not want to think about it, and she did not have to, because they had everything under control. They were working on him.

Her eyes flew open. *They were working on him?* Slowly, her head began to clear, her senses began to sharpen. They were working on Kyle because *his chances were slim.*

His chances were slim because he was going to die.

He was going to die.

Die.

"Shall we go back to the waiting room?" Ben asked.

"You can if you'd like," the doctor said. "But I'm afraid it will be a long wait. You may prefer to go home and get some rest. I can call you to come back."

Rita looked down at her bony, freckled knees, at the tiny purple veins blotched together by blood, blood that was under her skin pumping, proving that she was alive. She was alive, and so, for now, was Kyle.

"I'm not going anywhere," her voice cracked.

"My son is here and I will wait here." It didn't matter if it took an hour, a day, or a month. No one was going to make Rita Blair leave her son.

"I'll stay with you," Ben said. "And someone else is here, too. She's out in the car."

She couldn't imagine what Ben meant.

"Jill," he said slowly. "Jill's here to be with you."

They hugged for several minutes. Jill stroked her hand through Rita's curls; Rita sobbed and sobbed until Jill feared her friend would come apart, limb by limb, seam by seam. Jill did not know or care where her tears stopped and Rita's began—she only felt wet salt against her cheeks, and knew that this was right. No matter what Rita's son had done, no matter what Rita had done, she was her friend, the one best friend Jill had ever known.

At last they moved to a corner of the waiting area and sat beside each another. Jill held firmly on to Rita's hands, trying in vain to ease their trembling.

"Think I'll go find some coffee," Ben announced, then padded off in his stocking feet, leaving them alone.

"Oh, God, Jill," Rita cried. "What am I going to do?"

"You are going to sit tight. And you are going to pray. We are both going to pray."

"I don't think I know how."

"Me either. I guess I should have listened to my mother after all."

Her comment brought a small smile to Rita's lips. "She never liked me, did she?"

Jill took her hands from Rita's. "My mother? Oh, I don't know, Rita. I don't think she liked anyone very much. Certainly not me."

"You had a good home though, Jill. With two parents, who loved each other."

Growing restless in her chair, Jill wished Rita would talk about something other than her parents. Other than her father, Kyle's father. "Yes, well," she said, "nothing's perfect."

Rita's eyes were glazed as she stared across the room into nothingness. "I always envied you—that you had a father. He was a wonderful man."

Jill rubbed one palm against the other. *Here it comes*, she thought. *Rita's hurting right now, so she's going to exorcise her guilt. She's going to tell the truth.* Jill tried to remind herself that no matter what her friend told her now, it would be okay. And that no matter what, she would stay here and be with Rita, no matter how much it hurt. Because nothing Jill might feel could compare to Rita's pain—the pain of having her only child, her son, lying down the hall, breathing his last breaths. Florence and George Randall were already dead. It didn't matter what Rita said now. It didn't matter if she needed to tell the truth. Jill looked down at her glittering diamond and wondered how she could make Rita's life easier. She wondered if she should mention it first, if she should open her mouth and say, "Rita, I know that my father was Kyle's father." But the glaze across Rita's eyes and the mascara stains down her cheeks told Jill that Rita needed to do this herself. For her own sake. For Kyle's.

"I don't know what I would have done without your father when I got pregnant," she said quietly. Then she turned her face to Jill. "You didn't know that, did you? You didn't know how much he helped me?"

I didn't even know you were sleeping with him, Jill wanted to shout, but shook her head instead.

"I was so scared," Rita continued. "Too scared to even tell you. I was so afraid everyone would find out. And that they'd think I was just like my mother."

Jill blinked. "Your mother?"

"My mother was a whore," Rita said flatly. "The father who left when I was ten probably wasn't even mine. My mother screwed every guy from the island to the mainland and back again. As soon as any man touched ground on Martha's Vineyard, they were fair game for Hazel Blair."

Pressure began to build at Jill's temples. "I didn't know that, Rita. I never knew that."

"Everyone else did. Your mother did."

"My mother? Are you sure?"

Rita attempted a laugh. "Come on, Jill. Why do you think she didn't like me? My mother worked for your father. Your mother knew who she was. She knew what she was."

Jill put her hand on Rita's once again. "Rita, I'm so sorry. Why didn't we ever talk about this before now?"

"What could you have done? Made my mother stop? Made me stop? Made it so I never would have gotten pregnant?"

"I don't know, Rita. Maybe if we'd talked . . ."

"You were determined to get away from here. There was nothing I could do to stop you."

"But you were pregnant . . ."

"It wasn't your problem. It wasn't your concern."

They sat in silence. Jill heard the clock tick once, then twice.

"Rita," she asked quietly, "you said my father helped you, but he should have done more."

"More? God, Jill, your father did more than you know. He gave me two thousand dollars to run away. To go off to Worcester. To have the baby. To have my Kyle." She shook her head. Tears spilled down her cheeks once more. "I don't know if it was because he felt sorry for me or what, but your father did more for me than the baby's father could have done."

Jill stared at Rita. She blinked again, then stared at the floor. She raised her eyes and stared at the wall, the clock. Had she heard her right? Had she really heard her right? "Rita," she whispered at last, "tell me about the baby's father. Kyle's father."

Staring across the room a moment, Rita answered, "He never knew. He still doesn't know. He was too good for me, Jill. I cared about him too much, and I wasn't going to ruin his life . . . ruin it by being stuck with me, of all people, and by having everyone around here talk."

"Ruin his life? What about *your* life?"

"My life wasn't ruined. I had Kyle."

"Rita," Jill said slowly, carefully, "there was no soldier in Worcester, was there?"

"No."

She swallowed hard; she clenched her jaw. "Rita?" she asked. "Who is Kyle's father?"

Rita hung her head. Her red curls were limp, damp, unraveled. She laced her fingers together, as though knitting the shards of her thoughts. "Kyle's father," she answered quietly, "is Charlie Rollins."

Chapter 25

Just before dawn, the doctor came and told them that Rita could sit with Kyle. "He's in a coma," the doctor warned her. "But you can stay with him if you like." Rita nodded and stood on shaky legs. "I have to warn you, he is heavily bandaged. We've brought a small bed into his room, in case you'd like to get some rest."

Jill and Ben walked with her to Kyle's room: it was small and dim, with a strong odor of antiseptic, the persistent beep of a heart monitor, and the mournful squish-squish of a respirator. The figure that lay on the bed was shrouded in white, with tubes going in and coming out of different parts of him . . . of *Kyle*, Jill realized and took a step back.

"Rita," Ben whispered, "I think Jill and I should leave you alone with him. But we'll come back later, okay?"

Rita did not look back to Jill and Ben. She simply stood by the bedside and stared at her son. "That would be nice," she said. "Kyle would like that."

Jill gazed out the window as Ben drove down Water Street, thinking about Rita, thinking about Kyle. She wondered if her mother had ever learned the truth, or if she had died believing that her husband had cheated on her, had fathered a child by a young island girl. She was glad she had not told Rita about the diary. She was glad she had not upset her friend more than she already was. Some secrets, Jill thought, were best left alone. Or shared with someone as objective—as kind—as Ben.

When they reached the intersection for the road to the tavern, Jill turned to Ben. "You can drop me off here," she said, "I want to go to the tavern. I'm going to leave a note for Charlie and tell him what has happened."

Ben gestured to the early pink sky. "It's a little early for him to be open, Jill."

"I know how to get in."

He pulled to the curb.

Her body ached and her mind was numb with exhaustion. Jill walked down the alley and went to the Dumpster, where she quickly found the crowbar in its place. As she pried open the lock, she realized that the one person she hadn't blamed was her father. Perhaps she believed that her mother deserved to be betrayed. But that had been before she had known the real Florence Randall—the woman concealed within the pages of the diary, the vulnerable, sad woman, stranded in pain.

The latch popped and Jill opened the door. She stepped into the quiet kitchen, the way she and Rita had done only a couple of weeks before. But now there was no laughter, no sounds that would haunt her, perhaps, for the rest of her life. She looked quickly around for a piece of paper, then decided to check in the dining room near the waitress station.

As she pushed open the swinging door, Jill stopped. Seated at a table, his head bent, a mug of coffee in front of him, sat Charlie.

"Jill," he said, looking up. "What are you doing here?"

"Charlie," Jill said and walked closer to him. "Are you all right?"

"I was up half the night."

"Me, too." She pulled out a chair and sat beside him. "Charlie, there's something you might want to know."

"I heard about Kyle."

Jill nodded.

"How's he doing? Is he . . . ?"

She shook her head. "He's still alive. But it doesn't look good."

He picked up a spoon and stirred his coffee. "Is Rita with him?"

"Yes. I'm going back later."

"He's mine, isn't he?"

His words came so quickly, she didn't know how to react. She hadn't planned to tell Charlie that Kyle was his son. She'd decided to leave that up to Rita, if Rita felt he should know.

"Perhaps you should go to the hospital," she said. "I think you and Rita have a lot to talk about."

He nodded slowly. "She never wanted me. All these years I've loved her, but she never wanted me."

"Maybe she felt it was you who didn't want her," Jill said. "Maybe she felt she wasn't good enough for you."

Charlie raised his eyebrows. "I'd have done anything for that woman."

Jill stood. "Then do something now, Charlie. Go to her. Be there for her. Right now, Rita needs all the friends she can find."

Carol Ann was standing in the kitchen when Ben returned. In her plain cotton robe and terry slippers, she could have been Louise. She sipped from her coffee cup and turned to face him. Tears coated her eyes. "Dad," was all she said.

Ben held open his good arm. Carol Ann walked forward and leaned into him, wrapping both arms around his back, squeezing him tightly, as she had not done since she was a little girl. Ben closed his eyes and let her love flow into him—this wonderful daughter who was very much his, very much here, and very much alive.

"Dad, I've been so worried," she cried. "If anything had happened to you . . . well, I just love you so much."

He pushed down his own tears, wondering how long it had been since she'd said those words, if she ever had at all. He realized now that for two people who had not been born in New England, he and Louise had sadly adopted the tradition of not speaking their feelings, of holding back their emotions. He made a pledge to put an end to that now, right here, in Carol Ann's kitchen.

"I love you, too, honey," he said, "more than you'll ever know."

She squeezed him gently, then pulled back and touched his cheek. "You need coffee."

"I'll make it."

Carol Ann laughed. "You can't make coffee with one arm."

Ben looked down at his dangling white plaster. "Right," he said. "I forgot."

She smiled and touched his other cheek, then went to the sink and took the coffeepot from the burner. The red button, Ben noticed, was on, though the pot was almost drained.

"Looks like you've already had a few cups," he noted.

"I haven't had much sleep," she said, rinsing the pot and refilling the basket with dark Colombian blend, Ben's favorite. "Terry Clarkson stopped by last night. He told us what happened. And about Kyle."

Ben pulled out an oak kitchen chair and sat at the table. He took a banana from the ever-present centerpiece of fresh fruit and began to peel. "Kyle's holding his own. But he's in bad shape."

"Do you think he'll pull through?"

"No." He blinked as he peeled back the skin. It was the first time he'd said it out loud, that Kyle wasn't going to make it, that Kyle was going to die. He hoped to hell he was wrong.

"Well, it's in God's hands, Dad."

Ben set the banana, uneaten, on the woven placemat. "Menemsha House is gone. Completely gutted. Burned practically to the ground."

She turned from the sink and sat beside him, then covered his hand with hers. "I'm so sorry, Dad."

He nodded and examined her long fingers, her short, clean nails. "It looks like it was Kyle. It's so hard to believe. I thought he was such a good kid . . ." Ben ran his finger around her plain wedding band, her small solitary diamond. "I guess it was him all along. Kyle who assaulted me, who sent the threats, who set the fire. He did it all."

Carol Ann shook her head. "No, Dad. That's not entirely true."

Ben pulled back his hand. "What do you mean?"

"Terry told us that when Carrie learned that Kyle had been caught in the fire, she became hysterical. She fled to the police station. She told them the truth."

He felt the muscles wrench in his gut. "Carrie? Sam's daughter?" The same Carrie who had stood on his back steps only nights ago, who had tried her damnedest to come on to him?

"Yes. Apparently there's a Saudi Arabian man named Ishmale or Isham or something like that who's been staying at the Wilkins place this summer.

From what Terry said, the man was going to put up the money for Sam's comeback. I guess no one else would, on account of the questions about his wife's death."

Ben nodded, not really caring if Sam Wilkins had killed his wife or not, only caring that Kyle—the boy he had trusted—now lay close to death.

"According to Carrie," Carol Ann continued, "this Isham person wanted the land where Menemsha House was. He made a deal with Sam: you get me the land, I'll finance your world tour."

He picked up the banana peel, then split it in half. "How did Kyle fit in?"

"Carrie's father was going to pay him to get rid of you and the house. I guess Kyle—or Kyle's mother—needed money."

He rose from the chair, poured himself a cup of coffee, and stared out the kitchen window at the scrub pines that dotted the backyard. A fat gray squirrel scooted across the bed of needles, in search of an acorn, in search of survival. Ben knew the feeling. He had searched this island for twenty years to survive; he had been convinced it was a futile battle. The one islander he could depend on—the only one—had been Kyle Blair. "So it *was* Kyle."

"Apparently he never meant to hurt you. The night he attacked you he thought you'd already be at the zoning board meeting. He went to your house to steal your duplicate plans so Sam could see them."

"Kyle knows I always make two sets of plans."

She nodded and continued. "You surprised him by being there. After . . . after it happened, he backed out of the deal."

Ben nodded. Of course Kyle hadn't wanted to hurt him. He had come to the house unarmed. *I'm sorry,* Kyle had said last night. Ben swallowed back tears. "Go on," he said to Carol Ann now.

"Illumination Night, he told Carrie to tell her father to forget it. They had a fight about it."

Illumination Night, Ben thought, taking a slow sip of his coffee. The night Kyle was with Amy. Drunk, confused, and probably scared. "Men do the damnedest things when they're scared," he muttered.

"Carrie went to Kyle's house to try and get him to reconsider. When she told him about her father's picnic, I guess Kyle put two and two together and decided it might be the night Sam would make his move."

"Who set the fire?"

"Carrie. Afterward, when she was sneaking back to the party, she saw Kyle's truck go up the driveway. He must have seen the fire. He went inside and started trying to put it out. But Carrie had doublebacked. She found him in the house: they fought. Then she whacked him over the head with a paint can and ran."

He took another drink, letting the rich blend soothe his insides. "Why do you suppose Carrie spilled the beans?"

"She said something about not being able to stand any more lies."

Ben watched another squirrel fighting for his life. "I knew Kyle wouldn't do it alone. All night I've been wondering if he was paid off by Ashenbach or some other yahoo on the zoning board. I thought none of them wanted me to succeed. I decided it had more to do with me than with Menemsha House."

"That's not true, Dad. The town fathers want you to rebuild."

Ben turned from the window and looked at his daughter. "What?"

"I said they want you to rebuild. Terry Clarkson said it has nothing to do with bad publicity, whatever that means. Anyway, a lot of the men are willing to pitch in and help."

He frowned. "Why?"

Carol Ann shrugged. "I guess they decided you belong here after all."

Jill sat at the rolltop desk in her parents' living room; Christopher sat in the wing chair, her father's wing chair, worn now on the armrests, worn by a man who had been a good man, who had been a loving husband, despite his wife's shortcomings, despite her pain. George Randall had done the best he'd known how, to sustain his family, to give them his home, to share his roots.

She ran her finger across the top rung of the ladder-back of the cherry chair—the antique cherry chair, which would soon belong to Mrs. Sherman, who would know what to do with it, who would appreciate its worth.

"You had quite a night," Christopher said.

"I'm sorry that all this had to happen with Maurice here. That it all had to happen on the night we should have been celebrating."

"Life happens, Jill. When we least expect it, we get clobbered. The important thing is to keep our focus."

Slowly, she nodded. "Is Maurice still sleeping?"

Christopher laughed. "He's gone clamming with Jeff."

Jill smiled. "That boy surely has taken to the island."

"Well, he only has until tomorrow. As sad as he'll be to leave, Amy will be glad."

"I wonder how she'll feel when she learns about Kyle."

Christopher shook his head. "It's over and done with, honey. She's young. Believe me, she'll soon forget that Kyle Blair or Martha's Vineyard ever existed."

"She'll be excited about L.A."

"She already is. I told her last night."

Jill raised her eyes to meet his. "You told her?"

He leaned forward, placing his elbows on his pressed khaki pants. "I thought it was best. Maurice and I stayed up late talking about the new show. I was afraid the kids would overhear."

Jill nodded. She wanted to tell him he shouldn't have done that, that it should have come from her, that she was their mother, that he was not their father. Then she remembered that soon he would be their father—*step*father—and that she was probably overreacting again. Overreacting, this time, because she'd had no sleep. No sleep, and a damned stressful night. "Is she excited?"

"An understatement."

Jill stood up. "I guess that's good."

"Honey, I know you two have had your problems these past few weeks, but things will change once we get away from here. Once you're able to put all this nonsense behind you."

Nonsense? Jill wondered. Is that what he thought about the fire last night, about the fact that Kyle lay close to death, that Rita—her friend—was now alone, sitting by his bedside, praying for a miracle that probably would not happen? Is that what he would have thought if she'd told him about her mother's diary?

"I'm going to take a shower," she said. "Then I might try and get a nap. If you don't mind, I'd like to go back to the hospital later on."

"Is that necessary? I thought you'd want to start packing for our trip home tomorrow. And Maurice wants to take us to Falmouth tonight to the Regatta for dinner. Amy and Jeff included."

The Regatta was an exclusive French restaurant that hugged Vineyard Sound, and was well known for its celebrity patrons and pricey cuisine. "He wants to go to Falmouth?" she asked, annoyed at the thought of making the trip.

"We can get a cab out of Woods Hole, then come back on the ten forty-five ferry. Maurice checked it out last night."

Jill tried to straighten the wrinkles of her sundress.

"There's more," Christopher continued with a smile, "Addie's driving down from Boston to join us."

What little energy she had remaining now drained from her body. It apparently didn't matter about Kyle. It apparently didn't matter about Rita, or that a good man had just seen his dreams go up in smoke. Then Jill reminded herself that Rita, Kyle, and Ben were part of Jill's life, not Christopher's. Not Maurice Fischer's. And not Addie's. She cleared her throat. "Well, it sounds as though you two have worked everything out." She didn't care now whether or not her annoyance showed.

Christopher stepped close to her. "Honey, when we leave tomorrow, Maurice goes back to Atlanta to draw up the contracts."

"So I need to be nice until then, right?"

He winked his wink. "That's my girl."

She wanted to tell him she was not his girl, that she was a grown woman who didn't like being talked down to, who liked being her own person and making her own decisions. She would need to work on this once they were married. But right now, she needed to take a shower. And get some sleep. "I'll run over to the hospital before we leave. I'll be back in plenty of time."

Christopher kissed her cheek. "Wear that little black dress with the sequins tonight, okay?"

Jill nodded, thinking that it would be different to be dressed up again, to have something on her feet other than sandals, and to wear her hair in a way that she wouldn't need to worry about getting wind-blown. It would be different, and, she supposed, it would be nice.

She blinked and headed for the stairs, wondering how long it would take her to readjust to reality, once they were home in Boston again.

Chapter 26

The door to Kyle's hospital room opened. Rita looked up, expecting to see a doctor or a nurse or, worse, the police. But instead Charlie Rollins stood there, his eyes swollen and red, almost as if he'd been crying. Rita quickly turned her head back to Kyle.

"Charlie," she said, "what brings you to these parts? I hope you're not sick."

His footsteps moved toward her. Rita closed her eyes, knowing she should put up her armor, pull all her defenses closely around her, the way that had become her habit around Charlie—a habit for so many years. But now, she didn't have the strength.

"I came to see you," Charlie said. "And Kyle."

Rita studied her son's face, trying to remember what it looked like beneath the layers of bandages. "He looks like a mummy," she said.

Charlie walked to the chair where Rita sat close to the bed. He knelt down and took her hand. "I'm so sorry, Rita. I'm so sorry this happened."

She sucked the inside of her cheeks and nodded. "Did Jill call you?"

"No. She came to the tavern. But I'd already heard. The Vineyard grapevine, remember?" he added, as though trying to lighten the mood.

Nodding again, she wondered how much Jill had told him.

"Rita?" he asked then, in a tone that told her what was coming next. Her thoughts flashed like lightning as she struggled to put the pieces of her story into place, the pieces of the lie she'd told so many times, so long ago. But she couldn't remember . . . she couldn't remember . . .

"Rita," Charlie said again, "he's mine, isn't he?"

She flicked her eyes to the respirator, to the heart monitor, back to Kyle's face. What used to be Kyle's face. She wanted to flee, to run from the room, to race home and drain a bottle of scotch. She wanted to flee, but she couldn't. Charlie was between her and the door. And Kyle, she thought. Kyle needed her here.

A tidal wave of tears drenched her cheeks. She quickly put her hands to her face; she would not have believed there were any tears left inside her.

Charlie put his arm around her shoulder. "You know," he said quietly, "I've watched Kyle grow up. All these years, part of me wanted to think he was my son. Our son. Yours and mine. I'd watch him fly past the tavern on his bike, or see him come in after school to wait for you, and I just always wished, I just always hoped . . ." His voice faltered. "Why didn't you tell me, Rita? Am I that . . . repulsive to you?"

She lay her hands on the edge of the bed. "No, Charlie. Maybe that was the problem."

"Sorry. I don't understand."

"You are Charlie Rollins. The hardworking son of a well-respected family. The guy who went on to do something with his life. The guy with the one thing that Rita Blair was deprived of at birth. Respectability."

The respirator squished. The heart monitor beeped.

"Jesus, Rita. I don't believe this. I love you. I have loved you since we were kids. I always thought I was the one who wasn't good enough for you."

She turned to him. Charlie's red, swollen eyes were level with hers. "Thanks, but I'm too old for bullshit, Charlie. Especially now."

He wove his fingers through her curls. "It's not bullshit, Rita. I love you."

Rita turned back and looked at her son, thinking of her years of struggles, her years of trying to protect Kyle from the wrongs she had done. Maybe, she thought now, that had been her greatest wrong of all.

"Tell me, Rita. Just tell me. Please. Is Kyle my son?"

She lightly touched the gauze wrapped around Kyle's arm. She remembered his arm, so strong, so nice when he wrapped it around her and said things like "Everything will be okay, Mom," or "I love you, Mom." She wondered if that arm would ever hug her again. She thought about the other arm around her now. Charlie's arm. Charlie Rollins, the man she had fought all this time to forget. The man who loved her still.

"Yes, Charlie," Rita said finally. "Kyle is your son."

Charlie leaned close to her and enveloped her in his arms. Together they cried and cried, the pulse of the heart monitor and the soft squish of the respirator weeping with them in their grief.

Late in the afternoon, Jill stood in the doorway of Kyle's room. She did not want to interrupt Rita and Charlie: they seemed so peaceful, sitting side by side, watching the motionless figure that lay shrouded in white. She put her hand to the large diamond necklace at her throat and smiled with the knowledge that it had been the right thing to tell Charlie to come.

"Why is it you always look as though you just stepped out of a magazine?" a voice behind her asked.

Jill turned and faced Ben, who was now scrubbed clean and wearing shoes, though it didn't look as though he'd had a chance to sleep either. His baseball cap was back in place, and he wore a new sling—a makeshift-looking brace stitched from denim. Jill wondered if his daughter had made it for him, or the "friend" he had mentioned. She glanced down at herself and suddenly felt foolish for standing in the hospital corridor in her skimpy black dress with the short sequined jacket, an outfit for Hollywood, not the Vineyard. "We're going over to Falmouth for dinner," she explained. "I wanted to stop in and see Rita before we left."

Ben looked past her, into the room. "Any word?"

"I just arrived. I didn't want to interrupt them." She followed his gaze. They stood quietly a moment, watching, waiting.

"I wonder if Kyle knows they're here," Ben said.

"I did a story once on people who had emerged from a coma. Some said they were aware of voices, of loved ones being there. I confirmed it by checking with the families. They said after coming out of the coma, the patients related conversations they would have had no way of knowing otherwise."

Ben smiled. "Ever the reporter."

Jill felt embarrassed. "I guess," she said softly.

"I'd like to go in now," he added, taking off his Red Sox cap. "Do you think it's all right?"

"I don't know why not."

She rapped on the door frame. Rita looked up.

"Hey," she said as she stood, "you guys came back."

"Of course we did," Jill said, walking toward her and kissing her cheek. "Is there any change?"

Rita glanced back to the bed. "No. None."

"Hello, Charlie," Ben said.

Charlie nodded and stood.

"Rita?" Ben asked. "Could I say a few words to Kyle?"

Rita scowled. "Sure. If you want."

"You may want to listen," he said as he moved close to the bed and pulled the chair closer.

Jill held on to Rita. Charlie moved to her other side and held her other hand.

"Kyle," Ben whispered, "it's me, Ben. How're you doing, buddy?" His voice cracked a little; Jill's throat started to close. "Kyle, I know what happened." He held his cap in his hands and studied it now, tracing and retracing his finger along the brim. "Thanks for trying to save the house. That means a lot to me. And forget about everything else. You had your reasons. The only thing that matters is that you did the right thing in the end."

Jill looked at Rita who shook her head. "I have no idea . . ." Rita whispered.

"We're going to rebuild, Kyle. We got the approval. And you know," Ben continued with a short laugh, "you're not going to believe this, but they're all going to help. Clarkson included. So you'd better hurry and get out of this bed, because you've got work to do. Can you hear me, kid?"

From under the gauze, there was no response.

Ben stood up and wiped his eyes. He walked back toward them. "He's a good kid, Rita. No matter what, always remember he's a good kid. And he did the right thing." He stepped forward and hugged Rita. Jill fought back her tears.

Suddenly the room grew curiously silent. The respirator beat out its thump-squish. But there was no other sound. Nothing. Then, an alarm rang. Rita pulled quickly from Ben.

"Kyle!" she screamed and raced to her son. "Oh, my God, his heart stopped beating!"

Jill froze. Ben flew out the door. Charlie ran to Rita's side.

"Kyle!" she cried. "Kyle! It's Mom. I'm here. Please. Oh, God, no."

A nurse rushed in, followed by a doctor. "Everyone please leave," he said firmly.

Jill leaned back against the wall. Rita turned rigid, her body like stone, unblinking, unmoving. Charlie cupped his arms around her and whispered, "Come on, Rita," then guided her past Jill and out the door. Jill followed them into the hall where Ben was standing.

She looked at him. "Is he . . ."

Ben held out his arms. Jill sunk into them.

And then the doctor came out of the room. He walked to Rita. "I'm so sorry, Mrs. Blair," he said, "please know we did everything we could. It's better this way. It's better for your son."

"I want to see him," Rita said after a few moments. "Can I see him?"

The doctor nodded. "Of course."

She took a deep breath and started back toward the room. Then she stopped, turned around, and held out her hand. "Charlie?" she asked. Charlie went to her, and together they went to say good-bye to Kyle.

Jill could barely stand the pain that coursed through her. She leaned against Ben and silently watched Rita and Charlie stand by Kyle's bedside, silently watched as Rita got down on her knees and folded her hands in prayer. Jill suddenly thought of her mother . . . her mother, who, too, had watched her son die. Jill's father—like Charlie—had been there to help her, but he had not known her pain. Perhaps her mother had been too ashamed to let it show; perhaps because they had lived in a different era, a different time, no one had realized how important it was to support the ones left behind.

Jill looked at her watch: it was five-ten. Tomorrow she would be leaving Rita again, going back to Boston, then on to L.A., onward with her life. But tonight Rita needed her. Christopher and Addie and Maurice Fischer could make do without her: there were plenty of nights for dinner that lay ahead for them: there was only one night left that she could spend with Rita. Rita. Her best friend. Her best friend who needed her now.

Jill stood up straight. "I'll be right back," she said to Ben, then headed down the hall in search of a pay phone to call Christopher and tell him to come pick up the Range Rover and go ahead without her.

Ben drove through the traffic after leaving the hospital in Oak Bluffs.

Jill tried not to think about Christopher, or the fact that he'd been angry when she called. She'd deal with him later—tomorrow. She looked out the window at the homes that passed by—the gray-shingled Capes, the clean, white colonials. They drove along the beach road, past the dunes, and the beach grass, and the clusters of beach plums—now ripened and ready for another year of picking. Then they moved into Edgartown, her town, and turned down West Tisbury Road, headed toward Rita's house, the one place that had always seemed like home.

Rita and Charlie were already there. Jill and Ben joined them in the warm, comforting kitchen: Jill made coffee that no one drank, and sandwiches that no one ate. Still, it was good to be together, each sharing their own form of pain, each perhaps feeling their own share of guilt. Rita insisted that Ben tell her the details of what had happened: when Jill heard about Carrie's part in the plot against Menemsha House, and that she'd set the fire, she recoiled.

"I checked with the police before going back to the hospital," Ben finished. "They're in custody now—Carrie and her father. The Saudi Arabian will most likely be deported."

A small part of Jill was glad that Carrie had been caught, that Carrie and Sam Wilkins would be punished, though no part of her would ever have wanted Kyle to die. Not even after all he had done, Kyle hadn't deserved to die. Then, she thought about her story on Sam, and wondered how Maurice would react when she told him it could never be aired. She wanted to ask Ben what he thought Carrie meant when she'd said she couldn't stand any more lies. But now was not the time. And Ben was not the one to ask.

By eight-thirty, Rita was exhausted.

"I think you should try and get some sleep," Charlie said, then turned to Jill and Ben. "I'll stay with her tonight. You guys go ahead."

Jill went to Rita and hugged her tightly: Rita, her brave, brave friend. "I know you'll be all right," Jill said, "I know you'll be all right, in time."

Rita cried into Jill's sequins.

"Have you thought about a funeral?" Jill asked.

"Kyle wouldn't have wanted that. He would have wanted to be cremated. To have his ashes scattered across the sea."

A true islander, Jill thought, and hugged her friend more tightly.

Then Rita pulled back and, with a long red fingernail, brushed away Jill's tears. "You're leaving to-morrow, aren't you?"

Jill nodded but could not speak.

"Will you ever come back?"

"Yes, Rita. Of course." Even as she said the words, Jill knew they were probably untrue. She knew her life would take up where it had left off; she knew she would be soon far from the Vineyard, far, even, from Boston. But she could not tell that to Rita now. She combed Rita's curls through her fingers and smiled. "There's no reason you can't come to see me, either," she said, and had a brief, magical picture of Rita in L.A., living it up. Then Jill looked back into Rita's wet eyes and wondered if Rita would ever laugh again, would ever find pleasure and release from her pain. She leaned down and kissed Rita's cheek. "I'll phone you," she said quietly. "That's a promise."

"I'll drive you home, Jill," Ben said.

She pulled away from Rita and shook her head. "No, thanks, Ben. I'd like to walk."

She said good-bye to Charlie and went out the door, with Ben close behind. "It's a nice night for a walk," he said. "Do you feel like company?"

They walked without speaking, Jill's black satin heels clicking against the brick sidewalk, Ben's good arm steadying her as they sidestepped the window-shopping tourists, who still crowded the streets, though the stores had long since closed for their short Sunday hours, and the sky had grown purple now, nearly dark.

When they reached her parents' house, Jill noticed the lights were off. She didn't know why that surprised her; she supposed she had hoped Christopher had stayed behind, or canceled the dinner, postponing the celebration until they could all be together.

Then she remembered that Addie would have driven down from Boston. Still, it would have been nice.

"It's been quite a day," Ben said as they walked to her front door.

"Thank you for everything you've done," she said, retrieving her key from her purse. "For me. For Rita."

Ben nodded, and as Jill looked into his gray eyes, she realized this may be the last time she'd ever see him, then realized the thought made her sad.

"I'll call you from Boston. You know," she stammered, "to make sure things go all right with Mrs. Sherman."

"Don't worry, I'm sure they'll be fine. If anyone can get a good price for you, the Shermans can."

She bit her lip and looked into the dark window, then up at the small glass inlaid whale over the door. "I like that," she said, pointing up. "I don't think I ever told you how much I like the whale. It's your trademark." She bent her head and toyed with the key. "I still think doing a story on you was a great idea."

Ben laughed. "I'm not sure your expanded audience would have agreed."

She smiled into his eyes. "They would have been wrong."

Silence fell between them. The peepers began to sing.

"Peepers," Ben said as he put his cap on his head. "They're getting louder. It's almost fall."

"Yes," Jill answered. "Almost."

He looked around the front of the house. "Will you be okay?"

Jill shrugged. "Sure. I'll be fine."

The peepers sang again.

"Well," she said, inserting the key in the lock, "I guess I'll say good night."

"Yes," Ben answered. "And good-bye."

"Yes," she replied. She turned the key and pushed the door open, then turned back to face him. "Will you check in on Rita from time to time?"

"Absolutely."

Jill nodded again. "Good. She'll need her friends now."

Ben reached up and touched her cheek. "We all need friends, Jill." Then he leaned forward and gently, softly, touched his lips to hers.

She closed her eyes and raised her hands to his shoulders. His kiss was so tender, so filled with caring. She parted her mouth a little. She kissed him back, surprised at the warmth that flowed through her, surprised at the peace that enveloped her every pore, her every nerve, her very soul.

"Good-bye, Jill," Ben said as he broke away.

"Good-bye, Ben," she answered quietly, then let herself into the dark house and closed the door behind her before she could tell him not to go.

She leaned against the door, stared up into the black staircase, and tried to catch her breath. Her vision blurred, her eyes grew wet. *Ben Niles*, she thought, *is like no man I've ever known*. She closed her eyes and, for a moment, tried to let herself feel the touch of his lips on hers again. The warm, wonderful touch of a sensitive, caring man. She brought a finger to her lips and gently touched them. They tingled. They parted. They wanted more. She frowned, the creases of her brow deepening, the yearning inside her rising.

Just then there was a knock on the door. Her heart fluttered. Quickly Jill turned and opened it.

Ben stood there, a small grin on his face.

"Come in," Jill said without hesitation.

Once inside he pulled her to him without words. The strength of his arms enveloped her as he kissed

her face, her eyes, her neck. Never had Jill felt so
wanted, so needed, so loved.

They climbed the stairs. When they reached the
top, Jill did not go to her parents' bedroom, to the
bed she shared with Christopher. She needed this to
be special, so very special. She took Ben by the hand
and led him up to the widow's walk.

Over the floor, she spread the quilt of her ancestor's. She looked up at Ben. He stood watching, surrounded by moonlight that flooded in the windows
from north and south, from east and west. He took
off his cap and dropped it onto the trunk—the trunk
that held the diary.

Slowly, Jill removed her sequined jacket, then
slipped from her black sheath. She unclasped her
bra, let it fall to the floor, all the while watching his
eyes watch her. She slid down her panty hose and
her black silk panties. Then she stood motionless,
naked, in the moonlight.

He stepped forward and gently cupped her
breasts, his soft gray eyes locked in her gaze. Then he
bent his head and lightly flicked his tongue across
her aching nipple.

She cried out.

He raised his face to hers and kissed her once
again. Slowly, tenderly.

Her hands reached for his jeans. She unsnapped
the top, the zipper glided down. And then, she felt
him in her hand.

"This may be difficult with only one arm," he
whispered.

Jill studied his face, his warm, wonderful face. "I
don't think we have to worry." She sat down on the
quilt, then pulled him gently down beside her. "Lie
back," she said, "and let me do all the work."

He smiled, his soft gray eyes filled with longing,
his dimple deep with joy. "You are the most magnificent creature I have ever seen," he said, lying back.

Jill smiled back and raised up, then lowered herself onto him.

And in the glow of the moon's light, amid the depths of her past, Jill made love to a man—and was made love to by a man—with more love than she had ever known. Warm, tender love, a blending of life, a merging of souls.

They stayed in their embrace for what seemed like only moments, yet must have been hours. Then, Ben spoke. "I'd better leave. Your family will be home soon."

Jill did not want to respond, but knew she must. "Yes," she answered.

She wrapped the quilt around herself and slowly they descended the staircase. She tried to pretend that she was not filled with sorrow, that she did not ache inside with an ache that she knew would never go away.

At the front door, Ben kissed her again. And then he left.

Jill went into the dining room, and through the window she watched as he walked down the sidewalk, and out of her life.

Chapter 27

October 7, 1992

I was cleaning out some things today and came across this diary in that dusty old trunk. It's been more than a dozen years since I've written in it—there are few blank sheets left to fill. Perhaps I can. Perhaps I will today. I feel I must.

Much has happened in the last fourteen years. George has been gone now several years, and yet I still miss him terribly, I miss the way he made everything whole, I miss the way he held my hand at the most wonderful times right up until the end, right up until his death. Looking back over my life I see that he was, indeed, my rock—always there for me, always by my side, never doubting his love for me or mine for him.

Unlike me, who had been so sure that he had gotten Jill's friend pregnant. If Hazel Blair herself had not come to me before she left for Florida and thanked me for George's generosity, I never have would known the truth. I guess I'd been too afraid to ask George himself.

It was strange, that day when Hazel came to my door. I don't think she'd ever been in my

*house before: I don't think I ever would have
let her in. Judgmental, I guess I was. I feared
her reputation would somehow taint my house,
somehow taint my life. Yet when she came, I
saw such a different person from the one I'd
imagined, from the image of a woman I'd
heard so much talk about over the years.*

*Yes, she wore too much jewelry, and it was
cheap at that, glittery costume things that
should have turned her wrists and fingers green,
and perhaps they did. And, yes, her sweater
was too tight, her hair far too long for a
woman of her age, her lipstick much too bright.
Yet somehow God intervened and told me to let
her in.*

*We had tea (perhaps she would have pre-
ferred whiskey!) and we talked, like two
women, friend-to-friend. She told me what joy
my daughter had brought into her life: how she
missed Jill's laughter, how she missed being a
part of the silly things the girls did in their
early, growing-up years. Then, tears made her
dark mascara drip down her rouged cheeks. I
never thought a woman like Hazel Blair would
take the time to cry, or have the feelings to cry.
I felt so guilty then, and wished we had been
friends. I realize now what I have missed, by
shutting out so many people in my life, by being so afraid of life.*

*When Hazel told me that Rita's son was fa-
thered by Charlie Rollins, I nearly spilled my
tea. She had no reason to tell me: as far as she
knew I didn't even know that her daughter had
been pregnant before she left the island so
many years ago. As far as she knew, I believed
the story that she had married some boy who
was killed in Vietnam. Lord knows George
never would have told me the real story—he*

*would have wanted to protect me from know-
ing the scandal.*

Anyway, Hazel begged me not to tell anyone, to keep their secret, so that Rita and her
boy would be able to hold their heads up high.
She said she didn't want for Rita the kind of life
she'd had, with all the gossip and all the accus-
ing looks. To this day I have not told a soul. I
never even told my dear George. Or my daughter, Jill.

Yes, so much has happened in these years. I
have seen Jill only once—she came for George's
funeral. I wish she had brought her children—
my grandchildren—such beautiful children I
can tell by the photographs. I wish that George
had known them. I wish that Jill would let me
know them now. But some things, I guess, are
not meant to be. Jill did not want to come back
to the Vineyard: she did not want to run the
tavern, or save it for her son. I found that upsetting, yet, I cannot blame her. In truth, I
know my daughter feels no ties to me, and that
has been difficult to live with these past years.
But she has her own life now—a good life, she
says, though I worry about her, a divorced
woman, struggling to make a career, trying to
raise two children on her own. I pray for her. It
is all that I can do now. I cannot change the
past.

It's hard to see the page now—the light is
dimming, my eyes have gotten worse. I just reread what I've written here and realized that I
know the reason I came up here today and dug
this diary from the ancient trunk.

Mother died last week. The letter came from
Myrna today. I was surprised: I had no idea my
sister knew where I lived, or even if I was still

alive. There has never been a note from her—not even a Christmas card in all these years. We are both old women now; we have each chosen our separate lives. Mother was an old woman, too—she must have been ninety-six or seven, it's difficult to remember dates. I wonder if she thought of me before she died. I wonder if she regretted all the things she did to me, all the pain she caused.

I know that I am sorry I never had the chance to say good-bye.

I suppose I, too, will die soon. I hope I do not have to live another twenty-some-odd years the way my mother did. I would be so lonely without George.

Perhaps if I had been a better daughter things might have been different for me. Perhaps if I had been a better mother myself my life would not be as lonely now, as empty.

This is the last page of my diary, the last blank sheet to fill with memories of my life. It is perhaps the best place to capture the most important thing that I have learned in life: the importance of forgiveness.

It is sad to think it has taken so many, many years to learn this. But now I know that I must forgive my mother for the way that she was—for being so controlling, for shutting me out. After all, I do not know what caused her to do—or not do—the things she did. I do not know what kind of pain that she, herself, endured. I must forgive her now, though she will never know. And I must pray that my daughter, Jill, can at last forgive me, too, for all the things I did not do, for all the things I did.

Most of all, I think it's time I learned to forgive someone else, too. Myself. I now know *that no one's life is easy—not mine, not George's, not Hazel Blair's. Yet I suppose we all just try and do things right. And I think we can only hope that others will forgive us if we are not perfect in their eyes.*

As my own mother before me, I only did the best I could.

"Jill? What are you doing sleeping up here?"

Jill rubbed her eyes. Christopher stood over her, looking down. She pulled the throw pillow close against her shoulder, then remembered where she was, what she had done. An empty mug of hot chocolate was on the floor beside her; the quilt insulated her against the cold wood floor; and she was tightly wrapped inside her mother's old chenille robe. The robe and the hot chocolate had warmed her after Ben had left, after the air became chilled by his absence.

She closed her eyes again. "I came up here after I got home last night. I was going through some things." She was not going to tell him that Ben had been here, too, that she had made love to him, and he, to her.

"I didn't hear you come in. I assumed you were still with your friend."

Rita. Jill's head began to ache. "No. I was home. I was here."

He stood in silence.

"How was dinner?" she asked.

"Fine," was all he said.

She opened her eyes and sat up. "I guess you're angry at me."

"Not angry, Jill, just confused. I can't believe you slept up here. On the floor."

She wondered what Christopher would have done, if his best friend's son had just died.

"Did you forget we're leaving at noon?"

Jill ran her hands through her tangled hair. "No. No, I didn't forget."

"Then I suggest you get a move on. We've got places to go, things to do, and the career of your dreams to get under way." He looked around the widow's walk, then his eyes fell on the diary. "What were you reading?"

Jill quickly picked up the diary, lightly caressing the unsealed lock, the cracks of the leather, the edges of time. "Nothing special," she said as she replaced it in the trunk. "Just some old family recipes."

She pulled herself up and closed the lid of the trunk, then followed Christopher down the stairs to prepare for her new life.

Ben stood on the cliffs of Gay Head and stared out across the sea. "I fell in love last night," he said to his friend, Noepe. "Kyle died and I lost Menemsha House, and I fell in love last night."

"Love is good," Noepe answered. "It is what keeps us all alive."

Ben tugged the visor of his Red Sox cap closer over his eyes. "She cannot love me back. She is in love with someone else."

"Perhaps," Noepe answered. "Perhaps not. The important thing is that you feel again. Your inner soul has now returned."

Rita turned on her side and stared into the morning light, surprised that she had slept at all, surprised she had not awakened screaming, crying out for her only son.

She did not know how long the pain would last. She did not think that it would ever go away. She stared into the hollowness of the room where she'd been raised, and wondered what life was all about, and why it was at all.

And then she felt an arm around her, Charlie's arm. Charlie's safe, warm arm. Still clothed in yesterday's now-wrinkled shirt, not groping for her body, only there to hold her, only there to bring her peace.

"Good morning," he whispered quietly. "I'm glad you slept."

"Have you been here the whole time?"

He laughed. "Except when I answered the door."

"The door? Who was here?" A thought flashed into her mind. Had it been Kyle? Was he still alive? Then, the pain returned.

"Well, Jesse Parker for one. And Hattie Phillips. And about a dozen others—neighbors, people you've been supplying with fudge all these years."

Neighbors, Rita thought. Good island neighbors. "What did they want?"

"Let's say there's enough food downstairs to feed the tavern customers for a whole week in August. Breads, cookies, casseroles."

Rita sucked in her cheeks. "For me?"

"For you," Charlie whispered softly and kissed her hair. "For us."

The tears spilled from her eyes and the ache grew once more in her heart, and then Rita let herself move close against him, where she was safe, at last.

Chapter 28

 "This is the hottest story of the decade, and you're saying you won't do it?" Maurice Fischer's eyes popped as he spoke, their pupils jumped up and down. He aimed a piercing look at Christopher. "Talk to your bride-to-be. I think she needs a lesson in the facts of life."

They were crammed into her dressing room, awaiting the first show after her return. Jill hugged her back against the chair, and did not dare look at Christopher.

"Ten minutes until *Good Night, Boston*," came a voice from the tin speaker in the ceiling.

"Honey," Christopher's voice tried to sound soothing, "it's only one story. It's a once-in-a-life-time break. We can't walk away from it."

"I can," she answered. "I can, and I will. I refuse to exploit my best friend for the sake of my career."

"Sweet Mother of God," Maurice moaned.

"If you don't do it, someone else will," Christopher continued. "Would you rather have a stranger hound Rita? Someone with no compassion for what she's been through? They'll chew her up, Jill."

"It won't matter what I do. The media sleazeballs will find her. Rita can handle it."

"But you're the one with the goddamn exclusive!"

Maurice screeched as he bolted from the vanity stool and pounded his fist on the dressing table. The tiny white bulbs surrounding the mirror rattled. His neatly trimmed mustache quivered as he spoke. "You're the one he lied to, you're the one his daughter told the truth to. You're the goddamn one, Jill. Nobody else!"

She rose from her chair and walked to the window. From the thirty-second floor, Boston looked small, insignificant. It hadn't always been that way. Once, it had seemed so big, so awe-inspiring, that her greatest goal had been to own it, to ride the wave to media stardom, to catch the all-American dream.

"Talk some sense into her, Christopher. And do it goddamn fast. We've got a show to put together. It seems your young lady doesn't understand the stakes."

"She knows what they are, Maurice, and she knows what to do," Christopher said. "Come on, I've got a bottle of bourbon in my dressing room. Jill? I'll be back in a few minutes."

She did not turn to face them as they left. Instead, she folded her arms around her waist and thought about all that she had done to rise to meet the stakes: agreeing to the *Lifestyles* article, agreeing to write the Sam Wilkins story, agreeing to subject her daughter to a world that was out of touch with Jill's values, and out of sync with reality.

She knew the stakes, all right, and this time she was standing firm. Standing firm, the way she promised herself when she walked out of the Gay Head Police Station, three days ago.

Carrie had agreed to speak to Jill before they left the island, to give her the answer to one final question: what had Carrie meant when she'd said she was tired of all the lies?

"Did my father tell you I was a crack addict?"

They were seated on hard wooden chairs in a

small brown room at the station. Carrie was dressed in a loose blue smock; the dark roots of her hair were evident as it hung over her shoulders like a limp spaghetti mop.

"Yes," Jill answered.

Carrie gnawed at a fingernail. "It's not true," she replied. "It's a lie."

Jill didn't know what to say.

"It was part of his comeback plan," the daughter of one of the world's most cherished rock stars confessed. "He came to me one night and said he had it all worked out. That all I had to do was go along with it, and we'd be filthy rich again. It would help my career as an actor take off."

"What was the plan, Carrie? What was the rest of it?"

"He said he'd explain that a private detective had found me in a crack house, that he wasn't home, and that my mother, wild with rage, jumped in her car and took off to get me. That would have been when she had her accident."

Jill bit her lip. "And you're saying none of it was true?"

She shook her head. "He said the world would forgive him their doubts if they felt he was trying to protect his daughter. As long as he found a sucker reporter to be on his side. You fell into it, Jill. Hook, line, and sinker, as the Vineyard fishermen say."

A knot formed in Jill's stomach. "What happened to your mother, Carrie?"

The room grew silent. She lowered her head. Her hair hung down, covering her face. "All I know is they had a fight that night. I was there. She stormed out of the house and peeled down the driveway. I've always suspected he tampered with her brakes. But the car was demolished. No one but him will ever know the truth."

"So all these years, you've been the one protecting him."

She raised her eyes. "He's my father, Jill. I'd already lost my mother. I didn't want to lose him, too. But after all that business with Amy . . . and when I realized what I'd done to Kyle . . . that I left him trapped in the fire . . ." Her voice trailed off, her confession complete.

Jill stared out at the skyline now, at the glass and gray buildings, at Boston Harbor beyond. Maurice, she knew, was right. The story of Sam Wilkins had erupted into one of sensational international scope: from the Saudi money man who tried to blackmail Sam for the Menemsha House property; to the island boy who was killed trying to save the land and, perhaps, save his conscience as well. Add to that the mix of the scandal over the mysterious death of Sam's wife, the wayward daughter's need to protect her father, and the near death of Ben Niles, an acclaimed celebrity home renovator, and it was definitely the stuff of which juicy television features were made.

But Jill McPhearson was not going to be the one to make it. It would hurt too much those people whom she loved: Rita, Charlie . . . and, she admitted to herself, Ben.

It would also turn the Vineyard into Chappaquiddick all over again.

And, no matter how much she tried to deny it, Jill was not a sensation-seeker. She was a journalist. Nothing bigger, nothing more. The daughter of George and Florence Randall, who both had loved her after all.

"Five minutes 'til air," the ceiling screamed again.

Jill glanced down at her gold Movado watch. Soon, it would, indeed, be airtime, another show, another night.

Then the door to her dressing room opened. Christopher stomped in.

"Are you nuts?" he asked. "Why are you being so stubborn?"

She took a deep breath, then let it out. "I'm not being stubborn. I'm doing what feels right. For me."

His handsome face twisted in anger. His cheeks reddened. He walked to the vanity and picked up a brown package that had arrived earlier that afternoon.

"Does it have anything to do with this?" he demanded to know.

Jill stared at the package. Her hands grew moist. "Put that down, Christopher."

He laughed. "I knew it," he said, untaping the end of the box that Jill had opened earlier. "What's in here, anyway? I wasn't aware that builders sent going-away gifts."

She wanted to lunge at him and rip the package from his hands. But it would not, she knew, make a difference. She doubted he would even care once he discovered what it was.

She watched as he tore back the brown paper, then opened the lid of the box. Then he pulled the contents out.

"Please be careful," she said calmly. "It's quite old."

He held it in his hand a moment, then turned back the leather cover. "What the hell is it?"

"It's a diary," Jill answered. "My mother's. Ben found it when he was packing up my mother's things for Mrs. Sherman. He knew that I would want it."

Christopher smiled. "You are far too sensitive, Jill. It's amazing that you ever got into this business."

Crossing to her vanity, she took the diary from his hands. Then she sat down. Her eyes moved to the black-and-white photos tucked around the edges of the mirror: Jill and Christopher accepting a plaque from the Associated Press, honoring the "innovation, insight, and warmth" of *Good Night, Boston*; Jill and Christopher with Jeff and Amy, receiving congratulations from Senator Kennedy at a charity fund-raiser; Jill and Christopher in the Grand Ballroom of the Copley Plaza after the first ratings came out—smiling, celebrating, happy, with nowhere to go but up.

Her gaze drifted to her Emmy—the shining symbol of her success, her inroad to stardom, there, waiting, hers for the taking. She touched its cool, smooth edges, caressing what could have been the future. Then she reached for the pear-shaped diamond on her hand, slipped it off her finger, and held it out to Christopher.

"I won't be needing this anymore," she said.

In the mirror, the reflection of shock was on his face. "You really are crazy, you know that?"

"No, Christopher. I am not crazy. I am not part of this world of yours, I never could be. Give the ring to someone who will appreciate its worth. Someone like Lizette."

His nostrils flared. "There was never anything between Lizette and me."

Jill steadied her eyes on the glistening stone. "If she's not appropriate, then I'm sure Addie can find someone who is. You don't need me, Christopher. I am just an island girl after all."

He snatched the ring and stormed from the dressing room.

She closed her eyes and felt the pressure ease.

"Jill, we need you on the set," the ceiling called again.

Rising from the chair, Jill knew what she would do. She would do the show as planned, but it would be her last. There would be no L.A. for Jill McPhearson, no RueCom syndication. She was going back to the Vineyard, back to where her life had form and shape and substance, back to a place where she wouldn't be afraid to raise her children.

She would do some freelance stories—good stories, of the things she loved best, stories like the one about the Shermans and their household filled with love, and the one about the intriguing home renovator, with his tiny trademark whale etched in the glass over so many, many doors.

Then Jill closed her eyes and smiled, and hoped that when the ferry chugged into Vineyard Haven, an old Buick would be waiting on the pier, and a gentle man in a Red Sox cap would be there to welcome her home.

About the Author

A New England native, Jean Stone has spent considerable, memorable times on the Cape and Islands, including at her summer home in Falmouth for many years. Her previous Bantam books—*Sins of Innocence, First Loves,* and *Ivy Secrets*—have been translated into several languages. She currently resides in southeast Michigan, where she is at work on her next novel.